continued . . .

"A riveting read, with intriguing characters, page-turning action, and danger lurking around every turn. Ashley's Shifter world is exciting, sexy, and magical."

—Yasmine Galenorn, *New York Times* bestselling author

"Another excellent addition to the series!"   —*RT Book Reviews*

PRIMAL BONDS

"[A] sexually charged and imaginative tale . . . [A] quick pace and smart, skilled writing."   —*Publishers Weekly*

"An enjoyable thriller . . . [An] action-packed tale."

—*Midwest Book Review*

"Humor and passion abound in this excellent addition to this series."   —*Fresh Fiction*

PRIDE MATES

"With her usual gift for creating imaginative plots fueled by scorchingly sensual chemistry, RITA Award–winning Ashley begins a new sexy paranormal series that neatly combines high-adrenaline suspense with humor."   —*Booklist*

"A whole new way to look at shapeshifters . . . Rousing action and sensually charged, MapQuest me the directions for Shifter-town."   —*Publishers Weekly*, "Beyond Her Book"

"Absolutely fabulous! . . . I was blown away . . . Paranormal fans will be raving over this one!"   —*The Romance Readers Connection*

More Praise for the Novels of Jennifer Ashley

THE DUKE'S PERFECT WIFE

"Fabulous . . . A sensual, gorgeous story that was captivating from the first page to the very last."   —*Joyfully Reviewed*

"Ashley demonstrates her gift for combining complex characters; emotionally compelling, danger-tinged plotting; and a delectably sensual romance into one unforgettable love story."

—*Booklist* (starred review)

THE MANY SINS OF LORD CAMERON

"Big, arrogant, sexy highlanders—Jennifer Ashley writes the kinds of heroes I crave!"

—Elizabeth Hoyt, *New York Times* bestselling author

"A sexy, passion-filled romance that will keep you reading until dawn."

—Julianne MacLean, *USA Today* bestselling author

LADY ISABELLA'S SCANDALOUS MARRIAGE

"I adore this novel: It's heartrending, funny, honest, and true. I want to know the hero—no, I want to marry the hero!"

—Eloisa James, *New York Times* bestselling author

"Readers rejoice! . . . A unique love story brimming over with depth of emotion, unforgettable characters, sizzling passion, mystery, and a story that reaches out and grabs your heart. Brava!"

—*RT Book Reviews* (Top Pick)

"A heartfelt, emotional historical romance with danger and intrigue around every corner . . . A great read!" —*Fresh Fiction*

"For a rollicking good time, sexy Highland heroes, and touching romances, you just can't beat Jennifer Ashley's novels!"

—*Night Owl Reviews*

THE MADNESS OF LORD IAN MACKENZIE

"A deliciously dark and delectably sexy story of love and romantic redemption that will captivate readers with its complex characters and suspenseful plot." —*Booklist*

"Mysterious, heartfelt, sensitive, and sensual . . . Two big thumbs up."

—*Publishers Weekly*, "Beyond Her Book"

WILD WOLF

JENNIFER ASHLEY

BERKLEY SENSATION, NEW YORK

THE BERKLEY PUBLISHING GROUP
Published by the Penguin Group
Penguin Group (USA) LLC
375 Hudson Street, New York, New York 10014

USA • Canada • UK • Ireland • Australia • New Zealand • India • South Africa • China

penguin.com

A Penguin Random House Company

WILD WOLF

A Berkley Sensation Book / published by arrangement with the author

Berkley Sensation Books are published by The Berkley Publishing Group.
BERKLEY SENSATION® is a registered trademark of Penguin Group (USA) LLC.
The "B" design is a trademark of Penguin Group (USA) LLC.

For information, address: The Berkley Publishing Group,
a division of Penguin Group (USA) LLC,
375 Hudson Street, New York, New York 10014.

ISBN: 978-0-425-26604-5

PUBLISHING HISTORY
Berkley Sensation mass-market edition / April 2014

PRINTED IN THE UNITED STATES OF AMERICA

10 9 8 7 6 5 4 3 2 1

Cover art by Tony Mauro.
Cover design by George Long.

Thanks go to my husband,
without whose support my books would never get written,
or cats or humans fed. I couldn't do this without him.

Thanks also go to
my editor Kate, and my agent, Bob,
who help make these books the best they can be.

Finally, thanks go to the two Felines in my life,
the White Monster and his brother, the Natural Disaster,
for providing inspiration for the cub twins and their antics.

CHAPTER ONE

Graham McNeil slammed his massive fist into the jaw of the attacking wolf just as his cell phone rang.

He got the wolf into a headlock and tried to reach for the phone, but the wolf fought and clawed, drawing blood, its breath like sour acid. Graham's Collar sparked heavy pain into his throat, while the Collar on the wolf he fought was dormant.

Was this where things were going with the stupid-ass idea that all Shifters should have their pain-shocking Collars replaced with inert ones? Shifters at the bottom of the food chain would use their fake Collars as an excuse to try to claw their way up, like this Lupine was. The shithead was from the family of one of Graham's trackers and was supposed to be loyal to Graham, but today the wolf had decided to wait in Graham's house until Graham walked in alone, and jump him.

Idiot. Graham had territory advantage, even if he still wore his true Collar, which blasted pain into him with every heartbeat. Time to show the attacking wolf who was truly alpha.

Graham's phone kept ringing against his belt. Because Shifters were only allowed to carry "dumb" phones, he didn't have a fancy ringtone to tell him who was calling. The damn thing just rang.

Graham grabbed the Lupine by the throat and threw it against the wall. The wolf howled, but did it stay down? Not for long.

As the wolf prepared another attack, Graham yanked the phone off his belt and flipped it open. "What?"

"Graham," came the breathless voice of his more-or-less girlfriend, a human called Misty.

Everything slowed. Graham saw in his mind the curvy young woman with light brown hair she wore in a ponytail, her soft face, and her sweet brown eyes. Every thought of her was like a breath of air, snaking into his messed-up brain and trying to soothe him. Graham wished he was with her now, teasing her, kissing her, instead of trying to beat an insubordinate wolf into submission.

"I'm a little busy right now, sweetheart," Graham said loudly as the wolf landed on him. A wooden chair smashed under them as they both slammed to the floor—damn, he *liked* that chair. "You break my TV, you're dead," Graham snarled.

"What?"

"Not you, sweetie. I'll have to call you back."

"You can't. Graham, listen, I need you. They're . . . Oh, crap."

"What?" Graham bellowed. "Slow down. What are you saying?"

"I have to go. I don't know when I can call you again."

Graham's shift was coming. In a few seconds, he wouldn't be able to hold the phone, let alone talk. "Wait!" he yelled at her.

"I can't. I've got to go. Graham, I lo—"

The phone clicked, and Graham was shouting at a dead line. "What? Wait! Misty! Fuck."

He threw the phone across the room and lifted the

attacking wolf by the scruff of the neck. "Would you stop, you asshole?"

The wolf snarled, teeth snapping at Graham's throat. The wolf in Graham responded. He felt his body change, muscles becoming harder and leaner, face elongating to accommodate teeth, claws jutting from fingers that quickly became paws.

With an ear-splitting snarl, Graham went for the other wolf's throat, snapping teeth around fur.

At the last minute, the alpha in him told him not to kill. Graham was this wolf's protector, not its enemy. The wolf needed to be taught its place, not destroyed.

Not that Graham wouldn't rough it up a bit. But quickly. He needed to find out what was wrong with Misty. The fear in her voice had been clear, the desperation palpable. *They're . . .* What? *Here? Coming? Killing me?*

Graham's Collar kept snapping arcs into his neck. He held on to the throat of the fighting wolf, not letting the Collar stop him.

Dominance didn't have anything to do with Collars, or pain, or fighting. Dominance was about putting full-of-themselves, arrogant Lupine Shifters in their place. Graham got the wolf on the floor and stepped on it, and then shifted to human again, breathing hard, his clothes in tatters.

"Stay down." The words were hard, final.

The wolf snarled again, then became human—lanky, dark-haired, gray-eyed—typical Lupine. Except this one was female.

She looked up at him, rage in her eyes. "This isn't over, McNeil."

"Famous last words. Your dad sent you, didn't he? Thought maybe I'd mate-claim you if you couldn't best me, right?"

The way she looked quickly away told Graham he'd hit upon the truth. She was naked, and not bad, but Graham hadn't been able to think about any other female since he'd met Misty.

He hadn't mate-claimed Misty, or even had sex with her. Graham had never had sex with a human before, and he feared he'd not be able to gentle himself enough for Misty. The last thing he wanted to do was hurt her.

Also, his position as leader of the Lupines in this Shiftertown was precarious. His wolves expected him to mate with a Lupine, to provide a cub who would be their next leader. If he went into mating frenzy with a human, the more old-fashioned of his wolves might try to solve the problem by killing Misty.

But Misty's phone call had his gut churning. Graham climbed to his feet. "I've got to go," he said to the woman. "I want you out of here by the time I get back. No more ambushes. If you want a mate, go chase some bears. They're always horny."

Graham turned around and walked away. The best way to show submissives they were submissive was to indicate you didn't fear them jumping you the minute your back was turned. Making them know that if they did jump you, you'd stop them. Again.

His heart hammered with worry, the wolf forgotten, as he detoured to his bedroom to grab clothes to replace the ones he'd shredded with his shift.

Graham left through the back door, mounted his motorcycle, started it, and rode noisily away from his house and Shiftertown.

"I'm asking you one more time, where is he?"

"I said, *I don't know.*"

The gang leader who held Misty against the wall by the throat didn't believe her. He'd caught her running out of the back of the shop, and he'd taken her cell phone, thrown it to the ground, and smashed it with his boot heel. She'd never seen the man before, but she guessed who he was—a guy called Sam Flores who'd been in prison with her brother—and why he'd come.

"You do know." Flores's breath was foul with cigarettes and beer. "That him you had on your phone?"

"No—" Misty broke off with a grunt as her head smacked into the wall. "I don't know where Paul is. He took off."

"Lying bitch." Flores had blue eyes in a sun-darkened face, and dark hair streaked by strong desert sunlight. "I'm going to beat you until you tell me where that asshole is. Then my boys and me will make you understand why you don't mess with us."

Misty was so cold with fear, she couldn't feel anything anymore. She struggled, though she knew she'd never get away. Paul had been out making deliveries, and Misty really didn't know where he was. She'd called him before she'd called Graham, but she'd had to leave a voice mail, telling Paul to lie low. Paul had hiding places, but Misty didn't know where all of them were.

Flores held her in place, the prison tatts on his fingers up close and personal. Behind him, his friends were smashing up her flower shop. Baseball bats smacked into the clear glass refrigerator doors that held her stock; pots filled with arrangements were thrown against the counter. Glass splintered and flew; the flowers, innocent, scattered everywhere. Broken stems and a river of petals littered the floor.

The gang boys got into the refrigerators and smashed the vases there to the floor. Water gushed across the cement and tile along with all the flowers. Cool, dank air, scented with roses, carnations, calendulas, daisies, and baby's breath wafted across the shop.

"You know you aren't walking out of here," Flores said. "You might as well tell me where he is."

Misty didn't bother to answer. If she would die here, the last thing she'd do would be to keep her little brother, Paul, safe. She'd taken care of him all her life, and she wasn't about to stop now.

"I don't think you understand," Flores said. "It won't be

easy. You'll be in so much pain by the time we're done with you, you'll be begging to die."

Fine, then Misty would beg to die. At least she'd been able to hear Graham's gruff, take-no-shit Shifter voice one last time. She thought about his strength, the tatts of fire on his arms, his hard face, and buzzed dark hair. Everyone thought Graham too tough, too mean, and too wild to tame, but Misty had seen what was in his eyes when he was around the two orphaned wolf cubs in his pack.

She'd started to tell Graham the secret inside her heart when the man with the callused fingers had snatched away her phone.

They were going to do whatever they wanted with her, and Misty would die. She was scared, but at least Paul had gotten away, and Graham's voice had given her strength to face what she had to.

Not that she'd give up without a fight. *Go down swinging,* her dad had liked to say. He should know; he'd had to fight for everything his entire life.

The men in her store—five of them—were armed, carrying pieces stuffed into back holsters, knives in boots and on belts. Misty had nothing but her fists and her flowers.

"Cops're coming," one of the men by the door said.

Misty heard sirens. Probably Pedro at the convenience store across the lot had seen the break-in and called the police. But Misty knew better than to relax and be thankful the police were on their way. There would be a standoff, probably a gun battle, and someone would be shot. Most likely Misty.

She struggled to get away. Flores punched her twice in the face. Misty's head snapped back, and blood flowed from her mouth.

Flores clamped his hand over her throat, cutting off her breath. He squeezed, not enough to choke her, but blocking off enough air to make Misty dizzy and sick.

He dragged her with him out the back door to the alley, the other four following. Two of the guys had motorcycles; the other two and the man who held Misty went for a pickup—a Ford 250, all shiny and new. Big enough to shove Misty down into the backseat, tossing a cigarette-smoke-infested tarp on top of her.

The truck rumbled under her as it started. Then the pickup jerked, tires squealing, as it headed down the alley that ran behind the strip mall. Another turn onto the street, and they were off, carrying Misty who-knew-where.

Misty's pickup wasn't in her carport. Graham killed the engine on his Harley, stepped away from the engine's smell, and inhaled.

Every hackle he had went up, the wolf in him starting to snarl. Misty was gone—Graham could scent how she'd left the house through the back door not long ago, gotten into her truck, and driven away. All as normal. She'd have gone to her store, as early as it was, to do whatever it was she did before opening for the day.

Why hadn't the woman told him where she was calling from? Graham's cell phone had indicated what number had called him, but Misty had been on *her* cell, which meant she could be anywhere.

Graham scented no struggle here, no fear or worry. Just Misty's fresh scent, overlaid with the flowers she worked with all the time. Graham couldn't catch a whiff of roses these days or the strong odor of what she said were Asiatic lilies without thinking of Misty.

No, *thinking* of her wasn't the right way to put it. The scents conjured up her sultry voice, her uninhibited laughter, her soft face, and brown eyes that went shiny when she looked at him sometimes.

The images, sounds, and scents of her woke up Graham's needs too. He hadn't touched the woman, but he dreamed almost every night about running his hand up the loose skirts she liked to wear, freeing her hair from the ponytail, licking between her breasts . . .

Misty had sounded terrified. Someone had been coming for her, and she was scared out of her mind.

Graham swung back onto his bike, started it, and roared down the street again. He saw the people who'd come out of houses to watch him, wondering what the hell a Shifter was doing in their nice corner of the city, but Graham didn't care right now what they thought.

He turned out of the neighborhood and joined traffic on the 215 before he raced off on Flamingo, heading to the flower shop in this middle-class side of town. Shifters didn't come here much, confining themselves to the north side of Las Vegas and the desert not far beyond. The big hotels on the Strip and downtown didn't want Shifters scaring away tourists, so Shifters mostly stayed away, even though some Shifter women danced at nightclubs as the entertainment. Pissed Graham off, how Eric Warden, the Shiftertown leader, was all right with Shifter females doing exotic dancing for humans. One of the many reasons Eric was a dickhead.

Misty's flower shop—Flamingo Flowers—was in a strip mall with other small retailers, which should have been quiet this early on a Saturday morning. Graham knew something was seriously wrong, even before he saw the smashed glass in Misty's doorway and the cop cars all over the lot.

A couple of cops saw him, and Graham hesitated. He should get the hell out of there and have nothing to do with the city police, but if he left, he'd not be able to help Misty. She might be in there, and if she wasn't, he needed to get inside and sniff around to figure out where she'd gone.

He decided to approach as though he had every right to be there. Shifters weren't banned from *every* store in town, just most of them. But not this one. Misty had sense enough to know that Shifters were good customers.

Graham pulled his motorcycle next to one of the cop cars and dismounted. Next thing he knew, he was surrounded by five cops, who'd all pulled their weapons on him. One cop backed those up with a Taser.

Graham's wolf fought to get out, wanting to go into a frenzy that would land the cops on the ground, their weapons broken. He clenched his fists, fighting the aggression he always had a hell of a time taming. When he'd lived in middle-of-nowhere Nevada, in a Shiftertown where his word had been law, Graham had never bothered damping down his wolf instincts. Now he was expected to live in a city of humans who treated him like he was some big scary animal that had escaped from the zoo.

He wanted to grab the guns from the cops and break them, just to scare them, but Graham dialed it back. He needed to find Misty.

He lifted his hands to show they were empty. "Hey, this is my friend's store. I need to make sure she's all right."

"A human owns this store," the cop closest to Graham said.

"Well, no shit. Her name's Misty—Melissa Granger. She called me, scared. She in there? Is she all right?"

Maybe watching Eric deal with humans for the last eight months had taught Graham something. The cops still eyed him warily but believed his worried tone.

"No one's inside," the lead cop said. He had black hair buzzed short, a flat face with acne scars, and a big nose. He held his Beretta steadily, still pointing it at Graham. "Place is torn up."

"But her truck's here." Graham pointed at the black pickup sitting quietly in a space a little way from the cops. "She was here. Where is she now?" His fears mounted as he spoke. He couldn't stop the growl in his throat, couldn't stop the sparks on his Collar.

"This is a crime scene," the lead cop said. "You don't need to be here, Shifter."

"No? This store belongs to my *friend*. My *friend* might be in trouble. I don't see you doing anything about it."

The pistol didn't waver. "Why don't you go back to Shiftertown so we can do our jobs?"

"Why don't I go on in there so I can look around? Maybe figure out where she is?"

"Turano, call Shifter Division," the lead cop said. "We need to contain one."

Graham stared at him and then moved his gaze to the one called Turano, who was reaching for his radio.

"Aw, screw this shit."

The cops tensed, expecting him to charge through them, but Graham turned his back and walked away, making for his motorcycle. He made a show of starting his bike, giving the cops a collective dirty look, before he pulled out of the parking lot.

Graham rode down the street and around the corner, then took the delivery entrance into the alley behind the shops. There was one cop car back there, and one cop. Graham roared up, dismounted his bike, and headed for the back door.

"Hey!"

When Graham didn't stop, the cop drew. Graham whirled around and had the pistol out of the man's hand and broken into two pieces before the man could react.

When the cop opened his mouth to yell, Graham punched him, once in the face, then once in the temple. The cop folded up, and Graham lowered him gently to rest against the wall.

"Sweet dreams." Graham stepped around the cop and through the door, which led to the back office and storage.

The thick steel door hadn't been forced, which meant it had been opened from the inside. Probably by whoever had broken in taking the back way out. A glance into the shop revealed a mess: flowers, glass, and water all over the place. A dripper that ran constantly inside the refrigerated section had broken open, turning the refrigerator into a lake. The water wasn't gushing anymore, which meant someone had been smart enough to turn it off.

Graham stayed out of sight of the cops picking their way through the scene at the front door. He didn't have to go all the way into the shop though. He smelled Misty's blood, along with the scents of four—no, five—humans. Humans who smoked heavily, hadn't bathed in a couple of days, and one who'd been partaking of weed.

Graham got all that from a few long sniffs. He also scented that they'd taken Misty out back and loaded her into a vehicle. He growled, his blood heating with rage, and went back outside.

The day was already warm, August in southern Nevada. Heat made scents brighter. Graham smelled motorcycles and a car or truck, and these had taken Misty away. Too bad scent couldn't tell him the make and models of the vehicles and where they'd been heading. Graham only knew they'd taken Misty.

He stepped over the unconscious cop, started up his bike, and rode out. A mile down the road, he pulled into another empty parking lot, took out his cell phone, and made a call.

"Hey," he said to the Shifter who answered. "I'm gonna need some backup."

CHAPTER TWO

Misty half woke when she was carried from the truck and into a house. Outside it was bright and hot, the day warming to its usual late summer temps. The men hadn't bothered to blindfold her, but Misty had no idea where she was. Somewhere in Las Vegas, but it was a big city. Her vision was still blurry from the blows to her face and from the long, hot ride stuffed in the back of the truck's cab, and looking around at the generic buildings didn't tell her much.

The house was cooler than outside, though it smelled of damp garbage. Stale cigarette smells overlaid those scents, ashtrays overflowing.

The man who carried Misty dumped her on a couch that was strewn with clothes. The couch's springs were broken, the cushions made of scratchy material, stuffing coming out the edges.

The leader sat down beside her. "Do you know who I am, Misty?"

"Sam Flores." The words stuck on her tongue. She needed water.

"That's right. Do you know why I'm looking for your brother?"

Misty licked her lips, tasting salt and dryness. "You were with him in prison."

"Right again. And he screwed me royally. I just want to see him. To have a little talk."

"To kill him, you mean."

"Maybe."

Misty drew a breath, trying not to gag on the living room's odors. "He could have reported you. You'd still be in there if he hàd, maybe even in maximum security."

"Oh, yeah, Paul was a little angel." Flores put his face close to Misty's. "But I had a good thing going, until he screwed it up for me. He didn't think I'd get my parole, did he? Well, I have a good lawyer, who does what I want."

Probably in exchange for the money Flores got for coke. Misty didn't know the whole story, because Paul still wasn't coherent about it, but apparently Sam had been good at drug dealing inside prison. Paul, whether he'd meant to or not, had helped an even meaner drug guy take away Sam's business. Paul hadn't explained very carefully, only that he'd had to choose between two evils. The second guy had promised to keep Flores away from Paul—Flores and his boys had beaten Paul every day before that.

"You'll probably need that lawyer again," Misty said, her voice a croak.

"No, because no one's going to find you for a very long time, or your brother either." Flores held up a cell phone. "Now, I was so pissed off I crushed your phone before I thought about it, and now, I'm going to need Paul's number. So tell me what it is without making a big deal, and I might go easy on you."

"I'm not about to tell Paul to come running over here so you can kill him," Misty said hotly. "He's my brother. Would you do that to your brother?"

"Yeah." Flores grinned. "My brother's an asshole." He leaned closer. "You have a choice, pretty thing. If you give me Paul's phone number, I won't hurt you so bad. If you don't, I'll just kill you now and take your body out to the desert. All right?"

Misty wet her lips again. She needed water, but thirst was the least of her worries. If Sam stabbed her or shot her, a dry mouth wouldn't matter.

She decided to gamble. What did she have to lose? "All right," she said in a near whisper. "But give him a chance to explain. He had no choice."

"Everyone has a choice. Even you, sweetheart, and you made the right one. What is it?"

Misty closed her eyes, repeated the number, and started to pray. She heard the little beeps as Flores punched in the digits, then the phone rang on the other end. In a few seconds, a harsh voice said, "What?"

She opened her eyes as Flores jerked. "Who the hell is this? Where's Paul?"

Silence. Then the voice said. "He's in the bathroom. What do you want?"

"Tell him to get his ass on the phone."

"Shit." More silence. Then another voice. Not Paul, Misty knew, but one doing a close approximation of him. "Yeah?"

"If you want to see your sister again, you'll get out to where I might give her back to you." Flores gave directions down a highway then to a turnoff, way out of town, some remote place in the desert. "I'm not going to wait long." He clicked off.

Misty said nothing. Sam might decide to go ahead and kill her, and Misty would have to fight for her life. She would probably lose. But she had hope.

She had no idea who the Shifter was who'd answered as Paul, and she had no idea what Sam would do when he lured them out to the desert. But she knew Graham would be coming.

Graham rode out on his motorcycle, his nephew, Dougal, following. North out of town, then east on a county road, north on another dirt road, out into vast desert with knifelike mountains. The only vegetation was the creosote, with its long, slender white limbs and tiny gray green leaves reaching to the white blue sky.

The Mojave was a land of stark beauty, but it was deadly. The tourists who came to Las Vegas by the bucketload flew safely over this desert every day, but those who lived permanently in town knew its dangers. A human could die of dehydration and heatstroke out here quicker than he knew what was happening, and it wasn't much better for Shifters.

Misty had been smart to trick her abductors into calling Graham. He'd grabbed Dougal, who'd come out to help, and told him to pretend to be Misty's brother. Dougal had convinced whoever was on the other end that he was Paul Granger, which didn't feel right to Graham. The man who had Misty couldn't be that stupid. Or else the guy wasn't afraid of whoever would come to him out in the hole in the desert. So, either he was overconfident, or he had a nasty surprise waiting.

Either way, the man was dead. He'd taken Misty, and Graham was going to rip him open.

Shifters weren't allowed to kill humans though. A Shifter killing a human would bring human wrath down upon all Shifters.

All right, so maybe Graham would control his instincts and not do any actual killing. Maiming though—maiming he could do. It's what he *would* do, whether humans liked it or not.

The turnoff came up, and Graham swung his bike into it, Dougal close behind him. Graham wished he could have a little more backup than his messed-up nephew, but there hadn't been time. It was early in Shiftertown, when all the Felines slept heaviest, bears couldn't be bothered to get out of bed, and even the Lupines were sluggish. If he'd called Eric, who would have been the best backup, Graham would have had to waste a lot of time explaining. Eric loved explanations.

The rough dirt road narrowed with each mile and finally petered out. They were a long way from the paved county road now, even farther from the highway. The desert floor, Graham knew from long experience, wasn't the most stable of places to ride. What looked like solid earth could prove to be a crust for a giant dry hole, and washes hidden by brush opened out without warning.

Graham's and Dougal's motorcycles were leaving a trail any simpleton could follow, but Graham didn't have time for stealth. The men ahead knew they were coming, they'd be armed, and they had Misty. The whole thing smelled of a big fat trap, but Graham would trip it and to hell with it.

They reached the appointed spot, which was at the bottom of a mountain. Around here, mountains began abruptly, rising straight up from the earth. No miles of foothills or gradual change in elevation, just horizontal and vertical.

A mining shaft had pierced the earth here but had been filled in—a mound of debris and stones protruded around rotted wood framing. An old shack, left over from the early part of the last century, squatted about twenty yards from the shaft. The tiny building had been reroofed at some point with corrugated metal, which was now square pieces of rust.

Five human men stood around the shack, waiting, guns in hands. Graham stopped his motorcycle and got off, Dougal behind him.

The men ignored Graham and focused on Dougal, who was shorter and much lankier than Graham. When Dougal took off his helmet, giving them a good-natured and toothy wolf grin, the lead man shoved his gun into Graham's face.

"Where is he?"

"You mean Granger?" Graham asked. "He couldn't come."

"I want him. You were supposed to bring him."

"He was busy. I came to get Misty. If she's hurt, I'm going to kill you and not worry about it. We're a long way from town—the humans won't find your bodies for a while."

"Yeah, it is a long way, isn't it?" the gang leader asked.

Something was wrong. This guy, whoever he was, didn't look scared enough. He took in Graham's Collar and Dougal's. "Two Shifters. I only need one."

A growl formed in Graham's throat. "Need one for what?"

"I wanted Granger too," the man said. "But, oh well, I'll just grab him later."

What the hell was he talking about? Misty was inside the shack, Graham knew. He scented her in there, even over the fuel smell of the bikes and the rank odor of humans.

Flowers and spice. That's how he always thought of her. Sweet and sassy.

"Get out of my way," Graham said.

The gang leader touched the end of the pistol to Graham's nose. "No."

"I warned him, right?" Graham said to Dougal. "You saw me warning him? When Eric gives me crap about this later, tell him I warned him."

"You're funny, Shifter," the gang leader said, even as Dougal gave Graham a serious nod.

"Yeah, I'm a tub of laughs."

Graham ripped the gun out of the gang leader's hands and smacked him hard in the face with it. The gang leader went back with a surprised grunt, hands going to his bloody mouth. As the other men started forward, Graham called the strength of his wolf and twisted the pistol in half. Pieces of metal and bullets rained to the ground.

The gang leader lifted his head, his nose and mouth dripping scarlet blood. "That was stupid."

"But fun." Graham grabbed the man by his shirt, hoisting him high. Then he stopped being civilized and went for it.

He threw the leader into the knot of his men. They scrambled either to grab him or get out of the way, and Graham was on them. He punched, elbowed, jabbed, swept his boot across ankles to send the men to the ground.

Dougal joined the fray, laughing. Dougal had a lot of anger in him, and he loved the chance to work it off. These dumb-ass humans were the perfect targets. Let the kid take it out on them.

He heard Misty yelling from inside the shack, and thumping as she kicked the wall. Not in terror—she was pissed off, probably bound and trying to get loose. *You go, baby.*

Graham punched and kicked, spun and jabbed. He didn't bother becoming wolf or his in-between beast—it was a pleasure to kick ass without even shifting. His Collar sparked, driving pain into his neck, but he didn't care. He'd care later, but not now. Pain didn't slow Graham down; it galvanized him.

He heard the boom of a pistol, and then blood was running hot down Graham's side, soaking his shirt. *Damn.*

The man who'd shot him looked up in terror as Graham bore down on him, half shifting as he went. Graham tasted blood as he tore into the guy, and the pistol became a pile of broken metal.

Howls filled the air behind Graham, but not howls of pain. Dougal had shifted, his wolf furious that someone dared wound the only parent he'd ever known. Fur flashed by Graham as Dougal, now a huge black wolf, charged the remaining humans standing.

They never had a chance to shoot. Dougal fought like a whirlwind, his Collar throwing sparks into the bright morning light. Graham slowed, his side hurting like hell, and watched as Dougal clawed and bit until the tough inner-city gang boys were pools of whimpering terror.

The leader managed to limp to the pickup parked behind the shack. Graham went after him, but the pain of the shot slowed him. The leader got into the truck and had it started up while Graham was still a few yards away.

"You're screwed, Shifter," the man said. Then the truck leapt forward, spun a little on the dirt, and rocketed down the track toward the road, leaving his yelling gang boys behind.

What an asshole. He'd just run out on his own men.

The humans left didn't waste time standing around being mad. They ran for the motorcycles, Dougal's and Graham's included.

Graham spun and tried to intercept them, but one guy punched Graham in the side, right where the bullet was. Pain blossomed in Graham's body, his Collar biting deeper agony into him. Graham grunted as he fell to his knees, and the guy managed to twist away and keep running.

Dougal's jeans lay forlorn on the ground near the bikes—easy for one of the men to lean down and scoop up Dougal's keys. Graham leveraged himself to his feet, but the two men had reached Dougal's bike, starting it up. As Graham staggered toward his own bike, the second man on Dougal's motorcycle aimed his pistol at Graham's Harley and shot it again and again.

Graham had to watch his motorcycle, the Harley Softail he lovingly worked on every day of his life, become as wounded as he was. The gas tank punctured, fuel poured onto the ground, and more bullets lodged in the engine.

The man driving Dougal's bike moved it out, following the others, leaving them stranded.

Graham folded his arms over his stomach, trying and failing to draw deep breaths. He was in excruciating pain, and their way out of the desert plus all the water was racing toward the highway, a thin spiral of dust rising in its wake.

Misty kept tugging at the handcuff that held her to the one beam in the shack that looked stable. She'd been pulling and yanking to no avail, her wrist raw. She'd feared to pull too hard in case the whole shed came down on top of her.

She heard the vehicles roar away, and then the drawn-out howl of a wolf. "Graham!" she shouted.

Another howl came, holding a mournful note, and one of fear. Shifter wolves were supposed to be strong and ter-rifying, but this one sounded lost and alone.

"Graham!"

"I'm right here, baby."

Graham yanked open the door to the shack. His eyes held deep pain, the skin around his Collar was black, and blood oozed from behind the hand he pressed to his side.

Misty tugged at the cuff again. "Oh my God, you've been shot!"

Graham's voice was as strong as ever. "Stop screeching. You're hurting my ears. And you—" He turned and yelled over his shoulder. "Quit with the howling. I'm not dying. Not yet."

"I'll stop screeching when you call nine-one-one," Misty told him.

"Already tried. No signal."

Graham kept his hand on his side as he moved stiffly into the shack. He latched his fingers around the cuff that bound Misty's wrist, yanked once, and broke the handcuff.

Misty lowered her arm in relief. "Can you ride? I might be able to drive your bike if you help me. I've never ridden a motorcycle before."

"Nope. The assholes shot up my bike, and took Dougal's, and their fearless leader took off in his pickup. They left us out here without water, transportation, or phones that work."

He sounded so calm. "And you've been shot." Misty touched his arm, finding his skin hot and slick with sweat.

"Yep. But don't worry, sweetheart. I'm used to it."

CHAPTER THREE

Misty started to shake. "Oh, right. Don't worry. I was sitting here tied up, and you get shot, and you don't want me to worry." She swallowed, her throat dry. The thin-walled shack with its many cracks was like an oven. "You're a shithead, Graham."

"That's what everyone tells me."

Misty couldn't move her hand from his arm. She felt his strength beneath her grip, comforting her even now.

Graham was a big man, loud-voiced and full of arro-gance. Other Shifters were afraid of him, including his own wolves—his Lupine pack, he called them. Humans backed away from him, and even Shifter groupies only watched him from afar, too scared to approach him.

Misty, though, couldn't bring herself to be afraid of Graham—or at least, not terrified of him. She remembered the first night she'd met him, in a Shifter bar called Cool-ers. She'd found herself sitting on a barstool next to him, Graham all banged up from a bout at the Shifter fight club. He'd looked disgruntled, angry, and very lonely. She couldn't ever forget what she'd seen in his eyes that night, a man searching for something, though he didn't know what.

Not that Graham had ever showed Misty his softer side. But he'd let her see a hint that maybe he *had* a softer side—deep, deep, deep down.

Graham turned from her, and Misty's fingers slid away from him. "Dougal!" Graham bellowed as he banged out of the shack. "Stop whining. You need to take this bullet out of me."

"No, you need a hospital," Misty said, following him. "Maybe we can make it to the road, or at least close enough to find a cell signal."

"I'm not walking anywhere, sweetie. I have a bullet stuck in my side, and it could lodge in a bad place if it doesn't come out now."

"Can't you shift . . . ?"

"Sure. Then I'll be a wolf with a bullet stuck in my side that could lodge in a bad place. Dougal can take it out. He knows how."

Misty didn't know much about Graham's nephew, Dougal Callaghan, who lived with Graham. Graham had said that Dougal's mom died giving birth to him—*bringing him in,* Graham had called it. Dougal's dad had deserted him a long time ago, back before Shifters had been rounded up and put into Shiftertowns. Graham had never been able to find the dad, who'd probably gone feral, whatever that meant. Graham had raised Dougal himself, and apparently, Dougal had been a handful.

Dougal came running to them, in his human form now and stark naked. Misty's face went hot, and she spun around and faced the shack's sun-bleached wall.

"She's human," Graham growled at Dougal. "She expects pants."

"Goddess," Dougal said in disgust then ran off again.

Graham said nothing, making no apology. He leaned against the shack's doorframe and closed his eyes, his face losing a little color. Misty turned and laid her hand on his arm again, wishing she could do more.

But she wasn't an ER nurse, or a doctor, or anything useful like that. She ran a flower shop. She knew everything about flowers—their names, types, and popularity; how they were cultivated; traditional meanings of each flower; which ones were appropriate for what occasion; how to arrange them; and which ones sold the best. Great information for running her business, nothing that would save a Shifter who'd been shot.

Dougal returned, jeans on and belted. The morning had turned hotter—August days generally reached the triple digits. Clouds were forming over the mountains as well, signaling a monsoon storm that would be ready to come in during the afternoon. If the three of them were out here then . . . Storms had deadly lightning, high winds, and hail, not to mention the flash floods that tore along the washes and overflowed their banks. The three of them could be cut off until the washes ran dry again.

Dougal ducked under Graham's arm and helped him around the tiny shack to its shady side, where Graham stretched himself out on the ground. There wasn't enough room for him to lie inside the shack's small interior, especially when its floor was covered in rusty bits of metal.

Dougal peeled Graham's shirt from him, Graham grunting as the cloth came unglued from his skin. Graham's six-pack abs were covered with blood, which continued to seep from the slash in his abdomen. Dougal used Graham's shirt to wipe off excess blood then he stretched Graham's flesh apart and started to reach inside to pull out the bullet.

"Wait!" Misty cried.

"Can't wait," Dougal said. "He's going into shock. You have to help me."

Misty's head spun, but she knelt beside Dougal. "What do I do?"

"Hold this open." Dougal indicated the lips of the wound. "It's going to be messy."

"Not to mention not sterile," Misty said.

"We don't have a choice. Don't worry, I've done this lots of times."

"Really?" Misty put her fingers where Dougal guided her. "Graham gets shot often, does he?"

"Not always Uncle Graham. But other Shifters. Hospitals were too far away from our old Shiftertown, and hunters liked to take shots at us."

Graham gave another grunt. "Hunters and old Craig Morris."

Dougal snorted a laugh. "Yeah."

"Who was he?" Misty asked. She pressed down as Dougal showed her and spread the wound. More blood poured out, which Dougal mopped up with the T-shirt.

"Old Shifter," Graham said. "About three hundred years old when we were rounded up. He hated living so close to other Shifters—he should have stayed in the wild and died with some dignity. He'd been alone a long time, and bringing him in and giving him the Collar was tough on him. He used to shoot anyone who came too close to his house. His eyesight was going by then, so his aim was usually off, but once in a while, he got lucky. *Shit*."

Dougal had dug his fingers into the wound. "Press down hard," he told Misty. "We have to keep him still. This is going to get bad."

"Don't worry." Graham's words were tight and faint. "I'll try not to kill anyone."

"That's what you always say." Dougal put his hand on Graham's shoulder as he started fishing around for the bullet.

Graham roared, fingers sprouting claws as he reached for Dougal's throat.

"Grab him!" Dougal yelled. "Hold him down. No matter what happens, hold him!"

Misty caught Graham's wrists and quickly laid herself across his chest and shoulders. She knew she wouldn't have the strength to grapple with him, so she used her weight to keep him down.

Graham growled, his body rippling beneath her. Misty felt him change. Fur burst across his bare chest, his face elongated into a muzzle, and his eyes went silver gray.

"Don't shift!" Dougal shouted at him. "Hold him, Misty."

Misty pushed her face at Graham's terrifying wolf one, which was emerging from his human's. His eyes were white gray, and full of pain, rage, madness.

"Stop!" She tried to sound firm, but everything came out shaky.

"I'm touching it," Dougal said. "Just . . . trying . . . to grab it."

Graham's growls grew more fierce. Blue snakes of electricity arced around his Collar, the sparks stinging Misty's skin. She pressed him down, her head on his shoulder.

"Hang on," she said. "Almost done."

More snarling, but she felt Graham strain to hold himself back. All that strength—he could snap her in half and Dougal too, but he didn't. Graham's hands balled into huge fists, claws jabbing into his own skin.

"Hang on," Misty whispered.

"Got it!" Dougal lifted his hand, coated with gore, and held up a piece of metal. He whooped in triumph, then grabbed the T-shirt and jammed it over the wound.

"Keep pressure on that," Dougal said to Misty. "I'll try to find something to help patch the hole."

Misty pushed down on the cloth, which was already red and sopping. Graham's face gradually returned to human, and his Collar ceased sparking. But his skin was sallow, his breathing rapid.

Graham opened his eyes to slits, the silver gray of the wolf shining through. "Was it good for you?" he asked, his voice a scratch. "'Cause it sucked for me."

"It really sucked for me too," Misty said, giving a breathless laugh.

Graham reached for Misty's hand. She slid hers into his, his fingers barely squeezing.

"What do you know?" Dougal said, returning from inside the shed. "Duct tape."

Graham let out a chuckle, closing his eyes again. "One human invention that's useful."

"Lots of human inventions are useful," Misty said, babbling while Dougal peeled off pieces of tape and ripped them from the roll with his wolf teeth. "Cars, for instance."

"Paved the world and clogged all the clean air with crap," Graham said. "Destroyed Shifter territory and made us vulnerable to humans."

"Thanks, Graham."

"Sure thing, sweetheart." His eyes opened again. "Are you going to tape me up anytime soon? Like before my guts fall out?"

Dougal wiped the wound as clean as he could with the soaked T-shirt, then Misty helped him hold Graham's skin together while Dougal taped it closed.

"This will hurt like hell when you pull it off," Dougal said.

"Yeah, well, it hurt like hell going on," Graham said. "Now you need to get out of here and look for a spot with a cell phone signal. If you have to go all the way back to Shiftertown for help, do it."

Dougal stared. "You want *me* to go?"

"Yes, you. Misty will never make it across fifty miles of desert on foot, without water. Right now, I'm a wuss because I've been shot, had a hand dug into me, and am being held together with duct tape. That leaves you."

Dougal gazed out at the empty land, his fingers picking at the roll of tape in his hands, his face almost gray. Dougal, though in his early thirties, was considered barely an adult by the Shifters. Graham had told her Dougal had come through his Transition—whatever that was—and had been an adult for about a year. But though in years Dougal was older than Misty, in many ways he acted like a scared teenager.

"Your wolf can do it," Graham said. "Follow the scent trail back to the dirt road. Call Reid, tell him what happened. And for the Goddess's sake, don't tell Eric."

Dougal nodded, but numbly.

"Promise me," Graham said. "Not Eric. I don't want him all up in my face about this. He'll blab all over Shiftertown that I'm hurt, and we can't afford for some of my wolves to know that. Understand?"

Dougal's eyes cleared a little, and he nodded again. "Yeah, yeah, I got it."

"Now, go. It's getting hot, and I'm looking forward to that other human invention—air-conditioning."

Dougal plucked his cell phone out of his pocket at the same time he unbuckled his jeans again. "How am I supposed to carry this as wolf? If I have it in my mouth, I'll bite through it."

Graham grinned and pointed a shaking finger at what Dougal had dropped. "Duct tape."

"Shit," Dougal said.

Dougal at least hid in the shed as he shucked his clothes again and changed back to his wolf. In a few minutes, a black wolf with light gray eyes emerged from the shack, his fur shaggy and rumpled, his tail almost dragging on the ground.

He looked so dejected Misty wanted to put her arms around him and hug him, but she'd learned she shouldn't do that to a Shifter without permission. Shifters hugged each other all the time, including male-to-male hugs that would make some humans uncomfortable, but an outsider didn't join the hugging group until invited.

Misty did give Dougal a gentle pat as she started taping the cell phone between his shoulders. Dougal growled while she fixed the phone in place, but his Collar didn't spark, which meant it wasn't a growl of aggression.

Dougal went to Graham before he left, pushing his muzzle at Graham's face. Graham let Dougal touch his wolf nose to Graham's, and Graham brought his hand up to pat Dougal's side. "Go on," Graham said.

Without looking at Misty, Dougal turned away from them and trotted down the little hill and into the desert. Misty watched until the wolf slunk away into the shadows of tall creosote, and then he was lost to sight.

Misty knelt next to Graham, who had closed his eyes
again. "Don't go to sleep," she said sternly. "You lost a lot
of blood. You need to stay awake."

"Shifter metabolism is different from a humans'," Graham
said without opening his eyes. "I'll be fine."

"Then you need to stay awake to keep me from worrying about you. It's my fault you've been shot, so I need you
to live."

Graham's eyes opened a slit. "How is this your fault?
You didn't pull the trigger."

"You getting mixed up in my problems, that's my fault."
Misty hugged her arms across her chest, her shirt sweat-
soaked and dirty. "I gave Sam Flores your number."

"That was smart. Stupid human thought I'd bring Paul
out here so he could be ambushed and killed." Graham's
brows drew together. "Too stupid. Something's wrong."

"What's wrong is I need to warn Paul. If Sam tracks
him down, he's screwed."

"Let's make sure we're not screwed first, all right? It
will take Dougal a while to find civilization. Good thing
Shifters heal fast."

Graham already sounded a little stronger, but when
Misty took his hand again, his grip was slack. "All that
with Dougal—making him take out the bullet and then
sending him for help—you did that so he wouldn't be
scared."

Graham's grin cracked through dirt on his face. "Yeah,
you caught me."

"Will he be all right?"

"Probably. He's been through a lot, and he's learned to
be tough. Poor cub got stuck with *me* to bring him up. I'm
the alpha of the alphas, but Dougal's not that dominant.
Other cubs gave him hell for it when he was growing up,
and my pack still does. He's the natural choice to be my
successor, but they know he's not strong. The minute I drop
dead, they'll be all over him trying to throw him out and
take over."

Misty's mouth popped open. "That's terrible."

Graham shrugged. "It's a Shifter thing. They won't touch him while I'm around, and I'm coming up with ideas to keep him safe. But having to fight back all the time has made Dougal stronger."

Misty squeezed Graham's big hand. "You're good to take care of him."

"He's my sister's son. I didn't have a choice. That's another Shifter thing."

"I bet you did have a choice. You could have had someone in your pack help you with him, right? You did it yourself because you felt sorry for him. You were being nice."

Graham gave her a faintly startled look before his grin appeared again. "Don't tell anyone, all right? I've got a rep."

"You're nice to me," Misty said, stroking his shoulder.

"Because you're sexy as hell."

He was joking. Graham always joked. In all the time she'd known him, he was either yelling at someone or joking with them. A serious talk was not something Graham did.

Also, in the eight months Graham and Misty had been going out, he'd never made any move to take Misty to bed. He'd kissed her . . . Wow, had he kissed her. Blood-sizzling, she-could-have-an-orgasm-just-kissing-him kisses. But nothing more.

Mostly Graham took her to clubs, like Coolers, or to out-of-the-way restaurants and bars that allowed Shifters. Other Shifters were always present at these sort-of dates, and much of the time, Misty had to drive herself to meet him there. Graham was very attentive during the dates, sitting with his arm around her, interested in her talk about her day and her opinions on whatever they discussed. When the date was over, he'd walk her to her pickup, kiss her good night, and wait until she drove safely out of the parking lot. Then she'd go home—alone.

Misty had been to Graham's house, where he lived with Dougal, but Graham had never let Misty go to the fight club—an unofficial arena where Shifters battled it out with each other for fun. Misty also never stayed the night with Graham, and he'd never been inside her house, though he knew where she lived. He'd come to her flower shop once, but only once—some customers had been reluctant to enter when he'd been there. Graham had decided he shouldn't scare away Misty's business, and never went back.

They'd never talked about their relationship. Graham didn't seem to be the kind of guy who wanted to discuss relationships. Misty was afraid he'd start ignoring her altogether if she brought it up.

Misty had her own friends now in Shiftertown, like the party-happy Shifter girl Lindsay, and Cassidy, a wildcat who was the sister of the Shiftertown leader. Lindsay, the font of all Shifter gossip, told Misty Graham wasn't seeing anyone else, so that wasn't the cause of the distance he kept with her. He wasn't gay either . . . that fact would be all over Shiftertown too.

Graham might die today. The sun was reaching its zenith, the shade from the shed narrowing to a sliver. In a few minutes, it would be gone altogether.

"Stay with me, Graham," Misty said, massaging his shoulder.

"I'm not going anywhere, sweetheart."

The shade disappeared. The sun burned down on them, beating through Misty's thin tank top. She was in shorts too, which she wore when getting deliveries ready to go in the mornings, and the sun was hot on her skin.

Misty had lived in southern Nevada long enough to know what over a hundred degrees felt like, and this was it. It might get up to a hundred and ten today, and possibly higher than that. Out here, the temperature of the desert floor could rise to a hundred and twenty and more.

"We need shade," Misty said.

"No kidding," was Graham's helpful answer. "Not in that shed. Don't feel like lying on a rusty nail right now."

Blood poisoning would finish him. There was only so much even Shifters could take.

A nice cool cave with an underground spring would be

perfect. That was too much to hope for, but the mountain they were up against might have a niche or something out of the sun. The mining shaft was out, even if it hadn't been filled in. Old shafts were dangerously unstable and full of vertical shafts that could drop hundreds of feet.

Misty had done enough desert hiking to know that rocks in shade absorbed coolness overnight, and gave off that coolness during the day. Even on the hottest afternoons, a niche that had stayed in shadow all morning could be twenty degrees lower than the rocks just outside it.

Misty squeezed Graham's shoulder again. "I'm going to look for shade. I don't like to move you, but I don't want to watch you burn to a crisp either."

"I'm worried about you more." Graham reached for her hand, his brows drawing down. "Humans die fast in the heat."

"I'm not that delicate. I'll be right back. Don't go away."

"You are that delicate. And you think you're funny too."

Misty leaned down and gave him a soft kiss across his cracked lips, her own as dry. Graham could barely move his mouth in response.

When Misty lifted her head, she saw a flash of naked emotion in Graham's eyes. Need, longing, loneliness, the weight of his position as alpha. On top of that, a tenderness for her.

Misty stilled a moment, soaking it in. She'd never seen any kind of sentiment in Graham for her. Liking yes, and he'd charged out here to rescue her today, but she'd never seen this flash of stark feeling.

She hated that this might be the last time she saw it. If he died today . . .

Misty wouldn't let him. She kissed Graham one more time then rose and brushed herself off. Graham watched her, still frowning. "You be careful, understand me?" he rumbled.

"I will."

"If I have to come looking for you, I'll be pissed off."

"I know." She sent him another smile. "Be right back."

Graham didn't answer. He moved a little, grunting in pain, but Misty made herself walk away from him.

She started for the ridge above them, finding a narrow wash that gave her a clear path upward through the scrub. She went slowly, picking her way along, the wash full of loose rocks. If she fell and broke something, they could both die out here before Dougal returned.

Misty made for a fold of rock that jutted out into the slope from the desert floor. These mountains looked smooth from the distance, but close to, they were clumped with boulders, tough weeds, creosote, and critters. The critters were mostly lizards and birds for now—not too many bugs liked the hot, dry afternoons. But in the evening, crawly things would be everywhere, including snakes. Snakes liked dusk, when they slithered out in droves to soak up the last warmth of the rocks. When the snakes emerged, so would the coyotes.

Misty rounded one particularly large clump of boulders and was rewarded with the sight of a narrow opening between two big rocks. Going carefully, keeping an eye out for snakes that might have come out early, she squeezed herself through the niche.

It was a tight fit. Misty held her breath and inched along, promising herself she'd go back if it got too tight. She couldn't afford to get stuck, and if Graham couldn't fit, the shelter would be useless to him.

Once more step, and Misty popped through. She stopped, looking around in surprise.

A giant cave opened out from the rocks, lit by sunlight streaming through a hole in the granite wall high above. Reflections danced everywhere, caused by a burbling spring that spread out into a pool at the far end of the cave.

"A nice cool cave with an underground spring," Misty whispered. "What do you know?"

CHAPTER FOUR

Misty moved forward cautiously. The sound of trickling water made the thirst she was trying not to think about soar to life. Her tongue stuck to the roof of her mouth, and her lips were aching and cracked. She *needed* that water.

Misty wasn't stupid enough to rush to it, scoop it into her hands, and gulp it down. Water in wild places was likely to be contaminated, especially out here, between a city and a nuclear testing site. Misty might be dying for the water, but she'd be foolish to drink it.

The cave, however, was blissfully cool. If she could get Graham this short distance, they could wait for Dougal here.

The cavern was gigantic from what she could see, as though the whole inside of the mountain had been carved out. The cut in the rock high above, letting in light and air, kept the place from being too damp, but the water cooled it. The faint chill felt like the one in her flower room, always pleasant on a hot afternoon.

Her flower room was nothing but smashed glass and

petals now, Misty thought in sorrow. But she'd have to deal with her destroyed shop later. First, she needed to get Graham here where he could rest and cool down.

"Hey," a voice said.

Misty jumped, her hand going to her chest, her heart banging. A man rose from the other side of the pool of water, where he'd been crouching in the shadows. He wasn't one of Flores's gang boys, she saw to her relief. He was a hiker—tall, with blond hair messy from perspiration, wind, and dirt, and wearing a T-shirt, canvas shorts, thick socks, and hiking boots. A backpack, one of the huge kind that could hold supplies for a multiday hike, lay on the ground near him.

"You lost?" he asked, peering at Misty. "Want some water?"

Yes, she wanted water. "You didn't drink from that stream, did you?" Misty's voice came out a croak.

"Didn't have to." The man held up a bottle. "Brought it with me. You sound terrible. You need help?"

"My friend does." Misty went toward him, stepping carefully, her sandals not made for desert walking. "Some gangbangers shot him."

The man's eyes widened. "Oh, jeez. Are they still around?"

"No, they ran off. Leaving us stranded."

His eyes remained wide. They were dark eyes, a nice contrast with his light-colored hair. The man wasn't much older than Misty, she realized as she reached him. And in great shape. He was tall and lean, his muscles ropy, his skin tanned a liquid brown.

He handed Misty the bottle and watched while she took a sip. Then a gulp. The water tasted good, silken and smooth, cool from the insulated canteen. Misty kept on drinking until the last droplet flowed into her mouth.

"Sorry," she gasped. "Didn't mean to drain it."

"It's all right. I have more. The water is supposed to be inside you, not the bottle. Did you call for help?"

"Another friend went. We couldn't get a signal." Misty looked hopefully at the cell phone on his belt.

He shook his head. "Lost contact about five miles back. Let's get your friend in here, out of the sun."

"Thanks." Misty felt better, first with the water wetting her mouth like sweet nectar; second, because she had someone to help her with Graham. This guy was strong. Everything would be all right.

She handed the canteen back to the hiker, and he gave her another one. "Keep it. You need it, and so will your friend. Show me where he is."

The hiker followed Misty out through the crack in the rocks. The heat hit her like a wall, the sunshine seeming more intense after the cool relief of the cave.

"This way," Misty said as the hiker emerged behind her.

The shack was still in sight. Misty picked her way back down the wash, rocks rolling under her feet and those of the hiker behind her. Misty's soles were burning by the time she reached relatively level ground, her toes bloody from loose rocks.

Graham lay where she'd left him, on his back, eyes closed, one hand behind his head. Misty jogged the last few yards and dropped to her knees beside him, alarmed by the too-shallow rise and fall of his chest. The blood had dried around the duct tape, but the flesh looked swollen and angry.

Graham cracked open his eyes. His gaze was unfocused, and he could barely raise the lids. "You came back." He sounded surprised, pleased, relieved.

"Like I have anywhere else to go. I found some help. There's a cave not far away, out of the sun. There was a hiker there, and he gave me some water."

Graham blinked a few times. He sniffed once, twice, then turned his head and inhaled in Misty's direction.

"I don't like the way you smell," he growled.

"Thanks a lot. You're pretty rank yourself."

Graham didn't smile. "I mean you smell . . . wrong. What hiker?"

"Him." Misty looked up to point at the thin guy, but he wasn't there.

She stood up, scanning the wash and then the desert

around them. She didn't see him anywhere. "He was right behind me."

Graham struggled to raise his head, grunting with effort. Misty knelt beside him again. "Stop. Let me give you some water."

Misty unscrewed the canteen's lid, its slender chain clanking against the container's metal side. She put her hand behind Graham's head and supported him while she more or less poured the water into his mouth.

Graham made a face and tried to spit it out.

"No," Misty said firmly. "Drink it. It's more important for the water to be inside you than in the bottle."

The hiker had said that, but he was right. Graham held his breath and swallowed the water, scowling the entire time. "Rank," he said.

Misty had thought the water tasted good, possibly because she'd been parched. "Have some more," she said.

"No. I'll live."

Graham tried to sit up and ended up crashing down again. "Shit. Hurts."

"No kidding. Do you think you could make it up to the cave? It's getting hotter."

Graham looked up the rise to the boulders on the ridge and took a breath. "Yeah, I can make it. Give me a second."

He closed his eyes again. Misty looked down at him, at his hard, square jaw, firm cheekbones, forehead now creased with dirt. Graham's hair was black, but he kept it buzzed short, a thin wash of darkness on his scalp. Graham couldn't be called handsome, not like some of the other Shifters Misty had met, but there was something about him that made Misty like looking at him. His large body was hard with muscle, his face firm, eyes an intense gray that could pin even the boldest of people in place. A strong man, who even now strove not to show weakness.

After a few minutes, Graham opened his eyes again and nodded. Misty helped him sit up and then, after another time of rest, she helped him to stand.

Graham fell against her as soon as he gained his feet,

and Misty struggled to hold his weight. After a while, he was able to move, and Misty guided him back to the rise, Graham's every step labored.

Misty looked around for the hiker as they climbed up the wash, but she didn't see him. She hoped he was all right, but the desert could be treacherous.

It took much longer to reach the niche in the rocks again, but finally Graham and Misty came to rest on the level ground near the boulders.

Graham stiffened as he leaned against the rocks, and he inhaled sharply. "In there? Are you crazy? I'm not going in there."

"It's a giant cave," Misty said. "It's cool inside—it gets bigger after the entrance. What's the matter?"

She started through the niche. Graham gave a long growl, then sucked in a breath of pain as he pushed in behind her. She reached back and grabbed his hand, guiding him through.

They emerged into the cave . . .

But it was the wrong cave. The hollow in these rocks was cool, but nowhere near as big as the cave in which Misty had found the hiker. This niche was only about five feet deep, ending in a solid granite wall. There was no sign of the pool, or any water at all.

"Damn," Misty said. "That cave was perfect. But at least you can rest here out of the sun. I can look again for the other one. It can't be far away."

Misty turned to leave, but Graham clamped his hand over her wrist. For a wounded man, he had a lot of strength.

His eyes were clear now as he glared down at her. "Give me that water."

"What?" Misty fumbled with the canteen at her waistband. "You could say *please*."

"I'm not joking. Give it to me."

Graham was standing upright, without support, and no blood at all leaked around his wound. The tattoos on his arms were stark against his skin, almost luminous in the shadows.

Misty handed him the canteen. Graham jerked it from her, unscrewed the lid, and took a long sniff of the water inside.

"Shit." His expletive filled the little cave before he upended the canteen and poured the water all over the dirt floor.

"No!" Misty shot her hands out, catching the falling droplets in her cupped palms. She brought her hands to her face and slurped the water, not caring how dirty she was.

Graham slapped her hands down, and the last of the water was lost.

"What are you doing?" Misty asked in a near screech.

"The hiker, where is he?"

"I told you, I don't know." Misty licked her lips, needing every drop of the beautiful water. "He was right behind me. I didn't see where he went."

"Shit," Graham said. "Shit. Shit. Shit."

"Graham, *what* is wrong?"

"Damn it." Graham scrubbed one hand over his short hair as he paced in a circle in shallow cave. "I drank that water."

"So did I."

Graham stopped. He grabbed Misty by the shoulders and yanked her to him, not gently. He looked into her eyes, his brows coming together. "You seem okay."

"I'm fine. You're the one who was shot."

Graham released her and stepped back. "I know. And look at me." He put his hands on his hips, standing upright. His face was no longer drawn and gray, and the spent look was gone from his eyes. He looked hale and well, tall and strong.

Graham ripped the tape from his side. Underneath, his skin was whole, the only thing left of the wound a patch of dried blood. He was completely and undeniably healed.

Misty reached out and touched his side to find warm, firm flesh. "I guess Shifters do heal fast."

"Not *that* fast. There was magic in the water, and there's only one kind of magic going around these days. At least around Shifters."

"Magic? What are you talking about?"

"Bastards. They'll do anything to get Shifters under their power again, and you went and handed me to them. Damn it." He turned away, pacing again. "This is what I get for being nice to a human."

Misty took a step back. "What the hell do you mean I *handed* you to them? *Them* who? I didn't hand you to anybody."

"You forced that water into me. Now I'm screwed. *Shit.*" Graham balled both fists and slammed them into the rock wall.

He hit so hard Misty expected his fingers to break, but the wall chipped, and dirt pattered down like rain. Graham hit the wall again and again, the curse word sounding with each slam. He was enraged, and behind the rage on his stiff face, Misty saw fear.

"Graham, *what* is wrong?"

He swung to her. His eyes were white gray, a wolf's eyes, and his snarl filled the cave. "*You* are what is wrong. Don't you understand? You have *fucked me over.*"

Misty's lips parted, her breath hitching. He was furious, more so than she'd ever seen him, and he was mad at *her*.

Emotions tumbled through her. She'd been terrorized this morning, her fear for her brother overriding her fear for herself. She'd been rescued by Graham, who'd looked pissed off to do it. Then she'd been in danger of dying of heatstroke while she watched Graham start to expire with a bullet in his side. And now Graham was standing here, yelling at *her*.

Words wouldn't come, and neither would her breath. Misty turned her back and walked outside. The sun was beating down hotter than before, afternoon well underway, but she didn't care.

Graham came after her. He didn't bother to stop her; he pushed past her and started down the hill.

A plume of dust rose in the desert about a mile away, a vehicle approaching. Graham went on down the wash, stepping through the slithering stones with agility. Misty picked her way down, the soles of her sandals split, her feet burning.

The dark spot in front of the dust plume enlarged until it became a large black pickup. It skidded a little in the soft dirt as it turned off the track and headed for the shack and Graham.

Even before the truck stopped, Dougal leapt out of the back door of the four-door cab, clad in a new shirt. Dougal ran at Graham, hurtling himself into Graham's arms like a scared adolescent. Graham gathered his nephew into his embrace, holding him, rubbing his back.

The pickup halted, the driver's and passenger's doors opened, and two men got out of the cab. Misty recognized them as she drew near—Diego Escobar, a human who was the mate of her friend Cassidy, and Stuart Reid, a tall man Misty had met only a few times. Reid wasn't Shifter, but he lived in Shiftertown and didn't talk much about his past. He used to be a cop, as had Diego. Now they both worked for Diego's private security company, DX Security.

Misty pressed her hand to her side and hurried the last few yards, breathing hard. The two men and Graham turned to watch her, but Dougal kept his face buried in Graham's shoulder.

"Please say you have water," Misty said as she reached them.

Diego silently held out a sports bottle. Misty upended it, pouring the liquid in a stream into her mouth. The water didn't taste anywhere near as good as the water the hiker had given her, but it was wet, which was the point.

"We need to get out of here," Graham said.

"That's the plan," Diego said then turned to Misty. "You okay?"

"Fine," she said. "Now that there's water." She took another long drink.

Graham ignored them and pushed his way to the truck, Dougal still hanging on him. Without a word, he continued to the truck bed, where he convinced Dougal to turn him loose so Graham could lift his ruined motorcycle into the back, then they both climbed in with it.

Diego watched Graham, a puzzled look on his face. "I thought he got himself shot."

"He did," Misty said, too weary to go into details. "Can we go home now?"

Diego opened the pickup cab's back door. "Your carriage awaits."

Misty gave him a weak smile and let him help her up into the cool interior. Diego had the air-conditioning going full throttle, the icy blast making her blink. Misty leaned back into the soft leather of Diego's custom seats, thinking nothing had ever felt so good.

Diego slid into the driver's seat. Reid, who'd not said a word, was at the back of the truck talking to Graham. Misty couldn't hear what they said, but Reid wore a worried expression as he scanned the desert.

Reid then climbed into the pickup's bed, still conversing with Graham. Diego said nothing, only put the truck into gear and pulled out.

"Can I borrow your phone?" Misty said, her voice thin and tired. "I need to call my brother."

"Already taken care of," Diego said. "Your brother is safe, in Shiftertown, in fact. *My* brother and a couple of my guards are at your house, making sure no bad guys show up there. Paul's at Eric's house, which is where we're headed."

"No," Misty said sharply. "I want to go home."

Diego looked at her in the rearview mirror, surprise on his face. "Your brother's worried about you."

"Keep him safe, and thank you. But I need to be alone for a little bit. Tell Paul I'm fine, and I'll see him later. If my house is safe, I want to go there."

Diego still looked puzzled, but he didn't argue.

Misty dozed off once the truck left rutted road for smooth pavement. The pickup's deeply tinted windows kept out the sun and leather seats cradled her body.

The sleep didn't refresh her, though. Flashes of dreams struck her—Graham with blood all over him, Flores's pockmarked face when he'd pushed it close to hers, the despair when she'd been locked in the hot shack. Threading through these visions was the remembered sensation of the wonderful, sweet, clear coolness of the water. Misty wanted more. She had to have more.

The truck jerked as Diego slowed for traffic on the freeway, and Misty woke. The dreams fled, and she couldn't remember them when she reached for them. But she was still thirsty.

Diego pulled off the freeway and took the streets to the ordinary suburban neighborhood where Misty lived. In a short time, he was pulling into her driveway, the house a welcome sight.

Graham was up and out of the pickup's bed as Misty opened the cab's door and let Diego help her out. She started for her front door but realized in dismay she didn't have her keys. They'd be at the shop in her purse, still locked in her desk drawer.

Didn't matter. Diego's brother Xavier pulled open the house's front door from the inside, looked around, then gave a thumbs-up to Diego.

Graham got in front of Misty as she went up the walk. "Where the hell do you think you're going?"

"Inside." Misty motioned to the door where Xavier waited. "I live here."

Diego raised his brows, looked at Graham, and then turned and moved discreetly back to the pickup, pulling out his phone to text someone.

"You'll be safer in Shiftertown," Graham said, his voice a growl.

"But I want to stay here." Misty shook her head. "Thank you for helping, Graham, and I'm sorry you got hurt because of me." She paused. Xavier had retreated inside the house, as discreet as his brother, leaving her and Graham relatively alone. She drew a breath. "But don't call me again."

"What?" Graham's focus shot to her, the distraction of his fear and anger gone. His eyes burned, every part of his unnerving attention on her.

Misty stepped into the shade of her small front porch. "I said don't call me. I'm done."

"Done with what? What the fuck are you talking about?"

"Good-bye, Graham." Misty made herself walk inside the house and start to shut the door.

She thought Graham would grab the door at the last minute and charge in after her, raging all the way, but he only stood there, amazingly still, his wolf eyes going silver as she closed the door in his face.

CHAPTER FIVE

This is what I get for tangling with a human.

Graham repeated this to himself all the way back to Shiftertown. He and Dougal were now riding inside the cushy cab of Diego's truck, in the backseat, the air conditioning on too high for Graham's taste. But Graham wanted to ride inside because Dougal still needed Graham's reassuring hugs, and Graham didn't want the dumb-ass human police seeing Dougal basically on Graham's lap, and pulling them over. Dougal wouldn't last against human police right now—he might do or say something stupid and get them all arrested.

In fact, humans were pains in the ass all the way around. Graham would keep that fact to himself while Diego, a human, was driving them home. Plus Diego had found Graham a clean T-shirt, black with a tiny *DX Security* logo on it.

But for the most part, humans weren't worth the time. Misty was a distraction for him, and Graham didn't need distractions right now.

Her scent, that was most distracting of all. A scent Graham could wrap around himself until everything bad went away. Misty's smile was pretty good too. He remembered when he'd first seen her in the bar—she'd given him that sweet smile and asked if he was Shifter.

The smile had been completely absent this afternoon when Misty had said, *I'm done,* and closed the door on him. The finality of it bore into Graham's heart.

Like he needed a human in his life. Graham's day had been hell since he'd woken up. First the Lupine woman had attacked him in his own house, sent to try to get Graham to mate with her. Then Misty's scared voice on the phone. In the seconds he'd heard her, he'd known that nothing else mattered but finding Misty and making sure she was all right.

She hadn't been all right. He'd had to fight for her, which had led to him getting shot. Then he'd slowly baked in the sun until Misty made him drink water a Fae had given her.

Graham knew the "hiker" Misty had stumbled upon had been Fae. Reid agreed. The cave she'd described, which had mysteriously disappeared, screamed of Fae. They must have been on a ley line out there in the desert, one of the lines of magic that crisscrossed the world. Stone circles were found on them as well as other mystical places—Fae loved ley lines.

Graham remembered how the gang leader had smirked and said he only needed one Shifter. One Shifter for what? To give to the Fae lurking nearby? For *what*?

No wonder the human had been stupid enough to give Graham directions to his location instead of setting up a dead drop. The human had planned to give him to the Fae. Why, Graham had no idea.

Didn't matter though, did it? Graham had drunk the eff-ing water. It had cured his gunshot wound almost instantly, but Fae cures came with a price. Whatever else the water had done to him, he wasn't sure yet.

He'd planned to talk it over with Misty when they got to Shiftertown, where he'd explain everything to her. Diego, the traitor, had taken her home instead. Fucking humans.

I need her.

Graham banished the voice inside his head. He didn't need Misty. He needed to take a Lupine mate, and soon. Dougal wasn't a natural leader, and his wolves were getting restless because Graham had no other heir. He had to establish his dynasty, have strong cubs of his own who'd protect Dougal as family.

Plus, he needed to keep the wolves he'd brought to this Shiftertown under his control. The human government, trying to consolidate and save money, had closed the Shiftertown in Elko last year and shunted all Graham's Shifters here, expecting Graham and Eric, two powerful alphas, to decide who would lead. The humans had created a powder keg begging to explode. Some of Graham's Shifters were near to feral, having lived close to the wild for so long.

The few Lupines participating in the experiment to take off Collars were getting too big for their britches, like the female this morning. Collars didn't make or unmake dominance. The idiots needed to learn that. Collars just shocked you. Graham had decided to keep his Collar to prove no one would be able to best him despite the torture device around his neck.

No, he thought, as the pickup turned onto the streets of Shiftertown, *I don't need a human woman in my life to screw me up right now.*

I'm done, Misty had said.

Why did those words echo over and over inside his head?

Diego pulled the truck into the driveway of Eric's house. Eric Warden sat on a bench on his low-roofed porch, his bare feet up on the thick wooden railing. He didn't bother to rise when the truck pulled up, only turned his head to watch them stop and get out.

Eric was like that, acting all laid-back and too lazy to do anything. The truth was, he was the dominant Feline—the dominant Shifter—of Shiftertown, and he could switch from laid-back kitty cat to killing machine in a heartbeat.

His mate, Iona, came out of the house with a little more animation. Iona was a sassy sweetheart, even more so now that she was pregnant and about to drop her first cub. Her wildcat was mostly panther—which, everyone had explained to Graham, was a rare, black form of leopard. Explained why she and Eric, a snow leopard, got along so well. The pair of them could be scary as hell when they wanted to be, but mostly they sat around looking pleased with themselves. *Felines.*

Iona started to ask, "What exactly happened?" as Graham lifted his bike out of the back of Diego's truck, but Graham cut over her words.

"We need to contain those humans, Warden. They hurt Misty, and I'm not letting them get away with that."

Another human came out of the house—Paul, Misty's younger brother. He had dark brown eyes, like Misty's, and he was rawboned and lanky, like Dougal. He'd shaved off his hair during his time in prison, but he looked too young for the buzz. For a human, he was full-grown, twenty-three or something like that, but still he looked very young.

He'd been in prison for the last five years, serving a sentence for riding in the back of a stolen car when it had gotten into a wreck that killed other humans. Paul's lawyer had finally gotten him parole six months ago. Graham had been partly responsible for his parole—he'd growled at Eric and Diego until the two had used their influence in the law enforcement system around here to get the kid released.

"Is she all right?" Paul asked anxiously. "Where is she?"

"Home," Graham said. "She needed a break, all right?"

Eyes focused on Graham. Two pairs of Feline eyes, Lupine ones from Dougal, the human eyes of Paul and Diego, and the weird, black-hole eyes of Stuart Reid.

Graham had seen a glimmer of pure rage in Reid's dark eyes when Graham had told him about the Fae. Reid hated Fae—he called them *hoch alfar*—hated them more than Shifters did . . . Nah, that wasn't possible.

"She's *fine*," Graham said into the silence. "Xavier is looking out for her. But we have to cut it off at the source. If we get the leader, the rest will go down easy."

"Already being taken care of," Eric said mildly. "Diego?"

"DX Security tracked down Sam Flores and his gang

nursing themselves at their safe house. Looks like you and Dougal ripped them up pretty good. I dutifully reported Flores's criminal activity to the police. I know guys on the force who were happy to shovel Sam Flores and his boys back into prison. They broke their parole, so they're history. My friends found Dougal's motorcycle and are returning it to the DX Security offices as we speak."

Graham had meant something more permanent for Flores, like quietly breaking his neck and burying him somewhere no one would find him. That's what Flores had intended to do to Misty and Paul, and Graham saw no reason to be lenient.

But human justice was different from Shifter justice. Graham knew he had to let Diego take care of it, much as it chafed him. Diego had been a very good cop, with awards and everything, and the humans respected him, even after he'd mated with a Shifter.

Diego's Shifter mate came out of the house now, carrying their eight-month-old cub, Amanda. Attention left Graham and turned to the baby, who looked fearlessly out at the world from the safety of her mother's arms. She had Diego's dark hair but Cassidy's Feline green eyes. Diego had been surprised by the green eyes, but genetics worked a little differently for Shifters. Amanda would be Feline, like Cassidy, but because she was half human, she'd not change into her Feline form for a few years yet.

Cassidy smiled at Diego, her love for her human obvious. Diego had gone through a Fae magic ritual that would extend his lifespan to be close to what Cassidy's natural one would be. Graham had always wondered why the Fae had agreed, centuries ago, to perform this service for Shifters who took human mates, but he'd never bothered to track down a Fae and ask him. Graham stayed as far away from anything Fae as he possibly could.

Which brought him back around to the current problem. The shot he'd taken was a flea bite compared with what the Fae had potentially done to him.

And no one could know. Graham had told Reid, but Reid

could keep his mouth shut. If any hint got out among the Shifters that Graham might be Fae-touched, he'd be finished. His wilder Lupines might try to kill him and take over his power. Eric would try to stop them, and then there'd be a battle to the death, a bloodbath the Collars couldn't slow. Eric would win in the end, but a lot of good Shifters could die, including cubs.

This was turning out to be one hell of a day.

"I'm going home," Graham said. "Call me if you need help taking out the humans."

"Thanks, Graham," Paul said after him. "For helping her."

Graham made an indifferent wave. "Whatever." He and Dougal, who still didn't want to move more than a step away from Graham, went home, wheeling Graham's broken bike between them.

Graham lived in the new section of Shiftertown, where houses were still under construction. Graham's house and about six others were completely done, the others nearing completion.

Because Graham was a leader, he'd insisted on his house being bigger than the others. Eric might play *I'm-the-same-as-you* with his Shifters, but Graham decided to never let others forget his position. A Shifter played with fire if he did.

The newer houses were more modern looking than the ones on Eric's street, with stucco and tile, and lots of windows. Graham's house had a second floor. The older portion of Shiftertown had been built in the 1960s, when people kept out the heat with small windows set high under the eaves, thick outer walls, and flat, white roofs. Graham had insisted on more modern insulation and double-paned windows, and Iona, who owned the construction company that built the houses, had agreed.

All the new houses had air-conditioning that worked, so Graham walked into a cool haven. He shut the door behind him and Dougal and let out a sigh of relief.

Dougal was still stressed. Graham could scent it on the lad, sweat mixed with panic and exhaustion.

Graham turned to his nephew, who was starting to curl in on himself, straightened him up, and pulled him into another hard hug. Graham had been doing this for thirty years, he realized—holding Dougal while he grew up.

"You did good out there." Graham patted Dougal's back and tightened the hug. "You knew exactly what to do, and you brought help in time. We made it, and we're home, and whole."

Dougal nodded against Graham's shoulder. He stayed dormant in Graham's embrace for a time, then he took a deep breath, his strength returning. Shifter hugs were more than just comfort; they were healing.

"Better?" Graham asked, releasing him.

Dougal wiped his eyes as he turned away. "I'm fine. Don't worry about me. I have things to do, Shifters to see. Call me if you need me again."

Dougal walked to the front door, the swagger returning to his step. Graham hid his chuckle until Dougal had breezed out of the house, slamming the door behind him. He'd be all right.

Graham's laughter died as he made his way to the kitchen, thirst kicking him. He'd known the water was foul as soon as he'd smelled it, but his thirst had won over his common sense. And now he was thirsty again. He clenched his fists. If he gave in to a Fae curse, he might as well summon the Guardian and fall on the sword.

Misty hadn't seemed affected by the spelled water. Graham had looked into her face and hadn't seen anything but her clear, brown eyes, framed with thick, dark lashes. Lashes he'd love to feel fluttering over his skin.

Don't call me again, she'd said.

She hadn't meant that, right? So hard to tell with humans. Misty had gone through trauma today, been threatened, terrorized, and hurt, poor thing. When she felt better, she'd call Graham and ask if they could talk. Misty liked to talk. On the phone, in person, over e-mail. Graham had never talked much with his other females, but then, his previous relationships had been all sex and not much else.

Even with his mate, Rita, they'd spent most of the time in bed. They'd never really *talked*. Graham had never taken the opportunity to truly get to know Rita, and then she'd been gone, dead, the Guardian turning her to dust. Her death and his baby son's had left him stunned, barely able to think beyond his grief.

Brooding about Rita and Misty wasn't going to help Graham with his problems now. A Shifter had to push away grief and relationship worries and concentrate on immediate problems. That was the only way to survive. Right?

Graham walked into his kitchen, deep in thought . . . and stopped. Something was very wrong. He'd left the place trashed, yes, with his stupid fight with that Lupine, but not *this* trashed.

Someone had opened every single door of every single cabinet, and had yanked out every single drawer. Graham's pots, pans, and dishes, and cans and boxes of food were all over the floor, porcelain smashed, glasses broken, boxes opened, powder and grains spewed everywhere. The refrigerator door was ajar, and bottles and cans had burst open on the floor outside it, rendering the tiles a mess of ketchup, mustard, pickles, and beer. The refrigerator was shaking now too, as though it had taken on a life of its own.

No Fae spell was doing this. Graham roared as he yanked open the door.

Two fuzzy faces turned toward him, two pairs of eyes widened under two pairs of ears that managed to be pricked and flopping at the same time. Two little muzzles opened in identical, high-pitched howls, and two tails started moving rapidly, dumping over a half gallon of milk between them.

"What the hell are you doing in there?" Graham bellowed.

Matt and Kyle, the three-year-old wolves, yipped with joy, and launched themselves out of the refrigerator. They had a frenzied fight over who would reach Graham first, Kyle winning by a whisker. Both cubs scrambled up Graham's legs to his bare arms, wriggling with joy as though they hadn't seen him in weeks instead of about twenty-four hours.

Graham's back door opened, and a Shifter woman came in—Brenda Roberts, the cubs' foster mother. She ducked her head, as all Graham's wolves did when they faced their alpha, but her eyes held defiance.

"I can't do it anymore, Graham," she said. "I can't take care of them. I have my own cubs to look after, and I. Just. Can't. Do. It."

"What the hell are you talking about?" Graham asked, something like panic rising. "You're taking care of them fine."

Brenda shook her head and kept on shaking it. "No I'm not. I'm not sleeping, or eating, or doing anything but running around after those two little shits. I can't even go to the bathroom without them coming in and tearing down the shower curtain and eating the toilet paper. They need a firm hand, Graham, and mine's not firm enough."

"I don't have time for this," Graham said loudly. Kyle and Matt clung to him, small claws digging into his arms. "If you don't want to take care of them, fine. But they stay with you until I can find another foster."

Brenda was already shaking her head again. "I can't. When they had space to run around up in Elko, they were fine. Sort of. Now that they're more restricted, they're going insane and taking me with them. I've gone through eight months of hell, and I can't do it anymore. Punish me if you want to, but I'm not keeping those cubs another day."

Brenda still wouldn't look at Graham directly, but she had determination on her face. Lower dominance wolves never disobeyed their alpha—unless driven beyond normal endurance into something that would break them. Brenda had stood strong behind Graham and given a lot to the Lupines. And now this loyal wolf was being defeated by two adorable cubs who looked up at Graham with innocent eyes.

Graham could shove the cubs back at her and tell her to suck it up; he had that right. She could obey, or she could die.

But Graham wasn't leader because he was the loudest-voiced asshole in the pack, no matter what anyone else thought. He'd seen how worn down Brenda was, and it was true—she had four cubs of her own. She'd taken Kyle and Matt because of her soft heart, and Graham knew he'd taken advantage of her. So had Matt and Kyle.

"All right, all right," Graham said. "Just go."

Brenda's shoulders slumped in relief. She wouldn't have left the house without Graham giving her permission—not like Misty—no matter how much staying was upsetting her.

Brenda gave him a grateful look then turned around and marched out the door, the draft of its closing rushing over Graham and the cubs.

"Shit."

Graham grabbed both cubs by their scruffs and held them up, facing him. "What am I going to do with you two?"

Kyle and Matt squirmed in joy and wagged their tails.

"Shit," he repeated, softly this time. Raising Dougal had been the hardest thing Graham had ever done—he was still doing it. No way could he go through that again. "Tell you what; we'll go visit a nice Shifter lady whose cubs had to have been worse even than you two."

Fine with Matt and Kyle. Graham left the disaster of his kitchen and went out of the house again. He marched back through Shiftertown, the two wolf cubs on his shoulders clinging so tightly they ripped into the black shirt Diego had given him, cutting into Graham's skin underneath.

CHAPTER SIX

Misty surveyed the wreck of her store without being
able to feel much. She'd built the shop with nothing
but a little savings, a start-up grant for women in small
business, and a bit of know-how.

Her father had been great at starting businesses. He'd
absolutely sucked at keeping the businesses going after a
week or two, because his get-rich-quick plans never worked
out. But it had been so much fun for Misty and Paul to help
him out. When the three of them had been together, working, planning, and dreaming, they couldn't be stopped.

Dad had never succeeded, and had died in an accident
when Misty had been a senior in high school. Misty had
learned from him, though, how to get a business up and
running. She'd chosen a flower shop because people bought
flowers when they wanted to make other people happy or
cheer them up. Misty had had enough unhappiness shoved
at her in her lifetime that she wanted a career that would
take her away from that.

She'd discovered selling flowers was not as easy as it seemed, but she'd researched, worked hard, and got lucky when

this strip mall had a small slot to fill. Her shop didn't make millions, but Misty made a living, and she liked what she was doing. Now that Paul had his parole, he worked for her, doing deliveries and running errands, and he was enjoying it.

Misty had labored so hard for this business, and one person with a grudge had ruined it in the space of a morning. She might have to close, not just until she cleaned up the store, but for good. She'd had to cancel the orders for today that hadn't already been on the van, and she'd probably have to cancel the rest of the orders for the month and return her customers' money. One of Diego's security team had taken the shop's van, the only thing intact, out to make the remaining deliveries so Paul could stay safely in Shiftertown.

Misty knew she owed Diego and his guys for all their help. Graham too, even more so. She and Paul would have been dead today if it hadn't been for Graham.

Xavier Escobar had driven her down to the store and come in with her. "What a mess," he said, looking around. "At least we got the bastards who did this."

Misty nodded, her throat tight. "I really appreciate you taking care of Paul. If something had happened to him . . ."

"It wouldn't have been your fault," Xavier said quickly, putting a warm hand on her shoulder. "Guys like Flores think they own the world and everyone in it. They need to be taught they don't." He chuckled. "It's kind of fun to teach them."

Xav was such a nice guy, in a hard don't-mess-with-me kind of way. He too was a former cop, and had started DX Security with Diego to help people who couldn't otherwise find help, which Misty could respect.

"We can have a team in here to clean up right away," Xav said. "Make the place good as new."

Misty shook her head and moved away from him. "Insurance assessment first. That's why I pay for it."

"Okay, but if they start being a pain in the ass about it, you call me. I know people, Iona's family runs a construction company, Shifters like to build things . . ."

He leaned against the one clear spot on the counter as he spoke. Xav had brown black hair, dark brown eyes, liquid dark skin, and a square, handsome face. A hot man on a hot day. Why couldn't Misty fall for someone like him?

But no, she had to have a soft spot for a crazy wolf Shifter with a growling voice and a piercing gray stare. She shivered as she thought about that stare when she'd closed the door on him. But Misty had needed to be alone, to think, to worry about why Graham had been so enraged at her, why he'd said such things to her. And why was she so *thirsty*?

"Any more water left?"

Xavier looked into the little cooler he'd brought with him. "You drank the last one."

No problem. She'd go across to the convenience store. Misty was out the door and halfway across the parking lot before Xavier could follow.

At the convenience store, Misty nodded a hello to Pedro at the cash register then went straight to the drink refrigerators and started taking out bottles of water. If she was this dehydrated, she thought dimly, she should grab some Gatorade or something. But no, she wanted *water*. Buckets of it.

"Hey," a voice said beside her.

Misty looked up, her arms full of blissfully cool and moist bottles, to see the hiker from the desert. He was still in his hiking gear, a little more sweaty and dirty than before, and he was reaching for water too.

"You made it back," he said.

Obvious, since Misty was standing right there. "Yeah. We made it. What happened to you? I thought you were right behind me, and then you weren't."

The hiker shrugged. "Took a different trail. Didn't see you. When I looked for you, you were gone, so I figured you'd caught a ride."

Misty nodded. "Friends came and picked us up."

"Good." He plucked a bottle out of the fridge and smiled at her.

The smile was odd. His teeth weren't exactly pointed, but they didn't look right either. His hair, tousled and sweat soaked, covered his head to his neck. When his hair wasn't dirty, it would be very light blond, almost white.

"See ya," he said, and turned his lanky body to move to the cash register.

Misty took yet another bottle from the fridge and wished she'd thought to grab a handbasket. By the time she struggled up to the register, the hiker was gone.

"What are the odds?" she asked.

"What?" Pedro looked at her blankly, pausing as he rang up her purchase.

Misty realized she'd said the words out loud. "What are the odds that a guy I met out in the desert turns up at *this* convenience store? How many are in this city—say, thirty? More than that? But he comes to the one right next to my shop."

"Maybe he likes you," Pedro said, counting out her change.

"And followed me? Creepy. Did you see what kind of car he has?"

"Nope. Didn't see him get into a car at all. Or anything." He handed Misty the change. "Sorry about your store. Did they get the guys who did it?"

"Yes. They've been arrested."

"Thank God. That was fast. I worked at a store that was robbed seven times, and no one ever found anyone. Cops were all over your place though."

Misty didn't bother to mention the role Shifters had in taking down Flores and his little gang. She wasn't sure which way Pedro leaned on Shifters.

"Thanks, Pedro. See you."

Pedro said a cordial good-bye and turned to his next customer. Misty drank half a bottle of water walking back to her store, where Xavier met her and escorted her back inside.

"You shouldn't stay here," Xav said as Misty looked around at her ruined store again.

"I need to . . ." She stopped, and couldn't finish.

Misty felt Xav's warm arm around her. "I'll give you a

ride back home. Our guys will watch over this place better than any security camera or cops on patrol. You don't have to worry about a thing."

One of the "guys" he talked about was Shane, a bear Shifter who lived next door to Eric, who now grinned at her from the back and gave her a wave. Misty had never seen Shane shift into a bear, a grizzly, but his bulk at the door did make her feel better. Sam Flores and men like him would never get past Shane.

Misty gave Xav a smile and turned away, gathering up the cash from her register and safe to take to the bank. Flores had been so intent on his revenge on Paul he hadn't bothered to rob her.

One bunch of roses in her cooler had survived intact. Misty found a vase for them, and then Xavier helped her carry everything out to his truck, got her inside, drove her to the bank, and then home.

"Thanks, Xavier. Lindsay is lucky to have you."

Xavier gave a laugh as he followed Misty out of the truck and into her house, the vase under his arm. "Lindsay and I have fun, but she can take me or leave me. She goes out with other guys, and I learned a while ago either to be fine with it or stop seeing her at all."

Misty knew he wasn't wrong. Lindsay had told Misty that she wasn't ready to settle down yet and look for a mate. She was only fifty, for the Goddess's sake, she'd said, laughing. She had a lot of wild oats to sow, and female Shifters could sow some serious oats.

"Sorry about that," Misty said.

Xavier shrugged. "We're both young. I give her space, and she gives me space. Maybe one day . . ."

"Well, she should take what she's got while she can."

Misty headed for the kitchen and laid the roses on the counter, scarlet heads resting on paper towels. She took the vase from Xavier and started running water into it.

Cool, flowing water, reminding her of the water in the cave. Sweet, burbling, enticing water. Misty had wanted to strip off her clothes and dive her hot body into the pool, except the hiker had been there.

Truly weird how he'd happened to show up at the convenience store where she was. Made her shiver. Misty was grateful for Xavier's presence and reassurance.

"You're sweet," Xavier said, as Misty lifted the dripping vase to more paper towels on the counter.

"Hmm?" she asked absently, snipping the last inch or so from the roses' stems. "For what?"

"For what you said about Lindsay. Graham should appreciate *you* better."

"I dumped him," Misty said.

Xav blinked. "You what?"

"I said, I dumped him." Misty tore off low-hanging leaves with more force than necessary and stuck the roses into the vase. "I'm tired of him assuming I'll be there for him whenever he wants." She jabbed the stems in. "He expects me to be waiting, as though I don't exist when he isn't around. But I have a *life*. If he doesn't want me in his, then fine." She stuck in the last rose, cleaned up the mess, and carried the vase to a table in the hall. The roses filled the space with bright color and fragrance.

Xavier followed her. "I guess I get that."

"I mean, it's not like we have a sex life or anything. I don't know what Graham finds wrong about me, but he's not interested."

"Not interested?" Xavier looked Misty up and down with flattering interest. "Is he insane?"

"*You* know what it is to be a human around Shifters. I liked Graham as soon as I saw him, but he drives me *crazy*. What is wrong with me? I'm pretty sure he backs off me because I'm not Shifter. I bet that's why Lindsay keeps it cool with you too."

Xavier started to shake his head, and ended up shrugging. "Yeah, I figured that."

"Look at us. We're both two perfectly nice people. Why are we hanging around waiting on Shifters instead of finding other perfectly nice humans to be with? We're no better than the Shifter groupies."

Xav let out another laugh. "Are you sure you've only been drinking water?"

"Very sure. But I'm still thirsty. I must have gotten seriously dehydrated. I'll start on the booze as soon as I feel better."

"Why don't you drink some more water and lie down or something?" Xav said. "I'll be here, standing guard, so you don't have to worry about anything. You had an ordeal."

Misty sighed. "See? I'm right—you *are* sweet. Lindsay doesn't know what she's missing."

Xav actually started to blush. Misty went around him and back to the fridge to grab a bottle of water with electrolytes. On the way out of the kitchen, she paused next to Xavier, rose on her tiptoes, and kissed his cheek.

"That's dangerous," Xav said in a low voice.

Misty walked away from him, opened the bottle, and gulped down a third of the water on her way to the bedroom.

She fell asleep very quickly. She tried to think about Xav's handsome face, but it was instantly blotted out by Graham's hard, intense stare, and then she was asleep and dreaming.

Misty thought she was back in the huge cave she'd found. Water burbled in the middle of it, this time in an ornate, gigantic fountain that flowed into a river of water. Flowers and vines snaked around the fountain, up the rock walls, across the floor. These flowers shouldn't be thriving, not out here. Desert flowers could be gorgeous, but these were from a hothouse garden—large puffs of white hyacinths, climbing yellow roses, and red and pink dots of sweet william, mixed with tropical flowers like bird-of-paradise. Everything was beautiful in a bizarre kind of way.

Misty's mouth went drier than ever as she gazed at the fountain. She *needed* that water.

Come. Drink.

The hiker stood near the fountain. He was no longer the scruffy, dirt-stained, sweaty man who'd talked to her in the desert and the convenience store. His face was clean, sharp, and his hair, white blond, flowed to his waist in a long, straight wave. Some women would kill for hair like that.

Misty couldn't see what the hiker wore now, but whatever it was shimmered and caught the light.

"Come," the hiker said again. His voice was deeper than when she'd first heard it, the vowels long, consonants soft. "Rest. Slake your thirst."

Misty licked her lips, finding them dry and cracked, her mouth parched.

"Drink," the hiker whispered.

Misty took a step forward. Then she stopped. Everything inside her screamed at her not to go near that fountain, as enticing as it was.

The hiker spoke again, his voice smooth and coaxing. "The Shifter is dying. Take him the water. It is the only thing that will save him."

What Shifter? Then Misty saw Graham lying on the ground, flowering vines encircling him. His face was wan, blood coated his bare torso, and his breathing was rapid and shallow. He opened wolf gray eyes and stared right at her.

"Misty." The word was faint, scratchy, Graham's voice nowhere near as rich as the hiker's. "Help me."

"Only the water will cure him," the hiker said. "Take it."

He reached into the fountain then lifted his hand and let droplets trickle back into the river with a silvery sound. Misty's thirst jumped higher.

No, something inside her pleaded. *Don't.*

But this was only a dream. It didn't matter what she did in a dream, did it?

"Misty," Graham said again. "Please help me, love. I'm so sorry I hurt you."

Misty froze again, staring at Graham. He looked back at her, sorrow in his eyes.

Now she *knew* it was a dream. Because no way in hell

would Graham ever say in a cultured tone, *Please help me, love. I'm so sorry I hurt you.*

The dream Graham blinked, scowled, and took a deep breath. "Don't listen to the bastard. He's tricking you. He thinks humans are easy." He sounded much more like himself—gruff, gravelly, impatient.

The hiker's voice rose to drown out Graham's. "He needs the water. He will die. Would you let him die to assuage your pride? Save him, Misty."

No, she wouldn't let Graham die. All she had to do, at least in the dream, was take him a drink of that water.

Misty started forward. One little scoop, and Graham would feel better. Then the dream would go away, and she could sleep in peace.

A growl made her halt. The growl wasn't huge and fierce, like Graham's, but small, childish, and insistent. And at her feet.

Misty looked down. Two wolf cubs stared back up at her. Their muzzles were fuzzy, their eyes big, their ears perked. Both bared little wolf teeth in full snarls. When they grew up, those snarls would be frightening; right now, they were tiny but unceasing.

Misty had met these two before, Matt and Kyle, orphaned twins who lived in Shiftertown. They could shift into twin three-year-old boys, but they liked to stay in wolf form, better for running around and playing, they'd once explained.

"Where'd you two come from?" Misty asked.

Both cubs wagged their tails, but when Misty tried to step past them, they got in front of her again, little bodies vibrating with their growls.

"Leave them," the hiker said. "They don't understand."

One of the cubs, Kyle or Matt—she could never tell them apart—turned to the hiker, planted his little feet, and howled at him. The hiker hissed and pointed his finger at Kyle . . . or Matt.

Misty didn't like the pointing finger. She expected lightning or something to come out of it, and since this was a dream, it probably could.

Misty leapt between the hiker and the cubs. "Don't even think about hurting them," she shouted. "And get the hell out of my dream."

The hiker started for her. Matt and Kyle were going insane, trying to move around her to attack. Misty put her arms out in an attempt to protect them and Graham behind them.

"Leave the Shifters *alone!*"

The hiss turned to a snarl, a cold, nasty sound, and then all Misty could feel was ice. It coated the flowers and killed them instantly, then started toward Graham.

Misty snatched up the cubs under her arms—these little squirming guys were *heavy*. She flung herself and them on top of Graham, trying to shield him from the creeping ice.

"Hey, I'm starting to like this dream," Graham said, his voice still too weak.

Kyle and Matt wriggled out of Misty's grasp. Tails moving fast, they licked Graham's face. "Shit," he said, screwing his eyes shut. "Now I'm hating it again."

Kyle and Matt raised their heads and began growling anew. Misty looked up, and screamed.

The fountain had turned into a wave of ice, and now it was coming for them. The ice rose, frost white but with blackness in the center. It dove straight for them. Misty scooped Kyle and Matt underneath her, and stretched out on Graham's hard body. Graham's arms came around her, warm, strong, and caring.

The black wave washed over them, engulfing them, sucking them down into hideous darkness.

Misty screamed again and jumped awake.

Two men stood at the foot of her bed. One was Xavier. The other was Reid, tall and tight-bodied, like the hiker, but with dark hair instead of white blond. He had the same kind of eyes though, dark and mind-sucking, staring straight through her.

Misty yelped again and grabbed at the blankets. In her mad scramble, she tangled herself up, overbalanced, and rolled straight off the bed and onto the floor.

CHAPTER SEVEN

"You all right?" Xavier's firm hand was there to help her to her feet.

Misty pushed her hair out of her face, plopped back down on the bed, and let out her breath. She was wearing only a long T-shirt, which covered her underwear, thankfully. "How do you think I am? I just woke up with two men standing over my bed."

"Reid and I heard you screaming."

"Had a bad dream. Sorry, I'm still a little shaky. And thirsty." She licked the inside of her mouth.

Xav and Reid were staring at her as though they'd never seen a woman wake up from a bad dream before. Misty stood up, pushing aside the blankets, and started out of the room.

She heard Xav and Reid follow as she padded down her narrow hall and out into the kitchen. She opened the refrigerator, yanked out a bottle of water, and saw it was the last. "Need to go to the store."

"You're not going anywhere," Xav said. "I'll send someone shopping for you, until we're sure it's safe for you to go out."

Misty regarded him sharply as she pried open the water bottle. "You said you got Flores. Who else is after me?"

Xav exchanged a look with Reid. Xav started to say, "We're not sure . . ." but Reid cut him off.

"Tell me about the dream."

Misty took several gulps of water, letting the wetness slosh around her mouth before she answered. "I saw that hiker, and the cave again."

"Every detail," Reid said.

Reid looked a lot like the hiker. Not exactly, but enough to be unnerving. His build was similar, though the shape of his face was different. The greatest similarity was his eyes. Reid's coal dark eyes had the same kind of intense focus as the hiker's.

Misty related the dream to the two of them, remembering more of it as she spoke. She described the pool, Graham lying hurt nearby, the hiker's commands, the wave of ice, and the two wolf cubs trying to stop her.

Reid listened without blinking. How did anyone not blink for that long?

"Fae water," Reid said.

Misty glanced at her bottle. "What water?"

"Spelled. One drink holds you in thrall, giving the Fae a way to find you, no matter where you are. The only thing that will slake your thirst is another drink of the water. The Fae will make you his slave, forcing you to do his bidding in exchange for another sip. But the satisfaction doesn't last, and you will be as thirsty as before. More, even. Those enslaved end up parched and dying, no matter how much water they drink."

Fear worked its way through Misty. "But wait, that's not right. It was just a dream. I'm thirsty because I was stuck out in the desert for hours. I was starting to get heatstroke. It takes a long time to cool the body down again."

"No," Reid said. "The person you describe is a *hoch alfar*. How he got to the place in the desert you were, I don't know. There must be a ley line there."

"What the hell is a *hock . . what*?"

Xav answered. "A Fae. They come into human mythology as fairies. You know, as in fairy tales, fairy godmothers. But apparently, they're evil bastards, not the cute things with wings." He jerked his thumb at Reid. "He's a Fae."

Reid looked annoyed. "I am *dokk alfar*. Dark Fae. Not the evil-bastard kind."

"Depends on your point of view," Xav said without smiling.

Misty opened her mouth to argue some more—they had to be insane—but Xav's words made her remember something. "Wait a minute."

Sucking on more water, Misty left the kitchen and made her way back down the hall, the tile floor cool to her bare feet. The bedroom she used as her home office was comfortingly cluttered, her computer and sheets of invoices waiting for her to catalog them, her shelves filled with books on flowers and plants.

Misty scanned the shelves, which contained books about everything from scientific studies of rose growing to the meanings of flowers in Victorian times. She had books on the care of cut flowers, flower arranging, how commercial flowers were grown and cultivated, and the history of every flower imaginable and how to grow them.

Misty also collected unusual books about flowers, buying them at antique stores, flea markets, garage sales, and used bookstores. She'd found fascinating gems filled with flower lore from centuries past.

There it was. Misty reached to the top shelf and pulled out a small book, leather bound, with the binding still pretty good. The book had been published in 1907, and by the quantity of handwritten notes and underlining inside, had been used quite a bit. She'd found the book at the bottom of a cardboard box of old paperback romances; the indifferent flea market vendor had charged her a dollar for the entire box.

She sat down at her desk, opened the book, and scanned it for what she was looking for. Misty found the slanting pen strokes of the little volume's unknown previous owner strangely calming. Whoever it was had written such notes as, *Only attempt under a waxing moon; Make sure the flowers have bloomed three days on the bush and are cut in the morning; Scatter the leftover petals across water in the light of the setting sun.*

Misty flipped through until she found the entry she was looking for. *To counter Faery magic.*

She read, her heart beating faster. *Gather petals of red roses, washed three times, chopped with a fine-bladed knife. Immerse in alcohol, and drink by the light of the moon. Drink four quantities. Bury leftover rose petals in the earth, turn thrice, and open to the cleansing rays of the moon, the Mother Goddess.*

Xav and Reid were watching her, less curious than they were worried. Misty realized she was murmuring to herself, as she sometimes did when working here alone.

She held up the book. "It's an out-there idea, but you never know."

Reid reached for the book. Misty handed it to him, and his brows drew down as he read the page through. "This is—"

His words were cut off by a loud thumping on the front door, bangs like blows from a large and very angry hammer.

Xavier lost his friendly look, his hand going to the gun in his back holster. He stepped out into the hall, blocking Misty's way, and started for the front.

The door burst open, wood splintering as the lock gave way. A hulk of a man strode in, followed, incongruously, by two small boys.

"Misty!" Graham's bellow rocketed through the house.

Xav relaxed and took his hand from the pistol. Reid joined Xav, the two of them still shielding Misty as Graham came on like a freight train.

"I'm right here," Misty said between the two tall men.

Graham glared at the wall of Xav and Reid. "Get out of the way. I'm not going to hurt her."

Xav didn't move. "She said you split up. Now you tear

down the door and come running inside her house. What are we supposed to think?"

"Move, Escobar, or I'll break your ass. Misty, what the fuck was that?"

"What was what?" Misty squeezed around Xav, who let out an exasperated breath as he let her go. Misty eyed the hole where her door latch used to be and the splinters of wood that clung to it. "Graham, you broke my *door*. What the hell?"

Graham grabbed Misty by the shoulders and stared down into her eyes. The two kids, Matt and Kyle in their human form, grabbed onto his legs, one to each. "You were in that dream, right?" Graham demanded. "The one with the fountain and the Fae?"

Misty's mouth dropped open. "How did you know that?"

"I was there. The Fae bastard kept trying to get you to drink the water, and to give it to me."

"And the wolf cubs stopped me."

"Then you all jumped on me." Graham let out a growl. "Had to wash all the spit off my face when I woke up. They were licking me for real."

"This can't be right. How did we share a *dream*?"

"Because Fae magic is messed up. I saw the ice coming for you. I was afraid . . ."

Graham's fingers clamped down on her shoulders, and the lines around his eyes tightened. Misty saw the fear in him, stark and real, which he strove to cover.

"I'm all right," Misty said, softening her voice. "Xav woke me up, and it all went away."

Graham's fingers tightened more, his anger returning to drive out the fear. "*Xav* woke you? What the hell was Xav doing with you while you were asleep?" His glare shot to Xavier, who stood without flinching.

"Guarding me," Misty said. "What did you think?"

Graham's growl increased, his eyes turning very light gray. He said nothing, only fixed his wolf stare on Xav.

"Keep it cool," Xavier said, unruffled. "I'm not a shit-head who takes advantage of a lady in distress."

"The points to focus on," Reid broke in firmly, "are the shared dream, the Fae spell, and how to break it."

Misty shrugged out of Graham's grasp, much as she liked the comfort of his touch, even when he dug in. "That's what you made me remember, Reid—I'd found a book of magic spells involving flowers. I thought it was just nonsense, but now I'm willing to give the rose spell a try." Anything to break this thirst. She looked down at the boys, who were still clinging to Graham, being quieter than she'd ever seen them. "Thank you, Matt and Kyle, for helping." She glanced back up at Graham. "Were you all taking a nap?"

"I was walking across Shiftertown to take them to the bears," Graham said. "I woke up flat on my ass in the dirt, with two wolf cubs licking my face all over. Little shits."

Both boys grinned. Their faces were dirty, their T-shirts crooked, as though someone—probably Graham—had dressed them in a hurry. One boy had hair a lighter shade of brown than the other; one had brown eyes and one hazel. A way to tell them apart, Misty thought, as soon as she figured out which was which.

Misty leaned to them, her long T-shirt hanging to her knees. "You two want some ice cream?"

"Ice cream!" The boys released Graham at the same moment and hurtled toward the kitchen.

"No shifting!" Graham bellowed after them. "They don't need any more food, Misty. They already ate everything in my fridge. Don't know why they haven't gotten sick yet."

"Energy," Xav said. "Diego and I gobbled down everything in sight when we were kids. Still do." He grinned.

Misty ducked back into her bedroom to change into a pair of shorts and a tank top. By the time she emerged, the three men had gone into the kitchen after the cubs. Reid was sitting at the table going through the book, Xav leaned on the counter near the back door, and Matt and Kyle had planted themselves in front of the refrigerator door, eyeing it longingly. Graham, behind them, had obviously told them *not* to open it.

"Come on, sweeties." Misty took down bowls, fetched

chocolate-vanilla swirl ice cream from the freezer, and spooned it into bowls. After observing the frozen chunks of chocolaty vanilla cream, icy in the bowls, Misty scooped out a helping for herself.

"Xav?" she offered. "Reid? Want any?"

Reid held up a hand without looking away from the book. Xav shook his head, giving her a small smile. "Not while I'm on duty."

Graham didn't respond as Misty carried the bowls to the table, sat the little boys down, and gave them spoons. The two boys stared at the spoons, mystified, then lifted the bowls, and started licking the ice cream out of them.

"Hey!" Graham roared. "Be civilized."

"Don't yell at them." Misty sat down across the table from Reid and lifted her spoon. "Maybe they don't know. Like this."

Misty demonstrated how to hold the spoon and dip it into the ice cream, then she scooped some into her mouth. Frozen goodness coated her tongue, momentarily easing her constant thirst. Would be great if she could cure herself with ice cream.

As soon as she swallowed, the thirst came back, so she shoveled in more ice cream.

Kyle and Matt watched her, wide-eyed. "You can eat faster our way," one of them—Kyle?—said.

Misty wanted to. She could lift the bowl to her mouth and take all its contents in one gulp. The only reason she didn't was because Graham had sat down next to her and was watching her closely.

His gaze flicked to the spoon as she dipped it into the cream then followed it back to her mouth. He fixed on her lips as the ice cream went in, dropped to her throat as she swallowed, then returned to her lips, where a bit of cream lingered.

When Graham looked at her fully, Misty stilled, caught by eyes that held heat like silver fire. A shudder worked its way through her, besting even the thirst that popped back up as soon as she stopped eating.

Quench it with Graham . . .

The thought made her shake. Misty dug her spoon through the bowl, slowly lifting another scoop of cream. The ice cream was starting to melt now, its chocolate-stained vanilla droplets falling back into the bowl.

She lifted the spoon to her mouth. Graham's gaze fixed on her even tighter. Misty moved her tongue out and licked up a dollop from her spoon.

A growl sounded in Graham's throat, one so soft Misty knew only she could hear it. She took another lick of cream from the spoon. Graham sat so still he might have been carved into the chair, but his chest rose and fell sharply.

His face held the hardness of a man who'd survived on his strength alone for a long time, but Misty had always seen something in him besides the hardness. The tiny lines that feathered from the corners of his eyes, for example. He got them from laughing—Graham was a man not afraid to laugh. He could roar with it. Scars crisscrossed his cheek-bones, and his nose had been broken, several times, he'd told her. His face was sunburned from their adventure today, but even that was healing, his skin settling into its usual liquid tan.

The sun-bronzing made his eyes stand out even more, the gray turning to silver as he watched her lick another bit of ice cream. She moved her tongue around the mound on the spoon and drew it back between her lips . . .

Graham snarled. With one flick of his big hand, he sent the ice cream bowl flying across the table to shatter on the floor.

Misty could form only the first syllable of his name in protest before he was up and out of the kitchen, striding out the back door into her small, walled yard.

As she leapt up to follow him, she realized the entire kitchen had gone quiet. Matt and Kyle were staring, their eyes round, spoons frozen in place. Xavier, across the room, was watching as well. He didn't smile, but there was a knowing look in his eyes. Only Reid was oblivious, still poring over the little book.

Misty darted out the back door, pulling it closed behind her. Graham was striding through her small yard, which she'd filled with desert and tropical flowers she carefully cultivated. He was stomping around, hands clasped on his head, the sun beating down on him. He was about to ruin the clump of autumn sage she'd nursed back from frost kill last winter—she'd finally got the plant bushy again, the bright red blossoms cheerful against the green.

Misty marched to Graham and grabbed him by the arm. He swung around, the look in his eyes so wild and empty that Misty had to take a faltering step back.

CHAPTER EIGHT

He couldn't do this. Graham couldn't be around this woman, who smelled like honey and spice, who curled her tongue around the light and dark ice cream as though it were the sweetest aphrodisiac.

He had a hard-on that wouldn't stop. Xav Escobar knew it, the asshole. Graham had recognized the smirk. Of course, Xav probably had one too. And for that, Graham would kill him.

"I can't do this," he said.

"Can't do what?" Misty stood in front of him, hands on her hips. "Break my door? Smash my dishes? Trample my plants? You're like walking mass destruction."

She wanted him to apologize, Graham realized. But Graham never apologized. You said sorry, and people felt smug and justified, and started to take advantage.

Hard to look into those sweet brown eyes and say nothing, though. "I'll fix your front door."

"You bet your ass you will," Misty said. "Now, are we going to talk about it?"

There she went again. Talking. Always talking. "I thought you were done with me," Graham said.

"I am, but that doesn't mean I'm not still mad at you. Or not talking to you."

"Then we're not done." Not by a long way.

"Yes, we are."

Graham turned from her, not liking how fast his heart was beating. Or how thirsty he was. He fought it, having learned to work through hunger and thirst a long time ago, but he knew he couldn't banish it entirely. The Fae magic had gotten to him, but he couldn't give in to it. If he did that, he was dead.

To keep himself from thinking about the thirst, he focused on Misty's yard. It was like her—compact, neat, beautiful. She hadn't simply stuck clumps of plants everywhere. The yard had been landscaped, sculpted almost, with low mounds of grass and gravel hosting small flowering bushes and plants that bloomed fiercely under the hot sun. A false wash of river rock cut through the yard, crossed by a small wooden bridge.

Stepping stones led to the bridge and across the yard on the other side. Between the stones were gravel and scatterings of plants, blossoms moving in the summer breeze. The ugly cement block walls, so common in Southwestern cities, were softened by stands of hot pink and white oleanders on two walls, with a line of rose bushes, sheltered from the direct sun, on the third.

A pretty garden, with chairs and tables set out so Misty and friends could sit and enjoy iced tea or whatever women drank on summer afternoons. Graham was out of place here, a hulking creature in the diminutive space.

Misty seemed to be waiting for something. Graham did not understand her—anything female, in fact. She declared she was finished with him, then she ran after him. She said she wanted to talk to him, then she expected him to do the talking, when Graham wasn't any good at it.

"What do you want me to say?" he ended up almost shouting. Yelling—*that* he was good at.

Misty glared. Did she know how edible she looked in her body-hugging tank top, the shorts that stopped mid-thigh? She'd put on sandals, which showed her bare legs all the way to her toes. Misty wasn't a stick, thank the God-dess. Some human women starved themselves down to skin and bones and thought it looked good. Insanity.

Misty had round breasts, arms that were plump from shoulders to elbow then tapered into soft wrists and small hands. Strong hands—she worked hard in her store, carry-ing plants, heavy pots and baskets, armloads of flowers, buckets of water. Her legs were sturdy and curved, calves soft and kissable.

Her face—the one all screwed up with her scowl—was round, her nose in perfect proportion. Her eyes were a little too big for a human, but Graham didn't mind. They were soft brown and surrounded by thick black lashes.

Watching Misty tongue the ice cream had made every cell of him scream in need. She had a little bit of cream on her lips even now.

To hell with it. Graham closed the space between them, jerked her against him, and brought his mouth down on hers.

Misty made a little surprised sound in her throat, and fists contacted his shoulders. Graham tightened his grip, pulling her into him, and licked the cream from her lip in one firm stroke.

Misty stopped fighting. Her lips softened, hesitated, then formed to his.

Fire. Her mouth was heat and everything good. Graham laced his fingers through her hair, pulling it out of the ponytail she'd dragged it into. Soft goodness flowing over his hand.

He sucked her lower lip into his mouth, and Misty made another soft noise. No more protests, no more fists. No more *talking*.

Misty's body fitted to his, breasts tight against his torso. He moved his hand down her back, callused fingers catching on her cotton tank. The fabric was so thin he could feel the heat of her skin plus the strap of a bra, tight against her back.

Graham could savor her all day and all night. He licked

into her mouth, finding a bite of spice. Thirst went away as
he drank her.

Her small hands caressed his shoulders then moved to
the back of his neck, above the Collar. She liked to hold on
to his neck when they kissed for some reason. Not that
Graham minded. She also liked to run her fingers through
his short buzz of hair.

Graham kept on kissing her. Misty's mouth was a joy, her
breath warm, her body pliant against his. His cock hadn't
gone down; in fact, it had grown even more rigid. Misty
tasted like sunshine, felt like a soft cooling breeze.

If it could be just you and me . . .

We'd unmake the world.

Graham made himself ease the kiss to its end. Misty
gazed up at him, eyes warm, her lips parted. Her anger had
been erased for now, and what he read in her was desire.
Moisture lingered behind her lower lip, and Graham licked
it away.

It took all his strength to relax his arms around her, to
let go. Misty had been on tiptoe, and now she thumped
back on her heels. She stared up at him, unblinking, her
lips slightly swollen.

Graham pointed his finger at her face and ended up touching her lightly on the nose. "You and me," he said. "We're not
done."

He turned and walked away. Killed him to do it, but you
didn't say an exit line and then not leave the stage. You
didn't even look back to see if she stared after you, longing
in her eyes, no matter how much you wanted to.

Graham wouldn't go home. After his searing kiss and
the parting shot, Misty expected him to be long gone
when she came back inside the house, but no. He was talking to Reid in the living room, his loud, harsh syllables
drowning out Reid's quieter ones.

Xav had cleaned up the broken bowl and given the cubs
more ice cream. The two little ones could sure put it away.

They'd discovered that licking the ice cream from the spoon was even more fun than licking it from the bowl. They could lick the spoon all over before they scooped up more. After all, Aunt Misty had been licking it from the spoon. So it was all right, wasn't it?

When they finished, Kyle or Matt said, "Can we play outside, Aunt Misty? We didn't go out before, because you and Uncle Graham were kissing."

Xav laughed from where he sat at the table, and Misty's face went hot. "That's fine, but don't mess up my plants. They get hurt easily."

Matt and Kyle agreed they'd never do anything like that. They half wrestled each other trying to be first to the door, then they started yanking off their clothes.

Before they finished stripping down to their skin, they were shifting, fur rippling, tails popping out. Two fuzzy cubs barreled out the door they'd already opened, yipping all the way.

"They don't have Collars," Misty said out loud. She hadn't noticed that before, but when they'd shucked their T-shirts, she'd seen that their necks had no slash of black and silver Collar to mar them.

"They don't take Collars until they're older," Graham said, coming into the kitchen. "'Cause they're damn painful. Even humans couldn't bring themselves to be that cruel."

Misty let out a breath. "All humans are not that bad, Graham."

He gave her that look that said he'd lived a hundred years in the harsh wilderness, and she didn't know what she was talking about. "Yes, they are," he said.

"Then why are you still here?"

Another look. "Because a Fae is after you, and an ex-cop with bullets isn't going to stop him."

"And a Shifter is?" Reid leaned in the doorway. He still had the book, but he held it closed in his hand.

"Shifters won the Shifter-Fae war," Graham said. "Remember? We kicked your asses. You lost all your Shifter pets."

"That was more than seven hundred years ago," Reid said mildly. "I wasn't born then. And *dokk alfar* had nothing to do with Shifters."

"I know; I just say it to piss you off. Point is, this Fae targeted her—and me—and I'm not going to sit at home waiting for him to come get her."

Why did that make Misty feel better? She should want Graham gone. Out of here.

Instead she went to the sink and filled up a glass of water. Las Vegas tap water tasted terrible, but who cared? She needed the water, needed the cool wetness inside her parched mouth.

"This book." Reid held it up. "Where did you get it?"

Misty explained about the flea market. "I had it valued, but even though it's a first edition, it's in too bad a shape to be worth much. I kept it for the interest."

"Whoever wrote it knows much about the Fae." He flipped to the title page. A nice frontispiece with an etching of an heirloom rose faced it, the plate guarded by a thin piece of vellum. The title page itself didn't have much information.

"The author didn't put her name on it," Misty said. "Or his. They didn't always back then. This book has a date but no publisher or author."

"Maybe a Shifter wrote it," Xav suggested.

"Doubt it," Reid answered. "The spells in here against Fae are subtle but show a good understanding of Fae magic. Shifters are cruder when dealing with Fae."

"He means we just rip their heads off and spill out their insides." Graham strode to the back door and yanked it open. "Kyle! Get out of that damned tree! You're not a cat."

Kyle stopped squirming in the branches of the fruitless mulberry that overhung Misty's yard from her neighbor's, and dropped to the ground. He yipped once when he landed, then he trotted off, none the worse for wear.

Misty tried to memorize what he looked like, so she could try to tell them apart, but once he joined Matt, she gave up. The two, as wolves, were identical.

"Are you babysitting them?" Misty asked when Graham came back inside.

"Their foster mother dumped them on my doorstep," Graham said. "I was on my way to hand them to Nell and her bears when the dream hit." He regarded Reid speculatively. "You and Peigi have a bunch of foster cubs at your house. Kyle and Matt like them."

"No," Reid said quickly. For the first time since Misty had met him, Reid looked less like a mysterious being and more like an ordinary human. A worried human. "Peigi's got too much to deal with—the cubs, the other Shifter women from Mexico . . . You weren't here when we rescued them. They went through hell, and Peigi as their alpha feels the worst of it. Leave her alone."

Graham scowled at him a moment longer before he relaxed into a grin. "Why don't you just make the mate-claim on Peigi and get it over with?"

Reid looked embarrassed. "*Dokk alfar* don't do mate-claims."

"You'd better start. Shifters need females, and she's fair game. Even my wolves are eyeing her. They're going to start to Challenge for her, and they won't care if you're *dokk alfar* or tree bark. They'll use the Challenge as an excuse to kill a Fae, and won't care you're one of the good ones."

"I'll keep it in mind," Reid said, recovering his calm. Graham didn't seem to frighten Reid, and neither did other Shifters, Misty had noticed. Most humans, even Xavier sometimes, could grow nervous around Shifters, but never Reid.

"So we wait until moonlight?" Xav broke in.

Misty shrugged. "I guess."

"I guess we do." Graham moved back to the door, opening it again to watch the cubs. He wasn't about to leave, she saw. Misty would have to sit here with him for the next few hours, her nerves making her crazy, the sensation of his hard kiss lingering on her mouth. "Got any beer?" Graham asked over his shoulder.

"I told my guys to bring some," Xav said. "And we'll get pizza."

At the word *pizza*, high-pitched yips sounded in the backyard. One cub popped up from the riverbed, an eager look on his face. There was no sign of the other cub.

"Matt!" Graham shouted. "Get *out* of there."

The second wolf scrambled out from under the bridge. He gave Graham and Misty an innocent look, or as innocent as he could with a clump of Angelita daisies drooping from his mouth, their yellow heads bobbing in the sunshine.

Moonlight. The clear skies of southern Nevada ensured plenty of light once the three-quarter moon rose into the black night.

The moonlight poured down into Misty's backyard, rendering her colorful flowers pale ghosts of themselves. The neighbor's tree cast sharp shadows on the patches of grass, and the dry river's dark rocks took on a dull glow.

The cubs, unbelievably, were asleep. They'd dropped off fearlessly on top of Misty's bed after consuming more than their bodyweight in meat-lovers' pizza.

Misty's aching body begged for rest, but she was afraid to sleep, afraid to dream. What if she found herself facing the hiker again, the wave of ice? The cubs didn't worry, but then they hadn't drunk the Fae water. How the cubs had entered the dream, and whether they'd truly been there, neither she nor Graham knew.

When the moon had risen high, Misty and Graham went out to Misty's backyard. Graham had told Xav and Reid not to join them. He didn't know what the spell in the little book would do, if anything, and he didn't want it messed up by unspelled humans or a Fae—especially not a Fae.

Reid agreed without argument. Xavier didn't like it, but he stayed inside, saying he'd keep an eye on the cubs.

Xav's men had not only brought the pizza, but water— glorious water. A case of it, which Misty had drunk almost half of.

Graham had drunk nothing. She knew he was feeling the thirst, because he kept wetting his mouth, or swallowing and turning away as Misty had guzzled water. Why he wouldn't drink, she had no idea, and he wouldn't tell her.

Graham helped her carry the accoutrements for the spell outside. Misty had harvested petals from two of the roses she'd brought home from her shop, washing them thoroughly and rolling them dry in a towel.

"You eat flowers?" Graham asked when she told him imbibing the petals would be safe. "Humans are weird."

"Lots of flowers are edible," Misty had answered. "Cake bakers paint them with sugar water and use them for edible decoration. Roses, pansies, carnations, squash blossoms. I went to a restaurant where they made sweet corn tamales in squash blossoms. They were awesome. You have to be careful to choose the right kind of flowers, though. Olean-ders, for instance will kill you quickly." She waved her hand at the thick, dark green bushes along her fence.

Misty set everything up at a table on the other side of her yard, which was reached by the little bridge. She spread out a white cloth, scattered the cut rose petals on it, inhal-ing their fragrance, and consulted the book.

Gather petals of red roses, washed three times. Check. *Chopped with a fine-bladed knife.* Check.

Immerse in alcohol . . .

That had been an interesting problem. Misty and her friends drank mostly wine and beer, saving hard liquor for martinis on evenings out. Misty wasn't sure she wanted to gulp down rose petals in beer, or even in the nice white wine a friend had brought her last time she'd come over.

Then Misty had found a bottle in the back of her liquor cabinet. She hadn't noticed it in a while and hadn't drunk any for a long time. But it might work.

Now she put the chopped rose petals into two shot glasses, one in front of her and one in front of Graham.

"What is that?" he asked as Misty poured out the liquid. Graham only drank beer too.

"The good stuff." Misty sat down across from him, lifted her shot glass and waited for him to lift his. "Tequila."

CHAPTER NINE

Graham shrugged, raised his glass, and clinked it against Misty's. "Down the hatch."

"Cheers," Misty said. They lifted their glasses at the same time and drank in one shot.

The tequila burned Misty's mouth like liquid fire. The rose petals felt strange against her tongue, but she made herself not spit them out. Some stuck to the bottom of the glass, but that was all right, the spell said. They would bury the spent ones.

Misty swallowed, and the liquor shot down her gullet in a stream of flame. She coughed.

Drink four quantities.

Misty coughed again. One rose petal got caught on her tongue, and she fished it out and dropped it to the table.

Graham wiped his mouth, shaking his head. "What is this—lighter fluid? Humans actually drink this stuff?"

"All the time. Haven't you ever had a margarita?"

Graham made a face. "You mean that frothy shit in fancy glasses? I don't drink stuff with slices of fruit stuck in it. Drinks should be in a bottle."

"You have no soul, Graham."

"All Shifters have souls." Graham spoke without humor. "Can you imagine me with my wolves? *Hey, thanks for helping me fend off those hunters. How about we kick back, watch the game, and I'll make some margaritas?* Or mimosas. Or wine coolers. Girly drinks. They'd tear me apart and pick a new pack leader real quick."

"I get it. You're rugged." Misty sprinkled more rose petals into the glasses and added another shot of tequila to each. "Four times, the book says."

Graham studied the rose petals floating in the liquid. "I don't feel any different."

"Maybe we have to drink it all first." Misty lifted her glass, and again they clinked them. Graham's scarred fingers touched hers.

The second swallow was even more fiery than the first. Misty shuddered as it went down, her body feeling the heat.

"Lemon drop," Graham said. "Another girly drink."

"This is straight tequila," Misty said, licking her tingling lips. "It's plenty manly."

"Bellini," Graham went on as Misty doled out more petals and more alcohol. "I don't even know what the hell that is."

"Like a mimosa. Champagne, but with other fruit instead of orange juice—peaches or berries, say."

"Great. You ever seen me put berries in my beer?"

"Beer can be fruity." Misty raised the third glass. "Like hefeweizen. Bars serve it with lemon wedges. Or orange."

"I know. Ruins the head. It's *beer.* A hundred years ago, no one put fruit in it. We just drank it. By the barrel."

"You shouldn't tell me how old you are," Misty said, giving him a little smile. "Chin-chin."

Another clink, another shot dumped into her mouth. This time, Misty's entire tongue went numb. But the thirst was still there. The dehydrating alcohol was only making it worse.

"Let's hurry and do the last one." Misty's hand fumbled as she poured the last shot. She was almost out of rose petals.

"You are so beautiful."

Misty jumped, tequila sloshing from her glass. Graham was staring at her, moonlight on the thick glass in his hand throwing spangles over his face. His eyes were pale gray, wolflike.

"What?" Misty stammered.

"You heard me."

Misty thought of the searing kiss they'd shared this afternoon, under the equally searing sun. How he'd touched the tip of her nose and said, *You and me. We're not done.*

The gruff note in his voice tonight was the same. Graham wasn't comfortable with the words, but he'd said them anyway.

"Cheers," Misty said softly.

She clinked her glass against his. Graham reached over and brushed his fingers along her hand before he turned his glass and poured the shot down his throat.

Misty swallowed, wincing at the fire in her throat. Her mouth burned, and her tongue felt thick. Good thing the spell book said only four shots. Misty would be flat on her back if it had said five or six.

"I still don't feel any different," Misty said. "Except a little drunk."

Graham thumped his shot glass to the table and slammed his hand down next to it as he swallowed. "Nope."

"Maybe it really isn't a spell," Misty said. "Maybe whoever wrote the book is laughing at us."

"We're not done yet."

"That's true."

Bury the rose petals in the earth, turn thrice, and open to the cleansing rays of the moon, the Mother Goddess.

Misty stood up, and clutched the edge of the table. "You're going to have to help me dig."

Graham was less shaky than Misty, but he definitely swayed a little as he got to his feet. Shifters could handle alcohol a lot better than humans, he'd told her. Their metabolism burned it off quickly, same way they burned food. But they could still get drunk and have hangovers—it just took more doing.

Misty and Graham went together to the corner of the yard, where the ground was soft under the rosebushes. The jutting branches of the neighbor's tree plus the wall of Misty's garage shielded that part of the garden from the house, and the glow from her lit back windows was muted here.

Misty crouched down under the rosebushes. In spring and fall, these plants were a glory of red, yellow, pink, orange, and white. In August, it was still too hot for blooms, but even now, buds were showing in the shadiest spots.

Misty awkwardly poked at the dirt with her trowel. Graham closed his big hand over hers, shoving the trowel in and turning over the earth. The strength of him came through her hand and sent heat to her heart.

She scraped the last of the rose petals from the shot glasses and dumped them in the hole, adding the petals she'd cut but hadn't used. Graham's hand still on hers, they filled in the hole and smoothed the dirt over it.

Graham released the trowel and stood up. He reached down and pulled Misty to her feet, remaining close to her in the shadows. "Now what?"

"We turn around. Three times. Like this."

Misty stepped out into the moonlight. She opened her arms, lifting her face to the moon, *the Mother Goddess,* and turned in place once. Graham watched her, then he spread his arms and did the next circle with her.

Misty thought Graham might complain he looked stupid rotating in Misty's yard, but then, Shifters performed rituals all the time. Misty had seen a mating ceremony, which was a little like a human wedding, though much briefer and rowdier. They called it *mating under sun and under moon*—one ritual performed in daylight, the next under the full moon. After the full-moon ceremony, the Shifters were considered officially mated.

She had also seen a ceremony to celebrate a cub coming out of Transition to full adulthood. Sadder, she'd attended a Shifter gathering to recognize the yearly anniversary of a loved one's passing.

Graham and Misty did another turn together, then Misty stopped, and Graham did his third one alone.

When he finished, they looked at each other. "Now what?" Graham asked.

"I don't know."

The book hadn't specified whether the moon should be full, waxing, or waning. Or whether the roses had to be fresh cut, or other details like that. Could be the book was just the ramblings of someone who loved whimsy, and it wouldn't help at all.

Graham was watching her, his body quiet in the darkness, moonlight glinting on his Collar. He belonged out here in the night, a wolf, a being of the moon.

Other Shifters Misty had met could look and act exactly like humans, but Graham never quite could, not entirely. Graham was always a beast—tall, broad, raw strength in his bare arms. She had the feeling he kept to human shape only for convenience . . . his.

"Nothing's happening," he said.

"I know," Misty said glumly. "Maybe we—"

Pain choked her words to a halt. She bent in agony as blood surged through her veins as hot as the tequila had been, burning its way to her heart.

Misty thought she screamed, but only a faint cry escaped her lips. She pressed her hands to the hot core of her chest, struggling to breathe.

Not a heart attack. She couldn't be having a heart attack. Could she?

"Call . . ." Misty coughed, lungs begging for air. She clawed at her chest, trying to open it, to let the air in. What the hell was happening to her? She was falling, falling . . .

But Graham had caught her, solid arms around her, cradling her as she went down. He was on his knees with her, gathering her to him.

Misty felt Graham's heart hammering in his chest. He closed her in his arms, hands on her back.

"Stay with me, Misty." His voice was harsh. "Stay with me, love. Don't . . . don't . . ."

Misty opened her mouth—and found air rushing back inside her. She gasped out loud as hot desert night air flowed into her lungs, expanding them again. Oxygen pounded to her heart, filling her blood, which shot fire around her body again.

And then the burning eased, little by little, cooling as did the baking desert under a soft fall of rain.

Misty drew another breath, this one more natural. She licked her lips, tasting the residue of tequila, feeling moisture linger in the wake of her tongue.

Moisture. Not parched lips and dry mouth. The horrific thirst had vanished.

"I think it worked." Misty looked at Graham in relief. She smiled. "I think it actually worked."

Graham said nothing. He bathed her in another of his intense stares, then he cupped her face in one hand and kissed her mouth.

No slow starts and easing in this time. Graham's hand was hot on her cheek, thumb at the corner of her lips. He took her mouth in hard strokes, and Misty clutched Graham's shoulders, his skin hot through his T-shirt. He curved over her, sending her down into the ground.

Misty's body came alive. The kiss this afternoon had been burning, but *this* . . .

Gravel cut into her back until Graham thrust his arm behind her, lifting her to him. He moved himself over her, his large body engulfing hers. Misty met his kiss with hers, thrusting her tongue inside his mouth, wanting him.

She felt the rough of his palm on her shoulder then the skinny strap of her tank top moving downward, and with it the top, baring her to the night. With his other hand, Graham unsnapped her bra, pushing it and the tank down to her waist.

Graham never stopped kissing her. He closed his callused hand over her breast, her nipple tightening to meet his palm. Heat streaked from the cup of his hand to every part of her, settling at the join of her thighs.

Misty scrabbled at Graham's T-shirt, wanting to touch

him too. His skin was roasting, which worried her, but the worry was dim, buried behind the rush and roar of the kiss.

She worked his shirt upward, finding the smoothness of his back, the curve of his spine, the muscle of his shoulders. All the while, she kissed him. She tasted the bite of tequila, the sweetness of the rose petals, felt the burn of the spell beyond the insistence of his lips on hers.

Graham pulled back abruptly. Moonlight outlined the harsh planes of his face and glinted on his Collar. His lips were parted, eyes hard.

Misty lifted to him again, seeking his mouth. Graham raised his head away from her, but his hand remained on her breast.

His eyes narrowed, silver and gleaming. Then he said softly, "Aw, fuck it."

Graham tugged off his T-shirt in a few quick jerks and flung it away from him, and then pulled Misty up to him. His hands were hot on her back, kisses hard.

Graham took his mouth to her neck. A sharp pain, a love bite, then he licked his way to her shoulder, closing his teeth over the skin. Another bite, before he moved down to her breast.

Part of Misty's brain reminded her Xav and Reid were in the house and could emerge at any time. The other parts told her to shut up. She needed this.

Graham drew his teeth together over her firm nipple. Misty gave a quiet cry, the not-pain brushing white heat through her.

He licked and played for a time, circling her areola with his tongue, nibbling the tip. Then he pulled her breast all the way into his mouth and suckled, strokes firm.

Misty arched to him, a groan escaping her lips. Magic and moonlight, and Graham.

Graham traced her navel with his fingertips then popped the button of her shorts. Before Misty could say a word, Graham unzipped the shorts and slid his fingers inside.

He found her sweet spot right away. *God, did he find it.*

Misty's hips rose, she seeking the wonderful friction of his hand. She felt his fingers grow moist and slick, evidence of how much she wanted him.

Graham lifted his head, his lips damp from suckling her breast, his eyes alight. "You feel good, sweetheart."

Misty tried to respond, but all that came out were incoherent sounds. Graham smiled, and slid one strong finger inside her.

The stiff invasiveness made her tighten. At the same time, Graham brushed his thumb across her opening, drawing more moisture and more heat.

"What are you doing?" Her whisper came out a croak.

"What does it feel like I'm doing?" Graham slid in a second finger.

His fingers were large, stretching her. Misty drew in a breath, prepared to tell him to stop, but the words didn't come. She didn't want him to stop. For months she'd craved his touch, and now he was giving it to her.

Misty wormed her fingers under his waistband, finding his slick, warm hip. Graham yanked her hand out again.

"Not yet," he growled. "Feel *me*."

She couldn't *not* feel him. Graham slid a third finger into her, and Misty groaned. Her legs opened of their own volition, wanting this spreading, his large hand inside her. He was going to think she was no better than a Shifter groupie, begging with her body for the touch of a Shifter.

Who cared? Graham kissed her again, his mouth a place of goodness, while his fingers gave her pleasure. Her breasts were bare, pressing against his torso, and Misty pulled him closer. When he eased off kissing her, she reached up and caught the skin of his neck in her teeth, leaving her own love bite.

"Oh, yeah?" Graham's smile flashed, his eyes wicked.

He moved his fingers in and out, easy with how wet she was. Doing with his fingers what he'd never done with his cock.

Misty clung to him while she rose against him, wanting to drag him inside her. His hands awakened the desires she'd constantly pushed aside, telling herself she was happy with only his company and his kisses. What a lie.

Her desire built and built until it broke. As with the icy wave in her dream, Misty's climax rose over her and swept her away on a black tide.

She heard her own voice ringing until Graham silenced her with his mouth. She suckled his tongue, needing him inside her, squeezing his fingers that thrust into her.

Graham kissed her while she rode out the wave, then he increased the speed of his thrusts, sending her up into climax again.

Three times he took her there, and three times he held her while she went wild around him. In the end, Misty had no idea where she was or when, and she didn't care. She only needed Graham, and he was in her arms.

She hung on to him until the spinning stopped, then she fell back to earth, his large body coming down on hers. He didn't crush her, he only covered her with his warm length, shielding her against the night. Graham stroked Misty's hair, lips touching her face, the line of her hair, her lips. Incredible gentleness from this rough-edged man.

For a long time they lay together, stretched out on the ground, absorbing the warmth of the darkness. Graham said nothing, only nuzzled her cheek and lightly kissed her. He'd given Misty all the pleasure, demanding nothing in return.

As moonlight brushed his skin as he kissed her, an idea that had been tapping before Graham had driven her thoughts away started knocking for attention again. Misty looked into Graham's face.

"The spell cured me," she said. "I'm not thirsty anymore. But it didn't work on you, did it?"

Graham regarded her another moment, his gray eyes steady. "No," he said, voice quiet. "It didn't."

CHAPTER TEN

No, Graham wasn't cured. And that was going to be a problem.

He staved off the thought by brushing his lips against Misty's, but for the first time in his life, he faced the question—*What do I do?*

Graham always knew what to do. If he didn't, he made something up. Yelling at one of his Shifters or knocking them across the room usually helped. But this time, brute force and bullying wasn't going to work.

Thirst pounded through him. Kissing Misty calmed it, but as soon as he released her, his mouth grew parched again. He needed to drink.

Graham also knew, though he wasn't sure how he knew, that his gunshot wound was only temporarily healed. Fae magic had closed it up, but Graham would bet that, if the Fae chose, he could rip it open again. Shifter metabolism being what it was, Graham would still heal from the shot eventually, but he'd have to go through the agony of its infliction all over again. And maybe the Fae would keep reopening the wound, just to punish Graham.

Misty, though, was free. Somehow the stupid little spell with the roses and tequila had burned the Fae water out of her. Possibly the tequila alone had done it; humans were weak when it came to alcohol. Maybe that was the same reason it hadn't worked on him—Shifters had a high tolerance even for the strongest liquor.

"Graham?" Misty touched his face.

He loved this—Misty in his arms, a moment of peace.

Graham had left his mark on her. The dark love bites on her neck and breasts stood out in the moonlight. His mark, his brand.

He closed his fingers around her wrist and held on. "You can't tell anyone it didn't work. Swear to me."

Misty blinked in concern. "Why not?"

Graham didn't answer for a moment. He kissed her again, savoring her taste. He thought about moving his fingers back between her legs, where it was hot, sweet, slick. He could bring her to climax one more time, forget about spells and Fae. Only Misty was important.

"Graham?" Misty's voice was soft, but insistent. "We'll need help to figure this out."

"No," Graham said, his voice harsh, though he softened his hold on her wrist. "If my Shifters think I'm Fae-touched, they'll fall apart, and take me with them." They needed him, and that wasn't just arrogance. Most of Graham's Shifters hadn't adjusted to living in the city yet, with Shifters they didn't know. Most hadn't adjusted to living in a Shiftertown, period, even after twenty years. They'd have all gone feral, or died, or curled into little balls of whimpering fur if Graham hadn't done some of the shit he'd done. "If they know I'm under a Fae's power, they could turn on me, take me out—kill me—and maybe Dougal too. I know that's not allowed, but my Shifters are pretty wild and don't care. So, they can't know. No one can."

Misty gave him the startled look she always got whenever he told her how violent Shifters were. Why did humans think Shifters had been tamed? Making them wear the shock Collars was like putting a tiny bandage on a gaping wound.

"There must be someone you can talk to," Misty said. She caressed his face, as though she found something she liked in the scarred, harsh mess of it. "Reid, maybe?"

"I said, I need to think about it." Graham gentled his impatient answer by kissing the inside of her wrist. "This is the kind of problem a Shifter takes to his leader. Except I *am* the leader."

"Eric, then," Misty said. Sweet lady; she was so naive. "He's your partner."

Graham snorted a laugh. "Right. Don't think so." Eric had wanted Graham under his thumb since Graham's Shifters had been forced to move into Eric's Shiftertown.

Misty didn't look convinced. Graham kissed her again, letting the kiss turn lingering. He loved that the terrible thirst slaked a bit when his mouth was on hers.

He wanted to stay kissing her forever, the fragrance of the flowers she loved wrapping around them. Misty's scent was even better than the flowers', her soft body under his worth every second of his agony.

Graham had to fix this, and fast. And then figure out what the hell to do about his growing mating frenzy for Misty. He'd not be able to stave it off for long, and if the frenzy consumed him, it would be as dangerous to her as any Fae spell.

Graham stayed the night at Misty's, which entailed more pizza. The cubs ate most of it.

Reid departed before the pizza arrived, borrowing the book from Misty, intrigued by it, he said. Graham knew Reid's real reason to leave was his ache to get back home to the bear Shifter, Peigi. It had been more than a year since Peigi had been rescued from an insane, feral Shifter in Mexico who'd kept her and other women in a basement, more than six months since Reid had moved in with her. And still she and Reid weren't officially a couple, for some reason.

Graham stayed with Misty not only to protect her but also because it was clear Xavier wasn't about to leave. Xav might claim he was just doing his job, and had three other DX Security men stationed outside the house, but Xav was inside, with Misty.

In spite of her apparent recovery, Misty was still reluctant to go to bed, afraid to dream, but Graham eventually talked her into it. Misty needed her rest—she'd had a hell of a time. The cubs, as wolves, dashed into her room ahead of her, leapt up on her bed, and curled up on the foot of it. Misty let them, kissed Graham good night, and shut the door on him.

Good thing. If Graham went in there, he'd want to hole up with her and never come out. And then everything in the outside world would go to hell.

Thinking of Misty's scent, her warmth around his fingers, the taste of her when he'd touched his fingers to his lips, made him not care about the rest of the world. Let it go. Mating frenzy was more important, right?

He made himself turn away and leave her alone.

Graham didn't blame Misty for fearing to dream. Still under the spell, he didn't want to sleep either. He talked to Xav. He walked around the house on the outside, sticking to shadows. He checked the backyard; he checked on Misty and the cubs. Matt and Kyle were curled up on her feet, fast asleep, and Misty was breathing evenly, her face relaxed in slumber. Watching Misty lying there made Graham want to go curl himself up around her, but again, he closed the door and let her rest.

Graham watched Misty's TV, running through the three hundred or so channels he didn't get in Shiftertown. He looked through Misty's DVD collection and her downloads after that. As he already knew, Misty liked chick flicks, each of which featured a pretty heroine who blundered into embarrassing situations, had wacky best friends or zany coworkers, and fell in love first with the wrong guy—the bad boy who broke her heart—and then the right one, the nice guy who'd been there all the time. Graham had argued with Misty that females in real life wouldn't settle for the beta and would keep trying for the alpha, but Misty had rolled her eyes and told him he didn't understand romance. Well no, he didn't. Not the kind of romance in those movies, anyway.

But what the hell. Graham decided to give one a try, desperate to stay awake.

It was his downfall. On the heroine's third fumbled conversation with the geeky-looking nice guy—who didn't deserve to end up with her—Graham fell asleep.

He woke in the cave with the spring and the fountain.

"Shit." Graham scrambled to his feet. His side throbbed, and he looked down to see blood soaking through his T-shirt.

"You'll die of that." The Fae didn't enter with a bang; he was just *there*, when he hadn't been a second before. He gestured to Graham's wound. "You should tend it."

He had the look of all Fae—tall, pointy eared, white haired. He was dressed in silver chain mail, with a sword at his side, as though ready to run off and do battle with something. Over the mail he wore a shimmering silver cloak draped across his shoulders.

Graham deliberately did not press his hand to his wound, as much as he wanted to. "You know why the Shifters rebelled from the Fae?" he asked. "Your crappy fashion sense. You've been wearing the same clothes for a thousand years."

"Time moves differently in Faerie."

"Good for Faerie. Who the hell are you, and why are you stalking me?"

"You may call me Oison."

Not his real name, Graham knew. Fae had a thing about true names. "I don't care about calling you anything," Graham said. "Get the hell out of my dreams."

"I can't," Oison said. "You have been chosen."

Chosen. Fae loved to say crap like that. Anything dramatic. "So, *un*-choose me before I kick your sorry ass."

"I cannot do that."

Graham started toward him. Oison watched him come, unworried.

Stupid-ass Fae bastards. This Oison had hurt Misty, had tried to enslave her, and for that, he'd die.

The cave's floor was slick like glass—no, it was polished obsidian. Graham slipped, the gunshot wound hurting him, but he refused to fall.

The fountain burbled incessantly. Fat vines snaked up the walls and across the floor, turning the rock cave into a jungle of flowers. The scent was thick. Graham thought of Misty's small garden where the much sparser growth had smelled clean and sweet.

Graham reached Oison. The Fae was tall, like Reid, with the same eyes that tried to bore into Graham's skull. But Reid had proved to be smart, reasonable, and helpful, despite his Fae-ness, and he had a true fondness for Peigi and the cubs he'd helped rescue. Somewhere inside Reid was a heart, and feelings.

This Fae had used Misty to lure Graham to the desert, then tricked Misty into feeding Graham spelled water. Oison had caused Misty to be hurt, terrorized, and trapped. Therefore, he had to die.

Graham roared, shifting as he attacked. Who cared if it hurt like hell when his clothes fell from his bloody side? This was a dream.

Graham loved the look on the Fae's face as two hundred and some pounds of snarling wolf landed on him. *Eat this, shithead.*

Oison went down, scrabbling to draw his sword as he fell, but Graham ripped into him with teeth and claws. He met the metal of the mail, but it peeled back like tinfoil, and Graham tasted blood.

Oison struggled, the sword falling to the obsidian floor with a clank. Graham opened his mouth wide, clamped his teeth around the Fae's throat, and ripped. The Fae screamed, then the scream died to a gurgle in an eruption of gore.

Graham tasted lifeblood pouring into his mouth. He snarled his victory, raking open Oison's skin to find bones. Oison's coal black eyes fixed, then filmed over.

Graham scrambled off him. He sat back on his haunches, lifted his bloody muzzle, and howled. He'd defeated his enemy. He'd saved himself and Misty from the Fae's clutches and the damned water spell.

Sudden pain cut off Graham's breath. The echo of his wolf's howl bounced from the cave's high ceiling and evaporated.

Graham's Collar had come alive. Dormant while Graham had attacked the Fae, the Collar was now a hot band of metal, shocks arcing around it and straight into Graham's body.

He howled again, this time in pure agony. His body shifted of its own accord from wolf to his in-between beast, his strongest form.

The Collar's shocks increased, blasting him with hot pain. Graham clawed at the Collar, desperately trying to make it stop.

He saw movement out of the corner of his eye. Through his blurring vision, he saw the Fae, bloody and torn up, rise and draw his sword.

Fae swords were works of art. They were fashioned of bronze or silver—iron and steel were poison to the Fae. This one looked silver. As well, Fae swords were almost always full of spells. The Swords of the Guardians had been made by a Shifter centuries ago, but woven with spells from that Shifter's Fae mate.

Oison held his sword battle-ready as he made his way to where Graham fought his Collar. Graham reached his huge, clawed hands for Oison, ready to kill again—as many times as it took to put the asshole down.

Oison swung his sword, stopping when the tip contacted the Collar. Graham's agony increased. The Fae held the sword against the Collar, spells on the blade feeding into the Collar and then into Graham.

Graham was being baked alive. He roared, hands going for the Fae's throat, which still ran with blood.

Oison shouted at him in a Fae language, but Graham somehow understood it. *Monster, created of filth. I hold*

*you. By sword and by Collar, you are mine. You will give
them to me, the battle beasts, and Fae again will walk the
earth.*

Graham tried to jerk away from the sword but Oison
was merciless. Graham saw runes shimmer across the
sword's blade, heard whispering: *weakened, enslaved, ob-
edient.*

"That's what the Collars are," Oison said, his voice clear,
no matter that his throat was a bloody mess. "Chains that
will bring you back to us. You have enslaved yourselves."

Graham used all his will to wrench himself sideways,
finally breaking the contact with the sword. He fell down,
down, and the flowering vines reached up to pull him to the
slick floor.

He heard himself shout, *Fuck you!* then something
started hammering on his chest, dozens of blows, full force.

Graham dragged in a breath to fight this new threat . . .
and found himself lying flat on his back on Misty's couch,
the same stupid movie on her TV. Two little wolves were
standing heavily on his chest, beating on him with their
oversized paws.

M isty emerged in the morning to find Graham at her
kitchen table, red-eyed and irritable, his hands wrapped
around a mug of coffee. Kyle and Matt, in their human form
and dressed, their faces already dirty, bounced in chairs
opposite him. Xavier stood at the stove, a towel over his
shoulder, black T-shirt hugging his torso, as he cooked
something that smelled wonderful.

Misty poured herself coffee. She enjoyed leaning back
against the counter and taking a leisurely sip, happy to no
longer crave liquid by the gallon.

Graham, on the other hand, was still under the spell. He
lifted his coffee and took a sip, but his hands shook. He
pulled the cup from his mouth after one taste, as though
stopping himself from pouring the burning brew down his
throat.

"You all right?" Misty asked him.

"Do I look all right?"

His voice was harsher than usual. His eyes were blood-shot, lips dry. This was Graham with a hangover, under a thirst spell, and by the looks of it, little sleep.

"No, you look like crap," Misty said. "You need to drink something."

Graham growled. "I need to go back to Shiftertown. Only reason I'm still here is to feed Kyle and Matt. And to make sure you're all right for the day."

"Xav's making us chili killies," one of the twins proclaimed.

"*Chilaquiles,*" Xav said good-naturedly from the stove. "Mama's specialty. You'll love this, Misty."

Misty's stomach growled. After the tequila shots, she should be as dry-voiced and red-eyed as Graham, but she felt pretty good. She'd had a dreamless sleep, waking when the sun rose to find the two wolves curled up on the bed next to her.

They'd leapt out as soon as she'd opened the door, and she'd hurried through her shower and dressed, concerned about Graham.

Xav brought two plates filled with eggs, fried tortillas, cheese, and tomatillo salsa to the table and put them in front of the cubs. He'd already laid out forks, and fortunately, the cubs decided to try to use them.

Graham had pushed aside his place setting, his elbows where his fork and knife would be. The flame tattoos climbed up his arms—red, orange, yellow, outlined in black.

"You need to eat something," Misty said to him.

"No, I don't. I need to go back to Shiftertown."

Kyle and Matt didn't have to be told to hurry. They were already halfway through their meal. All the pizza last night obviously hadn't filled them.

"Well, eat something at home then," Misty said. "And drink." Just because Graham couldn't control the thirst didn't mean he didn't need water.

"Will you let me worry about that?" he snapped. "You

stay home. There's a crazy Fae running loose, and he might get pissed off because you broke his spell. I'm sending over reinforcements."

"I can't stay home," Misty said, watching Kyle and Matt shovel in the rest of the eggs and tortilla chips. "I have to talk to my insurance agent, make sure they receive the police report, call people about getting my store repaired, postpone incoming deliveries, and apologize to all my customers for having to cancel their orders. I'll be busy."

"Then you wait for my reinforcements." Graham shoved aside the coffee and thrust himself to his feet. "Come on, you two."

Matt and Kyle abandoned their places and licked-clean plates to barrel toward Misty. "Good-bye, Aunt Misty!" The two little boys hugged her legs, two eager faces turned up to her. Misty leaned down and hugged them back, kissing their foreheads. They gave her sticky kisses in return then broke away from her.

"Bye, Xav!" Another enthusiastic leg hug, and then they were out the door, heading for the small truck Graham had driven over.

Misty's broken front door had been temporarily repaired with a piece of board nailed over the torn part, plus it was guarded by another muscled man in a black T-shirt and black camouflage pants.

"Graham," Misty called as Graham strode out the door without another word. She caught up to him in the driveway, as the cubs climbed enthusiastically into the pickup. "Wait a minute."

Graham swung to her. She expected him to give her hell again about wanting to talk, but he said nothing, only waited.

Today he looked less human than ever—a wild animal posing as a human being. His light gray eyes were hard with anger and pain, his short hair mussed, and the scars on his tanned face and arms were stark white. He was battling thirst and need for sleep, and losing.

"You should stay here," Misty said. "You need to rest. Maybe Reid can find another way to break the spell . . ."

Graham's words cut over hers. "No. Until this is over, I'm staying far away from you. Stick with Xav and the Shifters I send over, but keep away from me."

Misty took a step forward. Her body hummed from his pleasuring of her last night, from the way he'd held her when they'd finished, her half-naked body folded into his. Graham hadn't forgotten that, his look told her, and he wasn't angry at her. He was scared.

"Graham . . ."

Graham raised his hands. "Stay. Away." He moved his hands as though physically shoving her back, and then he turned around, got into the truck, and slammed its door.

Without looking at her, Graham started up the truck, backed out of her driveway, and roared off. The cubs waved out the window, then the truck turned a corner and was gone, leaving Misty alone with the warming morning and the stench of exhaust.

"Warden," Graham said, walking into the Shiftertown leader's house. "We need to talk about the Collars."

Graham hadn't been invited in, and Eric's sister and his son, Jace, were in front of him before the screen door slammed, the soft snarls in their throats threatening mayhem.

"Good going, McNeil," Eric said from where he lounged on the couch. He was in T-shirt and jeans, his bare feet propped on the coffee table. "Why don't you charge into an alpha's territory and start giving him commands? That's the way to get your balls torn off."

Graham watched Cassidy and Jace, who continued to block his way, their eyes, so like Eric's, fixed on him with near-feral anger. Diego had come out of the kitchen, and now he paused in its doorway, also watching Graham. He was probably armed, like his brother, and Diego had less of a sense of humor than Xav.

"We don't have time for this shit," Graham said. "We need to get the Collars off the Shifters. All Shifters. Right now."

Eric finally looked startled, though the only sign he made was his Feline eyes widening a little. "And you know why we can't rush."

"Things have changed. Collars need to come off. Now."

"He's not wrong," Stuart Reid said from the other side of the screen door. Unlike Graham, he was savvy enough to wait outside until the alpha Shifter invited him in. "Or things are going to get bad for all Shifters, everywhere."

CHAPTER ELEVEN

Did Warden leap up, grab his son—who'd just spent a painful time learning about how Collars came off—and start running around Shiftertown doing it? No, he sat there contemplating Graham with his jade-colored eyes, and clasped his hands behind his head.

"You two want to tell me what you're talking about?" Eric asked.

"You want to call off your posse?" Graham growled, baring his wolf's teeth at Jace and Cassidy. "If I wanted you dead, I'd have attacked you and not let them stop me. Where's your mate?" he added, realizing he neither saw nor scented Iona.

"Busy." Meaning Eric wasn't about to tell Graham. "Reid, get in here and close the door. It's hot."

Reid obeyed. Showed how seriously he took this, because Reid usually gave Shifters who told him what to do a *fuck-off* glare. Now Reid only walked inside and shut the solid door, closing out the morning heat.

"All right, you have my attention," Eric said. "Talk."

Graham drew a breath. The last person he wanted to tell

he was weakened was Warden, but the risk went beyond him now. Being alpha, and leader, didn't only mean Graham could best all other Shifters. It meant he took good care of those he bested.

"I think we're all screwed," Graham said. "Because of the Collars. What I'm about to say doesn't leave this room, all right?"

He launched into the story of what had happened out in the desert, including him drinking the Fae water, the dream he'd shared with Misty, the way they'd tried to counteract the spell, and his dream alone with Oison. He left out the more intimate moments he and Misty had shared in her backyard after the spell had left her—some things were none of their frigging business.

As he spoke, Cassidy moved to Diego, who put his arms around her from behind, and Jace joined his father on the sofa. No one had changed position all that much, but just enough to show that fighting was no longer imminent.

"Oison," Eric repeated when Graham had finished. "Know anything about him, Reid?"

"Never heard of him," Reid said. "But Faerie's a big place."

"If you've never heard of him, how do you know I'm right about him and the sword?" Graham asked. Reid had never hurried to agree with Graham before.

"Because of Misty's book," Reid said. "It contains many anti-Fae spells. From what I gleaned from the notes and subtext, the Fae might once before have tried to use devices to bring the Shifters back into their power, I'd say about a hundred years ago. Except, the last time, they didn't have the technology available to them that humans have now."

Only Reid could use words like *gleaned* and *subtext* with a straight face. "I really want to know about this half Fae who designed the Collars for us," Graham said. "No, what I really want to do is break his face."

"He's dead," Eric said in a mild voice. "But his son is still around somewhere."

"I say we round him up and talk to him."

"I think we agree," Eric said. He unclasped his hands

and rested them on his abdomen. "Write it down. Doesn't happen often."

Diego spoke up from behind Cassidy. "Let me see if I understand this. This Fae, in your dream, had a sword that, what, connected to your Collar?"

"Yep," Graham said. "Like a key and a lock. Only the lock hurt like hell."

"And from this dream, you're guessing there are more swords that will affect more Collars?" Diego went on.

"I'm saying they figured out a way to manipulate the Collars," Graham said impatiently. "Figured it out even before the Collars went on us. Like electronic dog leashes. And they've been planning this for the last twenty years."

"Kind of a long time to wait," Diego said.

"Time moves differently for the Fae," Graham said. "At least that's what that asshole told me in my dream. And he wouldn't stay dead, which means he was there and not there at the same time, devious bastard. I bet the pain was there for him, though. Not that it makes me feel any better."

"We need a leader meeting," Eric said.

Graham's temper, which he'd barely been holding on to, splintered. "Whoa, what happened to *What I'm about to say doesn't leave this room*? I'm not letting other Shifter-town leaders know I'm spelled. They'll eat me alive. You know it, so don't give me that patient look."

"If you'll shut up," Eric said. "I'll tell you I agree with you. Again. That's twice in one morning. Amazing."

"If there's a leader meeting, I'm going to it," Graham said. "And you're going to say exactly what I tell you to say."

"I don't—"

Graham cut Eric off. "I'm *going*. There, we disagree on that, but suck it up. Set up the meeting, tell me when and where."

Before Eric could draw breath to speak again, Graham turned his back and walked out. His heart was thumping hard, in worry and pain.

What Oison had done scared him, not only for himself but for Shifters like Dougal, Lindsay, and others—Shifters who weren't strong enough to fight the Fae. They'd end up Fae slaves in a second, their wills taken away, made to fight Fae wars in the realm of Faerie, and maybe here too if Oison's cryptic statements were anything to go by.

Fae had difficulty in the human world because of all the iron and steel. But if they enslaved Shifters to fight the humans for them, the violence the humans feared from Shifters would come to pass. Shifters wouldn't be able to do anything about it, even if they loathed what the Fae made them do. And Graham knew plenty of Shifters, unfortunately, who *wouldn't* hate killing humans, even for the Fae.

Before Graham had met Misty, he might have been one of those not caring if humans suffered. But Graham *had* met Misty, and he'd kissed her, and he'd kill every Shifter on the planet, and every Fae in Faerie, before he'd let any of them touch her.

Paul met Misty at her store later that morning. Her brother leaned on a push broom in the main part of the shop and looked dejectedly down at the broken glass and ruined flowers.

He dropped the broom when he saw Misty and came to her, wrapping his rawboned arms around her in a deep hug. Paul had grown up too fast after their parents' divorce, and had tried to act tough, but underneath, he was still a frightened boy.

"I'm sorry," he said. "I'm so sorry, Misty."

Misty said nothing, only held him close. After a few minutes, Paul raised his head and wiped his eyes. "I'll make it up to you. I'll fix it. I'll get you money . . ."

"You don't have to do anything at all," Misty said quickly. "Not your fault Flores is a criminal. Don't even clean up. The insurance adjuster has to look at the damage first."

"Insurance guy is already here," Paul said. "In the back."

"Really? That was fast." Misty had known people with

property damage who'd had to wait weeks, even months, before their claims started to process.

She left Paul and went into her office to find a man in a white shirt and dark tie, holding a clipboard and making check marks on it left-handed.

"Most of the damage is in the front," Misty said. "Not much back here." Thank God. Her safe and most valuable vases had been in her storage room. Flores's gang had come for Paul and revenge, not petty cash.

"I see that." The man switched the clipboard to his left hand and stuck out his right. He did it a little awkwardly, as someone who had to practice doing anything with that hand. "I'm Kevin Foster, from your insurance company." He released Misty, plucked a card from the top of his clipboard, and handed it to her. "They really busted up the place, didn't they?"

"Pretty much."

Kevin smiled. He had dark hair and blue eyes that crinkled in the corners. "It's too bad. This is a nice little place. I hope you can get it up and running again."

"That's the plan. As soon as the claim gets filed."

"Which, I know, insurance companies can take a long time with." Another little smile. "But I'll do what I can."

"Can I start cleaning up? I'd love to get back to work."

"I'll clear it. Repairs have to be made by approved workers, though, keep in mind, or the company might not pay the claim."

Misty strove to remain polite. In the real world, things could move at a snail's crawl. Meanwhile, businesses went under because customers lost faith in them.

Kevin seemed to understand. "I'll do my best. Don't worry. Give it a week, tops."

"Really?" Misty's skepticism rose. "I don't mean to be rude, but . . ."

"But nothing. I'm a friend of Iona Warden's. She was waiting at my office this morning and pretty much wouldn't let me even grab my first cup of coffee before she made

sure I was headed out here. My company does a lot of work
with her family."

Ah. Iona, mate to Eric, ran a construction and contracting
company with her mother and sister. Humans had been kept
in the dark that Iona was half Shifter so she wouldn't have to
give up her livelihood. Shifters weren't allowed to own businesses, or run them, or even hold very high positions in
them. Such were the unfair laws governing Shifters.

"Tell her thank you," Misty said.

"I will." Kevin gave her another smile. He was cute,
really. A normal guy. "You start your cleanup," Kevin said.
"I can recommend a service to help you, if you want."

"I'll let you know. Thanks for coming."

Kevin gave her a final smile and departed. Misty followed him out of the store and watched him get into a con-
servative four-door car. He started up, backed carefully out
of his space, and used his turn signal when he left the parking lot. A guy who played by the rules.

Paul was sweeping the floor inside the store again, and a
few men from DX Security were helping scoop up and throw
away the glass and petals. When Misty tried to help with the
manual labor, Xavier told her not to—she might cut herself
on the shards, he said. They'd take care of everything.

Shifters were amazing, Misty thought as she went back
into her office. They banded together when any of their
own were in trouble and worked to solve their problems.
Cassidy's mate, Diego, had come to Graham's rescue in the
desert; Diego had made sure his security company and Xav
helped and protected Misty afterward. Iona had driven
across town this morning to urge the insurance adjuster to
start on Misty's store right away. Misty wasn't even
Shifter—she was Graham's girlfriend, and she wasn't even
sure of that status. But the Shifters had sent resources to
help her, even when Misty knew Eric and Graham didn't
get along much of the time. They pulled together as a community. It warmed her that they considered her part of it.

Misty spent the rest of the morning canceling orders,
e-mailing or calling customers, and apologizing until she

was breathless. This was so wrong. Flores had broken into her store and wrecked her business, and *she* had to apologize.

By lunch, she needed a break. Paul and the security guys had done a great job sweeping everything up and salvaging what they could. The refrigeration room and the watering system still worked, which was a blessing, but she'd need to replace all the glass doors, her counters, shelving, and the front door and window, which would be expensive, and who knew how much insurance would cover?

Depressed, she told Xav she was heading a few doors down to get herself an enchilada at the little café that served New Mexico–style Mexican food. Paul had already gone down there, Xav said and offered to walk with her.

Xav was another nice guy, Misty decided. He wore the same black T-shirt as the rest of the security men, the tight fabric showing off every muscle beneath it. Diego and Xav had probably decided on the shirts to reassure clients that DX Security hired only strong guys.

Misty focused on the DX men in an effort to not dwell on a Shifter who also looked hot in a tight T-shirt. Even hotter without it.

Graham hadn't called Misty all morning, hadn't said a word. *Stay away*, he'd told her forcefully. Misty thought she understood why—now that she'd broken free of the thirst spell, he didn't want her near him to get caught in danger again. He was hurting, vulnerable, and didn't want to drag her into his problems.

Well, she'd dragged him into hers first. They should work on this together.

But who was she kidding? Graham had never indicated he wanted anything more from Misty than dating, and not even serious dating. Even if they figured out a way to get Graham free from the Fae spell, Graham might tell Misty he wanted to call it quits. She'd already laid the groundwork by getting mad at him and asking him not to call her.

And look how long *that* had lasted. Graham had come charging to her house only a few hours later. And now *he* was deciding they should stay apart. He drove her insane, and she was never going to win a control battle with him.

She needed to forget about Graham, Misty decided. There were plenty of other men around—for instance, Xav, or Kevin the insurance guy.

But Graham wasn't someone she could easily forget, and Misty knew it. He lingered, like the taste of the best wine—or something with a little harsher bite, like the tequila last night.

You are so beautiful. The words had softened Graham's rough-edged voice. The tequila talking, Misty guessed. But the phrase had shot straight to her heart and lodged there. She had no illusions about what she looked like, but Graham had been talking about how *he* saw her. Misty would treasure his words for a long time.

Misty and Xav reached the restaurant. It was crowded, this place popular. Paul had already snagged a table. Misty ordered herself an enchilada with spinach and white cheese topped with green chile sauce, her favorite. Paul went for a chimi, and Xav had the *carnitas*, the restaurant's specialty.

Halfway through the meal, which Misty was too distracted to appreciate, Paul excused himself and went into the back. When Misty glanced at him in the rear hall of the restaurant, he beckoned to her.

He wanted to talk to her alone. Paul wasn't entirely comfortable in social atmospheres yet, and he often asked Misty to step aside with him while he worked out his nerves.

"What is it?" she asked quietly as she joined him. The restaurant's crowd was noisy today, Xav answering his phone and not watching them, but Misty didn't want anyone overhearing. Paul was easily embarrassed these days.

"A friend of mine wants to talk to you," Paul said. "Think we can ditch our bodyguards?"

Misty's alarm grew again. "What friend?"

"Don't worry, he's not from one of the prison gangs I had to sell my soul to." Paul made a face. "I met him after I got out. He knows my parole officer, actually. Probably wants to talk to you about keeping me out of trouble."

Misty let out her breath. "All right. Have him come by the store after lunch, and we can talk in my office. I'm sure Xav will let us have a private conversation."

"He's here now. Wants to talk right away. He's busy."

"Here?" Misty scanned the small restaurant. Xav glanced their way but looked unworried, still on his phone. "Where? Why doesn't he come and have lunch with us?"

"He's in the alley. He only has a few minutes."

Misty stepped in front of Paul as he started for the restaurant's rear door. "Oh, right. Because that doesn't sound suspicious at all. Who is this guy? If he wants to talk to me so much, he can come to the store. It's only three doors down."

Paul looked suddenly afraid, which rang even more alarms. "Misty, *please*."

"No," Misty said firmly. "I'm not stupid enough to meet some guy I don't know in a back alley, even in broad daylight. If he's legit, he'll come to my office."

Paul opened his mouth to argue more, but Misty broke away from him. "Let's go finish lunch. We'll talk about him later."

To her relief, Paul followed her instead of charging out after this person. Paul pulled out his phone and was texting, probably canceling the back-alley appointment.

Xav gave the two of them a sharp look when they returned to the table, but he didn't ask. Paul finished his meal without speaking, and Misty picked at hers, wishing she could enjoy it.

Back at the store, Paul followed Misty into her office. "He's legit, Misty," he said. He looked angry now instead of afraid. "He's on his way."

"Fine, then." Misty sat at her desk, turned to her computer, and pulled up her never-ending e-mail.

Paul stepped out and returned in a few minutes with a man who was on the short side, but broad-shouldered and buff, without an ounce of fat on him. In his thirties, Misty guessed as she looked up from her terminal. He had very short black hair and tatts that proclaimed he'd been in prison at least once.

"Hi," the man said, stopping on the other side of her desk. His voice was gruff, a little bit like Graham's, but he gave her a little smile and sounded apologetic. "I'm Ben. Sorry about that. Paul didn't think you'd want me coming here or even talking to you in the restaurant. I'm so obviously an ex-con."

Which meant Paul wasn't supposed to be talking to him. A friend of his parole officer? Really?

"What can I do for you, Ben?" Misty asked.

"It's not what you can do for me." Ben leaned on his hands on the desk, which made every muscle press against his sun-worn skin. "It's what you can do for your boyfriend, Graham McNeil."

"What?" Misty came alert, not pretending to give Ben anything other than her full attention. The man looked fairly harmless—well, as harmless as a tough man with prison tatts could look—but his brown eyes held only friendliness. He certainly wasn't a Fae, at least, Misty didn't think so. Did they all look like the hiker?

Paul had remained by the door, his back to it. He looked uneasy but not surprised that Ben was asking about Graham.

"McNeil is in a lot of trouble," Ben said. "You know that. He's dying. And you can save him, if you want to. Do you want to save him, Misty?"

CHAPTER TWELVE

The last Shifter leader meeting Graham had attended had been in Dallas, and he'd had to fly. Graham hated flying. An airplane was a machine, and machines could break. Vehicles on the ground were dangerous enough, but what if one broke twenty-thousand feet in the air? Humans were crazy.

This time, Graham wouldn't have to fly, to his relief. The meeting was in Laughlin.

Good choice, Graham thought as he headed out of town with Eric—on Dougal's Harley because his own still needed repairs.

A lot of bikers went to Laughlin, a town about an hour or so south of Vegas on the Nevada-Arizona border, the motorcycle riders mixing in with retirees who came for cheap food, cheap rooms, and cheap slots. A score of Shifters could blend in with the human bikers easily, and the human government never had to know Shifters had gathered there. Shifters weren't allowed to cross state lines without special permission, so the fewer humans who knew Shifters were traveling today, the better.

Only Shifter leaders and a backup were allowed to attend the meetings. No others. Backup tended to be trackers—those who ran errands for or guarded the leader. Graham wanted to argue that both he and Eric could bring one backup, because they were joint leaders, but no. Eric was considered the official Shiftertown leader, with Graham as his muscle. Stupid idea, because if Graham decided to, he could take out Eric quietly on this road trip and then make a play to rule Shiftertown himself.

Except, Graham wasn't sure how much he wanted to rule it anymore. Cassidy and Jace—Eric's second and third in command—would argue, probably with violence. Cassidy was a sweet-looking woman but one hell of a fighter. Jace had a mate of his own now, and neither were slouches in the fighting area.

The rest of Eric's Shifters would also instantly rebel against being led by Graham if he tried to take over. And Graham had Dougal and two little cubs to worry about. If he got himself killed trying to take over Shiftertown those three would suffer, and so would any other Lupines who'd backed him.

Responsibility. Graham was plagued with it.

The fact that Eric rode confidently along, letting Graham stick close to his back, was meant to show how much Eric had grown to trust Graham in the last year. Eric wasn't an idiot—he knew he was safe with Graham now, and he was right.

The town of Laughlin hugged the Colorado River, the bridge across it about fifteen feet above the water, in contrast to the giant bridge that crossed many miles north at Hoover Dam, where the river flowed through a huge gorge. Large hotels lined Laughlin's mini Strip, with buses disgorging tourists up and down the street. Men on Harleys shot around the buses with a roar of engines.

Shifters drifted into the bar at the far end of the main drag gradually, the agreement being that all of them didn't descend on a place at once. The bar's owner was known to Eric, and had agreed to let them meet there, the deal sweetened with a little cash. Graham had to concede that Eric had better connections on this end of the state than Graham could ever cultivate. Eric was a slick talker. Graham just commanded.

By four that afternoon, the room had filled with Shifters; or at least, with as many as could get here on short notice. That was still a lot—Shifters even from the other side of the country could move fast if they needed to, including Bowman O'Donnell, a Lupine from North Carolina; Aaron Mitchell, bear Shifter from the Canadian Rockies; and Eoin Lyall, a Feline from western Montana.

Most came from Shiftertowns located outside cities—as Graham's Elko Shiftertown had been—easier for them to disappear for a time without humans noticing. The city Shifters had a harder task moving around undetected. Of course, the smug Irishman, Liam Morrissey, and his terrifying tracker, Tiger, had managed to get here from Austin.

The meeting started by Eric standing up and saying, "Graham has something to tell you."

All eyes moved to Graham, and most of the stares weren't friendly. A lot of these Shifters were barely on this side of feral, in spite of the Collars, in spite of the rigid hierarchy of Shifters. Eoin Lyall, Graham knew, hadn't agreed to take the Collar until his entire clan had been threatened with execution. Twenty years later, he was still pissed off about it.

Graham told his story. He left out the part about drinking Fae water and being under the spell, but he saw the Shifters fill in those blanks on their own. They weren't fools. They might not guess exactly how Graham had come under a Fae's thrall, but they knew the Fae wouldn't have been able to make Graham dream about him otherwise.

Bowman said, "I agree. We find the Fae-get who makes the Collars and ask him a few questions."

"That supposes we know where he is," Eric said.

Liam Morrissey cast his blue gaze over Graham and rested it on Eric. "We know."

"Do you?" Aaron asked in his bear rumble. "And how do you?"

Liam shrugged. "I've made it my business to keep tabs on him all these years. I'll send someone to round him up."

The other Shifters muttered or growled. Only Eoin didn't look surprised. "You shouldn't keep information like that to yourself, lad," Eoin said in his Scottish accent. "But no matter—we'll not have to waste time on a search. The question is, where are we going to keep him for interrogation once we extract him from wherever the humans have stashed him?"

Graham liked how Eoin thought. "The Vegas Shiftertown, of course," Graham said. "I'm the one who wants the answers."

Bowman spoke up. "And have the humans find him? They keep a close eye on city Shiftertowns. And your Shifters aren't exactly tame, McNeil. They might rip him apart if they know he's there."

"Aw, wouldn't that be sad?" Graham shook his head in mock sorrow. "Don't worry; I'll make sure we get some answers first."

"No ripping," Eric said. "Morrissey, you bring him, we'll question, and then we'll return him."

"And keep him from running back to the humans and telling them all he knows, how?" Eoin asked.

Liam gave everyone his self-assured, shithead grin. "You let me worry about that."

"Have the Tiger talk to him," Graham said. "If the Collar maker is sane enough to remember his own name after that, he'll be braver than I thought."

Tiger hadn't said a word—backup wasn't supposed to talk unless asked a direct question. Graham always ignored that rule himself, but Tiger obeyed it. Graham knew damn well that was because Tiger didn't feel like talking, not because he followed any rules but his own.

Tiger was gigantic, with black and orange hair and yellow eyes. He wasn't quite right in the head, having been created in a laboratory instead of being born in the wild. Tiger was one of a kind, and growing up in a cage hadn't exactly made him sane.

Most Shifters were wary of him, even though Liam vouched for him. Tiger had calmed a *lot*, Graham had noticed, since taking a mate.

The mention of Tiger moved attention from Graham to Tiger, which had been Graham's intent. The other Shifters had been studying Graham a little too closely. A Shifter's natural instinct when near anything Fae-spelled was to kill it.

"It's settled then," Eric said. "Morrissey will put his hands on the Collar-making Fae and bring him out here—subtly. I know a place near Las Vegas we can keep him. McNeil is right that we need him near us, but Bowman's right that we need it to be far from Shifters with a grudge plus prying human eyes. We'll let you know."

"And you need to let us talk to the human woman," Bowman said. "Her name is Misty, right?"

Silence. Graham stood up, growling as he went. Tiger rose with him, but moved to Graham's shoulder, as though backing him up, not stopping him.

"Why do you want to talk to Misty?" Graham asked, his voice soft but savage.

Bowman kept his seat, not looking intimidated. "This woman has seen the Fae, in the real world, twice. You've only met him in a dream. I want to know why this Oison singled her out."

"She has no idea," Graham said, a snarl in his throat. "She has nothing to do with this."

"I want to judge for myself," Bowman said. "If she shared the dream with you, and the Fae contacted her, she must be important somehow."

"Doesn't mean she needs to stand in front of a bunch of Shifters and explain herself," Graham said, his growl more pronounced. "She's an innocent bystander. Leave her alone."

Eric could jump in anytime and help out, couldn't he? But Eric sat back, looking as lazy as ever, and let Graham talk. Only Tiger had come to stand at Graham's side.

"My mate is human," Tiger said now, his voice like broken gravel. "Our mates should not be made to face other Shifters."

"But the woman Misty is nae his mate," Eoin pointed out in his Scottish lilt. "Is she?"

"Not yet," Graham said.

Bowman said, "I hear your Lupines are pressuring you into taking a Lupine mate. So the human woman must be a passing thing. Yet she already knows Shifter secrets, such as our connection with the Fae."

"Hell, *I* don't even know much about our connection with the Fae," Graham snapped. "But I wouldn't care whether Misty was a groupie I shagged once and dumped— I'm not forcing her to face a Shifter interrogation squad."

"Neither will I," Eric said mildly. He hadn't risen, but such was the other Shifters' respect for him that they all went quiet and let him speak. "I'll monitor Misty. I too think she's significant if the Fae sought her, even if only to ensnare Graham and the rest of us. But leave it to me. If she knows nothing, she should be left alone."

Bowman considered a long time, but he nodded in the end. The others seemed to conclude that what was good enough for Bowman was good enough for them.

"I'll find the Collar maker then," Liam said. "And get him to Eric in Las Vegas. We all should be able to have access to him."

"Agreed," Eric said. He stood up.

And that was it. Meeting adjourned. A few Shifters walked out right away, but the others took their time. A few went into the bar for a refreshing beer. Thinking about cold beer made Graham's unnatural thirst kick in, and he fought it by marching out the door into the bright heat of the parking lot.

"We rode all the way down here for that?" Graham asked Eric as they went to their motorcycles. The sun was hammering down, this stretch of the river racking up the hottest summer temperatures in the country. Not helping with the thirst.

"Phones aren't secure," Eric said, mounting his bike. "Neither is e-mail. The Guardian network is secure, but this isn't Guardian business."

"Yeah, well, if I don't find some way out from under this spell, it might become Guardian business," Graham said darkly. "As in Guardian's sword, inside me."

"Spell, is it?" Liam had materialized out of nowhere, or so it seemed, and now he studied Graham with his too-knowing blue eyes. "You're ensorcelled still, aren't you? Don't worry; I'll keep it to myself. You think the Collar-making Fae can help *un*-ensorcell you?"

"I haven't the faintest fucking idea," Graham said. "I'm more worried about what the Fae bastards are up to with our Collars. They need to be stopped. If I die in the process, then I do."

Liam's Feline eyes narrowed as his gaze fixed hard on Graham. "Huh," he said finally. Nothing more.

Graham looked behind Liam at Tiger. "Hey, crazy. How are you?"

Tiger took a moment to consider. "I'm well," he said. He put a lot of conviction into the short answer.

Eric laughed. "Glad to hear it. Having a cub on the way changes a Shifter, doesn't it?"

Tiger nodded once and gave Eric a faint smile. Scary, watching that big man smile. Graham had seen Tiger tear apart a human man without even trying—Graham had shot Tiger with two heavy bursts from a tranq rifle before Tiger even slowed down.

Having a cub on the way changes a Shifter, doesn't it? Eric's question hit Graham as Liam and Tiger moved off, and Graham and Eric started their bikes.

Graham remembered sharply how proud he'd been back in the day to have gotten his mate belly-full. He'd been so protective of Rita, and both had been happy and excited. *I was so young,* Graham thought. *Sure the world would do anything I wanted it to.*

He and Eric rode out of Laughlin, heading for the rugged hills that lined the river. On the other side of those would be Searchlight and a flat, almost alien-looking desert landscape that stretched for miles. Down on that desert floor, it was hard to guess that a glittering city full of people craving entertainment existed less than a hundred miles away.

The ride gave Graham plenty of time to remember Rita, how into her Graham had been, how proud of his unborn cub. Graham's father had been clan leader then—seventy-five years ago. The old man had been hard-bitten and quick to punish, but he'd held the wolf pack—the extended clan—together. Out in the wilderness of Montana, that had been important. Graham, as his second, had been wild and untamable. Rita had been just as wild as Graham.

And then she'd died bringing in Graham's cub. Just like that. One day there, full of hope; the next day, Rita and the stillborn boy cub had been taken away from him. The Guardian had thrust his sword into both Rita and the cub, and their bodies had crumpled to dust. Graham had scattered their ashes in the mourning ceremony, but he'd been numb, unable to weep.

He'd spent the next year alone out in the woods, living rough. He'd returned to find his father dying, other wolves in the pack ready to try to take over the minute he drew his last breath.

Graham had proved he was leader by preventing the takeover and punishing the instigators. He'd nursed his father through his last days, sending for the Guardian while the elderly wolf still lingered, to let him go out with dignity. Another mourning ceremony, but this time, Graham hadn't had the leisure to go grieve for a year in the wild. He'd had to kick plenty of ass to stay leader, and had earned the reputation of being a mean bastard.

Graham had survived by learning to push away his pain. Now, during this ride through the waves of heat back to the city, the pain rushed at him and washed over him.

Graham had to hold himself together—for Dougal, for the orphaned cubs, for his clan and all the Lupines—whether they liked it or not. But he was achingly lonely.

Misty was a sweet spot in every day. And damned if Graham would let any of the Shifters come for her, question her, touch her, even look at her.

Now, Graham might be dying, or worse, taken as slave by the Fae. If that happened, he hoped Eric or someone would just kill him. He'd had a full life, didn't matter.

Graham's one regret was that he'd not had any time to spend with Misty. Always something else distracted him, plus Graham had backed off her because his pack didn't want him taking a human mate. He'd always agreed with them—until Misty had smiled at him at a bar nearly a year ago.

Graham needed to talk to her. To see her. To immerse himself in her. He needed to find her, touch her, kiss her.

But when Graham stopped for gas inside the city limits, and his phone rang, it was Dougal, frantic and half crying. "Matt and Kyle are gone," Dougal said, his voice blasting through the phone. "They disappeared, and I can't find them anywhere."

Misty stared up at Ben. "I think you'd better tell me exactly what you mean."

"Just what I said." Ben kept his fists on her desk, his brown eyes focused on her. He didn't have the same black-hole stare of the Fae—Ben appeared to be human, but that didn't mean he was safe. "McNeil is going to die, unless you help him."

"How the hell do you know that?" Misty demanded.

Paul stood behind Ben, his arms folded, looking ashamed but making no move to stop Ben. "Listen to him, Misty. He's a friend."

"I'm waiting for him to say something worth listening to." Misty kept her voice hard, as she'd learned to as a kid when other kids bullied her. She'd learned how to put on the hard shell while protecting her softer self. She'd protected Paul as well.

"I know all about the Fae's spell," Ben said. "You cured yourself somehow, Misty. For that I say—respect." He gave her a nod. "But that counterspell only works on humans. Shifters aren't cured by it. Helping Graham will be harder."

Misty's worry rose, and with it anger and fear. How did

Ben know about the spell and whether it had cured her or not? "What are you?" she asked.

"No Fae in me," Ben said. "No Shifter either. But I've made it my business to know about these things."

"Can we get back around to Graham dying? Why are you saying I can save him?"

"It will be dangerous. I can't lie to you, Melissa Granger. But I'll help you. I'll lead you on this quest and keep the path as safe as I can."

"Quest? What quest?" Misty got to her feet. "Did I wake up in *Lord of the Rings*?"

Ben chuckled. "The journey won't be that long. You won't have to leave the city, not really."

"Not really?" Misty glared at him. "You haven't told me anything I want to hear yet."

"That's what happens to messengers," Ben said. "We're hated if we bring bad news, loved if we bring good. But I'm more than a messenger. I'm a guide."

"I learned a long time ago not to blindly follow anyone," Misty said. "If you can't give me exact details on how I can save Graham, I'd like you to leave. The last person who coerced me into 'helping' made me poison Graham with Fae water. Forgive me for not instantly trusting you."

Ben lifted his fists from her desk and shrugged. "That's to be expected. Ask around about me."

"I will." Misty started to reach for the phone, as though ready to start making calls now.

Ben's smile vanished. "Don't wait too long to trust me, Misty. This Fae you met, Oison, he's powerful, and he's vindictive. He wants Graham because he'd a good leader. If you want to save Graham from him, you'll need help, and that help is me."

Misty lowered her hand from the phone and sat back down in her chair, Ben's declarations spinning around her thick and fast.

"Graham saved me from Flores," Paul broke in. "I wanted to help him. Ben said he could."

How Ben had been so handy, Misty wasn't sure. She needed

the full story before she decided anything, which meant talking to Paul alone.

If Paul had a weakness, it was in being too easily coerced. He tended to believe in people stronger than he was, and he let them talk him into things. This was why he'd been joyriding in a car with his friends when an accident had occurred that had sent Paul to prison. In prison, he'd been bullied by Sam Flores until an even bigger bully convinced Paul to trust him.

Ben could be fine, or he could be shady. Paul wasn't the best judge of character, unfortunately.

"I'll get back to you," Misty said. "Now, I have a hugely busy afternoon ahead of me, as you can probably guess."

"I'm sorry about what happened," Ben said. "All of it. But I get it." He lifted a sticky note from the top of her pad, grabbed a pen from her pen holder, and scribbled a number on it. "This is me. Call me when you decide—or about anything. Just remember, McNeil needs you. You can save him, but it has to be your choice."

He stuck the yellow note in front of her, dropped the pen, gave Misty a nod, and left the office, touching his fist to Paul's on the way out.

Paul closed the door. He faced Misty with the defiance he'd learned as he'd changed from scared teenager to a young man who'd had to grow up overnight.

"He's legit, Misty."

Misty spread her hands on her desk. "Where did you meet him?"

"Told you. Through my parole officer. Ben's rehabilitated. Is doing well for himself."

"What does he do?"

"Construction work mostly. But he knows what he's talking about." He gave her the little smile that reminded her of the young Paul who'd been taken away. "I wouldn't have believed him either if I hadn't met the Shifters and Reid. If he can help, listen to him."

Misty lifted her hands. "How did he get in touch with you? And how did he know about what happened to me, and Graham? That's what's bugging me. What did you tell him?"

"Not much. He called me this morning, said he'd heard about Flores, and you and Graham getting stuck in the desert. That wouldn't be hard to figure out, if one of Flores's boys talked about it. Ben hears a lot about the criminal world."

"I can see that, but what about the spells? And the Fae?"

Paul shrugged. "I have no idea, but he helps people. That I do know."

He looked earnest, pleading. Misty let out a quiet breath. "I won't dismiss him out of hand." Misty's instincts were telling her to, but she'd seen things in the last year to make her doubt her instincts. "But I need to talk to Graham first."

Paul relaxed and gave her a nod. "Sure. Thanks, Misty."

Paul really didn't need to thank Misty when he was trying to do *her* a favor, but she understood. "Now get out of my office, kid," she said, growling the banter they'd always used to use. "You're distracting me."

Paul gave her a grin and walked out, a swagger in his step.

As soon as he closed the door, Misty picked up her cell phone and punched Graham's number. He was near the top of her favorites, right after her mother in Los Angeles. How pathetic was that?

Graham didn't answer, and a recorded voice came on to tell Misty that the number couldn't be reached. That worried Misty enough to call Cassidy, who told her Graham and Eric had left together on Shifter business.

"Tell him to call me," Misty said. "It's important."

Cassidy promised to, then hesitated. "You all right?"

"Not really. Cass, can you or Diego find out all you can about a man called Ben . . ." Misty picked up the sticky note, ". . . Williams. I have his phone number if that helps." She read it off.

"Sure. Who is he?"

"I have no idea. He might be fine. But I just want to know."

"We'll check him out." Another pause. "If you need to talk, Misty, you know you can always call me."

"Thanks. I think if I talk right now though, I'll end up

blithering or crying. I need to keep it together." As she'd done her whole life.

"I get it," Cassidy said. "Let me know."

Misty hung up and sat a long time staring at the name and number on the sticky note. What she knew and didn't know wrapped around each other, tangling with her emotions and making her slightly sick to her stomach. Or maybe she'd had too much green sauce at lunch.

Pressing the note back to her desk, Misty left the office. "Xav," she said, approaching him where he was helping his guys lift shelves back onto brackets. "What did you think of the guy who just left here? Ben, Paul's friend."

Xav's dark stare fixed on her, and his end of the shelf sagged. "What guy?"

"Shorter than you, hefty, dark eyes, tatts. With my brother?"

"I saw your brother, but no one else. When was this?"

"A few minutes ago. Right before Paul came out of my office."

Xav's focus sharpened. "I didn't see anyone. Before or after. And I've been watching."

"Oh."

"Damn it." Xav handed his end of the shelf to one of the other security men and moved away, taking out his phone as he stalked through the back to the alley.

CHAPTER THIRTEEN

"Would you all calm down?" Graham roared. "I can't hear myself think."

Dougal had been wolf by the time he got home, sitting on the floor of Graham's still-trashed kitchen, his muzzle lifted in howls. Nell, the she-bear who lived next door to Eric, was trying to get him to calm down, her voice as loud as Dougal's howling. Nell, a grizzly, was a big woman, and she could yell.

Graham had learned to outshout anyone else long ago. Nell shut up, but she scowled at him. Nell was the alpha bear in Shiftertown—not that there were many bears at all—but she was in dominance about the same as Graham and Eric.

"I haven't seen them," Nell said. "I have Cormac and my boys out looking for them." Nell's "boys" were full-grown grizzlies, Shane and Brody. "Most of Shiftertown is, in fact. And Misty's looking for you. Cassidy said she called."

Graham had ditched Eric at the gas station and ridden hard and fast to reach Shiftertown. He'd found Dougal in the middle of the kitchen floor, wailing to the ceiling.

"Damn it." Graham wanted Misty with every breath. His throat was so dry it ached, but even the thought of her brought a bit of ease. "Dougal, when did you last see them? Stop howling and tell me."

"He was bringing them to me to babysit," Nell said. "They ran off when Dougal wasn't looking."

"Wasn't looking?" Graham swung on her. "What the hell was he looking *at*?"

"Lindsay in a bathing suit." Nell said. "Well, half a bathing suit."

"Shit." Graham threw up his hands. "That female needs to be hosed down. Dougal, you idiot."

"Don't be so hard on him," Nell said. "He's just come through his Transition, and his mating instinct is high. You're the one who left two little helpless cubs with him."

"*Helpless?* You're talking about Matt and Kyle, right? They're hiding. Playing. Must be." Graham hoped to the Goddess they were only playing.

"We're looking," Nell said grimly. "We'll find them."

But with all the Fae activity, and Matt and Kyle featuring in the dreams—or entering the dreams, or whatever the hell was going on—Graham went sick with worry. The Fae Oison had enthralled Graham, a big, badass alpha Shifter. Kyle and Matt were tiny and vulnerable. If Oison had touched them, Graham was going to kill the Fae *outside* a dream and make it stick.

"Dougal will you shut up!" Graham bellowed. At the same time, his phone rang. "What?"

"Jeez, Graham," Misty's voice came to him. "Do you ever just say hello?"

"Misty. Sweetheart." Graham tried to pull back into a normal speaking tone. "I'm really busy right now."

"You're always busy. So am I. We need to talk."

"I can't talk. Matt and Kyle are missing. I find them first, talk later."

"What?" He heard her concern escalate. "Graham . . ."

"I gotta go, Misty. I'll call you back."

Graham closed his flip phone so he wouldn't keep

talking to her. He'd stand here and pour out all his troubles and beg her to come to him. To mate with him. To be his forever. He'd do it in front of Nell and Dougal too and not care.

He would call her back, once he sorted out what happened to Matt and Kyle, and everything else. And they'd talk as much as she wanted to.

"Dougal, do you at least have an idea which direction they went?" he asked.

Dougal finally stopped howling—thank the Goddess. Graham's ears were going numb. Dougal didn't shift to human, but Graham could understand what he wanted to say.

The answer was no. Dougal had been fixed on Lindsay, walking around in a bikini with no top. When Lindsay had disappeared inside her house, Dougal had looked around, and the cubs had been gone.

Yes, he'd gone to Brenda's to see if they'd run back there, and he'd checked all over Graham's house, and he'd called Nell. Dougal knew he was a shithead. That he screwed up. That he should be punished. But why had Graham run off and left Dougal alone? He hadn't known what to do.

"Dougal, you're grown," Graham snapped. "You don't need me around all the time."

Dougal's muzzle was down, almost on the ground, his ears back, tail tucked underneath him. Graham balled his fists in frustration. Dougal needed reassurance, not more yelling. But damn it, the cubs, Graham's responsibility, were gone, and there was an evil Fae on the loose.

Graham laid his hand on Dougal's head. "The mating instinct is harsh. Trust me, I know this. It's going to mess you up all the time. But that doesn't matter right now. I need you. You have the cubs' scent. Help me find them."

Dougal lifted his head, looking slightly better, but he still cringed as he slunk out of the house and started sniffing around.

"Poor kid," Nell said.

"I don't know what I'm going to do with him." Graham went out the door after Dougal, Nell behind him.

Outside, they met Cormac, a huge, blue-eyed bear Shifter. He'd recently mated with Nell, and the two had stuck together since then like contact cement.

"If they're in Shiftertown, we haven't found them," Cormac said.

Graham swallowed the raging curses that wanted to come out and said, "Thanks for looking."

"We'll look again," Cormac said. Nell nodded, and moved off with him.

Shiftertown was abuzz. During the day, Felines usually napped, and bears did too—bears always found some excuse to sleep. But now Shifters were out, many in Shifter form, noses to the ground, helping search for the two little ones.

Graham shucked his own clothes, changed into his large black wolf, put his muzzle down, and sniffed.

What he mostly smelled was a maze of Shifter scents, going every which way. This was the problem with Shiftertowns—too many scents from different clans, packs, and species tangled together. Wolf packs needed to have their scents around them and no one else's. Other scents meant danger. But here, with everything mixed up, Shifters couldn't tell danger until it was too late. Which was probably what had happened with Kyle and Matt.

They searched. Dougal stayed close to Graham, both of them keeping to wolf form while they hunted, Dougal still needing reassurance.

A hatchback car came into Shiftertown, pulling up in front of Graham's house. The door opened, and Misty's scent came to him, even across the field where he searched. Misty didn't drive a hatchback, and the scent of it was wrong for her, but that fact was peripheral.

As soon as Misty's shapely foot touched pavement, Graham focused on her and nothing else.

It had happened. Last night had triggered it, or maybe the dreams or the spells had.

As Graham watched Misty, taking in her long legs under a loose, calf-length skirt, her shapely breasts hidden by a white tank top with a little pink bow at the neckline, he knew his mating frenzy hadn't come out of nowhere. It had started the first night he'd met her.

Graham had always told himself that he could give her up, walk away from her at any time. He needed a Shifter mate, Misty was human—and so it could never be.

Graham had reasoned that if he didn't have sex with her, didn't spend any nights with her, and kept her at a distance, he'd be fine. Then, when the time came for him to pick out a Lupine mate, he'd be able to tell Misty, *Thanks, it's been fun.* Or better still, say nothing at all. She'd get it.

Now, more than ever, Graham needed to cut her out of his life. She was free of the spell, free of the Fae, free of Graham's problems. Misty could go, and Graham would focus on his dilemmas and move on.

But Graham knew, watching as Misty walked around to the back of the car, her skirt swishing around her tanned legs, that he'd never, ever be able to send her away. She was rapidly filling every empty space inside Graham's heart, and cutting her out of it would kill him.

Graham sat down on his haunches, wanting to point his nose to the sky and howl as miserably as Dougal had. He was so, so screwed.

Shiftertown was busier than Misty had ever seen it, except on ritual days. But all rituals, even mourning ceremonies, carried the element of a party. Right now, the Shifters were on alert, roving everywhere, tension high.

She had a feeling she knew why. Misty unlocked and opened the hatchback, reached in, and lifted two wolf cubs out by the scruffs of their necks.

They didn't want to come. The cubs curled in on themselves, trying to cling to Misty.

The Shifters closest to her saw. They stopped, eyes and ears fixed on Misty, the ones in human form freezing to look.

The awareness that Misty had the cubs spread like a ripple, rolling outward from her and around the giant black wolf who'd stopped and stared at her before she'd opened the hatch.

The Shifters weren't rejoicing. Not laughing in relief that Misty had brought the cubs back home. They were angry. She heard growls, rumbles, the soft snarls of animals debating whether or not to attack.

If this had been Misty's first ever encounter with Shifters, she'd be diving back into the car and racing the hell out of there. These Shifters were enraged Misty had the cubs, and they didn't look as though they cared about explanations.

Misty tried anyway. "I found them. I didn't take them. I'm bringing them back."

She tried to gently set down the cubs so she could back away, showing she meant no harm. But as soon as she turned loose their scruffs, Matt and Kyle scrambled back into her arms, their little bodies shaking. They were terrified.

The black wolf had started forward as soon as Misty lifted the cubs from the back. Now he moved rapidly between her and the Shifters who were advancing on her.

The Shifters in front of the pack, mostly wolves, drew back a little, but their growling didn't cease. Graham turned to face them, baring his teeth, his snarl menacing. The Lupines moved backward, heads lowering, but still they growled, unhappy.

One Lupine didn't obey. He stood up, anger in his eyes, his ears flat on his head, wolf snarls matching Graham's. With a harsh sound that was almost a roar, Graham went for the wolf, his charge swift, his jaws opened for the kill.

Graham landed on the wolf and had his body flipped over in the space of a second, Graham's mouth going toward the wolf's throat. At the last moment, Graham snapped his teeth an inch from the wolf's fur, then eased his jaws around the wolf's throat. Graham held the wolf there for about thirty seconds, then released it and touched its nose with his.

Graham stepped back, then began to shift. His legs and arms became human as he rose on his hindquarters. In a

short time, Graham stood over the wolf, who also had
morphed to human—a dark-haired man—both of them stark
naked.

The man remained on the ground, curled in on himself,
his defiance gone. Graham stepped to him and laid his
hand on the man's head. Graham said nothing, only kept
his hand there, until the man finally looked up at him. The
man's eyes, wolf gray, held contrition.

"Sorry, Graham," he said.

Graham leaned down, putting both hands on the man's
head now and ruffling his hair. "We'll both get over it.
Misty!" Graham straightened up and turned away from the
Lupine, finished with him.

Misty couldn't speak. She'd been staring at Graham's
muscled back, which tapered to a firm mound of buttocks.
Now he faced her, which meant she saw his equally firm
torso, his strong arms, and the cock that hung, thick and
long, between his legs.

Graham was a large man, his body sculpted for running, hunting, fighting. No polished edges on him. He was
raw, rippling with strength, beautiful.

"Misty, what the hell is this?" he demanded.

Graham's voice was gravelly from all the snarling, the
hint of the wolf still in it. And he sounded dry. Thirsty.

"I found the cubs," Misty said, making herself raise her
gaze from his hips. "Obviously."

Graham's eyes narrowed. "Is that what you were trying
to tell me on the phone?"

"No. I didn't find them until I went out to my parking
lot. I was trying to tell you something else on the phone,
but you hung up on me."

"Because I was looking for these damned cubs!"

Graham reached for them. Kyle and Matt shrank back,
whining, clinging to Misty. One of them had climbed onto
her head, his claws raking through her hair.

"Who are terrified of you," Misty said. "Look at them.
What did you do to them? Ow, Matt—or Kyle—stop
that. Which is which?"

"Kyle," Graham said, pointing to the cub on her head. "Matt." His finger moved to the other one.

"Why are they so scared of you?" Misty asked. Not that she hadn't seen Graham a few moments ago terrorize another large wolf into cringing submission.

"I don't know. Where did you find them? That's not your car."

"Nothing gets past you, does it?" Misty tried to cuddle Matt and pet Kyle so they'd quit with the clawing. "Matt and Kyle were in the back of that car. One of the DX Security men found them in there when he was at the end of his shift. No idea how they got there—his car didn't leave the lot all day."

Graham looked over the dark red hatchback with its curvy lines and dented fender, his brows drawing together. "*That* belongs to a guy from DX Security?"

"It's his mom's. He was borrowing it for the day. I told him I'd bring the cubs back to you. Well, actually, I just grabbed his keys while he and the others were debating how to return the cubs, and I brought them back. I figured you'd be worried."

Misty decided *worried* wasn't a strong enough word. Most of the Shifters were relaxing now, especially the wildcats, who were changing back to human form, strolling home, or loping off in their animal forms. Kyle and Matt were all right, and Graham apparently wasn't going to kill anyone over it, at least not now. The Lupines who'd confronted Misty were still there, but not looking directly at her or Graham.

"Did they think I'd kidnapped them?" Misty asked Graham. "Or that I would hurt them? I never would." She raised her voice to carry to the others. "I'd never hurt them. Or any kids. Or cubs."

"They know that in here." Graham tapped the side of his forehead. "At least, they should. But instinct is a bitch. They see someone with cubs who've been missing, and they want to kill first, ask questions later. But they won't do it again."

"I called when I was on my way," Misty said. The cubs were calming now, tails moving a little as she petted heads. "But you wouldn't answer your phone."

"I was a wolf, trying to hunt a scent. Had to leave my phone at home." He turned to someone behind Misty, across the street. "Nell! Come and take these brats. I need someone to look after them for me."

"Forget it, Graham!" the large, dark-haired woman yelled back. "I don't have time, and I don't have room. You have that huge house with only you and your nephew. You take them."

Graham put his hands on his hips. "Wait, I can't raise twin cubs *and* run Shiftertown!"

Nell turned her back, put her arm around the huge man, Cormac, and walked away with him. "Suck it up, Graham," Nell said. Cormac looked back at him and grinned.

"Shit." Graham folded his large arms and glared at the two cubs, whose tails had started moving faster.

Behind Graham, his Lupines watched, faces softening in relief, but they were still wary. Misty realized that while Graham could stamp around and let himself be made fun of, he'd showed that, when need be, his word was law. His Shifters disobeyed at their peril.

"Don't think you two can get out of this by being cute," Graham said to the cubs. "Bring them, Misty. We need to talk." He growled as he turned away. "Hell, now you've got *me* saying it."

Graham threw open the door of his house, went inside, and signaled Misty to follow. No one was in the kitchen, but the place was the disaster area he'd left. Misty stopped, looking around in dismay.

"The servants all quit," Graham said, deadpan.

Misty stood motionless while Matt and Kyle crawled down her and dropped to the floor. No longer afraid, they started running in circles between Misty and Graham, chasing each other, fear forgotten.

What Graham liked about all this was that Misty wasn't shying away from his nakedness. She wasn't exactly staring at his goods, but she didn't avert her eyes, flush, turn away, or yell at him to please get dressed.

Graham was the one who left, to step into the living room and grab some sweatpants he'd left in there. He didn't mind Misty seeing everything, but if his thoughts kept rampaging, he'd never hide his growing hard-on.

When he came back into the kitchen, Misty was at the sink, sorting dishes, scraping them, running the water.

"You don't need to do that," Graham said quickly. "I'll get Shifters in my pack to do it; or have Dougal get his butt home and help. Here, I'll call right now."

Misty kept on rinsing and scraping dishes. She never, ever simply obeyed Graham, as everyone else did, which both intrigued him and drove him crazy.

"My mom and dad divorced when I was ten and Paul was five," she said, for no reason Graham could discern. "We lived with my dad a lot because my mother remarried right away, and her new, successful husband didn't want the bother of kids around. He was nice to us, but it was pretty clear he wasn't interested in my mom's kids from her previous marriage. I had to learn very fast how to take care of men. My dad was always buried in his next business idea, and Paul was too little." Misty had the dishes sorted out, scrubbing them in one side of the sink, rinsing them in the other. "I learned early that men aren't good at taking care of themselves."

"Shifter males are different," Graham said, leaning against the counter. "We *have* to take care of ourselves, our families, and everyone in the pack. We're good at it."

Misty glanced around the wrecked kitchen, gave him a wry smile, and returned to the dishes. "No, you're not."

Graham loved how her nose wrinkled when she smiled like that, loved how one strand of her hair had come out of the ponytail and fallen to her bare neck.

"Are you going to tell me why you tried to call me before?" he asked. "And how the cubs got into the back of that car?" His gaze swiveled to Matt and Kyle, who were trying to lick dried ketchup off the floor. "Leave it!"

Matt and Kyle jumped, looked guilty for about one second, then started running around the kitchen again.

"We don't know how they got into the back of the car," Misty said over rattling dishes. "They were just there. The car was in the parking lot all day; the guy who owns it didn't take it anywhere, not even on his lunch break. He ate at the convenience store."

Graham stepped in front of Kyle and Matt's next wild circle of the room. "Stop!"

The cubs came to a startled halt but looked up at him without fear. They knew the difference between Graham as alpha, disciplining the pack, and Graham the irritated babysitter.

He fixed them both with a scowl. "How did you get into that car?"

A series of yowls and yips followed as both cubs tried to excitedly explain. Misty turned around from the sink, concerned.

Graham held up his hands. "Quit that. You sound like a bunch of coyotes. Speak human, so Misty can understand."

The wolves morphed almost instantly into boys. They were good at shifting. Not all Shifters were—some struggled with the change—but these two had a natural ability.

"We don't know," Matt said. "We were playing hide-and-seek with Dougal."

"We were hiding," Kyle clarified. "And Dougal was looking at a female." His confused look told Graham Kyle didn't understand why.

"Then Dougal was mad, and yelling," Matt said. "And we fell asleep."

"Woke up in the car," Kyle finished.

"Where were you hiding?" Graham asked.

The cubs looked at each other, their big eyes filling with fear again. Fear made them fall silent.

"Just tell me," Graham said.

Kyle curled into a ball and hid his face against his knees.

"You're scaring them," Misty said. She wiped her hands on a clean towel she'd found and came to the cubs. Crouching down, she reached out for Matt's hand. "It's okay, Kyle. We just want to make sure you weren't hurt. And that no one else gets hurt. You're not in trouble."

"I'm Matt."

Misty blinked at him, taking in his hazel eyes. "Sorry. Matt. You can tell me."

Matt considered for a time. Then he squeezed Misty's hand and leaned forward confidentially. "A house," he said. "A house that isn't done. In the basement."

Kyle raised his head and smacked his brother on the arm. "We promised!"

"Ow! We said we wouldn't tell any *Shifter*. Aunt Misty ain't Shifter."

"Who did you promise?" Graham said above them.

"Don't know," Matt said. "But Shifter spaces are secret, aren't they? We're not supposed to tell."

"You'll tell me." Graham's growling grew stronger. He knew Misty was right—if he terrified the little guys, they'd never say a word. But the wolf in him was worried. *"Now."*

"Can't," Kyle whispered. "Secret."

CHAPTER FOURTEEN

Misty felt waves of fear from the cubs. "Graham, leave them alone," she said.

Graham only rumbled some more. She wished he didn't look so sexy in the drawstring sweatpants that rode low on his hips, exposing the glory trail that pointed to what he'd hidden. He was dusty and sun-bronzed from his ride wherever he'd been and also from running around looking for the cubs. Tatts hugged arms replete with muscle, biceps hardening as he folded those arms, a stance he liked.

Misty knew Graham was a complicated man. He had responsibilities pulling him every which way and no time for sentimentality. A girl who fell in love with him would have to understand that.

Graham had made it clear after they'd gone out a few times that he expected to take a Lupine mate; he'd probably choose one of the Shifters who'd been cringing on the green today. Misty knew she should walk away from this relationship and let him do what he needed to—that she should have a long time ago.

Misty looked at Graham again and knew she'd have to

summon all her strength if she decided to go. A few days ago, she'd been angry enough to tell him to leave her alone. But now, she wasn't sure she had that kind of strength.

McNeil needs you, Ben had said. *You can save him, but it has to be your choice.*

My life sucks.

Graham pointed at the cubs. "You two, upstairs, and into the bathtub. You're filthy. I'll get you some dinner, then you're going to bed. Understand?"

Kyle and Matt both looked up, their fear easing a little. "Are we going to live with you, Uncle Graham?" Kyle asked.

"Looks that way."

"Yay!" The boys jumped to their feet, gave each other high fives, then both dove at Graham and gave Shifter hugs to his pants-clad legs.

Graham growled again, but gently. Both boys changed to wolf even as they clung to him, and Graham reached down, lifted them with his big hands under their bellies, and carried them out, rumbling at them all the way up the stairs.

Later, after the cubs had bathed, eaten their fill of another pizza, and curled up in bed, asleep with noses buried in tails, Misty returned to the dishes. Two little boys and Dougal, not to mention Graham, could sure make a mess. Dougal had come in when the pizzas arrived, eaten a whole one in about three minutes, and breezed out again.

On the prowl, Graham had said. Males right after Transition were always on the hunt for mates. Females were choosy and made males work for it, but that didn't keep males from trying.

Graham needed to talk more to Dougal, Misty thought as she moved another plate into the drying rack. Dougal had avoided Graham's gaze and refused to speak about the cubs and his role in losing them. No one had talked about it, in fact. Graham hadn't let Misty tell him about Ben either. He'd been waiting to speak to her about everything alone, she understood.

Well, now was his chance. The cubs were asleep, Dougal gone, the night darkening, the house quiet. Shifters were moving around outside, but inside, Graham's house was calm. And much cleaner now.

Two scarred hands planted themselves on either side of Misty on the counter. Graham's strong arms hemmed her in against the sink, and his body, in a T-shirt he'd donned for dinner and the sweatpants, covered her back. The heat of his lips brushed the side of her neck.

"Goddess, you smell good."

Misty lost hold of the last slippery plate, then caught it, lowering it back into the water. "I notice you didn't drink anything at dinner," she said, her voice not working right. "And barely ate."

"Nope." Graham skimmed his mouth over her skin, his breath hot. "Not gonna do it."

"Graham, you have to drink *something.*"

"No, sweetheart." His lips moved against her neck as he spoke. "If I start, I won't be able to stop. I'll drink myself to death."

"But if you don't have any water, you'll die."

"Wolves can go a long time without drinking. I'm finishing this before I give that dickhead Fae the satisfaction of making me desperate."

Misty tried to look back at him. "I hate seeing you like this."

Graham licked her neck up to the ticklish place behind her ear, which her ponytail bared. "When I drink you, I'm not thirsty," he rumbled.

Heat shot to Misty's intimate places and rested there. "I need to tell you things," she whispered.

Graham nuzzled her. "They can wait."

"Probably shouldn't."

"I don't give a damn right now." Graham turned her face up to him, keeping her body facing the counter, and bit her chin. Then he bit her lower lip and kissed her.

A hard, commanding kiss, gentleness gone. His hands moved from the countertop to her abdomen, pulling her back against him, his fingers hard on her belly. He kneaded the soft flesh there, moving one hand up between her breasts.

Misty reached up to touch his neck, twisting in his arms, forgetting her hands were wet. She brushed the Collar, thick and cold, the silver and black chain marking him as enslaved.

Graham opened her mouth with his, sweeping his tongue inside. His tongue was rough against hers, his mouth hot, strong.

Misty rubbed his Collar then traced his cheek, her thumb at the corner of his lips. Graham turned his head and sucked her finger into his mouth, licking off the clean water.

He reached in front of her and turned on the faucet. His sink had a sprayer hose, and he lifted this and squirted Misty up and down her front.

Misty squealed and tried to spin away. Graham held her firmly and soaked her tank top and her skin beneath. Water trickled between her breasts, and it was *cold*.

"You want me to drink?" he asked. "Then I'll do it like this."

Graham lifted the nozzle to his mouth and squirted some water inside. Then, one-handed, he pulled off Misty's sopping tank top, unhooked her bra and slid it off, held the sprayer nozzle close to her skin, and pressed the trigger again.

The water wasn't on full blast, so it poured down her rather than showered. Graham snapped off the water, turned Misty around, and lifted her onto the edge of the counter.

One strong arm behind her pulled her up to him. Graham lowered his head and licked across her chest, his tongue trailing fire. He raised his head, nose-to-nose with Misty, and a slow smile spread across his face. Misty touched the smile, liking how it creased the corners of his mouth.

Graham lowered his head again and scooped up the water on her breasts with his tongue. His warm mouth sent fierce tingles through her, pins and needles of heat. Graham licked around the mound of Misty's right breast and sucked her nipple inside his mouth.

The heat increased to incandescence. Misty groaned as Graham bit down on her nipple, the small pain erotic. He leaned her backward, dragging his tongue from her breasts to her belly, licking water as he went.

Misty felt her skirt loosen. She forced herself upright then, the breath she dragged in cut off when Graham kissed her again. As his mouth moved on hers, she hooked her fingers around the waistband of his sweatpants and tugged at the drawstring.

"Not this time," she said, breaking the kiss. "You're not undressing me unless you're bare too."

Graham stared at her. He was going to say no, back away, not go through with it. Misty's heart squeezed, pain seeping through her excitement.

Graham took a step back, grabbed the back of his T-shirt and pulled it off, and then shucked his sweatpants in one short movement. He wore nothing underneath. Unlike when he'd been naked outside, in front of everyone, Graham's cock was hard and lifted straight at her.

A male like Graham, rampant for her, was the sexiest thing she'd ever seen. Misty reached for him, liking the way black hair curled at the base, how the head was flushed with wanting.

"Don't tempt me," Graham said, moving her hand away. "We're doing this my way."

Misty curled her fingers into her palm. "Cassidy told me Shifters could have sexual partners without mating with them. And often do. Mating is different from just having sex."

Graham's growl vibrated the window behind her. He closed the few inches of space between them, his arms slammed to either side of her before Misty could say another word.

"I'll never *just* have sex with you. If I take you, it will be a mate thing, and nothing less. You know that, damn you."

"I don't know anything about you, Graham." Misty

rested her hand on his chest, feeling his heart banging hard beneath his hot skin. "You never tell me."

Another growl, this one rumbling long and low. Graham twisted her skirt open, the buttons holding it pinging to the floor. Her panties came next, skimmed off over her legs before he sat her on the counter again.

"There's nothing to know," Graham said. "Nothing I want to talk about."

Shutting her out. As usual. His gray eyes held old pain, worry that went back to long before she'd met him. Misty caressed his face, wanting in, wanting him.

Graham slid his fingers behind her buttocks and tugged her to the front of the counter. At the same time, he dropped to his knees, spread open her thighs, and plunged his mouth over her opening.

Misty choked back a scream. The cubs were asleep upstairs—Graham had to be insane. At least she'd pulled the blind down on the window behind her. Other blinds were open, though, the light in the kitchen haloing Graham while he licked her.

Misty's thoughts fizzled off into nothing. All she knew was sensation—Graham's strong tongue finding her depths, his hands hard on her thighs, his mouth on her. Drinking, licking, suckling.

She wound into dizziness. The water in the sink slowly drained, the stopper having worked loose, a little droplet from the almost shut-off faucet spattering on the water's surface. Misty curled her toes, her legs swinging as heat poured over her. She pressed her fingers into Graham's short hair, holding on, her head thrown back. The light made spangles on the ceiling, reflections moving softly.

The water's ripples became waves of sensations Graham poured into her. Misty heard moans come from her mouth, and she pressed her fist against her lips to stop them.

Before she knew it, she was bumping against the counter, barely able to stay on, her moans turning to little cries, still muffled by her fist. Graham was merciless. He kept drinking her, tasting, driving her wild.

She was going to die, and he'd be laughing. Graham went on, suckling, drinking, thrusting into her with his tongue. No sex had ever been this good, and it wouldn't be again, unless it was with Graham.

Misty's first climax finished, and another came hard on its heels. She heard herself begging him, and felt his laughter against her thighs. After the fourth time, Graham finally rose to his feet, gathering Misty to him while she shuddered and clung to him.

"Damn you," she whispered.

Graham's chuckle rumbled wonderfully beneath her ear. "I was thirsty."

Misty raised her head. Graham smiled down at her, his eyes dark, something in him relaxed and loosened.

Still, he looked way too smug. The smile said Graham knew he'd taken her to new heights, and he could do it again if he wanted.

Misty reached up and closed her teeth around his earlobe. Graham's hold loosened while he took a sharp breath, and Misty slid off the counter. She kept going, all the way down to her knees.

"No." Graham's hand fell heavily on her shoulder, but too late. Misty grasped the base of his long cock and quickly closed her mouth around it.

*N*o. *No, no, no.*
      Graham had to stop her. Tell her to get up, dress herself, and get her ass out of his house.

He balled his fists as Misty's mouth moved, lips stretched to take him all in. He groaned. "Holy Mother Goddess."

Misty pulled him closer. The Goddess wasn't going to answer Graham's prayer, but maybe she *had* answered it. Misty kept on with him, moving her tongue across the underside of his cock, licking him, nibbling a little.

Graham's burning thirst, now that he wasn't drinking Misty, had come roaring back, but for the moment, he

didn't care. His lower body was spreading its pleasure to
the rest of him, rendering his dry throat a minor issue.

Graham's hips began moving, slowly at first, then faster
as Misty continued. She pulled him into her, tighter, en-
couraging him.

Damn the woman. She was torturing him. Punishing
him for making her come four times and liking it.

Graham clenched his fists harder, feeling his nails
crease his palms. The small pain was lost in the swamping
need that poured through him, making every good inten-
tion evaporate like water from the desert floor.

He wanted to mate with this woman, take her in every
position he knew and some he'd never tried. He wanted to
curl up with Misty in the night, letting down every guard
he'd ever put up, then wake up and take her again.

*I want to mate with you under the light of the Mother
Goddess and the Father God. I want you with me until we
find the Summerland, and then float into brightness with
you after that.*

*I want you sun and moon, body and soul. Joined. For-
ever.*

Graham wanted her sweetness, her smile, her softness.
And he wanted sex. Pure, wild, raw sex.

He touched Misty's sleek hair, stopping himself from
bunching it in his fist. He was too strong; he could hurt her.
He stroked the satiny length of it, breaking the binding that
held it in the ponytail. Long, flowing, warm. Graham
would make her wear it down all the time.

Misty's tongue rubbed him, and her mouth pulled, teeth
scraping a little. She pressed her fingers into the firm flesh
of his buttocks, and then he felt one finger slide between
his cheeks.

The feeling was explosive. Graham threw his head
back, words coming out of his mouth, but he had no idea
what they were. He thought he said *love* in there, as well as
plenty of swear words.

"*Damn,*" he said, and then he came.

Graham stopped himself pressing Misty to him, urging

her to take him. But she didn't let go. She drank him down as Graham spilled his seed, knowing he had to have this woman forever.

He rocked against her for a long time, the house around them silent except for the soft sounds of their pleasure. The intense joy that gripped him eased down into a warmth that was no less joyful.

Misty drew back, releasing him, and picked up a fallen towel to wipe her mouth. Graham found himself on the floor with her, gathering her to his lap, closing his arms all the way around her. He rocked her there, kissing her hair, drowning himself in her warmth and scent.

Misty brushed fingertips over his rough, unshaven cheek, her smile quiet. "There," she said. "I knew I could wipe the grin off your face."

CHAPTER FIFTEEN

Misty had asked, "Do you want me to to go?"

Offering, knowing Graham had been trying to push her away, out of his problems. Except Misty kept landing right in his problems again.

"Stay," Graham had said into her hair, and he'd carried her upstairs.

Graham's bedroom was the neatest in the house. Dougal's room was a disaster area, Graham always surprised his nephew could find his own bed. Many times Dougal didn't, sleeping on the floor as wolf. The twins were snuggled down together in a spare bedroom, which Graham supposed was theirs now.

Graham lay Misty in his own bed and covered her nakedness with blankets. She gave him a sleepy smile, one a little bit smug. She'd gotten Graham to let down his guard.

Wasn't that hard, sweetheart.

Graham debated whether to join her. He'd want to touch her again if he did, wrap up in her, have sex with her. Mate with her.

Then he'd have to keep himself awake somehow, or he'd

slide back into the dreams with the Fae. He had the feeling that the more encounters he had with Oison in his dreams, the more hold the Fae would have over him.

Graham adjusted the light blanket over Misty, the ceiling fan and blow of air-conditioning making the room cool. Out the window, he saw the sweep of Shiftertown, the darkness that was desert and mountains beyond, the moon, even fuller than last night, and six Shifters waiting for his attention at the edge of his front yard.

They were all Lupines, five male and one female—three clan leaders and three seconds. One of the leaders was from a clan from Graham's Elko Shiftertown; the other two had been living here under Eric.

Graham growled in his throat, left Misty, who'd drifted off to sleep, grabbed a fresh pair of sweatpants and T-shirt, and went downstairs and outside.

The Lupines hadn't moved into the yard—this was Graham's territory, and they wouldn't approach without invitation. They'd stand at the edge of the sidewalk instead, willing him out by sheer force of glare.

The leader of the Elko clan took one step forward. He'd probably lost the coin toss as to who got to address Graham and risk being attacked without mercy.

Graham stopped in the middle of his yard, remaining firmly on his territory and not inviting them in. "What the hell is this?"

"Are you going to mate with the human?" the Elko clan leader, Norval, said. He inhaled, the hot Nevada wind easily carrying to him Graham's scent and everything he'd done with Misty. "We saw you."

Graham folded his arms. "Can't a Shifter get sucked off in his own kitchen without his neighbors having a meeting about it? It's my business who I mate with."

"A Lupine, you said," Norval went on. He'd gone white about the mouth, and Graham smelled his fear, but Norval was angry enough to stand and not run away. "You got us down here with the promise that you'd take a Lupine mate from my clan or the Las Vegas ones. I can barely hold my clan together, McNeil. They're ready to shove you out of power unless you start your dynasty."

"I got you down here any way I could, because the humans were forcing us to leave," Graham said. "If I didn't agree that all my shithead Lupines would get on the buses and haul their asses to this Shiftertown, the humans were going to round us up and kill us all. Humanely, they said. Only humans could name a kind of killing after themselves. Notice they only apply it to animals."

During the speech, the others moved uneasily. The sole woman, the second to one of the Las Vegas Lupine clan leaders, was the only one who kept still, her gaze on Graham. Females tended to be braver than males.

"You need to choose," the woman said.

"I won't choose you, Muriel," Graham said. "You're a total bitch."

He kept his tone and stance casual, as though his clan leaders ganging up on him meant nothing to him. Inside, Graham's heart was pounding, his mouth dry with the incessant thirst, his body heat high from the near-sex he'd had with Misty. He was drowning in feelings for her, mixed with annoyance at his Shifters and fear of what the Fae was doing to him.

"I wouldn't touch you, Graham," Muriel returned. "I'm already in a mate agreement."

With another poor Lupine in Graham's clan. An *agreement* they called it. She'd made the Lupine do that instead of outright mate-claim her, because Muriel wanted to keep her options open, in case she got a better offer.

"There are four unmated Lupine females among our three clans," Norval said. "We expect you to choose one before the end of our first year in this Shiftertown. Such was your promise."

"Things have changed." Graham had been convinced once upon a time that any dilution of Shifter blood weakened the pack and could drag down an entire clan. But since moving here, he'd found his old ideas rearranging themselves. He'd met Iona, the half-human, half-Shifter woman Eric had mated with. He'd bet Iona could wipe up all six of these Lupines and have energy left over to take on Graham. Graham didn't bring this up, because all Shifters had agreed not to talk about Iona's half Shifterness. But they knew.

"You need to decide," Norval said. "The clan leaders aren't going to wait forever."

Graham walked to Norval, stepping from grass to sidewalk, effectively leaving his territory to face Norval and the others on neutral ground. He didn't need territory advantage to intimidate.

"That's right," Graham said. "*I* decide. And if I decide a human mate is the best thing for me and my clan, then you'll have to live with it."

"Or we challenge your leadership," Norval said.

"Or you challenge my leadership." Graham gave him a nod. Challenging a leader who endangered Shifters was every Shifter's right. "But you'd better be prepared to win. And Goddess knows what Eric would say about it if you did win. You know what an interfering asshole he is."

He heard growls from the Las Vegas Lupines, anger at Graham for talking about Eric like that. They *liked* Eric leading them, Goddess help them. *Lupines giving themselves over to Felines. What's the world coming to?*

"Tell you what," Graham said. "You all go home and decide among yourselves which clan you think should be dominant. Because if I pick a female from one of your clans, you know that clan will increase in power. I hope you're all cool with that. Once you figure out which of you should outrank the other, come back and present your females. Then I'll give you my final answer."

The leaders didn't look at each other, but Graham saw them move a little bit apart from each other. Subtly.

That should shut them up for a while. They'd been so focused on forcing Graham to make a decision—or refuse to, giving them the incentive they needed to try for a leadership grab—that they hadn't thought about the fact that Graham's mate would increase dominance of her clan.

It was all stupid anyway, because the humans didn't like Shifters changing leadership. The humans thought *they* assigned leadership; they'd barely accepted Graham to stay leader of his Shifters. Eric and Graham had talked long and hard to convince them that Graham was best at keeping the Elko Shifters under control. The humans wanted the Shifters to live quietly and not cause trouble, so they'd agreed.

Shifters knew who led and who didn't, regardless of what humans thought, but they sometimes had to be covert about it.

"Go chew on that," Graham said. "And stop looking in my windows."

"You have to take a mate sooner or later," Norval said. "You know that."

Norval delivered his declaration with a sharp nod of his head, then he walked away, carefully not turning his back in Graham's direction. His second drifted after him.

The Las Vegas leaders walked away too, only Muriel giving Graham any kind of deferential farewell.

Graham knew Norval was right. If Graham's son had survived—he'd be full-grown and powerful by now—then his Shifters wouldn't give him so much grief about his mate. Eric's choice of half-human, half-Shifter Iona hadn't caused a murmur, because Eric had Jace, a strong son, plus his sister Cassidy was very dominant.

Graham had no one. Only Dougal, his out-of-control nephew. The few other members of his clan were distant relations, and several were equal in dominance with each other—no clear path to clan leadership. If Graham dropped dead, there would be a battle. The only way to prevent it was to take a strong Shifter mate and start putting out cubs. The more cubs the better.

Graham waited until the Lupines had faded into the darkness, their scents growing fainter. Only when he knew they were truly gone did he return to the house, wanting Misty.

He glanced up at the house and saw two small wolf

faces peering down at him from the spare bedroom window. Little shits. They were supposed to be asleep.

But they watched him all the way in, and he knew they'd heard every word. When he opened the door of their bedroom upstairs, Kyle and Matt were curled up on the bed again, head to head, tail to tail, pretending to snore.

Misty woke to early-morning sunshine pouring through the window, a stiffness in her body, and strange satisfaction. For a moment, she didn't remember where she was, then she saw she still lay in Graham's bed.

Of Graham, there was no sign. The bed bore only Misty's imprint and rumpled covers. Graham must have slept elsewhere.

Misty climbed out of the bed and headed for the bathroom. She was completely naked and had no idea where her clothes were. Still downstairs in the kitchen?

No, they'd been hung over the back of a wooden chair near Graham's bedroom door. Well, dropped haphazardly over the wooden chair. Graham wasn't the kind of man who sent out his lady's clothes to be cleaned and pressed then greeted her with breakfast in bed, including a rosebud in a vase.

Graham was himself. Misty had the feeling that, to him, *romance* was a word in an ancient, lost language.

The bathroom was clean though. New and nice. Misty showered, using plain bar soap and generic shampoo. No frills for the McNeils.

She dressed and went downstairs, hoping she could find utensils and ingredients for breakfast. The kitchen was as she'd left it, no change. The cubs weren't here or frolicking in the yard. They weren't in the house at all—they hadn't been in bed, and no way were they in here and not making noise. No one was in the house but Misty.

No sign of Graham, cubs, or Dougal in the backyard or in the front. They'd left, going who-knew-where, without bothering to leave so much as a note.

Not Misty's business, right? She should walk out, get into her borrowed car, and drive back home.

Disappearing without saying good-bye, though, especially after what she and Graham had done last night, felt wrong. She wanted to see Graham, to kiss him good morning, to see his smile and hear his rough-voiced teasing.

Matt and Kyle had confessed they'd gone to a basement of an unfinished house, and from there had somehow made it to Misty's store. Had someone snatched them, drugged them, carried them off? And why dump them in a car outside Misty's shop?

It was six o'clock, but the sun was up, the temperature already climbing. In the summer, desert dwellers did anything outdoorsy early, and then stayed inside with the AC for the hot afternoon. If Graham wanted to explore the scene of the crime in daylight, he'd have done it now.

Not her business, Misty repeated silently.

Oh, screw it. Misty wanted to know whatever it was they found. She cared about the cubs too, no denying it. She cared about Dougal and Graham, and her Shifter friends. Misty was in this now, no going back, no matter how much she and Graham danced back and forth on their relationship.

Misty put on her sandals and walked outside through the kitchen door. A step led down into a backyard with a patch of grass and a path connecting it to a common area between the houses.

Unlike many of the neighborhoods in Las Vegas, a block wall did not surround every yard in Shiftertown. Graham had told her Shifters didn't need walls. Each Shifter knew where his territory ended and another Shifter's began. If humans had as good a sense of smell as Shifters did, he said, they wouldn't need walls either.

Misty stepped into the common area and headed toward the first unfinished house she saw down the way. Two seconds later, a woman was in front of her, one tall and gray-eyed, her dark hair a bit shaggy. A Lupine, Misty guessed.

She eyed Misty coldly, and Misty stopped.

"Stay away from Graham," the woman said.

Misty hid a sigh. Facing jealous females was not something she liked to do. It always made her feel twelve years old, confronting a mean girl in the school cafeteria.

"That's for me and Graham to decide," Misty said.

"No, it isn't." The Lupine woman came close, invading Misty's personal space. Shifters did that when they decided they were dominant to you. Graham did it all the time. "Graham mates for the good of his clan, for Shiftertown," the woman said. "You're not good for us. So go away."

"He isn't mating with me."

The woman inhaled, her eyes narrowing. Misty knew she'd washed thoroughly with the deodorant soap, but Shifters had phenomenal senses of smell. They could strip scent down into layers and time, like archeologists uncovering civilizations.

"You reek of sex and his seed. Don't lie with him again. A by-blow will help no one. Might even hurt you."

Misty had also learned that when faced with a mean girl, she should look said girl straight in the eye and not back down. Sometimes this had led to Misty getting beaten up, but she'd always fought back with gusto, which had earned her a little respect.

"I'm not sure I like that you know what Graham's seed smells like," Misty said. "But it doesn't matter. It's Graham's business, and mine. Not yours."

"That's what you think, bitch."

So some of the mean girls in the cafeteria had said. But those girls hadn't had Shifter strength, or the huge, clawed hands that now came at Misty's face.

Misty ducked, shielding herself with her arms, hoping she could fend off the woman and not die. But the blow never came. Misty peeked out from under her arm, and found Dougal shoving the woman backward, his face half shifted to wolf, his claws extended, his voice guttural.

"Don't touch her."

"Stay out of this, cub," the woman snarled.

"*Not* cub. Not anymore. She's Graham's. You touch her, you answer to him."

The woman had stopped, also half changed to wolf. Her growl was furious, but Misty saw her realize that Dougal had a point. Graham never bothered with calm negotiation when he was angry.

"Tell Graham she's got to go," the woman said, her voice harsh. "If the other Lupines decide to take her out, there's nothing he can do."

Take her out? Not something Misty wanted to hear.

With a final sneer, the Lupine woman receded to human form and jogged away. Dougal, also back to his human shape, returned to Misty.

"You all right?"

"Yes." Misty dragged in a breath. "Thank you."

"Tell Uncle Graham I saved your ass, all right?" Dougal said. "He thinks I'm a complete wuss. If you're looking for him, follow me. I know where he is."

CHAPTER SIXTEEN

Graham peered around the darkness of the dug-out basement once the cubs had figured out which house they'd been exploring. They'd taken a while deciding, which had involved dashing back and forth, running in circles around Graham, and sitting on their small wolf butts and howling.

Finally the two agreed that they'd been exploring the basement in the second unfinished house from the end. The stud walls had been raised on the main floor, and now workers were putting in the plumbing and other pipes needed to fit the houses for modern living.

The basements were a secret. Most houses in this city were built on solid concrete slabs, with wiring and pipes in the walls and ceiling. Basements around here could fill with noxious gasses, not to mention desert creatures looking for places to nest.

Shifter basements were different though, whole other worlds. Shifters had dug out the basements of these houses at night, using equipment Iona made sure her construction workers left behind. They hid the evidence by constructing a solid ceiling that could be reinforced enough to take the concrete slab and weight of the house later.

Shifters had been building secret places for centuries. Territory could be invaded by other Shifter clans or encroached upon by humans at any time, so they'd made sure they had places to go to ground and survive, and to keep their most important treasures safe.

To invade another Shifter's secret territory could be death to the invader. It had been in the old days. Most Shifters, however, weren't foolish enough to try to enter another's secret hideaway, sensitive to the fact that they had their own hideaways to guard.

Cubs, on the other hand, needed to be taught. These basements weren't finished yet, and held no secrets. But the Shifters who moved in here would be itchy for a long time because of the scents Graham and the cubs were leaving.

And Dougal's and Misty's scents. Graham smelled them coming, even before he heard Misty's light footsteps as she climbed down the ladder. Dougal was more surefooted and quiet, but he was talking.

To Misty. The usually silent, sullen Dougal was talking to a female. But then, Dougal and Misty were about the same age. Misty acted much older than Dougal, but humans matured quickly. Had to.

Graham waited for them to catch up. "What?"

Misty gave him the look that said he was hopeless. "I was worried about you and the cubs. There's a Fae on the loose, remember?"

"I know," Graham said in a hard voice. "Exactly why I left you safely in my house. Which you're going back to now."

Misty folded her arms, which pushed up her breasts under her little tank top. "You know, when I was growing up and raising Paul, he had a favorite saying when I told him what to do too often."

Graham wrenched his gaze from her breasts and moved it to her face. "I'm going to regret asking what it was, aren't I?"

"He'd say, *You're not the boss of me.*"

"That's funny." Graham came close to her. The nearness of her almost knocked him over. He needed her. Needed to touch, to taste, to feel her under him. "Guess what? When you're a guest in Shiftertown, I *am* the boss of you. Dougal, take her back home."

Instead of leaping to obey, Dougal stood his ground and put on his obstinate face. "Tell him, Misty."

Misty blinked at Dougal, her angry look fading. "You mean *now*?"

"Tell him. I'm tired of him treating me like a cub."

"Tell me what?" Graham's voice echoed through the basement. The wolf cubs stopped their frantic running around and sat down again.

Misty was calm as could be. "That Dougal is not a wuss. He saved my life."

Graham's fears roared to the surface. "What the hell are you talking about?"

"Jan was sniffing around," Dougal said. "She tried to go at Misty. I stopped her."

Graham stilled. Dougal's fists clenched, and he looked shaky and sick, but he was alive and whole, not a pulp of Shifter dust on the ground. "I bet Muriel sent her," Graham said, but distantly.

"Probably," Dougal said. "Misty stood up to her though. Told her to stay out of your business."

Graham pinned Misty with a hard stare. She stared right back at him, straight into his eyes. Graham didn't like lesser beings who met his gaze, but Misty always had. He'd cut her some slack because she was human and didn't understand what the gesture meant, but the fact that she could do it intrigued him. Not many humans could withstand Graham's stare.

"Did you look at Jan when you said that to her?" Graham asked Misty. "The way you look at me?"

"Yes." Misty's brows drew down in puzzlement. "Where else would I be looking? The trees? She was ready to pounce on me—I thought I should keep my eye on her."

Graham relaxed a little, his worry receding even if his thirst didn't. "Dougal."

Dougal flushed, but his eyes held defiance. "I'm not apologizing to Jan."

Misty looked perplexed. "Why should Dougal apologize? Jan was the one threatening me. Dougal was just trying to help. Never let a bully get away with it, I always say. They'll just bully you some more."

Graham laid his large hand on Dougal's shoulder and yanked the young man into a hard hug. Dougal was shaking, but his shakes lessened as Graham held him close.

Graham released him after a few moments and patted his shoulders again. Dougal stepped back, wiping his eyes, but he stood a little straighter.

Misty had her hands on her hips. "What just happened?"

"Dougal went up in dominance," Graham said. "Thank you, Misty."

Misty was staring at him again. "What did I do?"

"Gave him the opportunity. And you showed your dominance too. I'm proud of both of you."

Misty kept staring. Any other Shifter would blush and show their pride at his praise. Misty only looked bewildered. "This is a Shifter thing I don't understand, isn't it?"

Graham put his hand on her shoulder. "Let me put it this way—you've just made my life a little easier. If Jan let herself get out-dominated by a human and a cub past his Transition, her alpha might keep her mating needs away from me." Jan's father was ambitious, which was why he'd sent Jan over to Graham's to fight him and "lose," so Graham would show his dominance by sexing her. Nice try.

"Anyway," Misty said, as though the very important issue had been a side note. "Is this the basement the cubs found? It's dark down here. Anyone bring a flashlight?"

Dougal snorted. "Humans."

"She's a guest," Graham said firmly. Moving up in dominance did not mean Dougal got to be a rude shit. "Look around for ones the humans might have left."

Dougal growled a little, but he walked away, the cubs scampering after him.

"Misty," Graham said.

Misty stood her ground. She'd moved her hands from her hips to fold them across her chest again. "I'm not going back."

"I know you're not, because you're an obstinate human woman who doesn't understand danger."

Graham stepped close to her, unable to keep himself from her any longer. Her scent filled him, her honey-spice that was even stronger after last night's intimacy. She'd bathed, but if she thought rubbing herself with the soap he used every day made her scent more distant, she was wrong. Now she smelled like him, his house, his bed, things that were a part of him.

Misty looked up at him, her brown eyes filled with uncertainty, confusion, and determination all mixed together. He liked that she could follow many trains of thought at once. Lupine women could be boringly single-minded.

Graham had to kiss her. Couldn't stop himself.

Her eyes softened as Graham bent to her, her lips parting for his. Misty's hands went to his chest, fingertips pressing into his shirt as Graham cupped her shoulders and pulled her up to him.

As soon as their lips touched, Graham's determined gentleness evaporated. He needed her. Pushing her away had grown too difficult, which scared the hell out of him.

Misty tasted of minty toothpaste, and herself. Graham opened her mouth with his, pressing her into his arms. He wanted her *now*, on the ground, in the dirt, her legs wrapped around him. He'd slide deep inside her and not come out until he'd satisfied himself again and again.

The longing swirled in his brain and through his body. Her kiss was as needy as his, but more tender. Misty kissed him for kissing's sake, as though she didn't care if it led to anything else. She simply liked *kissing* him.

Graham liked kissing *her*. He licked behind her lower lip, caught her tongue between his teeth and gently bit.

Misty laughed when he let go, then Graham scooped her up to him and started again.

Misty's body flowed into his, she softening to fit every plane of him. Graham ran his hands down her back to her buttocks under her loose skirt. Firm and sweet, like her, but soft enough for caresses. Her breasts flattened against his chest, unfettered behind her tank top. She hadn't bothered to put on her bra this morning.

Shifter women rarely wore bras, so the fact Misty had left hers off shouldn't have shot Graham's cock into the hardest hard-on he'd had since . . . well, since last night. He skimmed his hands inside her shirt, Graham's kiss intensifying as he drew his palms up to cup her breasts.

Warm, beautiful woman met his hands, her skin satiny, the slightest bit damp from her shower. He closed two fingers around each of her firm nipples, his cock fiery hot.

Misty had defied a Shifter woman for him. She had guts behind her sweet smile, and it made Graham's body hotter than August sunshine.

Graham broke the kiss to lick her throat. Bite it. The mark he'd left on her shoulder showed outside the strap of her tank top. Graham suckled her there again, darkening the mark. So all Shifters would know to back off. Even better, he breathed out onto her skin, scent-marking her.

For her protection, he told himself, so the horny, mate-needing male Shifters of Shiftertown wouldn't run after her. They'd know Graham protected her, and back off, unless they wanted to fight him for her.

But he knew, even as he did it, that the scent-marking was more than just for her protection. Graham was proclaiming that Misty was his and his alone. He'd been denying this to himself since he'd met her, but here in the unfinished, dusty basement, he knew. He wanted Misty, and no other, as his mate.

"My life is screwed up," he said softly.

Misty touched his face, turning him to her. "Hmm?"

"What am I going to do?" Graham asked, half to himself. "I can't stay away from you."

For answer, she kissed him, sweet and fiery. Graham tenderly squeezed her breasts, his hands still inside her shirt, the warm goodness of her coming through his touch. Graham wrapped his foot around her bare ankle. One tug, and she'd go down. He'd guide her, holding her, so she'd never fall, but only lie down while he came over her. He'd start making love to her by peeling off her clothes and licking her body, then he'd spread her legs with his hand and slide into her.

Goddess and God, he wanted that.

A light shone full in his face. The sudden glare after the fine darkness with Misty hurt his eyes. Bloody hell.

"I found flashlights," Dougál announced. The cubs, still wolves, sat on their haunches, looking interested to know why Graham had his hands up Misty's shirt.

"Good." Graham casually removed his touch from Misty's breasts, as though not worried Dougal and the cubs had caught him groping her. Misty didn't look worried, but amused Graham was embarrassed. "Give one to Misty. And don't shine the lights in my face—I don't need to be night-blinded."

"Thank you," Misty said graciously to Dougal as she took the lantern flashlight. The large, square glare lit up the corner of the basement. Dougal smiled back at her. He was going to hero-worship her, it looked like.

Graham glared down at Matt and Kyle. "All right, you little shits, where were you exploring?"

Graham kept hold of Misty's hand as they walked deeper into the basement. His grip was strong; she wasn't getting away.

His touch had been gentleness itself when they'd kissed, as though he'd been holding back his power to be tender with her. Misty loved that about Graham—his ability to soften himself when he needed to, to take care of the cubs, to help Dougal, to caress Misty. Everything he did made Misty fall for him a little more.

The cubs wanted to rush into the darkness, and only Graham's commands kept them close. Misty shone her light in front of her feet so she wouldn't trip, but she knew the cubs could see well without it. Shifters had good night vision and only needed the faintest glow.

The basement was enormous. It was more of a dugout, with rock and desert earth still above them rather than joists to support the next floor. As they walked forward, the bright daylight behind them quickly receded.

"Why is it so big?" Misty asked. "The house itself won't be this long. Or wide."

"She shouldn't be down here," Dougal said, a growl in his voice.

"No kidding," Graham said. "Remember me yelling at you for bringing her? Misty, you have to promise to keep quiet about what you see here. That we've put in basements at all. All right? It's very important. Could be deadly if you don't keep it secret."

One of the wolves—Kyle, she thought—came back and shifted into a boy. Yep, Kyle. "Will you punish Aunt Misty if she tells?" he asked, his eyes round. "You might hurt her. She's not as strong as Shifters."

"If I think Misty might tell," Graham said, "I'll tie her up, chain her to my bedpost, and . . ." Graham glanced at Misty, his eyes in the flashlight's glare holding wickedness. "Tickle her," he finished.

Kyle thought this over, perfectly serious. "That should be okay." He shifted back into wolf and ran after his brother.

"Tickle?" Misty asked.

"He means sex," Dougal said. Shifter hearing—she couldn't best it. "He wants sex with you in a big way. He's broadcasting it like crazy."

"Shut it, Dougal," Graham said with a growl.

Dougal went quiet, but Misty felt no contrition from him. Good for Dougal, having fun laughing at his uncle.

"Matt, Kyle," Graham called. "Wait."

The cubs came to an immediate halt. The fact that they

obeyed instantly, without question, told Misty how serious the situation was.

Graham turned in a circle, sniffing the air. "You sure this was where you were?"

One of the cubs shifted—Matt this time. "We came in here. We were exploring. Then we got dizzy. Then we were in the car."

"Mmm." Graham's acknowledgment was more of a grunt.

"Did you hear anyone behind you?" Misty asked. She imagined the hiker—the Fae—creeping up behind the cubs in the dark, tranquilizing them somehow. Had he used a tranq gun like the one Graham kept to stop Shifters who got too out of control? Or chloroform on a cloth?

"No," Matt said. "There was no one down here but us."

"If you're thinking of the Fae," Graham said to Misty. "They'd have smelled him. Fae really stink."

"Does Reid stink?" Misty asked. "I like him."

"He does, but we're used to him. And Reid's not the same as the High Fae, much as I yank his chain about it. In fact, we could use him here. Dougal."

Dougal turned around, his laughter gone, the defiant nephew returning. "Oh, come on, why do *I* always have to run the errands? Find flashlights, fetch Reid. Like I'm your bloody servant."

"Winning one dominance fight doesn't make you pack leader," Graham said, voice going harsh. "You do these things for me because that's what a good second does."

Dougal stopped, blinking gray eyes in the lantern light. "Second? I thought Chisholm was your second."

"I hadn't decided. But I want to keep it in the family, don't I? You're my tracker too, which means you do things to support me."

The look on Dougal's face was stunned, turning radiant by the time Graham finished. "Yes!" His shout rang around the large basement. "I'll get him. I mean, I'm on it. Be right back." Dougal bounded toward the light part of the basement. He whooped and punched the air, then scrambled up the ladder to the ground with amazing agility.

"That was nice of you," Misty said.

"Huh. It wasn't nice. I'm making him my pack and clan second, because I'm seeing that he's the only one I can trust." Graham watched until Dougal disappeared into the daylight, then he turned back to the darkness. "I'm going to need to go wolf now. Will you be all right if I do?"

CHAPTER SEVENTEEN

Graham was asking her. Showing concern. Not, *I'm doing this; too bad if you don't like it.* This was new.

"I'll be fine," Misty said, warming.

"Good. You can carry my clothes."

Figures. "Shouldn't you wait for Dougal and Reid?" Misty asked as Graham pulled off his shirt. His hard chest came into view in her flashlight's glare, wiry hair curling across it.

"I want to know what we're getting into. This basement goes back another fifty feet or so. Dougal will find us."

Graham yanked open the ties on his boots and pulled them off and his socks. Then, without shame, he unbuttoned and unzipped his pants and took them off, the loose gray boxers underneath following.

Graham wore his nakedness with the same comfort others wore their workout clothes. He stood easily with his feet in the gravelly dirt as he balled up his pants and shirt and thrust them at Misty.

Misty immediately shook them out and folded them neatly, pretending to ignore Graham rolling his eyes. She tucked the clothes under her arm but left the boots and socks, because Graham seemed fine on his bare feet.

In the light of her bright flashlight, Graham started his change. Fur rippled along his back and down his legs, his thighs bending to become the haunches of an upright wolf. His hands became giant paws very quickly, fur running up his arms, across his chest, and up his throat.

Finally, his face changed to the long nose and glittering gray eyes of a wolf. His ears pricked out last, popping up from his head so quickly that Misty let out a laugh.

Graham growled and charged her. Misty squealed and tried to sidestep, but Graham barreled into her. At the last minute, he pulled back the attack, ending up brushing her legs, his fur wonderfully warm.

Misty stroked him, loving the wiry heat of his fur, the strength of his wolf's body beneath it. Graham made a noise of what sounded like satisfaction, flowed around her again, and away.

The wolf cubs ran for Graham, yipping in gladness. They jumped at Graham's nose and rammed small heads into his front legs, until Graham lowered his head and bumped each in turn with his muzzle.

Family, acknowledging family, Misty realized. That was the most important thing, when it came down to it. Family taking care of each other, as Misty had taken care of Paul and her father, as Graham took care of Dougal and the cubs.

Graham growled at Matt and Kyle, and they seemed to understand him. They scooted underneath his belly, Graham so large that they had plenty of room. Graham started forward, the cubs giving a series of yelps. Guiding him in the right direction, Misty thought.

She came behind, careful not to shine the light in front of Graham. Once they'd gone a few more yards, the darkness was complete. Misty couldn't even see the square of light from outside behind her.

Graham stopped, and Misty nearly ran into him. He started again as soon as she drew near his big back, and he rumbled at her. She interpreted that he wanted her to stay close.

Another few steps, and she began to feel dizzy. The cubs whimpered. Graham stopped, and this time, Misty did run into him.

Misty put her hand on Graham's strong back, taking comfort in him. The cubs were whining louder, scared.

The flashlight's light snapped off. Misty shook the flashlight, but it was dead. Darkness fell upon her like a shroud. Her first instinct was panic, but she had Graham's warm body under her hands. She was safe. Graham could see in the dark, and he'd protect her.

Graham abruptly whipped around and snarled at her. Somewhere a glint of light shone on his eyes, or maybe his eyes glowed of their own accord. She saw his white teeth, all of them, bared. The sight was terrifying—eyes and teeth, snarls of a mad wolf.

Graham's wolf face shifted into a monster form, even more terrifying. He was snarling even as he changed. "Go back!" he yelled at her. "Run!"

Now was not the time to ask why or tell him again he wasn't the boss of her. Graham knew something she didn't, down here in the darkness, and Misty was ready to take his advice. She turned in the direction of where she thought the basement opening should be, and fled.

After three steps, she slipped, the floor having become slick for some reason, and went down, rocks cutting her knees beneath her skirt. It hurt, but wasn't incapacitating.

She scrambled up, heart beating wildly. Graham snarled again, a wolf once more, and Misty kept running.

This time, she made it five steps before another wave of dizziness hit her. She had no idea whether she fell to her knees or flat on her face, because there was just . . . nothing.

Except Graham's insistent voice, his hand on her abdomen. "Misty. Misty, damn it. Wake up."

Misty opened her eyes. The first thing she saw was Graham, his scarred face and broken nose over her, his gray eyes fixed on her.

"Thank the Goddess," he said in relief. "I thought—"
Graham clamped his mouth shut. His eyes, though, completed the thought and showed pain.

It was light where they were—lighter, anyway. Misty heard water running, a cool, soothing sound, but not from a faucet. More outdoorsy. More like . . .

Misty sat up, taking in a sharp breath. The wolf cubs were huddled together next to Graham, silent and shaking. They sat on slick rock, in a dim, cool cave, which was enormous. Vines snaked around them, out of reach, bearing small scarlet, purple, and light blue flowers. Misty swallowed. "Trailing petunias."

"What?"

"The flowers." Misty pointed. "They're trailing petunias. Grow on vines instead of in clumps."

"Oh, good," Graham said. "I needed to know that."

The water trickled pleasantly, but the sound put a chill in Misty's heart. They were in the cave where Misty had first met the hiker. Graham was naked, sitting on the black ground, his arms around Misty. She'd lost hold of his clothes, which were nowhere in sight.

"How did we get here?" Misty asked, pushing her hair from her face. "What happened?"

"I haven't the faintest fucking idea. I got dizzy, went down, woke up here. The cubs were fine, but you wouldn't wake up."

Misty swallowed. She didn't have the needy thirst anymore, but the water called to her. *Lovely. Cool. Drink.*

She gave Graham a sharp look. "You all right?"

"I didn't drink it, don't worry."

Misty blew out a breath. "Good."

Graham moved his tongue over his lips, but they remained dry. Since the ordeal in the desert, Misty hadn't seen him drink anything except a few sips of coffee, and the water he'd licked so erotically from her. She hadn't seen him sleep either.

"We aren't dreaming, are we?"

Graham shook his head. "Don't think so. It feels real, smells too real. That's good."

"Good? Why good?"

He gave her a grim smile. "Because if Oison shows up, this time I'll kill him for real."

Misty put her hand on his, finding his skin fever hot. "We need to fix you. You'll die like this."

"Not if I kill the Fae first."

"But what if even that doesn't release you from the spell? I never got to tell you about Ben."

"Ben?" Graham asked sharply. "Who's Ben?"

Misty related what had happened the afternoon before, Paul bringing Ben to her office and what Ben had said.

Graham listened, eyes narrowing. "Like I said, who the hell is Ben?" he asked when she finished.

"I don't know, but if he has a legitimate way of curing you, I'm willing to listen to him."

Graham gave her a dark look. "You're too trusting. How do you know he wasn't Fae?"

Misty shrugged. "He didn't look Fae. Not like the hiker, anyway. Or like Reid."

"Yeah, well, half Fae can look very human and be just as deadly, rotten, jerk-ass bastards."

"Like I said, I don't know," Misty said, holding on to her patience. "I asked Cassidy to have Diego check him out, but I haven't heard back yet."

"And it's not like I have a cell phone on me now," Graham rumbled. "You didn't happen to bring one, did you?"

"I left it at your house," Misty said. "Anyway, they didn't work out here before."

"Before, we were in the desert north of Las Vegas. Are we there now?"

"Have you tried to find out?"

"Look around you," Graham said. "See a way out?"

When Misty had been in this cave before, she'd approached the fountain from the entrance between the rocks, then turned around and went back the way she'd come. But the cave was gigantic. She couldn't tell if she was in the same place she'd been before or not.

"How did we get in here?" she asked. "You can't expect me to believe Shifters dug a basement that leads fifty miles out of town."

"No." Graham tilted his head to gaze at the ceiling, which was lost in darkness. "I think it's on a ley line."

"A what line . . . ?"

"Ley line," Graham said. "Magical lines that radiate around the world, many with gateways to Faerie. The sucky thing is, Shiftertowns are sometimes built on ley lines. The Austin Shiftertown has one. My Shiftertown in Elko didn't, but Bowman's in North Carolina does. I didn't think the Vegas one did; but I know there's a ley line up by Hoover Dam. Probably the same one or a branch of it."

Misty listened in surprise. "Why would Shifters build on the ley lines if they're gates to Faerie? I thought you hated the Fae."

Graham moved his gaze to her, while he absently petted the cubs, who were still huddled against him. "We didn't build the Shiftertowns, did we? We were sent to them. Not our choice. Probably another Fae conspiracy—they've been trying from the beginning to make Shifters slaves to them. But I'm not letting Dougal or these little guys ever come under the Fae. Fae are cruel, evil shits, and we should eradicate them."

"I am pained to hear it."

Misty jumped. The tall Fae who'd been the hiker stood behind Graham, a long sword in his hands. He hadn't been there a moment ago, and he hadn't appeared with a bang or even a faint sparkle. One moment he'd not been there, and this moment, he was.

The cubs were on their feet. But instead of cringing against Graham, they were snapping and snarling at Oison.

Graham let out a sudden groan and clamped his hand to his side, right where he'd been shot. To Misty's horror, the wound began to flow with blood. Graham sat in silence after the first grunt of pain, but his face lost color as the blood poured out.

Misty was on her feet. "Stop it!"

"He was only cured of the wound because of me," Oison said calmly. "I can reverse the spell anytime I wish."

"Wasn't a cure," Graham said through his teeth. "A curse, more like it."

"I helped you, Shifter," Oison said. "I took away the pain. I stopped the bleeding and ensured you didn't take sick. That is not a curse. That is me helping the being I wish to see at my side. What I did is no different from you keeping your nephew safe from the wolves who torment him, or the cubs from predators. I look after my own."

"Don't even . . ." Graham rose to his feet, holding his side all the while. It pained him to stand, but he shook off Misty's hand and got himself upright. "Don't pretend you're my pack leader or anything like it. You know damn all about being a leader."

"And you know everything about it, which is why I want you."

Graham dragged in a breath. "Well, I don't want you, asshole."

Graham changed to his wolf so suddenly Misty blinked, and at the same time he leapt at Oison. Oison lifted his sword, and brought it down . . .

"No!" Misty screamed. She knocked into Graham. She couldn't impact much of his momentum, but she managed to change his path so the sword didn't reach him. The blade scraped across Misty's side as Oison swung it, biting deep before the Fae yanked it back.

She heard snarling, huge and ferocious from Graham, small and vicious from the cubs. Then pain. Nothing but pain.

It flooded her body, blotting out all sight, all sound, all other feeling. She must have fallen, but Misty didn't register it, only found herself facedown on shining black rock. She heard cries of agony she didn't realize she was making.

Kyle licked her nose, yipping in distress. Graham was roaring, his blood splashing down on her, or maybe that was her blood. The pain was complete, erasing past and future, any pleasure Misty had ever experienced. There was nothing but hurting, and she'd never feel anything but pain again.

The Fae shouted, and dimly Misty heard a clatter of his sword. Graham's snarling went on, and then his body landed next to hers, human once more, blood pouring out of him. He got to his hands and knees and put his strong hand on her head.

"Misty. Stay with me."

"I'm not going anywhere," Misty said. Or thought she said.

Kyle left off licking her face. He joined Matt, the two of them bracing themselves in front of Oison, who was still standing, minus his sword. Oison looked angry. He pointed at them, as he had in the dream.

"No," Misty whispered.

She had no clue what Oison's pointing finger could do—shoot fire? Cast another spell? Move back and forth while he admonished them? Misty wanted to claw her way to the cubs, to protect them, but she couldn't move.

Graham was moving instead. He was shifting as he dragged himself to the cubs, leaving a trail of blood smeared on the polished black floor. He leapt at Oison, his mouth wide, teeth bared. Oison spun out of his way nimbly, but Graham followed him with great agility, his claws going for Oison's throat.

Oison dropped, rolled across the ground, and came up with his sword in his hand. The blade hummed, runes on it glowing like fire.

He shouted a word, pointing the sword at Graham. Graham fell in midair, his body thumping to the rock floor with an awful sound. The cubs ran to him, positioning themselves on either side of him, howling furiously.

Oison kept shouting words Misty didn't understand. Graham was silent, but he rocked in pain. The intensity of the pain came to Misty as though threads connected her with Graham, squeezing her heart, making her ache for him.

She could stop this. She could kill Oison . . . somehow. If only she could get to her feet.

Matt darted out and sank his teeth into Oison's boot. The Fae snarled and brought his sword down toward Matt. Kyle howled.

Misty heard a popping sound, and a wiry hand closed over Oison's wrist. The chain mail shattered, and Oison dropped his sword again. Oison swung around, face dark with rage, to face a man as tall as he was but his opposite—dark-skinned to his pale, black-haired to his white. Only their eyes were the same, black voids into nothing.

Reid. The name whispered through Misty's mind.

Dougal, looking terrified, was right behind Reid. Dougal ran to Graham, but Graham gave a loud growl, and Dougal straightened up and hurried to Misty. "You okay, Misty? Can you get up?"

Misty could only look at him, her pain so strong even moving her eyes hurt. Dougal looked lost, not knowing what to do.

Reid, on the other hand, had shoved Oison away from the little group, and was grappling with him by the fountain. The cubs still yapped and growled, but they'd positioned themselves between the fight and Graham and Misty, as though determined to guard the fallen.

Reid raised a weapon—a tire iron, Misty's foggy brain registered. He brought it down on Oison, not hitting him, but pressing it onto Oison's bare skin.

Whatever was supposed to happen, Misty didn't know. Reid looked surprised when Oison turned and took the tire iron in both hands, tugging it away from Reid. Oison held it up, laughing, chanting words Misty didn't understand.

Reid took a step back, scowling. The two Fae looked so different and yet the same—one in medieval-looking chain mail and silver cloak, Reid in jeans, T-shirt, and sneakers.

Reid raised his hands, clenched them, and shouted in a guttural language. Oison's smile evaporated as the iron bar in his hands started to bend, then undulate, then came apart into dozens of tiny fragments.

These fragments slid out of Oison's hands, paused in midair, then dove at Oison like a swarm of ferocious bees.

The iron particles slammed into the Fae's face and neck, cutting into him anywhere the chain mail didn't cover.

Oison clawed at his face. Reid spun away from him and sprinted for Misty. He grabbed one cub by the scruff of the neck, fell on his knees beside Misty, and wrapped his other arm around her.

Misty screamed in pain, and then the cave went away. She was lying back in the basement, under the opening to the outside world, the warm Las Vegas sunshine touching her like a lover's caress.

CHAPTER EIGHTEEN

"You have to save her," Graham said. He was in excruciating pain himself and could barely get the words out, but he didn't care.

Misty lay on his bed, her eyelids fluttering as she moved into and out of consciousness. Reid stood on one side of her, Neal Ingram, the Guardian, on the other, and they both looked grim.

Reid, who possessed the very helpful skill of teleporting, had gotten them out of the cave. He'd taken Misty first with one cub then popped back moments later for Dougal and the second cub.

Reid had returned a final time for Graham just as Oison was struggling up and groping for his sword. Oison's face and neck had run with blood, the Fae looking as though he'd been stung by a thousand hornets. Graham had wished he didn't hurt so bad so he could laugh.

Reid had come in with a bang, grabbed Graham, and popped them both out again.

Graham knew they'd never have survived without Reid. Which sucked, because now he owed Reid a debt. A big one.

But Misty came first. "Can you fix her?" Graham asked Neal, who had some skill in healing. Graham didn't like the presence of Neal's sword, which leaned in the corner, glinting softly in the afternoon sunlight. The Guardian's sword turned dead or dying Shifters to dust, sending their souls to the Summerland. Neal wouldn't use it on Misty, she being human, but the reminder of loss was sharp.

"I don't know," Neal said. "This is a Fae wound, from a Fae sword. Healing her will be different from stitching her up and putting a bandage on her."

"But you'll fix her," Graham repeated in a hard voice.

"What about you?" Neal looked at the makeshift bandage wrapped around Graham's bare side, which was already stained with blood. "You need a healer."

"Misty first. She can't die."

She couldn't. Graham touched her white skin, his heart burning when her eyes flickered. She wasn't waking up, but not sleeping either.

Reid said, "A human hospital won't be able to help her."

"But you can, right?" Graham demanded. "You're Fae. You made iron slivers go into Oison. Can you counteract magic from a Fae sword?"

Graham knew he was babbling, but watching Misty lie in his bed, pale and sweating, made him sick. His fault. Oison had wanted Graham, and Misty had gotten caught in between.

Neal seemed to understand. His voice was gentle, without its usual Lupine growl. "The answer is, we don't know."

"Well, what the hell good are you, then?"

Reid and Neal glanced at each other, neither taking offense. Graham was terrified, and he knew Neal smelled that. Neal would also smell his weakness, plus the Fae curse that was killing him.

"The Guardian's mate in the Austin Shiftertown," Neal said. "She's a healer. I've already called her."

"She's half Fae, right?" Graham stopped and took a breath as more pain flashed through his side. "That's all we need, more effing Fae."

Neal didn't answer. There was no reason to. The woman would come, and Graham wouldn't stop her having a look at Misty. Graham knew things were bad when he would welcome a Fae-blood's help.

"Why don't you sit down until she comes?" Reid said. "You can't do anything for Misty standing over her, breathing on her."

"Shut it, Fae. She's my mate."

Neal blinked, turned his head, and pinned Graham with a Shifter stare. Guardians could get away with looking alphas in the eye, because Guardians were a whole other hierarchy of Shifters. They followed the dominance line of their packs and clans, but they had their own rules, and they got away with shit no other Shifter did.

Graham had no idea why he'd blurted out that Misty was his mate. Except that it was true. Misty was the mate of his heart. He knew it. His heart knew it. His brain just needed to catch up.

"You've mate-claimed her?" Neal asked.

"Yes. Right now. I claim her as mate, under the sun, the Father God, and in front of witnesses. That would be you and Reid."

Neal gave Graham the ghost of a smile. The man was taciturn—hell, dead silent most of the time. But right now he looked almost amused.

"The Goddess's blessing on you," Neal said. "Both of you. Your Lupines are going to be pissed off."

"They can bite me."

Another twitch of lips from Neal. "They probably will."

"You still need to lie down," Reid said, giving Graham a scowl. "You have a gunshot wound, freshly reopened. Dying of it won't help Misty."

"If I lie down, I'll sleep," Graham said. "If I sleep, I'll dream, and Oison will be there. Who the hell knows what he can do to me then?"

"Have you tried surrounding yourself with iron?" Reid asked.

"Our whole lives are surrounded by iron," Graham said.

"Or steel. Doesn't seem to help, does it? Besides, you smacked him with the tire iron, and he laughed at you. He shouldn't have been able to grab that bar, but he did. He was only hurt by it because you turned it into bullets. How did you do that, by the way?"

"I'm an ironmaster," Reid said. "At least, I was in Faerie. That cave is a little piece of Faerie, so I could work my magic there. I can make iron do whatever I want in Faerie. That's one reason the *hoch alfar* hate the *dokk alfar*."

"I bet there's more to it than that," Graham said. "What I don't get is how we got there. I wasn't asleep. And you teleported to it. I thought you had to see a place before you could teleport there. But you never said you'd been to the cave."

"I hadn't," Reid said. "I do have to see a place, yes— unless I'm moving along a ley line. Then I follow the ley line's pull. Several ley lines intersect in that basement, I discovered. I suggest you seal it up and build the house elsewhere."

Ideas came together in Graham's head. "When the cubs disappeared down there, they must have followed a ley line that came out . . . at Misty's store?"

"I haven't had time yet, but I'll go down and see where they all lead," Reid said. "One goes to the cave in the desert—which can be there or not, as Oison chooses, it seems. He must be working some powerful spells, including ones to help him resist iron."

"Great. Iron is the badass magical weapon against Fae," Graham said. "Without that, what have we got?"

"Spells that help resist iron are temporary," Reid said. "And Fae can't resist iron when it's embedded in their brains."

Neal gave a short laugh. The man was opening up in a big way today. "Wish I could have seen that."

"I don't know if I killed him," Reid said. "Since Misty and Graham are still hurt, I'd say I didn't."

"Too bad," Neal said.

"Tell me about it." Graham dragged in a breath that sent

agony through him. "You can leave. I'll stay with Misty until the healer gets here."

Reid and Neal exchanged a glance. "You sure?" Neal asked.

"You want me to rest. I'll rest with her. But I won't sleep."

Another glance. Goddess, they were like nannies. Finally Neal took up his sword and buckled it onto his back. Reid gave Graham a last look, and the two men left the room together.

"Thought we'd never be alone." Graham sat on his big bed, swinging his legs onto the mattress and adjusting himself to lean against the headboard. He wore only jeans, his feet bare, the bandage squeezing his side in an annoying way.

Misty didn't respond. Her hair was sweaty and damp, still in the ponytail. The first night Graham had met her, at Coolers, she'd worn her hair in a softer style, with wisps curling around her forehead. She'd regarded Graham with her dark brown eyes, unafraid, and asked him if he was a Shifter.

And look what he'd done to her.

Misty should have run from him that night and never come back. But she had come back. She'd met him the second time by chance on top of a parking garage at the county courthouse, and then she'd sought Graham out in Shiftertown to tell him a bad man had asked her to spy on Shifters. That night, Graham had kissed her for the first time.

He'd never been able to forget the taste of her. Graham had drunk her last night as well, finding an even sweeter taste between her legs.

If she died, Graham would force his way into Faerie, hunt down Oison, and chop him into a million tiny pieces.

Misty's wound wasn't very deep, so Neal had said when he'd cleaned her up and bandaged her. But with Fae wounds, it didn't matter how deep they were. A scratch could be deadly.

"Stay with me, love." Graham took her hot hand in his and caressed her limp fingers. "I can't let you go."

Graham had lost everyone in his life. His father and

mother, his sister—Dougal's mother—all dead in the wild. Graham and Dougal were the only ones left of the pack. And Rita had died, Graham's one cub with her.

Alone, always alone. Graham had found more Shifters in his clan, then they'd been rounded up into Shiftertowns, practically living on top of one another, but it made no difference. A wolf without a pack was nothing.

But a wolf could start a pack. He needed a mate, and cubs. When Dougal mated as well, there would be many little ones running around.

The idea of being alone forever terrified the hell out of Graham. He'd never told anyone that.

"Stay with me, Misty."

He leaned down and kissed her hair, squeezing her hand. Misty never opened her eyes, never acknowledged him. She was here next to him, but Graham was still alone.

No, not quite. Kyle and Matt pushed the door open, concern in their wolf-pup eyes. They preferred staying wolf these days, Graham noted, unless they wanted to chatter to Misty.

Now they put their paws on the bed, looking up at Graham's high mattress. Graham lifted them both. After wagging tails and pushing noses into his palm, the two cubs lay down at Misty's feet, one on either corner of the bed.

Guarding her, Graham thought. Guards who closed their eyes almost immediately, and started to snore.

Misty swam toward consciousness, but that way lay pain. She thought she heard her brother's voice . . . *Paul, I need to take care of him.*

She was twelve again, and sick in bed with the flu, fever making her delirious. Her father was off pursuing one of his wild schemes, her mother was in Newport Beach in her new house with her new life. Only Misty was there to take care of Paul. *I have to get up. I have to look after him.*

But Graham was there too. She heard him rumbling something and relaxed. If anyone could take care of Paul, it was Graham.

She heard other voices, ones she didn't know. A woman with low, almost velvety tones, a man with an Irish accent. What were they all doing here?

Present reality caught up to her. She'd been stabbed, with a wound that seared, and Graham had been hurt. Where was she? Was Graham all right? Were the cubs?

She started up to find a heavy hand pressing her back down. "Stay still," Graham said.

Misty subsided. Graham sounded as strong as ever, though she heard the weakness in his voice. Faint, but there.

The pain returned. Pain had seeped through the darkness of her dreams, but it had been muffled, like sounds through a thick blanket. Now it raced over her, spreading through her body from one hot core.

"The cut isn't too deep," the woman's voice said. "But deep enough. I can try."

"What is *that*?" Graham's voice held great suspicion.

"Something my father gave me. He thinks it will help."

"Your Fae father."

The Irishman spoke. "You knew that when you called us."

Graham growled something wordless. "You're a Guardian," he said. "Why do you have to be in here? You make me nervous."

"The sword helps," the woman answered in soothing tones. "Sean and I do this together. If you want her to get better, you have to stand over there and be quiet."

Misty wanted to laugh, but it hurt too much. Graham hated being told what to do, especially by a female.

The Irishman, who must be Sean, gave a low chuckle. "I'll let no harm come to her. Andrea knows what she's doing. Now I'm going to draw the sword, but I promise, I'm not stabbing anyone with it."

A faint *ting* as metal touched metal. Then a touch on Misty's side. She cried out, cringing away, as pain intensified.

"What are you doing?" Graham said immediately.

"Calm down." Andrea's voice again. "I can see the

spells. They're complex, a mesh. It will take a bit for me to untangle them."

"Just do it," Graham rumbled.

"She will," the Irishman said. "Stop interrupting."

Graham made another noise of impatience, but he subsided. He must be truly worried if he actually shut up.

Misty felt the cold of animal noses touching her arm. Little noses. Two of them. She wanted to smile, but couldn't move.

And then more pain. Misty started to scream. She heard the sounds come out of her throat, hoarse and cracked. Another touch, this one Graham's big, rough-skinned hand holding hers.

"Easy," Graham said, so gently Misty was surprised it was he who spoke. "Easy, now."

Misty tried to lie still, but the pain pulled her. She writhed, only to find Graham's warm strength holding her down.

"Poor lady," Sean said.

Andrea drew a breath. "Ready."

"Aye, love."

Did that mean they hadn't *started*? Dear God, how much more could Misty take?

She forced her eyes open a crack. Sitting beside her bed was a dark-haired woman with gray eyes and a lovely face. She had one hand on Misty's side, the other wrapped around the blade of a sword that looked much like Oison's. Misty saw the runes on the silver metal, which began to glow.

The sword's hilt was held by a man with black hair and very blue eyes. He had his arm around Andrea, his free hand resting over hers on Misty.

Andrea closed her eyes and tilted her head back, drawing in another breath. Sean kept his hand steady on Andrea's.

Graham lay half on top of Misty, his short hair tickling her chin. His hard hands held her arms in place. The wolf cubs were beside Misty's head, peering worriedly into her face.

It's all right, Misty wanted to reassure them. But she wasn't certain it would be.

Another wave of pain, white-hot. She thought she was being sliced in half. The screams came again. Graham tightened his grip on her, and one of the cubs whimpered and licked her cheek.

Andrea's head went farther back, her eyes moving as though she watched something behind her lids. "Now, Sean," she whispered.

Sean removed his hand from Andrea's. He reached for something out of Misty's line of sight, then clamped what felt like a poultice to Misty's side, Andrea at the last minute moving her hand to rest it now on top of Sean's.

Misty thought she was dying. The agony reached a peak, beyond which there was no feeling. After a very long time, she heard Graham again, his voice harsh. "It's not working."

"Patience," Sean said, but Andrea drew a breath.

"He's right," she said.

I don't want to hear that, Misty thought frantically. *I want everyone surprised but happy I'm alive.*

"Move." Graham again, his weight rocking Misty. "Let me."

"No, you don't know—" Sean began, but Graham cut him off.

"Tell me what to do. What is this stuff?"

Andrea answered. "Fae . . . medicine."

"Yeah, don't reassure me. Why is it hurting her so much?"

"The Fae magic in her is fighting it," Andrea answered. "It's strong."

"I'm stronger." Graham's voice was rough, breathy. "Misty, love." He wrapped his hard fingers around hers. "Hold on to me. Tight as you can. And fight. Fight it for me, sweetheart."

Misty had no strength to fight. Nothing. She didn't want to die, but right now living was so, so tiring.

Graham's large hand went to her side, and he pressed a cloth filled with something over the sword cut. Misty half sat up, trying to scream again, but her voice had gone. Her vision was blurred, but she saw Andrea and Sean collapsed onto a couch pulled to the bed, holding each other. Matt and Kyle sat up next to Misty, anxious, two pairs of wolf cub eyes fixed on her.

Graham was merciless. His eyes were the light gray of his wolf's, determined, angry. He pressed her side, holding Misty down while she tried to wrench herself away from the pain.

"Hang on, baby," Graham said. "I know it hurts. You can kick my ass later. But *hang on*."

Misty clamped down on his hand, clinging to it as though it was a lifeline. Graham forced whatever it was into her wound, the pain searing, something hot rushing to her heart. She couldn't hold it in—her heart would burst, and Misty would die.

Through the pain, a small dart of warmth touched her chest. The tiniest piece, and yet it was something outside the pain, something to focus on.

She heard Graham draw a sharp breath, saw his gaze go to the middle of her chest, as though he knew what she felt. He looked down at his own chest, and his look turned startled.

Misty had no idea why. Was he feeling what she felt? Was that possible? But strange things had been happening all day. Night. Whatever time it was.

The piece of warmth suddenly flooded her chest, spreading, widening, burning through her to engulf the pain from the wound. Her body seared hot, hotter . . . hotter than she could stand.

And then everything stopped. Misty dragged in a long breath that seemed to come from the ends of the atmosphere, and she realized she hadn't been breathing for the last . . . however long it had been.

As soon as Misty exhaled and blinked, the cubs went into paroxysms of joy, dancing in circles, yipping, tails moving rapidly.

Misty found herself drenched but realized it was with sweat. The sheet was soaked with it, and so was the big T-shirt she was wearing. Not hers.

The runes on Sean's sword, still in his hand, flashed out

once, then went dark. Andrea was up, her hand on Misty's forehead, her face relaxing. "It's gone," Andrea said. "I don't see the spell anymore."

Graham unfolded himself like a huge bear coming to life, his eyes silver white and wild. He wrapped his arms around Misty, picking her up away from Andrea, gathered her against him, and buried his face in her neck.

Misty held his shaking body, both of them rocking a little. "It's all right," Misty said softly, stroking him. "I'm here."

Graham lifted his head. The relief in his eyes went a long way down, along with pain and stark terror. He drew a breath.

"What the hell were you thinking?" he roared in his loudest voice. "Going for the sword like that?"

Misty closed her eyes, sinking into exhaustion. "Love you too, Graham," she murmured, and hugged him.

CHAPTER NINETEEN

The next morning, Sean made everyone pancakes, which he'd assured Graham were famous. Graham never thought he'd see the day he'd let a Feline into his kitchen to cook for him, but times were strange.

But nothing mattered anymore. Misty was alive. That was all he needed. Graham's heart lightened when she came into the kitchen, looking tired but rested. Bandages bulked up her side under her tank top, but other than that, she moved with a sure step.

The cubs, in little boy form again, were happy to see her too—that is, when they could lift their faces from their plates of pancakes.

Andrea had been explaining that while Misty was healed once again, and she'd closed up Graham's wound, he was still under Oison's thrall.

"But you took the magic out of me, right?" Misty said, sliding into the empty place at the table. "Can't you take it out of him?"

Andrea shook her head as she wrapped her hands around her cup of coffee. Andrea was a Lupine, a gray-eyed wolf who had agreed to mate with Sean, a Feline, in exchange for a safe move to a new Shiftertown. Somewhere along the way, the two had found the mate bond.

"The magic dust my father gave me counteracted whatever Fae magic touched you from the sword," Andrea said to Misty. "Graham's a different case. He's under a complete Fae spell that seeks to control every aspect of him. I knit up his wound, but I couldn't break the spell. I don't have that kind of power, and my father doesn't either. The magic that entered you, Misty, was incidental. The Fae is not after you."

"Just Graham," Misty said. She looked across the table at Graham, unhappy.

"Not just me." Graham rejoiced that Misty was here to look at him at all, even with sadness and worry. Her brown eyes were free of pain, her face pink with health. "All Shifters."

Sean said from the stove, "Liam told me about the connection between Oison's sword and your Collar. I agree, we need to get the Collars off if the Fae have a big 'enslave the Shifters' plan. But, unfortunately, it's going slowly. The element we need to remove the Collars safely is rare. That's why the research."

"Yeah, I know," Graham growled. "Why do anything when you can think about it for years, have meetings about it, *talk* about it?" He pinned Misty with a stare. "Too much damned talking."

"Get over it," Sean said. "Here you go, Misty."

Sean flipped a stack of wonderful-smelling pancakes onto a plate and carried it the few steps to the table.

Sean and Andrea's cub, Kenny, ten months old, sat at the table in a high chair borrowed from the Lupines next door. The cub, who would maintain his human form until about age three or four, had dark hair like Sean, and gray eyes like Andrea.

Matt and Kyle eyed Kenny speculatively. They didn't like the little Shifter in their territory, even though Graham had explained the concept of *guests* to them. Kenny watched them, unworried, nonchalant, even. An alpha in the making.

Misty's eyes lit when she saw the pancakes Sean set before her. She poured a stream of syrup over them and then dug in.

Graham would love it if Misty would look at *him* in the same eager way she regarded the pancakes. And then reach for syrup and pour it all over Graham's body.

He tightened. His cock started rising, and Graham cleared his throat, moving in his seat, willing the thing to go down. Not that it mattered; Sean and Andrea would scent the change in his hormones right away. They already did, from the smirk Sean sent Andrea.

Misty didn't notice, intent on her pancakes, stopping to dribble more syrup onto the stack. A sticky droplet clung to her lips, and it took all Graham's self-control to keep from going over the table and licking it from her. Graham felt better since Andrea had patched him up—except for the continuing thirst—and his relentless need for Misty had returned, full force. Plus he'd mate-claimed Misty last night, which fanned the spark of his mating frenzy into a raging blaze.

"Want any more, Graham?" Sean asked, returning to the stove.

"No. Thanks." Graham had conceded to eat a little, knowing he had to keep up his strength, but filling his stomach had seemed to make made the magical thirst worse. "Can you go now? I need to talk to Misty alone."

Misty licked syrup from her fork. "Don't be rude. They've traveled a long way, and they helped us."

"And I'm grateful. Now I need to talk to you."

Misty gave him the eye-rolling look, which warmed Graham's heart, because she was alive to do it.

Sean clattered his cooking accoutrements into the sink. "Eric and Liam will want you with us when we question the Fae."

Liam had found the Fae-blood human he'd promised to round up at the Shifter meeting, Sean had told him last night. Eric and Liam had stashed him in Eric's hideaway out in the desert, ready for interrogation.

"I'll come out later," Graham said.

"And Graham really needs to talk to Misty alone," Andrea said. She rose and lifted her son out of the chair. "We'll take the cubs out too."

"We will, will we?" Sean asked. But he didn't look annoyed, he looked amused. "If you say so, love." He dried his hands and came to bend over the cubs. "Want to go walkies?"

Matt and Kyle growled, Lupine for *Who is this fool?*

Andrea laughed. "Come with me, little loves. We'll go play. Don't worry about Sean. Though I know he smells like a cat."

Matt and Kyle started eagerly out after Andrea, bumping into each other as they went. Sean shook his head, took up the high chair, and followed. "You want to watch yourself with this mate thing," Sean said to Graham as he went. "The females, they take over." He glanced from Graham to Misty, grinned, and strolled out of the house.

Graham left the table and locked the back door. He went out and locked the front door as well. Dougal had gone out early and had his key, but Graham didn't need his guests deciding to charge back in while Graham was having a heart-to-heart with Misty.

When he returned to the kitchen, Misty was washing the dishes again.

Graham paused, remembering what had happened when he'd come up behind her doing dishes the last time. He pictured how he'd wet her with the spray then licked her skin, how he'd drunk her, how she'd made him feel incandescent joy.

He was rock hard again—not that he was ever very flaccid around her.

"Leave it," he said.

Graham knew she wouldn't stop, and Misty didn't. "It's not a lot," she said. "Sean's much neater than you are."

"He must be a joy to live with," Graham said. "Neat and clean, Irish accent, bloody Feline grin."

"He is pretty good-looking," Misty said without turning around. "I can understand why Andrea is madly in love with him."

"He's *Feline*. She's Lupine. It's wrong. Of course, she's got Fae blood in her, which probably messed with her head."

Misty stacked the clean plates in the drying rack and started scrubbing down the griddle. "I know you're thankful they came and helped. You're just being a shit. You can't *not* be one."

"It's traditional with me."

Graham leaned on the counter next to her. If he came up behind her, he'd bend her over, lift her skirt, and do her right there. To hell with dignity.

Misty cleaned, rinsed, and dried the griddle and rested the heavy thing back on the stove. It was the kind that stretched across burners, using the stove beneath to heat it. She washed her hands, dried them on the towel, then hung the towel neatly on the towel ring that had come with the house.

"What did you want to say, Graham?" Misty asked. "If you're going to meet with Eric, I need to get back to my store. I have a ton of things to do." She let out her breath. "I hate to leave you alone, but Eric can take care of you. Sean looks pretty capable too. I'm going to try to find Ben, and ask him again about curing you. I should have Reid talk to him with me—"

"Misty, would you *stop*?" Graham thrust his hand over Misty's mouth. She looked up at him over his large fingers, indignant. "First, your brother went to your store with Xavier, plus I sent Shifters to help out. You don't need to worry about it. Second, you're not talking to that Ben person without me there—who the hell knows who he is? Third, I need you here."

And now Misty was getting mad again. She moved her head so she could speak. "No, you need to go with Eric. If we both work on this problem today, we can pool our information later."

But that would mean Misty not being here when Graham got back. "You have to stay," he said. "I mate-claimed you."

Misty's eyes widened. "You what?"

"Mate-claimed. It means—"

"I know what it means. I've hung around Shifters long enough." Misty spun away from him, her skirt swishing. "It means you're saying you want me to be your mate and do the ceremonies. And have me live with you and have your kids—cubs." Misty ran out of breath and stopped. "Are you insane? I know everyone expects you to mate with a wolf Shifter. One of your wolves even tried to attack me, remember?"

"And she'll be disciplined. Things are different now."

"What things? No, they're not."

Graham looked into Misty's stubborn eyes and knew the truth. Everything *was* different. His life had changed the moment Misty had turned to him on the barstool at Coolers and asked, *You a Shifter?*

"I've been lying to myself," Graham said. "I thought I could keep it cool with you, go out with you for the fun of it, to enjoy being with you. Then say good-bye when I chose a mate. But I can't. Letting you go is something I can't do. All right?"

When Graham had mate-claimed Rita, she'd nearly passed out in shock that the son of a clan leader had chosen *her*, then she'd recovered and thanked him for the great honor.

Misty only stared at him and didn't look honored at all. "You can't change your mind like that." Her voice was shaky. "I know your Shifters won't shrug it off and say, *Oh well, our great leader knows best.* They'll fight you."

"I'm prepared for that."

"I'm so glad. What about me?" Misty pressed her hands to her chest. "I'll have to fight too. That Shifter woman—Jan—who tried to attack me, was very angry. And her Collar didn't go off, so that won't slow her down, will it? And what about the other women who hope they can be with someone so high in Shiftertown? I've learned a lot about Shifters since I started dating you. You're a good catch, apparently, and they're not going to step aside so I can have you."

Graham gave her a growl. "What you don't understand is that I'm alpha. They do what I say."

"And what *you* don't understand is how someone *not* alpha thinks. Sure, they'll obey you—until they can figure out a way to get rid of me, permanently. Or replace you with someone who will do what they want."

"And *you* don't understand how leaders get chosen. I have to die before another one takes my place."

"Exactly my point."

Graham started to say that would never happen, but he stopped. Of course, it could happen. Challenges for leadership had occurred a lot in the wild—not to Graham, but to others. It happened less often now, but Collars were gradually coming off and some Shifters were hoping for changes. Liam Morrissey had fought his own father and won, thus replacing him as leader. Dylan Morrissey was a hard man with a lot of experience, so Liam besting him said something.

Graham didn't think any of the Lupines here could win against him, but now Graham had been spelled by a Fae.

"They're not going to kill me," Graham said, trying to keep his voice steady. "Eric won't let them."

Then again, when Graham had arrived here last year, he'd been a total shit to Eric. But Graham had been fighting to keep his position, fearing Eric would force him out. Graham couldn't stand the thought of having to be a kiss-ass, so he'd been a dickhead instead. Had Eric forgiven Graham enough to help him stand against his angry Shifters? Graham wasn't sure.

"And anyway," Misty said. "We should figure out this Fae problem first."

"No, I want to do this mating now, before the Fae problem kills me." Graham started to reach for Misty then forced himself not to touch her. "I want you mated to me, to know we're bound. Don't you think that will make me stronger?"

"No, I think it will be more distracting. Having to learn to integrate our lives, plus trying to get your Shifters to go along with it, will take a lot of work. Throw in trying to find a cure for this spell—that's lot to put on your plate."

"Damn it!" Graham's roar burst out. "What *distracts* me is seeing you around, with your gorgeous legs, and your lips I want to suck on, and your scent driving me wild. The touch of a mate heals—did you know that? It's why you're up and walking around today. Andrea's cure wasn't working until I took it away from her and dosed you myself. I need you. Even if we get rid of this Fae, not being with you is killing me."

He faced her, his hands clenched. Misty's lips were parted, red and kissable.

"Graham, I want to be with you too," she said in a rush. "But I don't want to make things hard for you."

"Well, too late. I'm already hard for *you*." Graham grabbed her hand and pressed it against the front of his jeans. "This is what you do to me, every time I look at you."

"That's just lust." Misty didn't move her hand, which warmed his blood. "Wanting. I want you too." She smiled a little, and Graham's frenzy skyrocketed.

Graham gripped her shoulders. "I need you. It's killing me. Don't refuse the claim. Please, don't leave me alone. Again. *Please.*"

CHAPTER TWENTY

The *please* shot into Misty's heart.

Graham was glaring at her, looking more angry than filled with love. His fingers bit into her shoulders, his grip desperate.

Don't leave me alone. This from a man who found it hard to admit he needed anything. Or anyone.

Misty lifted her hand away from his jeans, where his long and formidable cock waited. She remembered the feel of it against her tongue, the warm taste of it. She touched his arm, resting it on one of the flame tattoos.

"Graham," she whispered.

"Don't walk away from me, Misty. I'm going to die."

"I won't let you," Misty said.

Graham let out a sound like a groan. His grip grew harder still as he yanked her to him and brought his mouth down on hers.

The kisses he'd given her before had been powerful, but Misty now realized he'd been holding back a little to keep from hurting her. He'd played games with her, stopping himself from doing what he'd meant to.

Not this time. The holding back had gone. Graham had Misty against the wall in the space of two seconds. He held her solidly, his mouth on hers, while he pushed up her skirt and yanked down her underwear.

The cool of the room's air touched her bare skin, except where Graham covered her, his body hot. More than hot. His skin was feverishly warm, dangerously so.

The rough of his jeans brushed her thighs, while one of his hands held her shoulder, the other, her waist, lifting her from the wall and against him. All the while Graham kissed her, his mouth opening hers without respite.

Misty ran her hands along his bare shoulders, his muscles hard under his sleek skin. Down his arms, over the firm round of his biceps, to the smoother skin of the tatts. To his back, to feel the flat of his lower back and the waistband of his jeans. Dipping inside to the warm flesh of his buttocks.

Graham broke the kiss. "Run now if you want," he said, voice harsh. "I won't be able to stop if you don't go. Not today."

Misty debated a half second. But she couldn't fool herself. She wanted Graham, wanted this, wanted him forever. She shook her head. "I'm staying."

Graham said nothing. No triumph, no smile of conquest. The only thing in his eyes was need.

Graham tugged at the button of his jeans then his zipper. The jeans flowed off, over his bare buttocks to the floor. He stepped out and kicked them away, naked in his kitchen with sunshine pouring through the windows.

He was a beautiful man. Perfectly formed. Life had scarred his face and body, but the whole of him sang.

Graham had Misty up against the wall again. He hooked her leg over one arm, stretching her up, opening her wide. He lifted her with his other arm around her hips, looking down into her eyes as he slid the tip of his cock inside her.

Misty's eyes widened. Graham was large, his firm tip already pushing her open. She drew in a long breath, her body tightening. She wrapped her legs around his, her skirt draping them both, her bare feet on his thighs.

Graham lifted her higher, holding her steady, as he slid a little more inside. Misty's breath gave out. She tilted her head back, meeting the wall, opening her lungs for air.

Graham kissed her chin. "You are so beautiful."

Graham's whisper echoed what he'd said the night they'd drunk tequila and roses, looking for a way to end the Fae's spell. This morning, sober, he looked at Misty and said the same words.

Misty touched his face. Graham's eyes drifted closed as he slid the rest of the way inside her.

Fully inside her. Graham drove high, his large cock invading her. Her body gripped it, instinct overriding coherent thought.

He held her like that a moment, she against the wall, he straight up inside her.

Then Graham lifted her into his arms, holding her on him. He turned in a slow circle in the kitchen, looking into her eyes, the sunshine dancing on them. They were whole, together. One.

Misty felt him solidly inside her, pressing her in pleasure. She shuddered, her hips wanting to rock, but in the tight position, they could do nothing but be still and be joined. And that was no bad thing.

Graham kissed her. He said words between the kisses, but she didn't understand them. Soft little words of tenderness, or so she thought. Misty ran her hands through his short hair, smiling into his face. The warmth of the sun, the heat of Graham's body, the stiffness inside her, were the most wonderful things she'd ever felt. She'd longed to be this Shifter's lover since the first night he'd kissed her and changed her world forever.

Another turn around the middle of the floor, Graham's strong body holding them, then another and another. Dizzy joy, circling with the man Misty had been falling in love with, joined with him at last.

Graham slid his hands over her back, up under her tank top, pulling her to him for another kiss.

His last slow turn brought them to the table, bare now,

since Misty had cleaned up. Graham supported her back as he laid her down on the table, the length of it taking Misty's body.

Graham slid her hips to its edge, the two of them still connected. Misty glimpsed where his large cock disappeared high into her body, before Graham drew back, exposing the dark length of it. He was wet and slick from being inside her, still hard for her.

A moment, a glance, and then Graham slid back inside. He nestled there for half a second, then drew out, then in again. Then again, faster this time.

His thrusts increased, one after the other, beautiful friction. Misty propped herself on her elbows so she could watch Graham, his hands on her hips, drive into her. Wild feeling like music took away her thoughts.

She knew nothing but warm sunshine, Graham firm and thick inside her, pulsing hard joy into her. The scents of cinnamon and sugar, syrup and frying pancakes lingered in the room. The mouthwatering scent of food and the feeling of Graham twined together, one layering over the other.

Misty lifted her hips, her eyes half closing, while Graham continued thrusting into her. He was sweating, body glistening in the sunlight. The tatts moved on his arms, flames curling around muscle.

"You are so beautiful." Graham's words were hoarse. "Nothing else matters when I look at you."

Graham. Misty tried to say his name, but her tongue didn't work. She was gone on feeling, pleasure, glory. Her hips bumped the table, and she reached to twine her fingers around his wrists.

Back and forth, rocking, silent now but for the sounds of him going in and out, the creak of the table, the faraway laughter of cubs playing in the common yard behind Graham's house. There was so much life here, always movement, laughter, joy.

Joy. It wound up inside Misty and spilled out. A dark wave of feeling picked her up and washed her away, the room spinning around her as it had when Graham had turned with her.

Graham grunted. His hips moved faster and faster, his grip on her tight. He pumped into her in a frenzy, sweat dripping from him, his head back. He was a wild man, huge and strong. This was more raw than making love—this was pure, animal-like sex.

Graham's thrusts came even faster, Misty lost in the friction of it. She couldn't breathe, couldn't move. A scream came from her throat, echoing against Graham's shout.

Graham slammed into her one last time, groaning, his seed scalding inside her. His hips started moving again, the rhythm pounding, his hands sliding on her hips, slick with sweat.

He opened his eyes, his last shout of pleasure dying down into a groan. "Misty," he said. "Goddess, help me."

Graham lifted her again, gentler this time, and gathered her into his arms. Her legs went around his hips, he still inside her.

He turned with her in another circle, slower now, Graham kissing her with warm lips. He held her close, the fire gone from his eyes, a dark glow taking its place.

"Mate," Graham whispered. "Mine."

Misty touched his hair and kissed his lips, drifting on a cushion of happiness.

Graham carried Misty upstairs to his bedroom, where she'd lain in so much pain. Someone—probably Misty herself—had already stripped the bed, leaving the plain mattress ready for clean sheets.

Graham laid her down, stripped the rest of her clothes from her, parted her legs, and slid inside her again. He was not done sexing her. Not by a long way.

Misty lifted her body to meet his. She wasn't a shy virgin—she liked sex, and she wanted Graham. Graham felt no triumph over this. It was just . . . *right*.

Goddess, she was beautiful. He couldn't help saying it.

Her round breasts, tipped with dusky nipples, tightened as he loved her. Sweet plumpness he could sink his fingers into, her brown hair spread across his pillow. And her eyes, lovely liquid brown eyes, watching him without fear or shame. Eyes a man could drown in.

He pressed inside her, unable to slow his thrusts. He wanted her fast and hard, again and again. The mating frenzy. Sex until they couldn't walk, until she was heavy with his cub.

Something tightened inside Graham. He wanted her to bear his cubs. Craved it. If they had to stay in this bedroom and screw for days until then . . . Oh well.

Too soon, Graham came. Misty groaned with her own pleasure, she pouring heat over his cock.

The pain he'd had since he'd drunk the Fae water hadn't left him, but Misty around him let it recede. The mating frenzy broke through it, swelling Graham's cock again. More.

Misty laughed as Graham started thrusting again. She looked tired and spent, but he couldn't stop.

He lay down on her and rolled with her so Misty was on top of him. Graham liked things this way, where he could look up at her, her eyes heavy with pleasure, and cup his hands over her breasts while she rode him.

Face-to-face on their sides was good too, Misty's leg wrapped around his, Graham pumping into her. Again and again, Graham loved her, in every position he could think of. Misty laughed, pleaded that she needed to rest, and laughed again. Every time, she came with him, her body growing more and more pliant.

The sun was moving to the west when Misty dropped into sleep, not waking when Graham kissed her cheek. His mating frenzy was still high—he was a male Shifter in his prime who hadn't had sex in many months—but he had some compassion. He let her sleep, dressing himself and walking outside to the heat of the late afternoon.

"You done with sex?" Dougal asked, appearing from the green behind the house and falling into step with him. "Took you long enough."

"I'll never be done with it," Graham said. He walked along slowly, a bit chafed, but that would be gone by the time he went back into the house. Shifters healed quickly. "Mating frenzy won't let me be."

"Eric is looking for you. You need to go talk to the Collar-making Fae."

Graham shook his head. "I'm not leaving Misty alone. My wolves will know I mate-claimed her soon enough."

Dougal stepped in front of Graham, stopping Graham's long-legged pace. "You made the mate-claim? That's awesome. Did she accept?"

"No, she tried to refuse. But I think I've changed her mind."

"With sex?"

"No, I made her spaghetti," Graham said impatiently. "What do you think? Of course, with sex."

"So she's going to be your mate?" Dougal grinned, excited.

"You're okay with that?"

"I like Misty. She's nice. The total opposite of you."

Graham cuffed Dougal across the head, but gently. "I have to get my wolves to accept her. That won't be easy." When Graham had told them to try to decide which clan would dominate through one of their daughters, he'd temporarily eased the situation, knowing they'd argue among themselves. But when Graham presented them with his choice of Misty, they'd band together against him.

"I'll help," Dougal said. "I'm your second now. I've got your back. And if Eric approves, he'll have your back too. Everyone listens to Eric."

"So I've noticed."

If Misty refused Graham, on the other hand, end of problem. Something burned into his heart. If Misty refused, Graham would be lost. She completed him, made the other half of his world.

"Anyway, Eric is waiting," Dougal said. "Says he'll take you out to see the Collar maker. Liam's got him hidden."

"So no one will kill him." Graham stretched his fingers, cracking his knuckles. "Might be fun to put this guy in the rings at the fight club, to see how long he lasts. Against Shifters with working Collars, that is. Would be fun."

"Yeah." Dougal loved the fight club. He'd be the first one in line for a bout.

"But I'm not leaving Misty," Graham said. "You go in my place, tell them I'll come later."

Dougal looked behind Graham. "Looks like Misty's leaving you instead."

Graham pivoted. Misty was getting into the boxy car she'd borrowed to drive over here. She started it as soon as Graham turned, and pulled away from the house. She'd seen him, damn the woman, but she didn't stop. Misty even smiled and waved as she drove around the corner.

"Shit!" Graham headed for Dougal's Harley, waiting in the driveway next to Graham's still shot-up bike. His thirst kicked in as he lost sight of Misty's car, and so did the pain in his heart.

"Where are *you* going?"

Eric materialized next to the bike before Graham could kick the starter. Eric couldn't teleport, but the bloody Feline knew how to move softly.

"I'm going after Misty," Graham said. "Too dangerous to leave her alone."

"No, *I'm* going after her." Eric gave him a pointed look. "You go question the Collar maker. I'll take care of Misty."

Graham slammed his fists to his handlebars. "Screw you. Mates come first."

"Yep, you reek of the mate-claim," Eric said, nodding. "And sex. I'm thinking Misty didn't quite say yes, the way she hauled ass out of here. But I'll bring her back. You go take care of your curse."

"Eric, you are not my alpha."

"No. I'm your co-leader. I'm telling you this for your own good. Let me talk to Misty. I'm good at being persuasive. And I'll keep her safe. You know that."

Eric was a good fighter, strong and smart. And talky. Misty liked talking.

Graham sighed and started the bike. "Fine. I'll go.

Dougal, you make sure Matt and Kyle are being taken care of. And stay out of trouble."

"Aw, that's no fun," Dougal said. He lost his smile and walked away.

Graham watched him go, the bike throbbing impatiently under him. "Damned cub. How did you do it, Eric? Raise a cub to adulthood without killing him? Or him killing you?"

Eric shrugged, his lazy look in place. "Jace is a different person. And my son, not my nephew. He's . . . Jace."

"Yeah, well." Graham glided the bike forward and lifted his feet. He rode off without a good-bye, but when he checked his rearview, Eric had disappeared.

CHAPTER TWENTY-ONE

Misty took the turn out of Shiftertown onto the quiet street that led to it. Not many people were out this late in the hot afternoon. The people who lived in or commuted to Las Vegas rarely came to this back corner of it.

A large pickup pulled abruptly in front of her, blocking her way. Misty slammed on the brakes. At the same time, another truck pulled up beside her on the passenger side. A man got out, opened her car door, and slid inside. He closed the door, the truck ahead of her moved, and he pointed.

"Drive that way."

The man in her car was Eric Warden. Misty stared at him, making no move to obey. "What the hell are you doing?"

"Asking you to go that way." Eric pointed down a side street.

Misty gripped the wheel. "This is kidnapping."

"No it isn't," Eric said. "It's having a chat. Now will you start driving?"

The two trucks roared off. Misty caught only a glimpse of who was in them, but she thought she recognized the bear Shifter Shane driving one, his brother Brody the other.

Misty pushed the accelerator and moved the car down the street Eric had indicated. "All right. You've kidnapped me. For a chat. What do you want?"

"Accept Graham's mate-claim."

Misty slammed on the brakes again. Eric braced himself on the dashboard, then grabbed the seat belt. "If you're going to drive like that, I'll buckle up."

"Did Graham send you?" Misty demanded.

"Graham tried to stop me. I sent him off to take care of his Fae problem."

"Good." Misty started driving again, slowly. "Why do you want me to accept Graham's mate-claim? I think it would be a bad thing for Graham if I do."

"I don't know. You'll have to fight for acceptance, and he'll have to kick a few asses before everyone calms down. But I've watched Graham now for almost a year. Trust me, I keep a close eye on him. When Graham's around you, he's at ease with himself. He's a loud, arrogant, obnoxious shit—always has been, and will always be—but with you, he seems to find peace. A reason for living . . . besides his determination to be the biggest dickhead in the room."

"He's not a dickhead," Misty said hotly. "If he wasn't like he is, he'd have lost everybody in his life, more than he already has. He doesn't say that out loud, but I know it. Dougal would have been killed in the wild a long time ago—I understand that now—and the Shifters in his Shiftertown wouldn't have survived. Graham fought to keep them all alive."

"You're not telling me anything I don't know," Eric said. "He kept those Shifters together up in Elko, when all of them could have easily gone feral. One hell of a task. I commend him for it."

"And so you want me to cause more trouble by staying with him?"

Eric leaned back in the seat and rested his arm along the

window. "They'll come around. Shifters are all about what's for the good of the pack, or clan, or whatever community they're in. Might not seem like it most of the time, but they are. The only reason Shiftertowns work is that we've dedicated ourselves to making them work. We want survival, and we want our cubs to grow up safe and happy. We took the Collars, instead of letting ourselves get wiped out, for the sake of the cubs. Graham's Shifters will understand, in time, that Graham having you is the best thing that can happen for them. All the crap about hierarchy and Shifters breeding with Shifters for strength is bullshit."

"I see." Misty drove in silence for a time. She turned onto a main street, heading for her store. "You know, you've never once asked me what *I* wanted."

Eric made a lazy gesture with the hand along the window. "I don't have to. You want to mate with Graham."

Misty shot him a look. "Excuse me?"

"I've been watching you too." Eric leaned even farther back in the seat and rested one motorcycle-booted foot on the dashboard. "You're a sweet young woman, and when you're around Graham, you're happier, stronger. More self-assured. And I see the way you look at him. Trust me, no one else in Shiftertown looks at Graham as though they want him to stay exactly the way he is."

"Really? That's kind of sad."

"It means he needs you, and you need him. End of problem."

Misty turned down another street, navigating heavier traffic. "Was it that simple when you were going after Iona?" She sent him a sweet smile. "Graham told me you looked like you'd been hit with an anvil."

Eric didn't take offense. "True, I denied my need to be with Iona for a long time. I'd been grieving my mate for so many years I didn't know how to fall in love again. Iona taught me. Besides I had to save Iona from . . . other Shifters who considered her fair game."

Misty's smile widened. "Don't worry, I know Graham tried to Challenge you for her, so you don't have to spare my feelings. For a man who doesn't like to talk about personal things, Graham has told me a lot. I met him the night you two fought, and you lost."

"I didn't lose," Eric said indignantly. "I was incapacitated by something else. It was a draw."

"Graham tried to claim it was a draw too. But you both lost, didn't you?"

Eric sat up. "Hey, this is supposed to be your kidnapping. Me telling you what you should do."

"I'll think about it. Meanwhile, I need to return this car and make sure the rest of my life is all right. Including my brother."

"Paul's a good kid. He'll be fine."

"You have a lot of optimism, Eric."

"I've been around a while," Eric said. "It's experience, not optimism."

"Do you want me to drop you off somewhere?"

"No." Eric laced his hands behind his head. "I should check up on what the Shifters are doing at your store. Shane can drive me back."

"We're doing this, with or without my dad," Jace Warden said.

Jace, Eric's son, stood straight and tall, looking much like his absent father with his dark hair and green eyes, but more alert, more *present* than Eric ever let himself seem. Since Jace's mating—he'd recently taken a mate from the Austin Shiftertown—he'd stood even straighter, with more authority than ever.

Graham stood with Jace, facing the Shifters who were annoyed that Eric hadn't showed yet. Eric wasn't coming, Graham realized. He'd sent Jace to do this, letting his son take authority. Talking to Misty had been an excuse. Eric had made sure Graham was here to back up Jace if necessary. Cagey Feline.

The Shifters stood in an old airplane hanger forty miles from town, in remote desert, where a human called Marlo kept his planes. The former drug runner now made his money carrying Shifters where they wanted to go. Shifters couldn't travel outside a state without special permission, but as usual, Shifters had learned how to get around the rules. Marlo did a brisk business hauling Shifters back and forth. He was discreet, reliable, and knew how to avoid problems.

The Fae-blood human who'd been captured sat in a straight-backed chair at the end of the hanger. He'd been bound in chains of silver, spelled, Graham guessed. Sean Morrissey stood with him, the Sword of the Guardian on his back, his father, Dylan Morrissey, at Sean's side.

Couldn't be easy for the Fae-blood, facing a roomful of grim-faced Shifters who'd figured out he'd helped screw them in more ways than one. Couldn't be easy sitting in a room with Dylan either, one of the most formidable Shifters ever born. No one could predict what Dylan would do.

Bowman had come, as had Eoin from Montana. A couple of Shifters from Shiftertowns in Utah and New Mexico were also there, plus Liam and Sean—basically whoever had been able to get there on short notice.

"He won't tell us his real name," Liam said, starting without preamble. "Afraid this will give us unfair advantage."

A rumble of laughter came from everyone but Dylan and Bowman.

"In the human world," Dylan said, "he goes by Lorcan."

The Fae flinched slightly. For the most part, he maintained his arrogance, even though he was outnumbered by angry Shifters ready to kill him. Technically Lorcan was employed by the human government, and Lorcan must have believed the humans would rush to his rescue. But if Liam and Dylan had been true to form, the humans wouldn't even realize Lorcan had gone.

Lorcan's father, a half Fae, had come up with the concept of the Collars for Shifters, convincing humans twenty years ago, when the existence of Shifters was revealed, that these were the best way to keep the wild and dangerous Shifters under control. Collars used a combination of

technology and Fae magic to react to a Shifter's adrenal
system, giving them shocks when they became violent—in
the Collar's opinion.

Dylan's rumbling voice silenced the Shifters. "Graham
has recently discovered that the Fae in Faerie have created
swords that can work in conjunction with the Collars—the
swords set off the Collars at the will of the sword's wielder.
Is that correct?" Dylan bent to Lorcan, waiting for him to
answer.

Lorcan moved in his seat, but his eyes remained haughty.
"If a Fae told you that, that Fae is no longer one of us."

"Huh," Graham said. "He told *me*, because he thought
he had total control over me. Thought I'd surrender right
there and be his pet, then rush out and bring all my Shifter
friends back with me to him."

"You are *Shifter*," Lorcan said to him, his arrogance still
present. "You have always been a captive. I am not and
never will be."

"You are now, laddie." Liam picked up one of the spelled
chains binding Lorcan and shook it. "These don't bother
me, but they hold you pretty good. Why don't you tell us
what we want to know?"

"And then what? You kill me? If I am to die, then you
can live ignorant."

"We're not going to kill you," Dylan said. His tone was
quietly calm, deadly. Graham, who didn't intimidate easily, wanted to shiver. "You will go back to the Fae and tell
them that their experiment failed."

"Will I?" Lorcan asked, disdainful.

Lorcan, born of a human mother and a half-Fae father,
looked human, even more so than most half Fae. He was
slender, but his features were very human, his hair wheat
brown instead of the severe pale fair of most Fae. His hair
covered his ears, but Graham was pretty sure those ears
weren't pointy.

"You will," Dylan said.

"We know what you're up to, asshole," Graham said.
"You and your dad made the Collars, and I'm willing to bet

you made or helped make the Fae swords too. Now, what's the master plan? Or did you just want to make Shifters more miserable? Fae are still pissed off that Shifters won the war against them all those years ago and took their freedom. Get over it, already."

"This is a waste of time," Bowman said impatiently. "Break some bones and get some answers. How many of these swords exist? Where are they? Why have the Fae waited to use them?"

"Let Dylan finish," Jace said sternly.

The other Shifters looked at him, falling silent. Graham saw them adjust their thinking from viewing Jace as an older cub to Jace as Eric's successor.

Air displaced next to Graham, and Reid was there. Graham had drawn back his fist, ready to punch, but checked himself at the last minute. "Damn it, Reid."

The other Shifter leaders had started forward, a few of them half shifting. "What the fuck?" Bowman asked. Not everyone had known Reid could teleport.

When Lorcan saw Reid, his assurance drained rapidly. *"Dokk alfar."* He continued with a string of weird-sounding words.

"Ironmaster," Reid said, in English. He held up his hand, which was clasped by a heavy black ring—iron— and advanced on Lorcan.

"What's he afraid of?" Bowman asked, a growl in his throat. "Iron doesn't affect mixed-breed Fae. And what the hell is *he*?" He pointed at Reid.

"A dark Fae," Graham said. "A pain in the ass. But handy to have around."

Reid didn't appear to care whether iron was supposed to work on mixed-blood Fae or not. He held up his hand, light sliding on the dark ring, and brought his hand down and wrapped it around Lorcan's throat.

Lorcan screamed. He tried to scramble away from Reid, the chains clinking, chair scraping. He yelled rapidly in Fae before settling down to English. "Make it stop! Make it stop! Please! Stop!"

The rest of the Shifter leaders watched in a mixture of surprise and unease. *Who the hell is this?* their body language said clearly. *And do I have to worry he can do that to me?*

Reid lifted his hand from Lorcan's neck, took a step back, and nodded at Dylan. Dylan didn't return the nod.

Graham went forward, tired of waiting. The Morrisseys could toy with Lorcan all day, like the cats they were, if they decided to. Wolves were more straightforward. "What is going on with the Collars and the swords?" he asked, pushing his face to Lorcan's. "I want to know everything, including how to keep the Fae from activating them."

Lorcan licked the side of his mouth, where blood had dripped. More blood dripped from his nose, thin streams of it. "It's too late. The High Fae have been making swords to match the spells in the Collars for many years. They're almost ready. My father and I were chosen to help prepare the way."

"Because Fae want Shifters back under their power?" Graham asked. "Guess what? They're not getting it."

"Fae wish to walk the earth again, as they once did. Shifters will fight the humans for the Fae—Shifters can fight iron."

"You mean Shifters kill all the humans, and the Fae pour out of their stone circles and rule the earth?" Graham leaned closer to Lorcan. "Do they realize how many humans are on this planet?"

"Fae aren't that good at math," Lorcan said, gray lips quirking to a little smile. "But there are many millions of Fae in Faerie. Only a handful of them ever lived on earth. It's getting crowded in Faerie, and they want the human world back."

"Using Shifters to get it?"

"The battle beasts, yes."

Oison had called Graham a *battle beast.* "If Shifters get wiped out in this little war, the Fae won't have their battle beasts anymore," Graham said.

"They'll make more," Lorcan said. "You have many cubs now."

Graham felt the blood drain from his face. Shifters started to growl, move.

Rage replaced Graham's shock. He grabbed Lorcan by his shirt. "They touch the cubs, and we'll rip off their heads, starting with yours."

"I told them that," Lorcan said desperately, more blood trickling from his nose and mouth. "I told them how protective you were of cubs. They don't care."

Reid said, "Sounds like typical *hoch alfar*. Cold *and* stupid."

Dylan broke in, his quiet voice even more deadly. "Why did they wait twenty years? In the first years of the Collars, we were weaker, more vulnerable. There was chaos trying to settle into Shiftertowns and find our feet."

"They wanted you stronger," Lorcan answered. "Shifters started to live longer, be more healthy, have more cubs. Multiply."

Graham shook Lorcan once, spraying blood. "So the Fae would have a bigger army."

"Larger and stronger."

"Shit." Graham released him, and Lorcan thumped back into the seat.

"What is the secret of the swords?" Jace asked around Dylan. "How can we break their effect?"

Lorcan shook his head. "You can't. The Fae made the swords to have the same technology as the Collars—they taught my dad how to make the Collars in the first place, and he taught me. The spells in the swords activate the Collars. They don't have to actually touch the Collars, but touching makes the control stronger."

"But swords and Collars have to be in proximity," Dylan said.

"For now."

The chill of those words worked their way through the Shifters. "How many?" Graham asked.

"Swords? As many now as there are Shifters."

Silence descended in the hanger. Graham remembered the pain that had encased him when Oison had touched his sword to Graham's Collar. Oison had been able to manipulate Graham's gunshot wound, healing and unhealing it at will. The water spell had been a way to bring Graham close enough to Oison, he realized, through the dreams—Graham would never have voluntarily walked into Faerie on his own. The Fae spell, through the water, had taken Graham to Oison, so Oison could use the sword . . .

"Inside Faerie," Graham finished his thought out loud. The other Shifters jerked attention to him. "Oison didn't come outside Faerie, with the sword, to where I was dying in the desert. He coerced me through Misty into drinking the water, to get me under his thrall first. He couldn't just come and get me with the sword—I already had to be weak and in his power. Which means the sword spells must not completely work yet."

Lorcan looked nervous. "Oison is impatient. He thinks we should move now. The leaders say the plan hasn't matured, but Oison wants to start immediately, before Shifters get *too* strong."

And Shifters were now learning how to control the Collars and even to remove them. Graham wondered if Oison knew Shifters had discovered the secret of removing the Collars, but Graham wasn't going to voice the thought to a man hand in glove with both the Fae and the human government.

"Oison jumped the gun, you mean," Graham said. "He gave the game away. That's what he gets for being a fuck-wad."

"No, *I* gave the game away," Lorcan said. "I'm doing it now. The Fae won't let me live for telling you all this."

Dylan almost smiled. "Then you'll have to trust Shifters to keep you safe and alive."

Liam grinned. "Ironic, isn't it, lad?"

"Keep him safe?" Graham growled. "You mean I can't tear him in half? Or watch Reid do the trick with the ring again?"

Liam shook his head. "We can't risk the humans investigating us if Lorcan turns up dead and shredded, or cut in half by a Fae sword. So he's now under our protection. Poor guy."

Liam was laughing, looking positively gleeful. Graham wished he could be so happy. "How do we deactivate the swords?" Graham asked Lorcan. "All of them?"

"You don't," Lorcan said. "Not from here. You'd have to take that fight inside Faerie, or lure the Fae out."

Bowman broke in. "So, there are as many Fae with the swords as there are Shifters with Collars? I could eat ten Fae and have room for dessert, but them controlling the Collars makes things different."

Going into Faerie wasn't an option, Graham knew. There weren't enough Shifters in fighting form to win a fight inside Faerie, even without the Fae having the Collar-controlling swords. Plus, gates to Faerie were tricky—no guarantee a Shifter army could get in. On the other hand, enticing a boatload of Fae out of Faerie to fight didn't appeal either . . . if they'd even come.

"What about Andrea's father?" Graham asked. "What's his name, Fionn? He's a Fae. What does he know about all this?"

"Nothing," Dylan said. "I already spoke with him, and what I told him made him very angry. Not all Fae see eye-to-eye. He fears those Fae who made the swords will not only want to walk the earth again, but rule all of Faerie. There are constant power struggles there. Fionn can help, but only if he can convince his clan it's necessary. Fionn's people might be happy to let the Fae use controlled Shifters to kill humans, good riddance to the humans."

"Good riddance to Shifters too, you mean," Graham said, and Dylan gave him a slow nod. "And then there's Reid," Graham said, turning to him. "Go tell your dark Fae to kick some ass."

"I will," Reid said. "Same problem though, getting my clan to agree about the threat. They might be happy to let the *hoch alfar* fight each other, or let them leave Faerie for the human world without protest. Dark Fae will shut the gates behind the *hoch alfar* and be glad. *Dokk alfar* are the original Fae, after all." Reid's black eyes glinted. "However, I might convince my people to keep the Fae busy while we figure out how to stop them."

"I know how," Graham said. "Without going to Faerie at all."

He didn't say it out loud. Lorcan might be under Dylan's thumb now, but he still could turn around and text someone in the human government as soon as he got his hands free.

The solution was getting the Collars off Shifters. The Fae couldn't manipulate what wasn't there. Collars were already coming off the weaker Shifters, the ones who couldn't take the pain and couldn't learn the techniques for control. The thought that Matt and Kyle, and whatever cub Graham would have with Misty, wouldn't have to wear true Collars made his heart sing.

"Is that enough information?" Dylan asked. "I'd like to get Lorcan back home before the humans miss him."

Liam, hands in his sweat jacket pockets, nodded. "I'll get Marlo, and we'll go. Sean and Andrea will stay a while longer, Graham, to make sure Misty's all right." Graham gave Liam a nod of thanks.

"That's it then," Jace said.

The fact that the Shifters didn't disperse until Jace gave the nod attested to his growing power. Without any more talk, Liam disappeared into the darkening desert, and Dylan, Bowman, and Sean carried Lorcan, silver chains, chair, and all, out. A plane's engines started up, lights flashing, the lumbering bird waiting for its passengers.

The other Shifters started to walk away, off to board the airplane or find their own transportation home. No one said, *Take care of yourself*, or even *Goddess go with you*. Such words might mean they'd never see each other again.

"How'd you do that?" Graham asked Reid in a low voice as the building emptied. "With the ring? If mixed-blood Fae don't have to worry about iron?"

"They still need to worry about it," Reid said. "But they have enough human blood in them to dilute the effects. I used the ring to *un*dilute the effects, going straight for the part of Lorcan that was true Fae."

"Really?" Graham rubbed his jaw, feeling stiff bristles. "Good to know."

Reid eyed him. "You couldn't do it yourself. If *you* pushed this ring against Lorcan's neck, he'd only feel a ring against his neck. Only I can make the iron work."

"Because you're Iron Man, I know."

"Ironmaster," Reid said. But he gave Graham a ghost of a smile, appreciating the humor. Then he walked away a few steps, and disappeared.

Graham couldn't help his jump when the air around Reid displaced with a little pop. "Damn, I *hate* it when he does that."

Jace waited to walk out with Graham. "We'll start with you," Jace said.

He meant taking off the Collars. Graham shook his head as he mounted his borrowed bike. "Dougal first. He'd never stand against Fae. Thank the Goddess it was me who got shot and water-spelled. Dougal would already be gone."

"I agree," Jace said. "But it's not up to me."

"Your dad thinks it's up to him," Graham said. "Your dad's wrong."

Without waiting for Jace's answer, Graham started and revved the bike and took off across the desert. To the west, the sky was crimson, gold, and brilliant blue, black mountains in silhouette—a desert sunset in all its glory. A perfect backdrop, Graham thought. Too bad this movie wasn't over.

Graham checked on the cubs when he reached Shifter-town, who were happy to continue hanging out with Andrea and Sean, who'd returned from the meeting. Sean and Andrea were looking after Dougal too, while pretending not to, to spare Dougal's pride. They were good people, Graham conceded, for Felines and half-Fae Shifters.

Graham left them and headed south into the heart of Las Vegas to Misty's store. He knew she'd gone back there in spite of Graham telling her not to, because that was the kind of lady Misty was.

Misty wasn't at the store when Graham reached it, however. Some of Eric's Shifters were, including Brody, cleaning up. Eric had arrived with Misty here, Brody said, then Xav had followed Misty home, and Shane had driven Eric back to Shiftertown.

Graham continued to Misty's house. Her truck was in her driveway, along with a couple of black pickups and SUVs from DX Security. Graham told the man working on fixing Misty's door to get out of the way and go home. The man stepped aside, but went back to his work on the door.

Graham ignored him, in too much of a hurry to be irritated. He let scent and voices guide him to the kitchen, where his mate was.

Except his mate leaned against Xav Escobar, Xav's arms around her, Misty's head on his shoulder. While Graham stood there for a stunned second, Xav stroked one hand through Misty's hair.

Graham was across the room, his Collar sparking, a roar leaving his mouth. He wrapped his hand around Xav's throat, and kept moving, heaving Xav up against the far wall before anyone could say a word.

CHAPTER TWENTY-TWO

It took Misty a few heartbeats to realize the whirlwind who'd rushed by her was Graham. Graham enraged, his Collar throwing off arcs of electricity. His eyes were white with fury, his hands turning to claws that gripped Xav's neck.

Xavier, face red, brought out a black device. "I'll tase you, McNeil. Tasers and Collars, not a pretty combination." He had to force out the words.

Misty rushed to Graham and tried to pull his hands from Xav, but Graham's arms were like steel bars. "Stop it, Graham. It's not what you think."

"You touched my *mate*," Graham said savagely to Xav. "You want me to kill you now? Or do you want to Challenge me, and I'll kill you later?"

"Fuck you," Xav said. He brought up the Taser, electricity crackling.

"No!" Misty cried. "Graham, let him *go*! I was talking to him as a friend. He was comforting me, *as a friend*. Three guesses as to who he was comforting me about."

Graham wasn't listening. "You never, ever touch a Shifter's mate. You'll be dead before you hit the ground."

Graham's Collar was still sparking, but he didn't seem to notice.

"Let him go," Misty shouted at him. "I haven't agreed to be your mate."

Graham swung his head around, pinning Misty with his white gray stare. "I mate-claimed you. You didn't refuse. You had all that sex with me; you made me think—" He broke off, pain momentarily flickering through his eyes. "You are my mate."

The DX Security man who'd been fixing the door had come in, his Taser also at the ready. Misty held up her hand to stop him but looked Graham in the eye.

"You are *insufferable*. Because we had sex, now I belong to you? I don't even know what to say to that." Misty didn't know much what to do either. She settled for making an exasperated noise and storming out into the yard.

Behind her she heard Xav coughing. "Welcome to women in the twenty-first century," Xav said, and laughed. Hoarsely.

Misty's backyard usually comforted her. She'd planted it so something would be in bloom every season, whether they were in the hottest triple-digit temps of the summer or the forties in the winter. Moonlight now shone on four-o'clocks that bloomed in darkness and the ghostly white blossoms of the oleanders.

Misty hadn't stood more than five seconds trying to find calm, before Graham barreled out the door after her. She hoped he hadn't broken that one too.

Graham had always been gentle with Misty, pulling back his strength for her. Now he grabbed her by the shoulders, hands biting down hard, and yanked her around to face him. The silver white glow of his eyes was even more pronounced in the moonlight, the anger in them plain.

"Let go of me," Misty snapped. "And stop trying to kill my friends. You don't own me."

Graham didn't release her. "I scent-marked you. I mate-claimed you. Yes, I do."

"You know, every time I realize I love you, you start to

be an asshole. You break my house, you threaten people, you even get hurt yourself. What is *wrong* with you?"

Graham's grip on her arm abruptly softened. His Collar had stopped sparking, but Misty saw the dark marks it had left on his neck.

"What do you mean, every time you realize you love me?" he demanded.

"I mean, whenever I acknowledge I care about you, you do something that makes me wonder why I do."

"No." Graham let her go. "You said *love*."

"I know I did." Misty rubbed her arms. "And don't give me any crap about Shifters not loving like humans do, or me not understanding what I feel, or—"

"Goddess. Misty." Graham's eyes filled with wells of pain that matched his rage. He stared at her for a long moment, moonlight playing on his hard face, the flame tattoos, the dark buzz of his hair. "I want you with every breath."

His eyes had darkened to their normal gray, which still held a hint of silver. He reached for her again, his hands landing on her shoulders, this time without the hard pressure. Graham caressed her, thumbs moving on her bare skin under her tank top.

"I need you," he said. "Now more than ever."

His voice was thick, gravelly, with dryness and emotion. He stepped against her, the tall warmth of him covering her, before he leaned down and kissed her.

The kiss was slow, almost tender, but it held Graham's strength. His lips were shaking, as though he wanted to take everything but stopped himself.

When he eased back, his grip tightened on her shoulders. He looked down at her but shook his head, as though he debated something inside himself.

"Aw, screw it," he whispered.

Misty's heart fluttered as Graham turned her around and transferred his grip to her arm. He walked her ahead of him, across her yard and over the little bridge, lifting her in both hands as they got to the other side. He set her on her feet on the grass beyond, where they'd done the spell, and turned her to him, cupping her face in his hands and kissing her, again with tenderness. Then he slid his hands down her shirt and skimmed it up and off over her head.

Misty automatically tried to cover herself, but Graham pulled her arms apart and gazed down on her.

"Moon kissed," he said. "Touched by the Goddess. Beautiful."

Graham gently tugged her nipples between his fingers, kissing her again, his tongue a slow caress in her mouth. Misty moved her hands to Graham's waist, popped open the button of his jeans, and slid her hand inside.

She found Graham's cock, hard and tight, hot against her hand. She squeezed, and Graham made a noise of pleasure in the kiss. He let go of Misty to unzip the jeans and drop them all the way, letting the denim pool around his ankles.

"You are the sweetest thing," he said.

She slid her hand along his cock, his tip firm against her palm. Misty loved looking at him like this, a strong man bared for her, his head going back as he enjoyed her touch.

Graham had never made any pretense of not wanting her. He'd looked at Misty the first night as though he wondered what she'd be like in bed. If her friends hadn't pulled her away, Misty might have found out what *he* was like. Once they'd started seeing each other, Graham had held back, for many reasons, one of which, Misty had come to understand, was not to hurt her.

Now, he was giving her everything.

Graham smiled as he pulled her into his arms, she still holding on to his cock. As he kissed her, he unbuttoned her skirt and let it and her underwear drop to the grass.

He pulled her closer, his fingers warm on her buttocks. "Stay away from that damned human."

"I told you," Misty said, kissing his shoulder, "he was talking to me as a friend."

"Friend, my ass," Graham rumbled.

"No, this is your ass." Misty pinched it.

"Little shit. Just for that . . ."

Graham wrapped one leg around Misty's, gently pulling her feet out from under her. Misty squeaked once and landed on her hands and knees. She had no idea what he meant to do, until he slid his arm around her from behind.

Graham's shirt landed next to her on the grass. He settled in behind her, covering her back with his large, hot body. He positioned himself at her opening, his tip touching her.

"I'm not sure I can," she said, sucking in a breath. "You're . . . big."

"Yes," Graham stroked her hair, his body warming hers. "But you can."

"I'm not a Shifter."

"I know. I love that about you." Graham laughed softly, as though to himself, and then he was pushing inside her.

Misty gulped air, all her muscles tightening. No, he couldn't. *She* couldn't. Another breath, and Graham slid in another inch.

He stroked her hair, then her back, making soothing noises. "Take me, Misty. Be mine."

Misty took another deep breath, and then she relaxed. Her body opened, and Graham slid straight into her heat.

"That's it," Graham's voice went quiet, the gravel turning to velvet. "Goddess, you're good. Tight. *Yes.*"

Misty closed her eyes and groaned as he started to thrust. In this position, she felt only *him*, and all thought dissolved. Nothing existed but Graham, thick and hard inside her, the night, the grass prickling her hands and knees.

He went faster, hands on her back, beautiful friction. His legs were strong against hers, his rhythm even, unceasing.

Misty heard cries coming out of her mouth, floating to the sky to echo against the moon. Dimly she realized others would hear, but she couldn't stop. What Graham did was so intense, so *right*, and her mouth wanted to let the world know her pleasure.

She grabbed his shirt from the ground and pressed it to her mouth, letting the cloth muffle the sounds. It didn't dampen all the noise Misty was making, and Graham laughed at her.

"Sweet, sweet woman. We'll go up into the woods and do this all night, and you'll scream as much as you want to."

Yes. Misty pressed back to him, wanting more. Graham kept up his thrusts, harder and faster. He held her, covering her with his warmth, his rumbling voice soothing.

Misty had no idea what he said, but she loved his voice, clung to the sound. It rolled over her like a warm wave, lifting her into the greatest pleasure.

More waves caught her, these of her coming apart. She dropped the shirt, bunching it in her fist on the ground as she supported herself against his onslaught. She heard her own voice, low and needy, *Oh, yes, Graham. Please. I love it. I love you.*

"You're beautiful, Misty," Graham whispered. "So fucking beautiful. *Damn it.*" His words wound into a tight groan, and he hung on, his fingers hard on her soft flesh.

He kept thrusting as Misty held herself up, gasping, laughing, groaning. Everything was slippery and hot, wild and bright.

"*Goddess.*" Graham rocked back, fists light on Misty's back, coming into her one last time.

Misty wriggled back on him, loving the tight fit, the heat, the crazy feeling. Then Graham fell onto her, bracing himself to keep from crushing her. He took her down onto the grass, and gathered her back into him, still joined with her.

Graham kissed her face, her lips, her hair, arms wrapping around her. "Damn," he said, and laughed. "That was fucking wonderful."

"Yes," Misty said, snuggling happily back into him. "Wonderful."

A lovely feeling. Misty hugged it to her as she held on to Graham, letting herself bask in the moment. Graham and the moonlight shining on her, on her garden, on the flowers around them. Misty snuggled back into him, bringing his hard hand up to her mouth to kiss it.

She'd been made for this night, she decided. And Misty was going to enjoy every last second of it.

* * *

Graham gazed down at Misty lying in her bed, exhausted after another round of lovemaking. He'd carried her in here, she already half-asleep. Xavier had decided to be discreet and guard the front, so Misty hadn't been embarrassed to be carried through the house, their clothes piled in a little heap on top of her.

She'd drifted off after their last time, but Graham didn't sleep.

He'd gone for days without sleeping before, but this was the longest time he'd lasted without true rest. Shifter wolves could lie in the sun and soak up warmth, relaxing to the point of sleep, but still being alert.

Now Graham was afraid even to doze. He knew with every dream, Oison grew closer, and he couldn't afford to let him win.

He'd make sure Misty was safe—even if Xavier, the traitor, had to guard her—then he'd get with Reid and Eric and figure out a way to find Oison and take him down. They couldn't wait much longer—Oison might even now be preparing with his Fae friends to round up Shifters and start controlling them. Jace could help Shifters remove Collars, but it was problematic, and Graham liked the direct approach, and he knew Eric did too.

For now, he'd enjoy his moment with Misty. Graham nestled down into her warmth. He loved her with his entire body, the mate bond snaking around his heart.

He'd suspected the mate bond had been growing for months now, but he hadn't let himself acknowledge it. He'd known it for certain when he'd helped Andrea cure Misty with the herbal poultice Andrea's Fae father had sent with her. Graham had felt the warmth in his heart, the burn that had touched him at the same moment Misty had clutched her chest as though something burned her too.

Graham reveled in it now, closing his eyes and drawing in Misty's scent.

Come to me . . .

Graham jerked awake. At least, he hoped to the Goddess he was awake.

Moonlight filled Misty's room, the moon at the full. Moonlight was magical. Even Shifters, who didn't much like magic, acknowledged that on the full moon, when the Mother Goddess was at her height, mystical things could happen.

Fae worshipped the Goddess too, just a weird aspect of her. Instead of the comforting mother figure, they liked the crone-like goddess who wove dark magics.

Shifter. You are mine . . .

Son of a bitch. Graham scrambled up from the bed. Everything in him wanted to go find the voice, to do as it commanded. He broke into a sweat as he fought the compulsion.

Was this what would happen to all Shifters? The Fae made a connection with the Shifter somehow—as Oison had with the water spell—then used the further connection between sword and Collar to make the Shifter come to him. To obey him without question.

Graham couldn't. He needed to fight with everything he had. If Graham, one of the strongest Shifters alive, could be gotten at this way, what chance did the rest of them have? He thought about Dougal, and went cold.

Well, if Fae had magic, so did Shifters, of a sort. They had mates. The touch of a true mate could heal, and the mate bond could protect against many things.

"Misty," Graham touched her shoulder.

Misty didn't respond. Her breathing was deep but so soft Graham had to lean over her to catch it.

"Misty. Sweetheart."

She didn't wake. Graham shook her. Misty's body moved, rubbery, and her skin was cool.

Fear lacing him, Graham shook her again, and again. She was alive, but slumbering deeply. Graham patted her cheeks then harder, but she never woke.

Oison must have done this—maybe the Fae's connection to Misty through the water spell or the sword cut hadn't been completely severed. Graham stopped shaking her and smoothed her hair, his hand unsteady.

"He can do whatever he wants to me," Graham said in a hard voice, "but he's not having you."

He leaned down and kissed her, and the mate bond tightened in his heart. Graham kissed Misty's forehead then her lips again, then he rested his fingers on her abdomen. If what they'd done this night and last had born fruit, Graham would at least have that.

Come to me . . .

The voice in his head was louder, more insistent, and Graham's body jerked. The words were in Fae, but Graham understood them.

Moonlight beamed brightly through the window, bathing Misty and Graham in white. "Goddess go with them," Graham whispered. He touched Misty's face then her abdomen again, and left the room.

In the hall, he called Reid but got his voice mail. Graham growled a message at him and flipped his phone closed. He entered Misty's room again, placed his phone on top of her dresser, then moved to her window and slid through it with Shifter stealth.

The pain inside him lessened as he left the house, the compulsion spell happy that Graham was moving in the right direction.

Graham took Dougal's bike from the end of the driveway and pushed it into the street. The DX Security man stationed here nodded at him, seeing nothing wrong in Graham leaving when he pleased.

Graham pushed the motorcycle quietly around the corner before he mounted and started it, its throbbing loud in the stillness.

Come to me!

"All right, all right, I'm coming," Graham said out loud. "Shut the fuck up already."

CHAPTER TWENTY-THREE

Misty woke when early sunshine slid its first rays into her window. Graham was gone, though the bed bore the indentation of his large body, and the covers were a mess.

She smiled, remembering the warmth of him around her, the wild passion of their lovemaking in the garden and later in bed. As her fog of afterglow receded, though, she realized she couldn't hear his voice rumbling through the house, or sense his presence as she often could. She also saw, sitting on her low dresser, the black outline of Graham's small cell phone.

Misty sat straight up. "Oh, God, no."

She threw off the covers and scrambled out of the bed, and at the same time heard loud voices down the hall. Voices accompanied by frenzied yips.

Misty quickly pulled on shorts and top, finger-combing her hair as she ran out of the room and to the front door. Xav was blocking it, he red-eyed and dark-chinned from staying up all night.

"Misty!" Dougal tried to lunge past Xav, who barricaded the doorway with his body. "You're all right."

"Yes, why wouldn't I—"

Misty broke off as two tiny wolf bodies hurled themselves at her, Matt and Kyle climbing up her to nestle in her arms and lick her face, their tails moving furiously.

"They came and found me," Dougal said. "I was in bed at home—they kept trying to say you were in danger. They wouldn't let me go back to sleep until I followed them. They had me worried." He bent to the cubs. "See? She's fine."

Kyle lifted his muzzle and howled. Matt nuzzled into Misty's neck, shivering.

"I'm all right, little guys," she said. "But Graham's gone."

Dougal's eyes widened, and he glared at Xav, his Collar sparking once. "Gone where?"

"No idea," Xav said. "Never said a word to me. I saw him take the bike." He gestured out the door where Dougal's motorcycle had been replaced by the small pickup Dougal must have driven to get here. "I assumed he'd gone home. He left of his own accord, looking fine to me."

"And you didn't think you should tell me?" Misty joined Dougal in glaring at him.

"You were asleep," Xav said impatiently. "Until Dougal came charging over, I didn't figure he'd done anything but gone back to Shiftertown."

Misty's heart pounded and her head ached. She knew Graham was in trouble, though she didn't know how she knew it. But the hollow in her heart, where the warmth had been, told her she needed to find Graham and find him now. The cubs had sensed the same thing, had herded Dougal over here to ask Misty what to do.

Dougal was watching her, worry behind the hard-faced, bad-boy look he tried to maintain. He was waiting for Misty to take care of him, of the cubs, of the situation. The cubs themselves clung to her. Even Xav waited, though warily, for Misty to decide what she would do.

McNeil needs you. You can save him, but it has to be your choice.

The words of the odd man, Ben, whom Paul had brought to see her, echoed in her head.

I can save him how?

Misty had no idea. She was a florist—she knew flowers and plants and how to sell them. Other than that, her specialty was feeding boys and absentminded fathers, and not being offended when they never acknowledged what she did. She'd known they'd appreciated it, in their own way, but had been too caught up in their own worlds to say so.

Misty wasn't a warrior, or a being of magical power, or even a Shifter. She didn't know anything about Fae—hadn't even heard of them until one had tried to take her and Graham.

"Oh, yeah," Dougal said, reaching into the back pocket of his jeans. "I forgot. Reid told me to give you this."

He handed her the little book of flower spells Misty had let Reid borrow. Misty shifted the cubs' weight to take it, clutching the familiar leather cover between her fingers.

Her heart beating faster, she stepped into her living room, still carrying the cubs. Dougal leaned on the wall in the hall, watching her with Xav.

Misty opened the book. Inside, she found the sticky note on which Ben had written his name and telephone number the day he'd come to the shop. She was sure she'd left that sticky note in her office, but here it was, inside the book on the vellum that separated the picture from the title page.

Beneath Ben's handwriting was another. *Call Ben,* it said. *Ask him to help you.* It was signed, *Stuart Reid.*

Misty stared at the note for a long time. Still looking at it, she went numbly into the kitchen, fished her cell phone out of her purse, and started tapping.

Graham looked around the shallow cave he and Misty had found when she'd been trying to take him back to the Fae one. He'd left Dougal's motorcycle near the shack at the bottom of the little hill and hiked his way up.

All the while, Oison kept up the noise in Graham's head. *You are mine, battle beast. Come to me.* Graham gave up trying to shut it out and fighting the need to go to him. He hadn't been able to ride the motorcycle anywhere but here without being in excruciating, dizzying pain. He'd explained everything carefully to Reid in the phone message—Graham could only wait and hope Reid did what he was supposed to.

For now, Graham stood in the dry, shallow cave, the temperature rising outside.

"I'm here," he called out. "Where the hell are you?"

Change.

Graham didn't want to. He wanted to stand upright and tell Oison what he thought, right before he strangled the fucking Fae.

"I've come to kill you," Graham said. "I'm going to beat down your body then drag it back up, and beat it down again. Sound like fun?"

Shift!

The command flashed through Graham like the worst of the Collar's shocking pain. Without him willing it, he started peeling off his clothes.

His body began to shift before he was finished. The last of his shirt and underwear fell in shreds from him as his wolf limbs took form, and Graham landed on all fours, a huge black wolf. He snarled, then lifted his muzzle and howled.

The mournful wolf's cry echoed through the small chamber. At the same time, the wall at the rear cracked, shards of stone rattling down to the cave floor.

Then the wall disappeared entirely and so did the dry cave. A black, glassy obsidian floor swallowed up the dirt one, the trickle of the fountain pounded into Graham's brain, and flowering vines flowed toward him, their scents strong. Graham backed up, but the vines reached him and twined around his feet, climbing up his legs.

Graham fought them, but the vines grew tighter, flowing back as soon as he pushed any aside. One wrapped around his muzzle, and he bit the vine in half.

These plants were relentless. In Misty's yard, he'd thought her flowers pretty, but the ones here were terrifying. Trumpet flowers opened like mouths, and the puffball-like flowers grew until they were smothering pillows.

Graham kept fighting. He didn't notice Oison until the Fae was standing in the middle of the cave, near the fountain. Oison wore his chain mail and silver cloak again, with the sword in his hand, his white hair hanging in braids to his waist.

He spoke in Fae, but Graham understood every word. "If you think your *dokk alfar* will help you, think again," Oison said. "You tipped your hand, playing your ironmaster too soon. I fortified myself against him. There he is."

Oison pointed with the sword. At one end of the cave, which Graham could barely see through all the damn flowers, was a wall of ice. The ice floe was huge, hundreds of feet high and at least fifty feet wide. In the middle of it was a dark smudge, only just discernable.

"*Dokk alfars* are beings of earth," Oison said. "They master it. I trapped him with the element *I* master—water. The *dokk alfar* is still alive, enjoying every pleasure of being frozen almost to death inside ice."

Graham snarled, still fighting the vines. He made himself shift back to his human form, though it hurt like hell. His Collar went off, driving pain into him, but Graham forced himself through, ending up on his human feet.

Fighting the flowers and vines was easier with his hands, and he managed to drag them from his face.

"I'm not fighting your wars for you," Graham spat. "Forget it."

"Not war. Not yet," Oison said, sounding far too calm. "My colleagues are right that it's too soon for war. But they're wrong that it's too soon to bring in the Shifters. You will pull others to me—you have a hundred of what you call Lupines under your command, do you not? I will train you to obey and to submit. You will also breed new Shifters for us. Once you have multiplied, in a few generations, then it will be time for war. Good thing we made Shifters to be long-lived."

Graham snarled, pulling another vine from his face. "Not gonna happen."

"Yes, it will."

Graham kept up his defiance, but his body felt as icy as the wall that encased Reid. The vines wove relentlessly around his limbs, pulling him down to the black floor. They doubled in speed, pinning his body to the ground, spinning over him in a mesh that soon blotted out all light.

Misty unloaded Dougal and the cubs from her truck, unlocked her store, and let everyone in. No one had come to work on the place this early, but Misty could see that DX Security and the Shifters had done a great job so far. The broken glass and ceramic had been swept away, the shelves rebuilt. The front doors still needed to be replaced as well as the main counter, but the store was coming along.

Xav had accompanied her, not wanting to let Misty out of his sight. He was responsible for her, he said. His job. He'd brought several security guys who stationed themselves around the front and back in the parking lot.

Misty took the cubs into her office and set them on the desk. "All right, you two. You said you were playing in that basement in Shiftertown, and all the sudden you were here, in the back of a car." She leaned closer to them. "Tell me now, how did you get there . . . *really?*"

The wolves looked up at her, innocent-faced, and Dougal growled at them.

One of the wolves shifted. He had hazel eyes—Matt. He hunkered down, hiding his body, but Misty had the feeling it was out of shamefacedness, not modesty.

"We hid in the car," Matt said, his voice small. "Kyle said you and Graham would be mad, so we had to hide. The car was unlocked."

"Was it?" Misty asked, giving them a skeptical look. The guy who'd been driving it had sworn up and down he'd locked it. He worked for a top security firm and was careful about things like that.

Matt glanced at Kyle, who was still a wolf. "Maybe Dougal taught us how to break into cars," Matt said.

"Hey, you little monsters . . ." Dougal began.

"Not important." Misty raised her voice. "I need you two to show me *exactly* where you came out."

"Okay," Matt said, and shifted back into a wolf.

He and Kyle scrambled from the desk, their bodies wriggling as they tried to land softly. Matt yipped when he hit the floor, but was up again, racing to the door to scratch on it.

"I didn't teach them to break into cars," Dougal said as Misty opened the door so the cubs could scamper out. He didn't look Misty in the eye, so he might be lying, he might not. "How to pick locks, yeah, but different kinds." He hesitated. "Don't tell Graham."

"I don't have to." Misty gave him an exasperated look. "Just . . . don't teach them anything else, all right?"

Dougal sent her a grin that showed he might in time become as hard and fearless as Graham. "I'm their honorary uncle. I'm supposed to be a little wild."

Misty patted his arm. "You're awesome, Dougal."

"Aw. You're just saying that."

The cubs, let into the main part of the store, immediately ran to the unlocked front door, pushed it open with body weight and determination, and started racing across the parking lot.

CHAPTER TWENTY-FOUR

"Hey, no dogs allowed in here." Pedro pointed a broad finger at Misty and Xav standing slightly behind her. "Sorry, those are the rules. Health department."

Matt and Kyle started around the counter of the convenience store, growling and snapping at Pedro, unhappy about being called *dogs*. Dougal lunged for them and grabbed one cub under each arm.

"They sure are cute little guys," Pedro said, looking them over. "What kind are they?"

The store was empty except for Pedro at the moment. No one was at the gas pumps this early, and traffic was sparse on the roads.

"Wolf," Dougal said.

"Wolf hybrids?" Pedro reached out to pet Kyle.

"No." Dougal said. "All wolf."

Pedro jerked his hand back at the same time Dougal's T-shirt moved to show his Collar above the neckband. Pedro lowered his hand and swallowed. "No Shifters either. Sorry. Owner's policy."

"We'll be out in no time," Misty said brightly. "Promise.

You two." She pointed a finger at first Matt then Kyle.
"Where? And no goofing around."

Kyle and Matt wriggled to get down. Dougal set them
on their feet then followed close behind the cubs, Misty
after him. Pedro stayed put, watching, but not moving to
stop them.

Matt and Kyle led them to a door marked "Private," then
behind that to the stockroom, and to where the refrigerated
goods were stored.

Both cubs sat down and started whimpering.

"They're saying the ley line comes out here," Dougal
said to Misty. "In the back of a convenience store?"

"Probably the convenience store was built over it."
Misty looked around. A stockroom was a stockroom—
shelves of things to replace what was bought, door to a
small office, door to a bathroom, large back door for deliveries. "Does the ley line automatically work, or do you
have to do something to activate it? I can't believe it's automatic. I think people would have started noticing employ-
ees disappearing from the convenience store stockroom
over the years."

"You have to do something," a new voice said. Ben was
standing in the shadows, the man's short, broad appearance making him look like a creature from fairy stories.
Which, in the circumstances, wasn't comforting. "This is
why you need me."

Xavier had his Taser at the ready, and Dougal growled
and stepped protectively in front of Misty. Ben came out of
the shadows, regarding Dougal and Xav fearlessly. The
cubs echoed Dougal's snarls and rushed at Ben, not holding back.

Ben took a step away and raised his hands. "It's all right,
little guys. I'm not going to hurt her."

Kyle and Matt eased off, though they kept up little
growls as they sniffed Ben's running shoes.

Xav didn't back down. "The cubs might believe you, but
I don't," he said. "Who the hell are you?"

"I'm Ben. Misty called me. She needs my help."

"You smell wrong," Dougal's nose wrinkled. "In fact, you stink."

"Yeah, I get that a lot, but only from Shifters." Ben grinned. "Humans like the way I smell."

"Not exactly," Xavier said.

"You're not human," Dougal said, looking at Ben's tight, flat face, scarred from whatever fights he'd had.

"No kidding," Ben said, but let that interesting answer hang. "Misty, do you want to save Graham or not?"

"Of course I want to save him." Misty tried to push past Dougal and Xav, but couldn't. Dougal stood fast, his body almost as solidly strong as Graham's. "You said on the phone he was in Faerie. How do you know that?"

"I know when a gate opens. And one did, early this morning. Then you called and said your boyfriend was missing—I put two and two together. The Fae must have compelled him to come. Only you can get him away."

"Me? How? I have no idea what do to."

Ben gestured to the book she'd brought with her. "It's in there. Everything you need to know."

Misty glanced at it then back at Ben, her eyes narrowing. "How do you know what's in the book? I didn't have it with me when I talked to you."

"Because I wrote it."

Misty looked Ben over again, the feeling of wrongness about him increasing. Xav made a noise of disbelief.

"*You* wrote it," Misty said, "back in 1907?"

Ben nodded. "Yep. I've been around. The Fae have tried to return to the human world before . . . the last time was early in the twentieth century. They used interest in the standing stones, the growing popularity of the occult, Ouija boards, mediums, whatever they could, to try to find a way back in. I wrote these spells for humans, so they could counteract coercive Fae magic if necessary. The book was very popular at the time, though most humans didn't realize how magical it was."

Misty ran her hands over the leather cover and opened

to the frontispiece and the color plate of an heirloom rose. "Did you do the pictures?"

"Nah, don't have the talent. I hired an artist. He did a good job."

Misty closed the book again. "I'm still stuck on the part where you wrote it in 1907."

Dougal broke in, his voice fierce. "Means he has something other than human blood in him. He's not Shifter, though. Are you Fae?"

Ben laughed. "No way. Ask your *dokk alfar*. I'm not *dokk alfar* either, but he knows."

Misty listened to the exchange in impatience. "What in this book lets me open the ley line, so I can find Graham?"

"It opens a *path* along the ley line. Page forty-six."

Misty flipped to it and read the words printed in a fancy typeface, surrounded by line drawings of flowers. *Violets, forget-me-nots, yellow roses, and a sprinkle of rosemary, scattered in a swirl. Call the blessings of the Goddess, turn thrice clockwise, and chant the letters of your name in reverse.*

Misty looked up at Ben. "Seriously?"

Ben shrugged. "Turning in circles and saying things backward was popular at the time. The important part is the type of flowers and the pattern, which you lay directly on a ley line. And call to the Goddess, because you will need her protection. Don't do this without her." Ben paused, his dark eyes in this dim light like pools of blackness. "Seriously."

"Misty," Xav said. "Who is this guy, and why are you listening to him?"

Misty faced Xav, her chest tight. She'd been holding herself clenched so that her worry for Graham wouldn't reduce her to a puddle of ineffectual nothing. "Someone who might help me get to Graham. I'm willing to do anything, no matter how crazy, to help him. Understand?"

Xavier looked down at her for a long time. He'd been guarding her in the house and store since her adventure in the desert, and he'd been witness to every shift in Misty's relationship with Graham. She saw in Xav's eyes now that he knew she'd chosen Graham and would never have interest in a human ex-cop. A Shifter had gotten under Misty's skin, and she saw that Xav understood.

"All right. But I'm sticking by you, and keeping an eye on this one." Xav gestured with his Taser to Ben.

"Fair enough." Misty turned from him and read the words again. "Violets and forget-me-nots. You didn't live in this climate, did you?"

"Ireland," Ben said. "At the time."

"Rosemary is easy. I have some growing at home, plus there's always the supermarket. These other two . . . Damn it."

"What?" Dougal asked in alarm. "What's wrong?"

"I'd have these flowers in stock, but the gang boys destroyed everything. This means I have to buy from a rival florist, one that would be happy to see me go out of business. I swear, when I get Graham back safely, I'll let him visit Sam Flores, wherever he's been stashed, and kick his sorry behind."

"I'll do it." Dougal flashed her his grin again, the one that said he liked any excuse for trouble.

"No, you won't." Misty punched numbers into her phone. "Hi," she said to the pleasant-voiced woman who answered the phone. "I'd like to place an order. A rush. In fact, I'll pick it up from you. Yes, I know a rush is extra . . ."

An hour later, Misty and Xav returned from the florist with bunches of purple, blue, and yellow flowers. The owner of the flower store had pretended to be very sympathetic to the vandalism to Misty's shop, saying she wouldn't blame Misty for closing. "So dangerous, sometimes, to run a small place on your own," the woman had said. "We could always find a job for you in one of our shops, if you want it."

"I'm not closing," Misty had answered, irritated. "I'm waiting for the rest of my repairs then I'm back in business."

"Oh," the woman had said, giving her a false smile. "That's so brave of you."

Misty had taken her flowers without further word and departed. Xav helped unload them from her car back at her own shop, where Dougal and Ben had waited with the cubs. Misty thrust the bunches of flowers into Ben's, Dougal's, and Xav's hands and told them to follow her back to the convenience store.

"I hope no one sees me like this," Dougal said. He glanced around, as though worried other Shifters, the grizzly brothers maybe, would pull up, point to Dougal with his arms full of blue blossoms, and laugh.

"Suck it up," Misty said. She gave Dougal a smile to soften her words. "Hey, Graham's right about that saying—it's useful."

She led the way back into Pedro's store. Pedro only sighed when Misty asked to use the back room for a few more minutes and agreed, as long the owner didn't find out. He didn't ask questions—Pedro had once told Misty he'd seen it all. Maybe Misty charging into his storeroom with two wolf cubs, a Shifter, an armed security guy, and a whatever-he-was carrying armloads of flowers wasn't the oddest thing he'd ever encountered.

Misty followed Ben to the spot he indicated, and started laying the flowers in the patterns specified by the book. It seemed a shame to toss the blossoms to the floor, when they would look beautiful arranged in a big vase—small purple blooms of the violets and the vibrant blue of the forget-me-nots against the large yellow roses.

The florist had carried rosemary sprigs as well, in bloom. Their spiky leaves and tiny, pale blue flowers would also look good in the arrangement. The pungent scent of rosemary mixed with the heady odor of roses as Misty worked.

She laid the flowers out in a swirling pattern, leaving enough room in the middle of it for herself and her companions. Then she stripped the rosemary from its stems, as the book told her, and sprinkled the little leaves over the rest of the flowers.

"Now the circles?" Misty asked, thumbing to the page in the book.

"The blessing of the Goddess first," Ben said. "That's the most important thing. The other stuff is . . . pizzazz."

Misty held the book closed, her finger on the spell. "How do I call the Goddess? I've never done that before."

"I know how," Dougal said. He handed the cubs to Ben and stepped to Misty in the circle. Matt and Kyle settled down in Ben's big arms, having decided he was a friend.

Dougal took Misty's hands. His were more rawboned than Graham's, but just as large and strong. "Think of deepest moonlight," Dougal said. "Close your eyes, and picture it."

As soon as Misty shut her eyes, she saw moonlight as it had poured into her backyard last night when Graham had lain over her, his weight warming. His eyes had filled with reflected moonlight as he'd thrust into her, his lovemaking rough, but his hands so gentle.

Misty thought she could feel the cool light here in this dim storeroom. A calm stole over her, one sweetly peaceful.

"The Goddess," Dougal said in a soft voice. "Be with us." He twined his fingers more tightly with Misty's. "I ask your blessings to be upon Misty, as she walks the dangerous path."

More peace. A breeze touched her cheek, one so tender Misty wanted to melt. "And on Dougal," Misty said softly. "And the cubs, and Ben."

A sigh, a breath, perhaps a faint laugh. Misty opened her eyes. The sense of the moonlight evaporated, and she stood again in the dingy storeroom, its fluorescent lights flickering.

"Well done," Ben said. He handed the cubs to Dougal. "Now the turning and the chanting. Has to happen. Dougal, stay close to her, so that when she goes through, you do too."

Misty stopped. "No, no, Dougal is staying here. With the cubs. I thought you'd be coming with me," she said to Ben.

Ben shook his head. "The way to Faerie is sealed for me and my kind. Was ages ago. Dougal can protect you—he's stronger than he knows."

"Not the cubs," Misty said firmly. "You can cub-sit."

"Yeah," Dougal agreed, and tried to shove the wolves back at Ben.

Ben took a step back and raised his hands. "Oh, no, you'll need those little guys. Trust me. They're essential."

Dougal and Misty looked at each other. "Graham will take my head off for bringing them," Dougal said, worried.

The two wolves stared up at Misty with perfect confidence. She reached out and petted each of their heads in turn. "Why do you want me to take them?" Misty asked Ben.

Except Ben wasn't there. He was gone, the half-empty shelves in the stockroom silent.

"Crap," Xav said, looking around wildly. "I don't like that guy."

Misty took a cub, Kyle, and cuddled him into the circle of her arm. "Doesn't matter. We might as well take these two," she said, heaving a sigh. "They'd probably just find a way to follow us."

Matt and Kyle wagged tails and squirmed in delight.

Dougal moved his head as Matt started licking his chin. "Why do we have to use this spell? When you went through the basement, and when the cubs did, you didn't have to use flowers and rituals."

"Don't ask me." Misty rubbed the top of Kyle's head. "But if this works, I don't care."

"Crazy Fae shit," Dougal said. "How about we worry about it after we find Graham? Start twirling."

"Clockwise." Misty held Kyle more firmly and turned to her right. Once, twice, three times. "Y-T-S-I-M."

She stopped. The air conditioner clicked on with a rattle. Another light flickered. But they remained in place, flowers scattered around them.

"Is that all?" Dougal asked.

Misty checked the book. "Yes." *No.* Names, those were important, the book said—the difference between what a person was called, and her true name.

Misty closed the book and did the turning again. "A-S-S-S-I-L-E-Mmm . . . Holy *crap.*"

She'd stopped moving but seemed to be still spinning in place. The flowers lifted around her, circling her, petals leading stems. Yellow, blue, violet, yellow, blue, violet. Faster and faster, making her dizzy.

In the blaze of petals and scent—rose, violet, rosemary, forget-me-not—Misty reached out and latched her hand around Dougal's wrist. Xav shouted. Misty felt Xav's warm fingers on her arm, and then they slipped away, disappearing.

The whirlwind increased, the vortex sucking them somewhere. Misty couldn't think or see, hear or smell anymore. She could only feel the steel strength of Dougal's arm under her hand, and the warm body of Kyle against her chest.

The whirling dropped away, the flowers falling at once. Dead, petals and leaves brown.

But scents and color lingered. Misty was in a cave with a smooth black floor, covered in vines of colorful flowers, their scents so strong they were sickening. The fountain she remembered burbled enticingly in the center of the cave.

Other than that, all was quiet. No one was there, not Oison, not Graham. Xav was gone too, left behind. Misty's hand remained on Dougal's arm. He moved closer to her, Matt whimpering.

"Where is he?" Dougal's whisper was loud in the relative silence.

Misty looked around the cave. It was dark, but again lit from above, as though cracks opened to sunlight. If she found the entrance to the cave, would she emerge in the hot Nevada desert? Or someplace strange to her?

"Matt," Dougal said frantically. "Son of a bitch."

Matt had wriggled hard out of Dougal's arms. Kyle kicked free of Misty at the same time and landed on his paws, running as soon as he hit the ground.

"Kyle, Matt!" Misty yelled. "Wait!"

She ran after the two cubs, who were loping off into the darker part of the cave. She jumped over ropes of flowers she swore reached up to grab her as she passed. Dougal came behind, his human snarls changing to wolf's.

The cave went on for a long way. The daylight faded, the only light a strange glow from beneath the fountain's water.

Misty heard Matt and Kyle's yipping ahead. She kicked at a Lady Banks' rose vine trying to wind around her foot, and kept going.

She found Matt and Kyle pawing at a huge mound of flowers. Ropes of stems wound tightly around themselves, topped with vibrant flowers that shone in the eerie light.

Kyle and Matt pawed vigorously, little bodies moving as they tried to shove aside the vines. Whatever was under there, they wanted it.

"Will you listen to me if I tell you to leave it alone?" Misty asked them.

No response. Frantic digging. Yipping that turned into wild howling as soon as they made a hole in the vines.

All Misty's breath went out of her. She fell to her knees, shoving aside the flowers Matt and Kyle had loosened.

Beneath them was Graham's face. His eyes were closed, his skin pale, the scars and shadow of dark beard stark on his bloodless skin.

CHAPTER TWENTY-FIVE

"No!" Dougal shifted back to human even as he dropped beside Misty, his big hands scrabbling to move the vines. "Uncle Graham. *No!*"

His last word ended in a long wail, which held the pathos of a wolf's howl. Dougal lifted his head and cried out to the echoing cave, then he put his hands over his face and bowed his body, rocking in grief.

Misty, her heart pounding until it ached, pulled at the vines over Graham. Graham—this strong, amazing man—couldn't be dead. Couldn't. Seeing him unmoving, not breathing, was a knife to her heart.

"Dougal," she said sharply, trying to cut through his wails. "Help me uncover him."

Dougal raised his head. His face was red and streaked with tears, and he sniffled, unashamed. He unfolded himself enough to pull at the vines.

The flowers were tough, and they fought back. Misty had spent years cutting flowers and sticking them into vases or baskets, where they'd last a while, then wither and die. She had the sickening feeling that the plants were taking their vengeance for all those flowers Misty had used.

"Harvesting flowers helps the whole plant," Misty said firmly to them. "Reinvigorates it, makes more buds."

The vines didn't care. They reached for her, wrapping around her hands and arms, trying to drag her away from Graham.

Dougal, with amazing strength, ripped them away. He growled as he changed into a wolf, a black beast, like Graham, with silver eyes.

Dougal's wolf tore the vines, dragging them out of the way. He revealed Graham's torso, his neck with its Collar, his naked chest, his arms bound by the vines, which followed the lines of his tatts.

Misty put her hand over Graham's heart. Through the pounding of her own pulse, she felt nothing. Barely able to breathe, Misty leaned down and rested her ear against his cold chest.

There. A flutter. A small but strong beat, a long pause, and another beat. Graham's chest rose the slightest bit before falling again.

Misty sat up. "He's alive. Dougal, he's alive!"

Dougal kept tearing away the vines. He didn't acknowledge her announcement but kept pulling, with teeth and claws, growling when a vine proved too tough to move.

The vines holding Graham's arms and legs refused to budge. Dougal and Misty pulled the rest of the flowers away from Graham's chest, but thick, tough stems wrapped his limbs and held him in place.

"Graham." Misty touched his face, patted his cheek. "Graham, wake up."

Graham didn't move. Dougal put one big paw on Graham's chest and shook him, his mournful howls returning.

Through it all, Matt and Kyle remained to one side, as though realizing they couldn't move the vines with their small paws. They sat together now, pressed tightly together, watching as Misty and Dougal tried to wake Graham.

"Now would be a *great* time for Reid to pop in and save the day," Misty said.

She waited, just in case. Nothing happened, no Reid, no response from Graham.

Dougal shifted back to his human form, snarling a little as his limbs jerked. "Reid left us to rot," he said. "Fucking Fae. They all stick together."

Rock clicked together somewhere, as though a spatter of gravel had fallen. Both Misty and Dougal froze, but the sound wasn't repeated.

Misty pulled away several determined vines that had crept back over Graham. "We have to wake him up."

"Don't you think we've been trying?" Dougal growled. "Uncle Graham! Wake the hell up, already!" He shook Graham, hard. Tears trickled from Dougal's eyes again, his fear stark. "He can't die," he sobbed. "I'll be alone."

"No, you won't," Misty said quickly. "You have these little guys. And me. And other Shifters."

Dougal shook his head. "If Graham leaves me alone, the other wolves will kill me. They know I can't lead them."

Misty put her arm around Dougal, then rested her forehead on his bare arm, pulling him into a hug. She'd been around Shifters enough by now to know how a touch and embrace could calm them. Misty stroked Dougal's long back until Dougal quieted a little.

"Graham won't let that happen," she said. "Because we're going to wake him up."

"How?" Dougal went back to his hunkering. "We don't know what's wrong with him. He's Fae-spelled. He's dying."

"Be quiet a minute."

Misty fished around in the fallen vines for her leather-bound book. She opened it, leafing through the pages. A few flowers raised their heads next to her, as though reading with her, which gave her the creeps.

The book had no table of contents and no index. Misty had to turn every page to find out if there was anything in the book that might help at all.

"Here we go." Misty paused on a page about halfway

through the volume. "For enchanted sleep. Did he mean to release from? Or to create?"

Dougal didn't answer, sinking into his own fears again.

"Let's see. Roses—no surprise—all these spells seem to have roses. Irises, a little trickier. Plus honeysuckle. *Blend petals together, mix in water, and sprinkle over the victim.* Hmm. I don't like the sound of 'victim.' *Call down the power of the Father God, and keep the victim warm.* What does that mean? Calling the power of the Father God. Praying?"

Dougal raised his head again, his voice hoarse with his crying. "The Father God is represented by the sun," he said. "Probably means Uncle Graham has to be in sunlight."

The cave was very dark, the patches of sunlight far behind them. "Well, we'll work on that," Misty said. "Plus the water."

The fountain burbled, sounding louder, as though enticing Misty to use it. But the fountain's water was how they'd gotten into this mess in the first place.

One thing at a time. "Flowers, I can do," Misty said. "I see roses, honeysuckle, and even irises. Over there." She pointed to a line of purple and white flowers sticking up from spearlike leaves not far from them.

"You're going to tear up the flowers in here?" Dougal asked. "Are you crazy? They'll try to strangle you."

"They'll have to deal with it. I'm trying this spell." How Misty would find safe water and sunlight, she didn't know, but as she'd told herself, one thing at a time.

"Hey—wait!" Dougal was on his feet, yelling. "Come back here, you little shits!"

Misty scrambled up as well, her fear intensifying. Matt and Kyle were running away, twisting and turning through the vines until they were swallowed in darkness.

"Matt! Kyle! No!" Misty screamed.

Dougal took a step forward, then back again, torn by indecision. "I can't leave you alone," he moaned.

"Yes, you can. Go find them. I'll stay with Graham. There's enough light. You'll make it back." Misty rubbed Dougal's shoulder as he hesitated. "You can do this, Dougal. You know you can. You're his second, remember?"

Dougal took a long breath, drawing himself up at Misty's words. He nodded at her, mouth set in a grim line, then he loped off in the cubs' wake.

Misty sank down again, still clutching the book, as though it were a lifeline.

Graham lay so still it broke her heart. Misty touched his face, trailing her fingertips along the rough of his beard. "I love you," she said quietly. She smiled as she touched his lips. "I love how you can't talk at anything less than a yell. I love how strong you are, and how gorgeous you always look. I love that you growl and snarl but let people laugh at you, especially when you know they're weaker than you are. I love how you agreed to take care of Matt and Kyle, and I love how you take care of Dougal without letting him know it. And I love how you touch me."

Graham didn't move. He lay still, no flush of life in his skin.

Misty drew her hands down to his chest. "When you touch me, I feel alive. I spent my life taking care of other people—I love that now you take care of *me*. You make sure I'm all right before you leave me. I used to think you didn't care when you'd send me home alone, but I know now that if it hadn't been safe for me to go, you wouldn't have let me. You'd have come with me or sent someone to make sure I was all right."

Misty ran her fingers over Graham's Collar, which was bone cold. "You snarl at me because I always want to talk, and then you let me do it. And you listen, even when you pretend not to." She leaned down and kissed his cool lips. "That's why I love you, Graham McNeil," she said. "Because you're a good man, even though you pretend not to be. You take me for who I am, and don't want me to be anything else." Another kiss. "And you make me feel so wonderful, I could lie in your arms forever. And I will." Misty kissed him again, gently, savoring the satin feel of his lips. "As soon as I wake you up, get you free, and take you home."

Misty heard scampering claws and Dougal's irritated tones, and the wolf cubs ran back to her. Dougal carried a backpack that he dropped at Misty's feet. Inside were sports bottles of water, along with bags of chips and a few candy bars.

Misty grabbed for a water bottle. "Where did you get this stuff?"

"The cubs. When I found them, they were dragging this between them."

The two wolves were wagging tails, clumsily digging into the bag to pull out various packets of chips. Misty eyed them severely. The cubs seemed to be able to walk the ley lines without spells, and she knew where they'd found the stuff.

"Did you two go back to the convenience store and take this out of the stockroom?" she asked. "That's stealing."

Kyle started yipping then changed to his human form to answer her. "We didn't take it *out* of the stockroom. We came on the ley line back here. So, it's sorta still *in* the store, right?"

"Not if you eat it," Misty said to Matt, who'd clawed open a bag of chips. But she needed what they'd brought too much to put much heart in her scolding.

Misty opened one of the waters and took a drink. It tasted clean with just a hint of plastic, as commercially bottled water normally did. She remembered the unbelievable clarity of the Fae water she'd drunk, and took another pull of the warm bottled water. She'd take the plastic taste anytime.

Matt had his head and half his body inside the big bag of chips, crunching happily, tail wagging. Misty handed the water bottle to Dougal. "Hold this. It's time for these flowers to give back."

She got to her feet. She'd feel better if she had a good set of shears and some gloves, but she'd have to do what she could with her bare hands.

Misty had never before cut flowers that fought back, and she hoped to heaven she never had to again. She grabbed at the yellow Lady Banks' rose that had tried to trip her before—its vines twined around her arms, thorns out. Blood dripped from her fingers, but Misty relentlessly seized blossoms and stripped three of their petals. The petals fell, inert, to the floor, though the vines still tried to grip her.

Dougal helped her fight her way free. Once Misty stopped trying to harvest the petals, the rose vines snaked away, lying still.

"They're only plants," she said in a loud voice. "Able to move on their own, but without a true mind to guide them. Instinct only."

Dougal pointed to the petals. "What do I do with these?"

Misty started sweeping them into a pile. "Find something for me to put them in."

Dougal looked around and came up with a shallow stone that was slightly concave. Misty piled the petals on it, then made her way across the vines to the irises.

The irises didn't fight her as much as the roses had, though the leaves mindlessly tried to drive themselves into her skin. Kyle, who'd followed her, yapped at the plant while Misty pulled off the blossoms, separating the mouthlike petals. The honeysuckles tried to entwine her when she plucked off the flowers, but these vines at least lacked thorns. They were strong, though. Dougal had to help rip her free.

Misty piled the petals on the stone, mixed them together, and poured water from the sports bottle over them. The runny, petal-y mush was pungent.

"How do I call the power of the Father God?" Misty asked. "The cracks for the sun are a long way from here."

"Um." Dougal sank down on his knees, gently pushing Matt aside to go through the backpack. Matt sat on his haunches, still crunching, his whiskers full of salt and chip dust. Kyle whined at him.

"Here." Dougal grinned in triumph and folded down a zipped pocket of the backpack. "Mirror." He ripped a small square mirror free of the stitching that held it in place.

"Will that be big enough? How far can light reflect?"

"Hang on." Dougal got to his feet and jogged away, his step exuberant. He came back wearing his jeans again, his wallet in his hands. "There's a little piece of mirror in here," he said. "Came with the wallet. Maybe we can set up a relay."

"You work on that—the cubs can help you. I'll do the sprinkling and try to get Graham free of these vines."

Dougal saluted her, a mirror in each hand. "You heard her, kids. Help Uncle Dougal. Matt, stop *eating.*"

Matt shook himself free of another bag of chips and trotted off after Dougal and Kyle. Misty mixed the petals in the water with her hands, then lifted the mess and dribbled it over Graham's body.

Water pattered down to bead on his skin. Roses and the wet stamens of honeysuckle, the purple and white streaked petals of iris dropped on him, sticking to his chest and arms, curling around his tatts. Misty knew Graham was truly out then, because he'd have snarled at *flowers* covering his tatts.

Something bright flashed into Misty's eyes. Dougal's voice carried across the cave. "Hold it still, move it to the right. The *right.* No, the other right. Goddess."

The light moved around wildly, winking in the darkness. A wavering beam slid onto Graham's body, faint but clear.

"There!" Misty shouted at him. "It's touching him."

"Now call the blessing," Dougal yelled back.

"What do I say?"

"Keep it simple. *The blessings of the Father God be upon you.*"

"The blessings of the Father God be upon you, Graham," Misty repeated quickly.

Her words drifted into silence. The beam wavered again, spearing the wall and falling onto a strand of vine. The vine shrank away from the reflection, receding into the wall. Weird, Misty thought dimly, because plants usually tried to push their way *toward* sunlight.

Somewhere in the darkness, she heard little voices say, "Hold it still." "*You're* moving it." "I am not!"

Misty started scooping more water and blossoms onto Graham, every drop, every petal. "Damn it, Graham. *Wake up!*"

The vines around Graham jerked. Misty sucked in a breath. The vine flowers watching her trembled, light flashed over them wildly as the twins struggled with each other over the mirrors.

The ground shook a little, the earth giving a groan before it went silent again. Graham's eyes popped open.

Misty stilled, hands balling into fists, droplets of water snaking down her wrists.

Graham's gray eyes were blank, unseeing, but his chest heaved upward as he took a deep breath.

Sunlight from the mirrors hit him straight in the face. Graham's fists balled, and he jerked his arms open, snapping a few vines that held him.

He sat up, dirty, wet, and coated with flower petals. His eyes cleared, and he looked down at his body, then up at Misty.

"Misty!" Graham roared in a voice that brought more pebbles down from the ceiling. "What the *fuck* are you doing here?"

CHAPTER TWENTY-SIX

Graham was weak. Dying—he knew it. The only thing that had kept him from going insane while the vines smothered him was the thought that Misty was safe.

Now Misty sat next to him, looking pleased with herself. She had dirt and yellow pollen smeared all over her, her hair a scraggly mess, and a big smile on her face.

Graham never seen her so beautiful.

"What the hell are you doing?" Graham demanded. "This is my fight. Get out of here."

"A fight you're losing. Why did you sneak off like that?"

"I didn't sneak off. I was summoned."

Misty lost her smile. "Leaving in the middle of the night without telling anyone is sneaking off."

"Stubborn little . . . I told Reid. And he told you, the asshole. He was supposed to keep you home and not let you come after me. He's dead meat."

"Reid didn't tell me anything. He left me a note . . . It's a long story."

"Misty did a spell," Matt said, running up to them. "She

spun around and around, and then we were here." Matt demonstrated.

"And you brought the cubs?"

"Yes," Misty said. "Stop yelling. You'll cause a cave-in."

A few more pebbles rained from the ceiling. Another faint groan sounded, as though rock shifted.

"I want you out of here," Graham said.

Misty didn't wilt under his glare. No, she knelt there looking all pretty and sexy. "We came to get *you* out. I have a lot to tell you, but we can talk later."

"Later? That will be a first. Usually you want to talk without delay."

"Very funny, Graham. Can you break away?"

"I've been trying. Then I got covered with the damn vines and passed out."

"Enchanted sleep," Misty said. "You were in an enchanted sleep. I got you out of it, you know, like in *Sleeping Beauty*."

Matt laughed. "Uncle Graham is Sleeping Beauty."

Graham grabbed at the vines that held him, but he'd lost so much strength he could barely budge them. Uncle Graham was more screwed than anything else.

"I can't leave," Graham said, even as he tugged at the vines.

"What are you talking about? Why not?" Misty grabbed the vines and pulled too.

Dougal materialized out of the darkness, holding a mirror in one hand, a wolf cub in the other. Graham thought he'd scented his nephew over there. He wanted to start roaring again, but he stopped himself. Yelling would only upset Dougal, and Dougal needed to keep calm and not go to pieces.

"I can't go, because Reid is trapped." Graham tore away another vine that had rewrapped his wrist. The fact that he was too weak to do much about it worried the hell out of him.

"He's trapped too?" Misty looked dismayed. "Where?"

"In the ice."

Misty stood up, which gave Graham a nice view of her

legs in her shorts. Her skin was scratched and abraded, but even that couldn't mar her. Some of the scratches were from last night with her, when Graham had made hot pounding love to her in her garden. The thought of doing that again someday was one thing that kept him from crumbling and dying as Oison wanted him to.

"Where?" Misty started walking away, toward the sheet of ice.

"Misty." Graham sat up, jerking at the vines. They still wouldn't let him go. Dougal tried to help, but to no avail.

"He's in *there*?" Misty stopped, horrified. "Is he dead?"

"Hell if I know."

Dougal kept trying to free Graham, starting to moan when he couldn't. Graham had to switch his attention to bolstering Dougal's confidence. When he looked back at Misty, she was leafing through a book.

Must be her little book about flowers. The one that had gotten him drunk on tequila, making him take another step in his relationship with Misty.

"There's nothing in here about melting ice," she said in frustration. "Or breaking ice. Nothing about ice at all."

"Anything about water?" Graham asked. "Oison said his element was water. Reid's is earth."

Misty turned pages, rustling in the stillness. "I don't know. Damn it."

Dougal called out to her. "Anything about making plants stop messing with us?"

More rustling. "Let me look. Why are they doing this anyway? I mean, they're *flowers*. Plants aren't magical or sentient. Their 'magic' is converting sunlight, water, and soil into food and oxygen. Photosynthesis. These plants shouldn't be alive at all. No sunlight, and these are all sun-loving flowers."

"But this is Faerie," Graham said. "So magical shit works. All the stories about magical creatures originated here. The stories are watered down in the human world, but the original incidents weren't."

"Oh." Misty looked back at Graham, her face losing

some color. "So all the scary stories about frost queens and witches putting children in ovens are true?"

"Yep."

"That's disturbing." Misty went back to her book, as though determined to find something to protect her from every fairy tale ever written.

"Why the hell are Kyle and Matt here?" Graham demanded. Kyle was trying to help pull away the vines, while Matt was busy licking the ground around a crumpled bag of what used to be chips.

"Ben said they had to come." Dougal shrugged. "I don't know why."

"Ben?" Graham roared. "Goddess, get me loose. I need to strangle some people."

"Here we go!" Misty actually jumped in delight, her feet leaving the ground. "*To train plants.* I thought it meant pruning. It kind of does." She started moving excitedly to the nearest clump of plants. "Matt, Kyle, Dougal, I need petals from every single type of plant here. All of them. Don't miss one."

Her legs moved as she ran about the cave, grabbing flowers and yanking petals free. She moved so fast the vines that reached for her didn't have time to latch on before she was at another plant. Matt and Kyle, turning human so they could hold the petals, ran every which way, making a game of it.

"I got the red one!" "No, I saw it first." "You can have the purple one. I got yellow!"

Dougal stayed put, pulling futilely at the vines that refused to let Graham loose.

"Help them," Graham said, keeping his voice firm but gentle. "If Misty's right, then she'll get me free. Go on. She needs you."

Dougal shook his head, still tugging. As a cub, when he'd been lost in his own fear and misery, Dougal would fix on a task and not be able to stop. Graham, the best he could, put his hand on Dougal's arm.

"I need you to take care of her for me," he said. "If something happens to Misty . . . I might as well die here."

Dougal looked up at him, meeting Graham's gaze for a fleeting moment. "You really are going to mate with her?"

"I am. Definitely."

"Good." Dougal gave Graham a nod, seeming to take heart from Graham's statement. He finally let go of the vines and leveraged himself to his feet, then with a final look at Graham, walked away to find Misty.

"Now help me put them in a pile," Misty said to the cubs. "Good. You've found so many, both of you. Let's see. One missing. Hyacinth." She looked around. "I'll get it."

Graham felt his compulsion spell kick in as Misty went toward the purple plants, a spring in her step. He knew, deep in his burning blood, that Oison was coming.

He rose as far as he could in the tangling vines. Dizziness smacked him, along with his Collar's shocks. "Misty!"

The earth groaned again. Dirt rained from above, more than before. Maybe this cave was about to give, burying them all.

As Misty reached for the lavender flowers rising from leggy stalks, Oison appeared right next to her. He raised his sword and brought it down sharply toward her neck.

Graham bellowed and fought the vines. Matt launched himself at Oison, shifting to wolf cub as he went. As the sword came down, he latched himself on to Oison's arm, foiling his aim. Kyle, also wolf now, slammed into Misty, making her sidestep. She lost hold of the hyacinths and fell, and Oison's sword swished over her, missing.

Oison, silent with rage, plucked Matt from his arm and threw him across the cave. Matt landed heavily on his back, cried out in a pathetic whimper, and went still. Kyle, yipping, ran to him.

Oison raised his sword again, but this time, Misty scrambled out of the way. Dougal was there, reaching for Oison. His hands went out as Oison swung, catching the blade. Dougal screamed as the Fae-spelled sword cut his skin. His Collar went off, snapping and sparking, Dougal continuing to scream.

Misty lunged for the purple plants again, grabbing a handful. She raced to her pile of petals in the middle of the cave, threw the hyacinths down, and lifted her book.

Oison shoved Dougal from him. Dougal fell, moving in pain, his Collar continuing to spark. Oison headed for Misty, who was walking around and around her clump of flowers.

"By east and west, by north and south," Misty read in a loud voice. *"By wind and water, fire and earth. By the Goddess and moonlight, by the God and sunlight—I command you to do my will."*

Oison was almost upon her, but Misty kept walking. She lifted the book. "I command you to do my will!"

The petals swirled with her passing, rising a little, then moved faster. Faster still. A vortex of them rushed around her, encasing Misty in its tornado.

The vortex of petals reached all the way to the ceiling. Then they exploded, bursting over the entire cave, raining down like colorful snowflakes. They carpeted the ground, spilling over the vines, the black obsidian, Oison, the fallen Dougal, Matt, and Kyle.

As soon as the petals started to fall, Misty sprinted back to Graham. "Let him go!" she yelled at the vines.

They shivered, leaves and flowers shaking. Then they withdrew, unwinding from Graham and releasing him.

Misty stared, her mouth open. "It worked!" She shouted in delight. "I can't believe it—it actually worked! I'm going to give Ben a big fat kiss when I see him again."

"The hell you will." Graham tried to pull himself up, but he fell again, weak and exhausted.

But Oison was coming. The Fae kicked aside vines and raised his sword again, swinging it hard at Misty.

Graham caught Oison's wrist, and the blade swung and met Graham's thick upper arm. Snarling, Graham let it cut him to the bone as he twisted Oison away from Misty, Graham's Collar sparking hard. He tried to change to his between-beast as he fought, his strongest form, but Graham found he couldn't shift at all. The sword, and his shocking Collar, combined to take the last of his strength.

Oison ripped himself from Graham's bloody grasp, and Graham fell to his knees.

Misty screamed at the plants, and pointed at Oison. "Take *him*, take *him*!"

The plants moved sinuously toward Oison, the vines that had held Graham prisoner now seeking the Fae. But too slowly. Oison spun out of their way, his black eyes filled with rage, and brought his sword down on them. The vines he severed shuddered, then turned brown and crumpled away.

Oison went for the source of his frustration—Misty. Across the cave, Dougal tried to rise, tried to help. Graham forced himself to his feet, dizzy and dying. But he'd stop the bastard from hurting Misty. No matter what.

The cave shook again, the earth emitting another groan. Rock and sand poured from the ceiling, hitting the flowers and obsidian, the Shifters and Misty, Oison. Dust rose to coat the air. Graham heard Oison cursing, which told Graham the tremors weren't of Oison's making.

The sheet of ice that held Reid cracked with the sound of a gunshot. Graham turned to it as the ice fell away in huge chunks, not so much exploding as pushing outward and shattering on the cave floor.

As the ice splintered into needlelike shards and more rock from the wall fell, Reid walked out from the rubble. His clothes were shredded, he had blood all over him, and he was mad as hell.

Reid shouted something in a language that was guttural and harsh, unintelligible to Graham. Oison, on the other hand, whipped around, his sword raised. Oison had stark fear in his eyes, which Graham would enjoy if he didn't feel so crappy.

Reid went for Oison. He bounded across the cave on his runner's legs, hands outstretched, those odd-sounding words pouring from him. Oison met him, swinging his sword. Reid shouted again, and the rocks that had blown out with the ice rose up at his command.

The plants were still going for Oison as well. They tangled his legs as Reid's rocks came down on top of the Fae.

Oison swung his sword at Reid, and rocks clanked against the blade. Oison whirled his sword again, and disappeared. Reid snarled something and disappeared with him.

The rocks were still spinning in midair. They stopped abruptly as soon as Reid vanished, raining down onto the cave, clacking against the obsidian.

"Time to go," Graham said. "Misty, help me with Dougal."

Dougal was still rolling in pain, his moans turning to wolf howls. He'd shifted again to human by the time Graham and Misty reached him.

"Come on." Graham thrust his arm under Dougal, lifting his nephew to his feet.

Dougal jerked away. "No, I have to help Matt."

"We'll both help him. But we need to move."

Graham had struggled to learn the exact combination of compassion and command to bump Dougal out of his despair. Dougal finally nodded and let Graham help him around the writhing vines.

The plants had drawn back from the two cubs, encircling them but not touching them. Misty leaned down and picked up Matt's limp body.

"He's alive," she said in relief. "But he's hurt."

"I should have made them stay at Misty's," Dougal said. He hung on to Graham, his face wet with blood and tears. "Damn it."

Misty cuddled Matt close and lifted Kyle, who was a whimpering ball of fur. "I don't think these little guys would have listened."

"We'll never get out." Dougal rubbed his hand over his face, crazed with fear. "He'll trap us here."

Before Graham could answer, Misty said, "Yes, we will. We're family. We can do anything."

Dougal blinked at her. "What are you talking about? We're not pack."

"Doesn't matter. Graham brought you up, and he's Matt's

and Kyle's honorary father. And I'm his girlfriend. Close enough."

"And you're going to accept his mate-claim," Dougal said with conviction.

"Can we talk about this *outside* this cave?" Misty tucked the two cubs firmly against her, gentleness itself. "Time to run, I think."

Graham chuckled as he helped Dougal, half supporting himself on his nephew at the same time. "Hear that? Misty, for once, doesn't want to talk."

"Suck it up, Graham," she said.

Graham's laughter echoed against the cave walls, which were still too damn eerie for his taste. He made himself follow Misty's cute butt through the darkness to the ley line, wherever it came out, and decided he'd follow that gorgeous ass anywhere.

They came out in the basement of the unfinished Shifter house. The ley line, Misty surmised, must decide its own direction, or else they didn't know how to navigate it. She hoped Reid, chasing Oison, was all right.

Misty emerged into the basement, blinking at full afternoon sunlight. They must have been in the cave for hours. Kyle shivered in her arms, Matt too limp.

Graham and Dougal supported each other behind her, both of them growling in irritation. The sound gave Misty heart. When Graham and Dougal were arguing, they were fine.

But they weren't. Dougal had been cut by Oison's sword, Graham still under his spell. Matt was hurt, possibly dying.

She climbed awkwardly up the ladder first, supported by Graham. She had to hold Matt, and had Kyle clinging to her shoulder, so the going was slow.

When she reached the top, she knew there was something very wrong in Shiftertown. Shifters were everywhere, and humans milled among them, wearing black fatigues and carrying automatic weapons.

But these weren't DX Security men. She didn't recognize any of them, and behind them, in the heat, she heard sirens and saw flashing red and blue lights.

"Damn," Graham said softly, and he disappeared back down into the dark basement. Misty started to follow, but too late. One of the humans had seen her, and they were running her way.

CHAPTER TWENTY-SEVEN

"What the fuck?" Graham said in the darkness behind Misty.

Misty stood straight at the top of the ladder, holding on to the cubs, trying to pretend she hadn't been down in a hole under a Shifter house, a hole that wasn't supposed to be there.

The human soldiers reached her, along with Diego and Eric. "Misty," Eric said in a loud voice. "There you are. See?" he said to the soldier in the lead. "Here she is. You all right, Misty? Where've you been?"

"Umm." Misty looked around, trying to assess the situation before she answered. "I was looking after the cubs?" She let the statement end with a questioning note. Eric nodded once, subtly, and Misty put on a smile. "You know how they like to run off."

Diego was looking hard at her, his eyes, so much like Xav's, holding warning. What kind of warning, Misty had no idea.

"Yeah, they do like to play," Eric said. "And get into so much trouble. You know how kids are." Eric gave the lead soldier his laid-back smile. "Thanks for bringing them home, Misty."

"Not a problem."

Eric had glanced into the basement, his eyes flickering when he saw Graham. He moved his body a little, barely changing his stance, but Misty knew enough about Shifters now to realize he must be saying something to Graham without opening his mouth. Shifters were masters of nonverbal communication. Misty wished she could read the signals, because she was swimming in the dark here.

One of the armed men turned to Eric. "What's down there?"

Eric shrugged. "Don't know. I'm not into construction. Where the plumbing and electricity will go, maybe?" He gave the perfect impression of a man who might be strong but kind of slow.

"Sir?" The man turned to Diego with a lot more deference.

Diego also shrugged. "Same answer. I really don't know. You'd have to ask the construction team."

"We need to lock it down," The soldier who seemed to be in charge said. "Corporal, take a team and check it out."

One of the younger men signaled to another, shouldered his weapon, and started down the metal ladder to the basement.

Misty glanced down in alarm, but saw no sign of Graham or Dougal. They'd vanished.

"Are these the ones who've been missing?" the commander asked Diego, gesturing at Misty. Diego gave him a grim nod.

"Missing?" Misty asked as Eric reached for Kyle. Kyle clung to his arm, a wolf cub, looking fearfully back at Misty and Matt. "We're not missing." Misty tried her smile again. "We're right here."

The commander answered. "Your mother in L.A. called in a missing-persons report on Melissa Granger five days ago. Said she couldn't get into contact with you, and your neighbors said you left with a Shifter at that time and haven't

been home since. Business owners around your store say
Shifters have been at your shop, but no one has seen you."
He looked her over, from her tank top and shorts, torn and
covered with dirt, to her scratched and gouged legs and
arms. "So you need to tell me, ma'am, exactly where you've
been and what happened to you."

Misty listened, her lips parting. "Five days . . . ?"

More humans came hurrying to join the commander, these
looking more like paramedics. One caught Misty by the arm
and tried to lead her toward an open ambulance. "We need to
check you out," the paramedic said. "Make sure you're all
right. Commander, interrogate her once we've taken her vitals
and given her some water, all right?"

"Five days?" Misty couldn't help repeating.

"You went through an ordeal," the paramedic suggested. "But you're fine now. We'll take care of you and get
you away from these Shifters. It will be all right."

"Wait." Misty held Matt closer. "This one's hurt more
than me. He needs help."

Eric reached for Matt and took him out of Misty's arms.
Kyle wriggled in Eric's arms, trying to lick his brother's
face. "Poor little guy."

"You need to come with us, ma'am," the paramedic
said, in his stern but friendly voice.

"I'm not hurt that much," Misty tried. "I—"

She broke off as a familiar man with broad shoulders
but not much height reached to Eric for Matt. "I'll take the
cub." Ben gave a wide smile to the commander. "I'm a vet,"
he said. "I specialize in Shifters."

Ben really did have a reassuring smile, in spite of his
prison tatts and once-broken nose. Plus, he didn't wear a
Collar, and obviously wasn't Shifter.

"I'll have to clear this," the commander said, not changing expression.

"Sure you do," Ben said. "My name's Ben Williams.
Look me up. I'm ex-con but served all my time. Now I take
care of animals."

If Ben truly was a veterinarian, this was the first Misty

had heard of it. Eric, however, seemed perfectly sanguine to hand Matt to him.

Ben leaned near Misty as he carefully took Matt, his movement putting him between Misty and the impatient paramedic. "Misty, you need to blow the basement."

Misty blinked at him. "Sorry?"

"Cave it in." Ben kept his voice quiet, his face set only in compassion for the cubs. "Bury the ley line; close the portal. Humans will be screwed if they find it, and Shifters will be screwed if these guys find the basement."

Misty understood the why. What she didn't know was . . . "How?"

"Roots," Ben said. "You did the mastering spell. I can see it in you."

"But . . ." Dougal and Graham might still be down there.

"Do it," Ben said. He straightened up, a cub on each arm. "I'll take care of these cuties."

He walked away.

Misty stared after him, the man looking no less human than the soldiers around her. But then, Ben had written the book, more than a hundred years ago, he'd told Misty how to use it, and to trust herself. He'd been right every time.

Was Graham still down there, hiding with Dougal? Why was he? Only one way to find out.

Misty gasped and slapped at her pockets. "My cell phone. I dropped it." She stared wildly at the hole behind her, then before the commander could reach for her, she swung around onto the ladder and descended to the basement.

She saw no sign of Graham or Dougal anywhere. They could be hiding, or they could have gone back through the ley line to the cave.

Misty darted under the darkness, but it was too intense after the first few feet out of the sunshine for her to see anything. "Graham," she whispered.

No answer. He was gone, Dougal with him.

"Corporal, find her," the commander snapped.

Roots. Misty looked up. The Shifters who'd dug out this cellar had carefully left the earth around the house whole above it. The basement ran a long way underground, well past the house for which it was intended. The planted trees as well as the native brush were intact above it.

Desert shrubs might look fragile and could even appear dried out and dead, but in truth they were tough and hardy. They had to burrow deep into the earth in search of ground-water and rain runoff in order to survive, and their root systems were extensive and strong. The plants could live for years in dormancy, looking dead from above. Then, after a good rain, the plant would become green and vibrant, beautiful and blooming. It would drop its seeds, which would lie in wait in the shade of the parent plant, until that life-giving water found them.

The part of the desert plant below ground was giant and complex, never seen, but networking through the ground in a powerful mesh.

Misty studied the tendrils sticking out of the ceiling above her and the wall around her. She thought of how she'd controlled the vines in the Fae cave, but she had no idea if the book's spell would work here.

But then, this basement was on a ley line, and in Faerie, magic was real. She agreed with Ben that she needed to collapse it—this place was dangerous for humans and Shifters alike, and humans didn't need to ask questions about why the hole was here in the first place.

Misty took a breath, and took a risk. "Pull it down," she said to the roots.

"Ma'am." The corporal behind her was polite but firm. "You need to come with me."

"Now," Misty whispered.

Nothing happened. Misty clenched her jaw and turned around. She knew if she tried to evade the soldiers any longer, they might question her too closely—where she'd been, how she'd been injured, who she'd been with, what was down here . . . She'd been gone *five days*? She needed to get with Ben and interrogate *him.*

"Oh, well," Misty said, giving the corporal a helpless little smile. "I guess I can always get a new phone."

A root moved. Rustled. Another trembled. As Misty stopped to look up, the entire mass of roots began to vibrate, and clods of earth came down.

Misty backed up swiftly. The corporal grabbed her by the shoulders at the same time and pushed her to the ladder. As Misty climbed ahead of him, her legs shaking, the entire ceiling of the basement caved in, pulling with it a line of trees, bushes, and the foundations of the house that was being built over it.

The ladder shuddered and started to collapse. Eric reached down from the top and grabbed Misty, hauling her up just as the ladder broke into several pieces. The corporal tried to hang on and pull himself up, but falling dirt and rock carried him back down, his hands struggling for purchase.

Eric pushed Misty at Diego, flowed into his snow leopard form, clothes falling away, and went for the hole. He climbed with feline grace down into the avalanche, grabbed the corporal by the back of the shirt, and hauled him up again. Eric's claws scrabbled on the shifting dirt, his muscles straining, as the hole continued to fall in around him.

Finally, Eric leapt like the cat he was, landing on firm ground, and dragged the corporal well away from the hole before he released him.

Behind them, the basement disappeared, a rush of broken foundation, dirt, rock, and trees filling it in.

Graham. Misty looked at the wreckage of the basement she'd stood in a few moments ago, wondering if she'd just buried alive the man she loved.

"Five days," Misty said to Diego as he walked her across the common yards after the paramedics had checked her. Xav had arrived while the paramedics were assuring themselves she was unhurt, his handsome face showing his relief.

"Reid told me that time moves differently inside Faerie," Diego said as they walked. "I guess we have to believe him. You've been gone five days, your mother called your brother, who is also worried sick. Since none of us knew where you were, we couldn't help."

Xav shook his head. "I couldn't exactly explain that you disappeared from a convenience store stockroom in a whirl of flowers. And I couldn't follow. Why couldn't I? I was standing right next to you."

Misty shook her head. "I don't know." She broke off, feeling the press of Xavier's shoulder holster against her. "Wait, maybe because you were carrying a gun. Iron. Maybe it didn't let that through. Reid could come in with a tire iron, because he's an ironmaster."

"Yeah, well, Reid is missing too," Xav said. "Peigi is about to go postal. My guys practically camped out at the convenience store, but we couldn't follow you, and I couldn't find that Ben guy. Trust me, I looked. And then he turns up here today, out of the blue."

Diego regarded Misty sharply. "What happened to Dougal and Graham?"

"I don't know." Misty's breath hitched. She wanted to break down and sob, sink to the ground and bury her face in her hands. "He was behind me in the basement. And then I—"

"Shh." Xav went to her and put a comforting arm around her. "Knowing Graham, he found another way out. I've learned that Shifter spaces are more complicated than just holes in the ground."

Misty wiped her eyes. "But I don't know. What do I do?"

"It's tough being in love with a Shifter," Diego said, his dark eyes quiet. "Trust me. They're wild and crazy, and wild and crazy things happen to them. But it's worth it. We'll find him. Shifters are hard to kill."

"But not impossible."

"I know." Diego gave her a sympathetic nod. "Stick as close as you can to the truth. I'll be there, and so will Xav. We can fill in the blanks."

"Thanks, Diego. Is my brother all right?"

"Fine. Paul's at your store, helping put it back together. Keeps saying if he doesn't, you'll come back and yell at him. It kept him from worrying. Xav has already called him and told him you're all right."

"Now he'll yell at *me*." Misty smiled. "I'm looking forward to it." She took a breath as they neared the knot of soldiers waiting to question her. "When they're done with me, I'm grilling Ben. He's got Matt and Kyle, and probably some answers, which he's going to give me, whether he likes it or not."

Graham found himself stumbling into bright light and high heat. He'd pulled Dougal with him as he'd tried to find the ley line again. Dougal was collapsing against him, his Collar shocking at random.

He'd hauled Dougal all the way to the back of the cellar. They'd been there when Misty had come and called to him. Graham had opened his mouth to answer, and found himself breathing dirt. The ceiling had started coming down, the dirt wall behind him seeming to open to suck him in.

It had spit him out through a crack in rocks, and now bright desert sunshine poured over them. He'd expected to land back in the obsidian cave—a place he never wanted to see again—but he was on a ridge in the desert, overlooking the abandoned mine and the shack, with Dougal's bike still parked beside it.

"At least we have transportation," Graham said.

Or tried to say. His throat was so dry, his thirst so great, his words stuck and wouldn't come out. He was weak, and Dougal was only half-conscious, his hand still bleeding from the Fae sword. It wouldn't be blood loss that killed him, but the Fae spells in the sword.

The thirst and their state told Graham that Oison was still alive. The Fae's spell would have died with him.

I hope Reid gets the bastard. Graham decided against

speaking the words out loud, saving strength and whatever moisture was left in his body.

They'd die out here though. If he couldn't get Dougal someplace safe, both of them would go.

Not Shiftertown, not right now. Graham wouldn't worry about holding his own against the Shifter Bureau's soldiers, but Dougal didn't need to be interrogated by them right now, not when he was hurt. Dougal would go to pieces. No, they needed to lie low, heal, and then decide what to do.

Misty, I love you.

Graham wasn't afraid to admit it anymore. He needed Misty in his life, as his mate, as his love.

He'd make her see that she needed to accept his mate-claim, and they'd live happily ever after. As happy as she could be shacked up with a Shifter, and sharing a house with Graham's nephew with confidence problems and two cubs who liked to tear the place down.

He dragged Dougal into the shade of the shed before he made for the motorcycle, hoping there was still gas in it.

Rock clicked behind him, and Oison appeared. This time he was in his guise of the hiker, in T-shirt, shorts, and hiking boots. He looked ordinary and evil at the same time.

Graham stood up. "I'm not being your battle beast," he said. "Not bringing other Shifters to you, not training to be in your army."

"I know." Oison said. He drew out his sword from the long pack humans would assume was for hiking poles or camping gear. "I gambled on making you a slave, because you're a strong leader and could pull other Shifters to me. But it looks like you're going to be a bad slave."

"Damn right," Graham said.

"I can barely control you. Therefore, I came to a decision." Oison hefted his sword. "I will kill you, and take your nephew instead."

CHAPTER TWENTY-EIGHT

The commander questioned Misty for a long time before he finally let her go. Diego and Xav had stood by her, the only ones allowed to stay with her, because they were human.

Misty, Diego, and Xav had come up with the story that the cubs had tried to run away—somewhat true—and Misty had gone after them, worried they'd get hurt. They'd led her out into the desert, where they'd all gotten lost. They'd found a cave to stay out of the sun, and there Matt had gotten hurt.

Why hadn't she called anyone? the commander asked. Her cell phone hadn't worked out there, Misty said. How did they survive? She'd brought plenty of water with her and snacks, knowing that Kyle and Matt, as wolves, liked to run off as far as they could. They'd been used to living half-wild up in Elko, and didn't understand they couldn't do that here. They were just little kids, weren't they? So everyone should cut them a break. How did she get back? Walked to the road and hitchhiked in. She'd been bringing the cubs, Matt hurt, back to Shiftertown when the soldiers had spotted her.

Xav and Diego confirmed everything she said.

Xav walked away with her to look for Ben while Diego stayed with the commander. The soldiers, who'd been sent by the Shifter Bureau, weren't leaving, it seemed. Someone had called in an anonymous tip this morning, Xav told her, that not all Shifters' Collars were working. Eric was being questioned about that now, surrounded by the soldiers. Xav had no idea who'd called in the tip, but Misty had a bad feeling about it.

Oison had vanished from the cave before Graham, Misty, Dougal, and the cubs had fled. Had Oison stirred up trouble with the human government as part of his efforts to control Shifters? Graham in particular? Oison had disappeared not long before they'd run out of the cave, but if time moved differently in Faerie, as Diego had told her, maybe Oison had emerged hours before they did.

Xav queried other Shifters as they went about Ben and the cubs—Lindsay said she'd seen a weird guy with both cubs headed for Graham's. She'd wanted to follow and make sure all was well, but the soldiers had pulled her aside to speak to her. Lindsay looked worried, not her usual laughing self. She put her hand on Xav's arm as she answered, and what was in her eyes told Misty that maybe she'd reconsidered pushing Xav away.

Misty thanked her and hurried away, pretending not to notice Xav lingering to stay with Lindsay.

As she approached Graham's house, Misty heard yelling. A woman on Graham's front walk was loudly telling three soldiers what they could do with themselves as they surrounded her and tried to cuff her.

Misty recognized Jan, the Lupine woman who'd attacked Misty after she'd spent the night with Graham. Jan's blustering was to cover her fear, Misty realized. Misty remembered that Jan's Collar hadn't gone off when she'd gone for Misty—perhaps she was one of the Shifters whose Collars didn't work right. If the humans discovered Jan wore a Collar that didn't stop her from violence, what would they do? Fit her with a new one? Cage her? Or worse?

Misty sped her steps to take her into the path of the soldiers and Jan. Jan saw Misty, and fury entered her eyes along with the fear.

"Come to gloat?" Jan demanded.

"Where are you taking her?" Misty asked the soldiers, ignoring Jan.

"To have her Collar tested," he said. "All Shifters are. Orders."

"Huh." Misty put her hands on her hips and gave Jan a disgusted look. "You don't have to test *that* one. It's real, all right."

"Why do you say that, ma'am?" the soldier asked, trying not to look irritated.

"Because I got into a fight with her the other day," Misty said. "She's jealous as hell. Her Collar started crackling before she even got in a punch at me. I smacked her a good one, and she ran off. Believe me, the Collar worked. The sparks got me—they *stung*."

Jan kept struggling. "Bitch," she yelled at Misty.

"See?" Misty said, wrinkling her nose. "She doesn't like me much. Thinks I stole her Shifter."

The soldier looked Misty up and down, his gaze lingering on the skin bared by her sleeveless top and shorts. "Why would you go out with one of them?" he asked. "Ma'am."

"For the sex." Misty smiled at him. "Try it sometime."

One of the other soldiers laughed. "She's not wrong."

The soldier holding Jan released her and stepped back. "How about we go after some of the more docile ones?" he asked his colleagues. "This is going to take forever as it is."

As soon as Jan found herself free, she took off, running in her long-legged stride. The first man gave Misty another once-over. "You get tired of Shifters, come and find me. I'm at the Shifter Bureau attached to the air base."

Misty only smiled at him and walked away. She heard the other soldiers' voices as they tramped on. "You don't have a shot with her," one said, laughing, "especially once she's been with a Shifter. Tell you what, I'll take you to this bar called Coolers. There are some hot Shifter women there."

Misty drew a ragged breath, feeling sick to her stomach, then hurried out of the heat up to the cool shade of Graham's front porch.

Jan stepped out of the shadows of the porch's corner. "Why did you do that?"

Misty stifled a shriek and pressed her hand to her chest. "Crap, don't *do* that. How'd you get here before I did?"

"I'm Shifter. I ran. Now, why did you help me?"

"So they wouldn't test your Collar." Misty leaned to her and lowered her voice. "It doesn't work right, does it?"

Jan's nostrils flared. "I'd think you'd want me to be caught. To be locked up, or executed."

"Why would I? I didn't like you wanting to beat me up, but sheesh. Killing you? That's just wrong."

Jan stared at Misty a moment longer then she inhaled. She let the breath out and looked thoughtful. "You aren't lying."

"No. I'm not." Misty chewed on her lower lip. "Are there other Shifters whose Collars don't work?"

Jan nodded. "Some. Eric has them safe. I waited too long to go to ground, and they caught me." She paused, her gray eyes moving as emotions went through her. "Thank you."

Misty gave her a nod. "You're welcome."

Jan dropped her gaze. "Yeah, well. I better go."

"Yeah, you'd better. Stay safe."

Jan glanced around at the empty street then drew a breath. "The blessing of the Goddess go with you." She said it quickly, in one go, then she turned, jumped from the porch, and loped away.

"Wow," Misty said softly. "That was . . . Hmm." She pushed open the door and entered Graham's house.

She paused inside the front door, an ache in her heart. The house felt so empty without Graham in it. He filled every space of it—the house knew Graham's laughter, his bellowing voice, his swearing, the way he thundered up and down the stairs and banged around in the kitchen. In that kitchen, he'd made love to Misty, rendering her complete for the first time in her life.

Misty walked into the kitchen and stopped. Ben sat at the kitchen table, a bottle of beer in front of him, Kyle and Matt sitting on either side. Both cubs were in human form, dressed in sweats and T-shirts, and shoveling down ice cream. They were even using spoons.

Ben looked up at her and grinned. Kyle said, with his mouth full, "Hi, Aunt Misty." Matt continued to eat, as though he'd never get enough.

"What . . . ?" Misty came into the room, moving faster with every step until she leaned down and buried the startled Matt in a big hug. "You're all right." Tears wet her cheeks.

"He was knocked around and bruised up," Ben said. "No permanent damage. I took them to Andrea. She did her mojo."

Misty released Matt, who grinned at her, and collapsed onto an empty kitchen chair. "Andrea's still here?"

"Her, Sean, and their cub. But safely hidden away. Andrea was glad to help heal the cubs, though she said Matt wasn't too badly hurt."

"Thank God," Misty said, heartfelt. "And the Goddess too, I guess. Do you know Andrea?"

"You should ask—did she know me? Answer, no. Not until I introduced myself. But I know who she is. I keep tabs on Shifters."

"Do you really?" Misty looked him over. Ben, as before, had an innocuous look, despite his ex-con appearance. If he really was an ex-con. "You've been to prison, have you?"

"Oh, yeah. I just didn't say whose prison it was."

"And that means . . . what?"

Ben looked thoughtful. "The Fae put me in prison for a while. They talked about horrible ways to execute me, then they decided banishment would be even better."

"Really? If Oison is typical, I can't believe they thought letting you go was satisfying."

"Well." Ben folded his hands around the bottle of beer on the table. "They didn't just banish *me* from Faerie. They banished my entire race. Walked us out into the harsh human wilderness, locked the gates and made sure they never opened for us again. Half of us died the first year. How do you think I feel, knowing that?" Something dark flashed in his eyes, endless pain that Misty guessed never went away.

"What did you do? To get put in prison, I mean?"

Ben shrugged, masking the anguished look. "I killed one of their emperors. I killed him because he was running a war that was slaughtering my people, whole clans at a time. I snuck into the emperor's tent, pretending I was a pathetic sex addict who wanted the joy of an emperor doing me. The emperor's ego loved that. He got all his guards to leave us alone, and then . . ." Ben sliced his finger across his throat. "I knew I'd never get away, and I was captured, but I didn't care. Worth it. When an emperor dies, the High Fae clans fight each other to the last man to see who controls the next one, but in a rare case of Fae agreement, all the clans decided to banish me and my people."

And *half* had died in the first year. Misty's heart squeezed. "Ben, I'm so sorry."

Ben shrugged, the flash of pain there and gone again. "Even so, more of us survived because that emperor was dead, and the Fae couldn't use us anymore. We never thrived again, but we're still around. We've been helping humans and Shifters survive encounters with the Fae for nine hundred years now."

"And what *are* you?" Misty asked. "If you're not Fae."

"Human mythology calls us goblins, hobgoblins, or gnomes. We were pretty ugly in Faerie." He grinned. "Or beautiful, depending on your point of view. We learned how to look like humans since we came out of Faerie, changing our appearance every so often so we blend in with whatever fashion of whatever century."

"Gnomes," Misty mused. "Like the little plastic men with pointy hats people put in their front yards?"

Ben laughed uproariously. Then his laughter died in an instant, and he said, "No."

"I was joking. I've barely gotten used to Shifters—it will take me a while to process this."

"Take your time. I'll be around."

Misty folded her arms on the table. "So, why don't you look like a successful businessman or a rich man of leisure? If you can look like what you want?"

"I can *almost* resemble any kind of human I want. But I look like what I truly am—a man who did a crime and paid for it. I'm never going to pretend it didn't happen. I sacrificed a lot of people with my stunt, and it wasn't their choice."

Misty went silent a moment. The twins were listening, in spite of continuing to scoop globs of ice cream into their mouths.

"What do I do now?" she asked after a time. "How do I find Graham? Is he even alive?"

Ben drained the beer bottle and wiped his mouth on the back of his hand. "You still have your book?"

Misty touched it in her back pocket. "Yes."

"Look in that." Ben stood up, carried the empty beer bottle to the recycle bin and tossed it in. "And take those two with you when you go. You'll need them."

"Why?" Misty got to her feet. "Safer to leave them here with Eric or Xav, isn't it? Or whoever isn't being hassled by the Shifter Bureau."

Ben shook his head. "You'll need the cubs. They're very special Shifters. Take care of them." He started for the back door.

"Where are you going?" Misty asked in panic. "Stay and help me."

"Can't. You'll be fine. You have your guards there." He nodded at the twins, who were watching him, round-eyed. "There are other people out in the world being hassled by Fae. I need to save them too. You have my number if you need me again."

He pointed both forefingers at Misty, walked out the back door, slammed it, and headed down the porch steps. There was a flash of sunshine, and he was gone.

"Great." Misty felt despair settle over her. "On my own again."

"We're with you, Aunt Misty," Matt said. "You saved me. Now we'll save you."

They were adorable, both of them. Misty fetched a spoon and the last carton of ice cream in the freezer and sat down at the table with them. As the three of them reached with spoons for the chocolate marshmallow ripple, Misty opened the book. "All right, I'll look through it. *Again*."

Not until most of the carton was gone did Misty stop on a page. She pressed her hand to it, her heart beating faster. The spell read, *How to Find Your Lost Love*.

CHAPTER TWENTY-NINE

Graham danced aside as Oison struck, but the sword blade caught along Graham's ribs and broke the skin. Oison ran for Dougal, who had slumped to the ground, but Graham dove over his nephew, protecting him. Like hell he'd let Oison take him.

Oison raised the sword again and drove it down into the place Graham had been shot. Graham shouted in pain, but he wouldn't move—Oison wasn't touching Dougal again with that blade.

But Graham wouldn't let himself die, not yet. He needed to live so he could tell Misty how much he loved her. *You woke me,* he wanted to say. *I'd been existing before. Surviving. With you, I learned about life again.*

And about laughter. Misty was always smiling or laughing about something, finding the lightness in any subject. And talking. Goddess, the woman could talk. Her sweet voice had poured over him every time he'd been with her, soothing all the hurts in his soul. How could he have ever thought of *not* taking her as mate?

Oison raised the sword again. Graham roared as it came
down, then he heaved himself up to meet it.

He noted with satisfaction Oison's look of surprise.
Graham was strong, stronger than any Shifter he knew, and
Oison was going to find out just how strong.

The sword was in him, but Graham wrapped his hands
around Oison's throat. The Fae's slim neck was sturdy, but
Fae were of the same basic composition as Shifters or
humans. They needed air to breathe, blood to flow through
their bodies.

Graham pressed his fingers into Oison's throat, cutting
off the airflow. If he crushed the trachea, no more Oison.
He hoped he could do it before his own breath ran out.

He thought he heard Misty's voice calling his name.
Graham!

Graham could barely see. He thought he heard the throb
of a Harley, which wound him into memories. He and Dougal
riding side by side, wind in their faces, charging down an
empty Nevada highway as fast as they could go. Riding hard.

Other voices joined Misty's. Eric. Diego and Xav. The
wild yips of Kyle and Matt. Two small bodies whacked into
Oison, and Graham lost his hold. Damn it.

Graham cracked open his eyes. Matt and Kyle were
growling and snarling, climbing all over Oison. Graham
seemed to see, superimposed on the cubs, two gigantic
wolves, their muzzles huge, eyes red with fury. They were
too thick of body and broad of chest to be regular Shifter
wolves—these were something he'd never seen before.

Graham blinked, and they were the cubs again, tearing
at Oison, who batted at them as though they were annoying
gnats.

"Misty, no!" Xavier's voice, and Misty charging past
Xav, not listening. Typical. When Misty got the bit between
her teeth, there was no stopping her.

Electricity crackled, and there was Misty, a Taser in her
hand. "Matt, Kyle, out of the way." The cubs turned to
stare, yelped, and leapt to the ground. "Get away from my

mate, asshole," Misty said clearly, and she shot a bolt of electricity into Oison.

Graham had to laugh to see the Fae jolt with the shot. Oison let go of the sword, but not before an arc had laced down the blade into Graham. Graham grunted and fell back, Dougal still beneath him.

Misty was crying, on her knees next to Graham. Graham had enough energy left to open his eyes, to lift his arm to reach for her.

Oison recovered—Fae were almost as tough to kill as Shifters. His black eyes like mouths to hell, Oison yanked the sword out of Graham, and swung it at Misty.

The cubs went crazy again, leaping at him. Xavier slid out his Sig, and aimed it at Oison, but he couldn't shoot because he might hit the cubs.

Air popped, and Reid appeared, out of breath, filthy, his eyes as merciless as Oison's. He shoved Oison away from Misty, and the sword blade went wide. Oison, furious, turned to face Reid.

The two Fae fought, Reid grappling with him for the sword, rage on his face. Xavier kept trying to aim, but he had no clear shot. Reid landed a hit across Oison's face, drawing blood, but Oison backed up, his grip on his sword true again, and rammed the blade at Reid.

Graham heaved himself up. Blood ran from his wounds, and his Collar was shocking him, but the wolf in him gave him strength. He felt himself Shifting before he realized it, into his in-between beast, a monster that was half wolf, half human. Misty, instead of running away in terror, came to Graham and steadied him on his feet.

Graham roared. He grabbed Oison's arm as his sword came down to Reid and ripped the blade away. As Oison spun to face him, Graham took the blade in both hands and broke it over his huge knee.

There was a flash, a sound like a broken bell, and the pieces of the sword fell, tarnished and jagged, to the ground.

Oison opened his mouth and cried something in Fae, but he only got a few words out before Graham grabbed him by the neck again.

As Graham had done in his dream, he ripped his claws into Oison's throat, no chain mail now to stop him. Hot blood poured out over Graham's hands. Oison locked his fingers around Graham's wrists, gasping for breath. The Fae gulped air and started chanting again, another spell, Graham knew.

Graham felt himself weakening, shifting back to human, whatever magic it was taking hold, but he refused to let go.

"Graham!" Misty, his mate, screamed. "Get out of the way!"

Graham saw her, and his eyes widened. He spun Oison around so his back would be to Misty, then Graham hit the ground as Misty, who'd grabbed Xavier's gun, unloaded every bullet in it into the Fae.

Oison faltered, but he kicked away from Graham and ran for the opening to the cave. Bullets were lead, not iron, so while they'd slow him down, he could escape to Faerie and live.

Graham wouldn't let him. He was on Oison in two strides, changing to wolf, bringing the Fae down flat on his back. He closed his mouth over Oison's throat, biting down. Graham tasted blood, and saw the life leave Oison's eyes.

Oison's head lolled, blood coming from his mouth, then all at once, he looked straight up at Graham.

"It's only the beginning," he said clearly, then he died. His body crumpled, dissolving into dust.

Graham shifted slowly, painfully back to human. Misty dropped to her knees next to him, the gun falling from her hands.

"Graham . . ."

"It's all right, Misty," Graham said, barely able to form the words. "I got the son of a bitch."

He collapsed into her arms, spent, but there was no place

he'd rather be. The hot summer wind swept down from the ridge and carried the dust of Oison's dead body into the vast open plain of the desert.

"Dougal first," Graham said.

The DX Security van they lay in rocked and swayed over the rutted roads back to Shiftertown.

"Graham, you have three sword holes in you," Misty snapped. "And a reopened gunshot wound." She clung to his hand, her heart slamming in her chest, not liking that Graham's grip was so weak.

"And Dougal got stabbed, plus he's got Collar fatigue." Graham's voice might not be up to his usual volume, but he'd held on to his strength of will.

"I'm better," Dougal said. He sat up beside Graham, leaning against the van wall. "What hurt was the magic. Now that Oison's gone, so is the spell."

"No kidding." Graham had his other hand around a bottle of water. He'd insisted on drinking, so happy to be able to again, though Andrea had joked it would all come out the holes if he didn't quit.

"He's not good." Andrea said now. The slim woman put her hand on Graham's bloody stomach. "Too much blood loss, too long under a spell, dehydration, exhaustion. All that on top of his wounds. I'm going to need a lot of help."

"I'm here," Sean said. He put his hand on his mate's shoulder, his other on the hilt of his sword, which rested tip-first on the van's floor.

"What can I do?" Misty asked, not liking the sword so near. She knew what the swords of the Guardians did—were used to release a Shifter's soul when the Shifter didn't make it. "There has to be something."

Graham tried to squeeze her fingers. "You've done everything, love. You found me. Twice. You rescued me. Twice. You tased Oison, then you shot him." He chuckled. "That was fun to watch."

"Shut up, Graham." Misty kissed his scraped and blackened cheek. "Save your strength."

"You're going to need it to heal," Andrea told him. "Misty, the touch of a mate helps. Put your hand next to mine, and think about how much you love him."

"She's not my mate," Graham rumbled.

The others in the van turned heads to look at Misty, and Xav glanced back over the front seat at them. Misty found herself pinned under Feline and Lupine stares, including those of the cubs.

"She never accepted the claim," Graham said. "Sucks, but there it is."

"What are you talking about?" Misty put her hand on Graham's chest, feeling his heart beating hard and erratically beneath her fingers. "We argued about this, remember? You said I *didn't* refuse."

"But you didn't accept, either."

"Well, shit, Graham, I don't know everything there is to know about Shifter rituals. I'm going out with a man who doesn't tell me *anything*."

"Hey, don't blame this on me, sweetheart—"

Dougal broke in. "Misty, you say, 'Under the Father God and Mother Goddess, and in front of witnesses, I accept the mate-claim.'"

"See?" Misty glared at Graham. "Would that have been so hard?" She took a deep breath and spoke quickly. "Under the Father God and Mother Goddess, and in front of witnesses, I accept the mate-claim."

"Oh, yeah." Graham grasped her hand again and squeezed it. "I feel better already."

The mood in the van lightened. Andrea's face softened into a smile, and Dougal whooped. Even Reid, in the front with Xav, gave Misty a quiet nod. Sean grinned, and Xav gave them all a thumbs-up as he kept driving.

Dougal launched himself at Misty and enfolded her in a hard hug. "Thank you, Misty."

The twins rammed into her other side, hugging her

tight. Sean and Andrea had brought their clothes, which they'd put on more or less right, except Kyle had his shirt on inside out. "Aunt Misty!" They shouted. The cubs let go of her and jumped up and down together, then ran at her and hugged her again.

All the while Graham lay there, his eyes softening. "Thank you, Misty."

Misty leaned down, being careful not to hurt him, and kissed his cracked lips. "Anytime, love."

Graham tried to kiss her back, the glint in his eye telling her when he felt better, she'd need to watch out. Misty didn't care. She loved Graham, she loved sex with him, and she yearned for him with every part of her.

Graham smiled the best he could as she rose from him, then he looked past her. "And you two," he said to the twins, with a hint of his old firmness. "Goddess help me. I don't know whether to lock you in your room for two months or take you out for pizza."

The twins sprang away from Misty and high-fived each other. "Pizza!" they yelled.

"Earplugs," Graham said, wincing. "I'm buying a bucket load."

Laughter began, and then healing magic, as the van rocked and swayed through the dusty desert night.

Andrea's skill, bandages, Misty's touch, and time healed Graham's wounds, though he was the most impatient patient Misty had ever dealt with.

Graham was up and down constantly while he convalesced, picking at the bandages, reopening the closed wounds, grumbling when they were bandaged again. He said he couldn't stay in bed when he had to take care of Dougal, and the cubs, and Shifter business, and run his half of Shiftertown, *and* fix his bike, which had gotten shot, if she remembered.

The Shifters would have to rebuild the house that had collapsed, *away* from the ley line this time. Plus, they needed to get the Shifter Bureau off their backs about the Collars—though the soldiers had tested every one and found them all functional. Still, the fact that a seed of doubt had been sown meant Shifters had to be very, very careful about the Collars. But Collars had to come off and be replaced with fake ones as soon as possible, now that Shifters knew about the Fae and their nefarious plots with the swords.

Then there was the question of arranging for the mating ceremonies with Misty, and Graham breaking it to his Lupines he was mating with a human.

The Lupines already knew, of course, because nothing could be kept quiet in Shiftertown. Wolves would walk by his house while Graham healed, staring up at his bedroom window, and not always out of concern for him. They left him alone for now, but Graham said that a time would come for confrontation.

Paul had taken over looking after Misty's flower shop and its cleanup, so Misty could stay with Graham and help him. Paul proved to be good at the store, and Misty decided that once Graham was healthy again, she'd ask Paul to go into it with her as a full partner. She could do that for him, and Paul could finally begin his life.

Ben returned a week into Graham's recovery to congratulate Misty on her victory. Graham almost ripped Ben's head off as soon as he stepped inside through the kitchen door Misty enthusiastically opened for him.

"You asshole," Graham said clearly when he had his hands around Ben's throat. Graham's Collar sparked, but he didn't seem to notice or care. "Misty told me all about you. You sent her straight into danger—alone. Never mind about your little spell book. If not for you, she'd have stayed the hell out of this."

"Maybe," Ben said, unruffled, even though Graham's fingers bit into his neck. "But she wouldn't have learned how to find you or fight the Fae's spells, and you'd be a Fae slave now. Or dead. Maybe both."

"I don't *want* her to fight the Fae," Graham snarled. "I want her to stay safe."

Ben brought his hands up between Graham's and snapped his hold away. Graham stepped back in surprise and glared at him, but didn't renew the attack.

"I want her to stay safe too," Ben said, his look serious. "That's why I taught her how to defend herself and save you."

"Yeah, well . . ." Graham's growl was low, and his Collar quieted.

Misty released a breath of relief. She knew Graham well enough now to know he'd gotten his initial rage out of his system and might start listening.

"So when I found the box of books at the flea market," she said, rummaging in the refrigerator. Now that Graham was done choking Ben, both men might want beer. "Did you make sure I'd buy it? Or was it a coincidence?"

Ben winked at her. "I don't believe in coincidences."

Graham rumbled. "Of course you don't, you cocky son of a—"

"What about Matt and Kyle?" Misty interrupted. "You said they were special. Very special Shifters, you called them."

"Ah." Ben accepted the beer. Graham grabbed the other from Misty and twisted off the top, his movements still a bit stiff.

"I came to tell you about that, actually," Ben said. "I didn't realize what they were at first. I didn't think there were any left. But I did a little research, and I'm right."

"Get to the point." Graham leaned against the counter near Misty, protecting her even now, and fixed Ben with a Shifter stare. "Damn creatures from Faerie love the cryptic."

"They're Guards," Ben said.

Graham stiffened. "Guardians?"

Ben shook his head. "Guards. Back when Shifters were created, Fae made a special breed of them they called Guards. They were a little bigger and more ferocious than typical Shifters, and created to guard the highest generals, the clan leaders, and the emperor."

"Rear guard, you mean," Graham said. "To take care of the cowards who wouldn't go out in actual battle."

"You got it." Ben nodded and took a sip of beer. "Unfortunately, the Fae made the Guards a little too good. When the Shifter-Fae war came along, the Guards turned around and defended the Shifters instead of the Fae. They knew a lot about the habits of the highest-ranking Fae, and they used that knowledge to take them down. They fought the Fae to the death. The main reason the Shifters won that war is because of the Shifter Guards. Unfortunately, 'to the death' meant literally. The Guards died to the last one. Extinct. Or so we all thought." Ben gestured with his beer bottle. "Those two cubs are Guards. I guess the genetics made it through. Who was their father?"

Graham shrugged. "I don't know. Their mother was one of my wolves—she died bringing them in, and she never would say who the father was. None of my other Lupines would admit to it, so I figured she'd found a wolf from another Shiftertown, or maybe one who'd stayed in the wild. She died without naming him."

"Hmm," Ben said. "Interesting. Well, keep an eye on them."

"Great," Graham said, though the anger in his voice had lessened a long way. "They're out with Dougal right now. Probably watching Dougal chase tail."

"They'll take care of Dougal," Ben said. "Who's babysitting whom, that's the question." He chuckled, took another sip of beer, and glanced out the window. "Hey, Graham, looks like your wolves are ready to parley. Enjoy yourself." Ben set his bottle by the sink, came to Misty and kissed her cheek, then grinned at the snarling Graham, and exited through the front.

"Crap." Graham slammed down his bottle, winced, and touched his side. Shifters healed quickly, he'd said over and over to Misty this week, but even so, Graham wasn't ready for a full-blown fight.

Graham walked out of the house to his back porch, Misty following. Graham pulled himself up straight to face the crowd of Lupines who'd gathered at the edge of his yard. "She accepted the mate-claim," Graham told them, his voice as strong as ever. "Get over it."

"We know." The wolf called Norval fixed his gaze on Misty. "We *don't* accept it."

"Don't care," Graham said. "I formed the mate bond with her. What am I supposed to do? Throw that away?"

Several of the wolves moved uneasily. The mate bond was an almost sacred thing—to come between two Shifters who shared it was cruel, not to mention dangerous.

"Other Shifters have given up the mate bond for the good of their clans," Norval said.

"True," Graham answered. "Other Shifters, not me. And that was in the wild, where those choices meant survival. These days, we don't have to deny a mate bond so full-of-themselves Shifters don't get their knickers in a twist."

A few of the wolves chuckled. Norval only looked more angry. "Watch it, Graham. I'll challenge for Shiftertown leadership if you break this faith."

"Go ahead." Graham shrugged his large shoulders. "I'll slam you down. Then your second will climb over your dead body to take the clan leadership."

More movement, some of the Shifters drifting away from Norval, others gathering behind him.

Misty saw Dougal approach and stand on the edge of the crowd. Graham shook his head ever so slightly, and Dougal nodded back, silently staying where he was.

"I accept the mating," a female voice said.

The Lupine woman Jan stepped out from behind Muriel. Her arms were folded, she wouldn't look at anyone directly, but she glanced defiantly out of the corners of her eyes. "Misty Granger will be a good mate for Graham," Jan said, her voice firm. "She'll have our backs."

Norval bristled. "You don't know what the fuck you're talking about."

"Yes, she does," Misty broke in. A hiss of distaste went through some of the Shifters—a female, human, speaking to dominant Shifters—unheard of. Misty jabbed a fist in

Jan's direction and grinned at her. "Jan and me, we're sisters under the skin."

"Misty saved me from being taken by the Shifter Bureau," Jan said. "For that, I stand by her."

"I do too," Muriel said. "Jan told me what happened. While you alphas were skulking around avoiding the Bureau men, Misty was saving Jan's ass. She also saved Graham's. We wouldn't have a leader right now if not for her."

"She also got Graham into trouble in the first place," Norval said angrily. "He got shot and nearly taken by the Fae because he went running after her."

"Pay attention," Muriel said. "The Fae would have grabbed Graham any way he could. Misty brought him home *and* kept the Bureau from finding out we're digging under the houses."

Norval's eyes narrowed. "Are you 'sisters' with her too?"

"No," Muriel said. "But I'm not stupid. You want Graham to mate for the good of his Shifters, or so you say. Or maybe you're trying to force a match that's for the good of you."

"Muriel," Norval growled, giving her his alpha stare.

Another young female Lupine came forward, followed by another, more reluctant, but with her shoulders squared. "We'll stand by Graham's choice too," the first one said. "We're a little irritated that our clan leaders are trying to mate us off to him. It's our decision who we pick as a mate, not theirs. We're tired of being treated like chattel."

Norval swept his gaze over them. "Is this what city living does to Lupines?" he asked. "Clan leaders let low-dominance females speak without permission?"

"Clan leaders can get used to it," Misty called to him. "If I'm going to be the Shiftertown leader's mate, I'll teach the ladies to not let themselves be pushed around. They should all be like my friend Lindsay."

Norval went almost purple. "Dear Goddess. Graham, control her."

Graham shook his head. "I can't. She's human. She does what she wants." He rested his fists on the porch railing.

"My decision's made. I mate-claimed Misty, she accepted, the sun and moon ceremonies will be soon. Suck on it."

Norval and a few others looked as though they wanted to continue the argument, but Graham did his Graham thing of turning around and walking away, showing them his uncaring back. Misty gave Jan a grateful smile and retreated into the house after Graham.

Graham grabbed Misty around the waist as soon as she came out of the kitchen and had her against the wall in the hall. "You've got a sassy mouth." He leaned to her. "I'm going to bite it."

"Mmm." Misty laced her arms around his neck as he took her bottom lip between his teeth. The little pain of the bite shot excitement through her.

"Mating frenzy," Graham said. "It's rising and doesn't care about these damn bandages."

Misty put her hand on his jeans and slid it down to his zipper. "I see that."

Graham rested his hands on either side of her head as he licked across her mouth. "I need you, Misty. I've been needing you . . . it's making me crazy."

Misty lost her smile. "I don't want to hurt you."

"It's supposed to be me saying that." Graham nipped her chin. "I want to do *everything* with you, love. I want you to suck my cock. I want to drink you. I want you riding me, and looking at me with your beautiful eyes when you do it. I want you on your hands and knees, like in your garden, in the moonlight. I want to be in you, buried there, and not come out. I want it all."

Warm excitement built. "I can go for that." Misty pressed her hand to his chest. "But not until you're well."

"I'm well. I'm with my mate." Graham clasped her hand, pressing it harder into his chest. "And I have the mate bond. It's hot inside me, connecting me to you. Can you feel it too?"

The look he gave her was so hopeful, so utterly raw, no barriers between them, that Misty's eyes stung. "I feel warmth right here." She pressed his hand between her breasts. "I feel happy whenever I see you, even when you're yelling. I love looking at you, and watching you look at me as though you want to devour me. I feel lighter whenever you're around me. I told you in the cave that I loved you, and why. Want me to tell you again?"

"I heard you," Graham said. "Even that far gone, I heard you." He touched his lips to hers, the kiss the gentlest brush. "It brought me back to you."

"Graham." Misty loved saying his name. She laced her hand behind his head, rubbing his short hair, and made the next kiss deeper. She loved doing that too.

Graham opened her mouth with his kiss, brushing her cheek with his thumb. His body came hard against hers, pressing her back into the wall.

When Graham broke the kiss and looked down at her, the tenderness had left him. "I'm done being nice." The strength and the savage growl had returned to his voice. "Can you take that?"

Excited heat spun through her. "I think so."

"Better know so." Graham took a step back and flashed her his most wicked smile. "Run, sweetheart. I want to hunt."

Misty's eyes widened. Graham's little growl made her heart flutter and then beat very fast.

Misty turned and ran, but not out of the house. Graham caught her when she was halfway up the stairs. Then her shorts were yanked down, her shirt wrenched off, and Graham was on top of her. He growled as he slid inside her, taking her with hard, merciless thrusts. All the while he cradled Misty in his arms so she wouldn't be hurt on the uncarpeted stairs.

Misty met his thrusts with her own. It was a fierce, wild coupling, and Misty wanted it. Wanted more. Mating frenzy didn't happen only to Shifters.

"I love you," Graham said, his voice the gravelly rumble she adored. "Mate of my heart."

"I love you too," Misty whispered, then she yelled it, her voice echoing up and down the stairs. "I love you, Graham McNeil! Mate of my heart."

Graham made a noise in his throat, and the emptiness that she'd always seen in his eyes fled. The light in them warmed, flared, then was drowned by a sudden wash of tears.

Graham's mouth came down on her in a savage kiss, one that held both his fierceness and his love. He protected her with strong arms while he kissed her and sought his pleasure, and he gave her pleasure back threefold.

Misty traced his flame tattoos, which danced and swirled like the fires in her heart.

Turn the page to read the first chapter of

FERAL HEAT

*A Shifters Unbound e-novella that tells how
Deni Rowe and Jace Warden fall in love,
available now from InterMix*

The fight club had moved since Jace Warden had last visited the Austin Shiftertown. The Shifters used to meet for their forbidden bouts in an abandoned hay barn nestled into folds of a hill, but the land had been purchased, and a developer had built over it.

On his borrowed Harley, Jace turned from the discreet plane that had flown him this far and headed down a highway that led to drier country away from the river. The world had darkened while he'd flown east from Nevada to land at an airfield that had supposedly been closed.

Dylan Morrissey, the Austin Shiftertown liaison, had left a message for Jace to meet him at the fights, and he'd also left the bike for Jace's transportation. Tired and hot, and having hauled himself halfway across the country at Dylan's request, the last thing Jace wanted to do was to ride out to the fight club. But Dylan had summoned him to work on the problem of getting the Collars off Shifters once and for all, and had extended his hospitality, so Jace hid his irritation, thanked the humans who had helped him get this far, and mounted the motorcycle.

Jace turned off where the directions had instructed, the paved road quickly turning to dirt, the bike bouncing and skidding over gravel and through ruts. The road grew narrower and narrower, until it petered to nothing. Jace continued down a short hill and around a bend, and found the Shifter fight club behind a slight rise that hid it from the road.

He smelled it long before he saw the electric lanterns, fire dancing in garbage cans, and flashlights. Anything that could be quickly doused was being used to illuminate the scene.

Jace would have known it was a place of Shifters, even in the pitch-dark. Shifters working off adrenaline rushes and fighting instincts had a certain interesting—and pungent—odor.

Jace killed the engine of the bike, parking it among the pack of motorcycles, pickups, and smaller cars. He hung the helmet from the seat and made sure his backpack was well stashed in the saddlebag before he approached the fight area. He wasn't worried about Shifters stealing his change of clothes and toothbrush—Shifters didn't steal from one another, because a simple snatch could end up in a fight to the death. Possessions were territory, and territory was respected. But humans also came to the fight clubs, and some liked to abscond with things.

The new fighting arena was a broad slab of concrete about a hundred feet long and just as wide. Probably an old building or an event area of some kind, abandoned by its owners when money ran out. Everything had been pulled away except the slab.

Rings were outlined by concrete blocks, and firelight flickered wildly, making it a scene from hell, complete with demons. But the demons were only Shifters having fun and working off steam; those not fighting were cheering, drinking beer, or finding hook-ups—human or Shifter— and sneaking into the darkness to work off steam a different way.

Jace made his way around cars—a few of them being

used for liaisons—and toward the firelight. He didn't worry about locating Dylan in the chaos, because Dylan, a Feline Shifter who was mostly lion, always made himself known.

What Jace didn't expect was the wolf who sprang out of the shadows in a deserted stretch of the parking area and landed on Jace full force.

Jace swung around with the impact, hands coming up to dig into the wolf's fur and throw him down. The Lupine landed in the dust, his Collar sparking and sizzling. The Collar's shocks didn't slow the wolf much, because he rolled to his feet and charged Jace again.

Jace didn't know who the hell the wolf was. Not that he had much of a chance of identification as the Lupine landed on Jace again, his Collar's sparks burning Jace's skin. The wolf went for Jace's throat, and Jace's hands turned to leopard's paws to rake across the wolf's face. The wolf took the blow, landed on his feet, shook himself, and sprang again.

Jace's Collar hadn't shocked him yet, but he felt the build-up. Collars were made to spike pain into Shifters as soon as they became seriously violent, but Jace had learned techniques to fool the Collar and keep it dormant. It was tough to do, however, especially when he was taken by surprise. Jace had to focus in order to keep the Collar quiet, and right now he was busy trying to keep this bloody Lupine from killing him.

Jace whacked the wolf aside again, spinning around as he shed his denim jacket and half shifted to his wildcat. His shirt split, jeans falling as his back legs elongated into powerful feline haunches. He emerged from his shredding clothes as a fully formed snow leopard—creamy fur, black spots, ice blue eyes—and thoroughly pissed off.

Jace went for the wolf. The wolf was bigger, almost twice Jace's bulk, but leopards hadn't made it to the top of the wildcat pyramid because of size. Leopards might be among the smaller big cats, but they were swift, agile, and smart, and they didn't take shit from anyone.

This wolf wanted to give him shit, though. He came at Jace again, fur up, his canine jowls frothing, his golden eyes filled with rage. The scent that hit Jace reeked of challenge. This was a wolf who wanted to move up in rank, never mind that Jace was a different species and not even from this Shiftertown. Dominance challenges weren't allowed inside the ring at the fight club; one of the biggest rules was that fights were for recreation and showing off—that, and no killing. Outside the ring was a different story.

Jace got ready to teach him a lesson.

As he drew back to renew his attack, another wolf sprang from the parking lot and hurled itself at the first wolf. A female, Jace scented, one he hadn't met before.

She wasn't rushing to defend the wolf, however. She attacked the Lupine in fury, teeth bared, near madness in her eyes.

The first Lupine swung to meet her, and the two went down in an explosion of fur and snarls. Jace sat back to catch his breath, surprised. The two wolves were evenly matched, the male a bit larger than the female, but the female was plenty strong and agile. Probably dominant to the male too.

Jace let the female get her first anger out of her system, then he waded back in to rescue his rescuer.

The male Lupine had the she-wolf on the ground by now. He pinned the female with one big paw, snarling as he turned to Jace.

Jace gave him a warning growl. The growl said that, up until now, Jace had been holding back; that Jace was dominant in his pride, his clan, and his Shiftertown; and the wolf might want to think about it before continuing the fight.

The Lupine ignored the warning and went for the kill. Jace met him head-on, his lithe body and fast paws taking the wolf down to the ground before the Lupine could use his superior weight to his advantage.

The she-wolf rose behind the male, landed on the wolf's back, and sank her teeth into his neck. Her Collar was sparking frantically, and she got hit by the arcs from the other wolf's Collar, but she kept biting.

Jace drew back his paw and whacked the male wolf across the throat. The wolf spun with the blow, knocking the female loose. The male Lupine rolled across the dust and dying grass a long way before he was able to stop. He righted himself but stayed down on his belly, panting hard, conceding the fight.

Jace walked to him with a stiff-legged Feline stalk. When he reached the Lupine, he lowered his head to the wolf's eye level and growled again. Stay the fuck down.

Whether or not the Lupine understood Feline rumbles and body language, Jace's glare must have gotten the message across. The wolf snarled, teeth bared, but he plastered his ears flat on his head and didn't move.

Jace turned back to the she-wolf. She lay limply on the grass, and Jace went to her, giving her a cat's lick across her face. She growled softly, and Jace licked her again, feeling a need to thank and reassure her.

The need didn't leave him when he shifted back to human. He stroked her head, liking the wiry fur of her wolf.

The female wolf looked up at him in a wash of confusion. She was a gray wolf, with gray eyes. She breathed in Jace's scent, wrinkling her nose, clearly wondering who he was.

Jace gave her head another stroke, wishing she'd turn back to human so he could talk to her. She'd run to his rescue, a Lupine taking the side of a Feline, and Jace wanted to know why.

The she-wolf remained wolf, still growling softly. Jace touched her head one last time and walked back to the male wolf. "New way of greeting guests in Shiftertown?" he asked. "Let me introduce myself. I'm Jace Warden. A guest of Dylan's."

Jace knew he didn't need to explain that his own father was leader of another Shiftertown. The fact that Dylan sanctioned Jace's visit should be enough for this wolf.

The wolf morphed into his human form, a man with short black hair and light gray eyes. "Hey, I saw a strange Feline trying to sneak into the fight club when he wasn't invited, and when no one but regulars are supposed to know about the new place. What did you expect?"

"So you were defending all the Shifters here?" Jace asked with evident skepticism. "Commendable."

"Ask that crazy bitch what she was doing," the Lupine said, scowling at the she-wolf. "Nurturing females, my ass. She's all spit and vinegar."

"Let me guess." Jace felt mirth. "She turned down your mate-claim."

The Lupine gave Jace an incredulous look. "I wouldn't mate-claim her. Not if she were the last female in Shiftertown. She's out of her mind. You can never tell what she's going to do." The man made a broad gesture in her direction. "You saw her."

"I thought it was nice of her to help me out."

"Nah, she saw a fight, it sparked her loony side, and she dove in. Look at her. She's not even sure what happened."

Jace turned his gaze to the she-wolf again and saw that the man was right. She watched Jace and the Lupine, trembling but trying to hide it with a growl and a glare. Jace saw fear in her eyes along with deep anger—a woman hurting from something and not wanting anyone else to know it.

"I keep trying to tell Liam she should be put down," the Lupine said. "She's a danger to the rest of us."

The she-wolf snarled again. Scent and body language told Jace what he needed to know—the female was dominant but of a different clan than the male wolf; the male was aggressive, cocky, and hated to be bested. The male wolf would be dominant in his clan as well. Jace outranked both of them, though.

Jace looked into the other man's eyes. "Why don't you shut your hole, get dressed, and go the hell home? You're too unstable to be here tonight."

The man tried to meet Jace's gaze. He did pretty well, but in the end had to slide his eyes sideways. "What, you want some privacy with her? Don't say I didn't warn you."

"Just go," Jace said.

The wolf snorted. "Whatever." He climbed to his feet and strolled away, not worried that he was naked.

514

The fight hadn't attracted any attention. A sudden roar of voices within the arena told Jace why—there must be an intense match going down. The human voices were accompanied by roars and growls, since half the watchers would be in animal form.

Jace retrieved his torn clothing, grunting in irritation. He'd only brought two changes of clothes, thinking he wouldn't be in Austin that long.

The jeans had escaped the worst of the shredding, and he pulled them on, the ripped seams stretching as he crouched down to look at the she-wolf again.

"You all right?" he asked her. "Who was that asshole?"

The disgust in his question reached past the feral fear in her eyes. He saw clarity return, and then the wolf shifted into a female with a lush, lovely body, close-cut wheat-colored hair, and large gray eyes.

She remained in a crouch, covering herself, but Jace's gaze traced the curve of her ample breasts, his natural need rising. She'd be worth sneaking off into the darkness with, maybe having a bounce with in the bed of a pickup.

No, she'd be worth more than that. This wasn't a lady Jace would use to relieve horniness and then forget. Not with that gorgeous gaze pinning him flat.

"His name's Broderick," she said in a voice Jace wanted to embrace. "He usually wins Asshole of the Month around here."

"No doubt. What did you jump in for? He's right about one thing—it was a crazy thing to do. Two males with their blood up could have hurt you."

"I saw him besting you. No one deserves to be pounded by Broderick for no reason."

"He wasn't besting me," Jace said, giving her a grin. "I had him. And then he started kicking your ass."

She frowned. "Oh, please. I was a few bites away from making him crawl away whimpering."

As Jace hoped, his needling made her irritation erase her fear and pain. "Not to mention, your Collar was going off," Jace said. "Are you sure you're all right?"

He placed his hand on the side of her neck, over the Collar in question. Ordinarily, Jace wouldn't touch uninvited, especially not cross-species, but something in this woman cried out to him. She needed soothing.

Her eyes widened a little, but she didn't jerk away. "What about you? Your Collar didn't go off. You can dampen its effect, can't you? Like Liam does?"

Jace let his fingers caress her neck as he chose his words. "That's not supposed to be common knowledge. Need-to-know basis."

"Maybe I need to know. Dylan's trying to teach me, but I can't do it yet."

"In that case, I'll give you some pointers." Jace traced her Collar to the front, pausing when his fingers rested on its Celtic cross lying against her throat. "But I'd better find Dylan and tell him I'm here before the payback for controlling my Collar hits me."

"Dylan's fighting right now," the woman said. "His bouts are always popular. But short. He should be done soon."

Jace placed his hand on hers. He wanted to keep touching this woman for some reason, as though breaking contact with her would lessen him somehow. "Come with me. We'll watch him win together."

"No." The woman started to rise, and Jace unfolded himself and helped her to her feet. She didn't hide herself anymore, a Shifter woman unembarrassed by her body. "I have to go. Are you Jace? You've been to Shiftertown before, haven't you?"

"Yeah, but why haven't I met you?" Jace still didn't want to release her hand. "I've made lots of trips out here, but I don't remember seeing you."

"I've been . . . sick," she said. "I'm Deni. Deni Rowe."

Deni watched him anxiously, as though gauging his reaction to the name. "Ellison Rowe's sister?" Jace asked.

"Yes." Deni still peered at him, waiting.

Jace tightened his hand on hers. "Why do you have to go? Stay with me and watch Dylan kick ass. You can keep other Lupines from jumping me."

Deni didn't smile. She glanced at the arena and the mass of figures there, and Jace scented her nervousness. "I can't. Sometimes the fighting . . ."

"Calls to the feral in you? Makes you lose control?"

She gave him a startled look. "How did you know that?"

"Because I saw your eyes when you attacked Broderick. You didn't dive into the fight only to rescue me. You did it because watching made you want to fight too. I was like that during my Transition." Jace caressed the hand he hadn't released. "All you have to do is hold on to someone. The touch will calm you and keep you tethered."

Another startled look. "That doesn't work. Even my cubs . . ."

"Bet me," Jace said. "You hang on to a dominant, and he takes the heat and cools you down. Works. That's what dominants are for."

A spark of pride returned to Deni's eyes. "And you're saying you're dominant to me?"

"Yep. It's obvious. You outrank Broderick—I bet you outrank a lot of wolves—but you're not dominant to this Feline." He touched his chest.

She gave him a half smile. "And you're not full of yourself about that."

"Just stating facts." Jace did not want to let go of her hand. "Let's find your clothes and go. Unless you want to watch as wolf."

Deni sent him another haughty look that made her eyes beautiful, but she didn't pull away. "I'll find my clothes."

"Good."

Jace left his shredded shirt behind—why bother with it?—but caught up his jacket and followed her into the darkness, her hand on his like a lifeline. A warm, sweet lifeline. He definitely wanted to know this Lupine woman better.

D eni's heart beat swiftly as she pulled on the sarong she'd thrown off to rush into the fight with Broderick. Broderick's scent of arrogance had enraged her, and she'd wanted to pummel him for jumping the other Shifter without challenge.

Then she'd felt her memory slide away, the feral thing inside her taking over. She shivered. Her wildness hadn't receded until Jace had smacked the wolf down himself, and Deni had fallen away from the fight.

Jace hadn't then turned around and kicked her butt, as he'd had a right to for interfering. Instead he'd touched her, licked her with his strange Feline sandpapery tongue, then held her hand after she'd changed back to human.

Deni was still shaky as they entered the fight club's main area. Jace kept hold of her hand. It was a big hand, warm but callused, his grip strong. He was a fighter, a warrior.

If Deni remembered right, Jace Warden was the son of Eric Warden, leader of the Las Vegas Shiftertown. Jace was third in command there, the second in command being Eric's sister. Jace would be in the most dominant Feline clan of his Shiftertown, and in the most dominant Feline pride of that clan. The top of the top.

Alphas usually bugged Deni, because they could be arrogant shits, but only concern and protection flowed from Jace. An alpha interested in taking care of others. What a concept.

The biggest crowd gathered around the central ring—the other two rings were empty. From throats, beast and human, came wild cries, delight in whoever was winning, groaning from those foolish enough not to back Dylan.

Jace moved through the throng to the ring. Shifters moved aside for him, most without noticing they did so. Instinct, Deni guessed—sensing that they should get out of Jace's way before he made it an order.

A large man stood at the perimeter of the ring, arms folded, the Sword of the Guardian on his back. Deni always felt a frisson of dread when she saw the sword, whose purpose was to be driven through the hearts of dead or dying Shifters. The sword pierced the heart, and the Shifter turned to dust, his or her soul following the pathway to the Summerland.

The sword shimmered a little in the flickering light. Other Shifters gave the Guardian a wide berth, also uncomfortable with him. Kind of hard on Sean, Deni always thought, but Sean had been much less haunted since he'd taken a mate.

A human woman stood next to Sean—not his mate. She was the scrappy woman who'd tied herself to Ronan, a Kodiak bear, who was even now in the ring, fighting Dylan. The woman—Elizabeth—danced on top of the cement blocks, cheering for Ronan at the top of her lungs.

Sean would be standing as second for Dylan, his father. A second's job was to make sure that no one interfered with the fight and that the other side didn't cheat. Dylan and Ronan would go for a fair, straight fight, but other Shifters could be cunning. The seconds were there for a reason.

Dylan was the black-maned lion snarling in the middle of the ring, his paws moving lightning fast as he battled the bigger bulk of the Kodiak. Ronan was fully shifted to bear, his ruff standing up, his eyes alight with fighting fury. Ronan's Collar sparked deep into his fur, but Dylan's was quiet.

"Unfair advantage," Jace said into Deni's ear. "Dylan knows how to keep his Collar from going off."

Deni had to turn her head and stand on tiptoe to answer into Jace's ear. His hand in hers was warm, and she leaned close. "That's why he only fights the strongest: Ronan, or Spike, who's the champion. Sometimes Dylan lets his Collar go off on purpose, to keep things interesting."

"But he usually wins anyway," Jace finished.

He had a rumbling baritone that tickled inside her ear, his hot breath making Deni tingle even more. She squeezed his fingers a little, and was rewarded with an answering squeeze.

Ronan roared. His Collar was sparking, his mate yelling her encouragement, but Deni saw her worry. These matches weren't to the death, but Shifters could be badly hurt in them.

Deni could scent and sense Elizabeth's excitement tinged with fear. She also caught Sean's tenseness as he watched his father battle. If something went wrong, if one of the Shifters was hurt so much the Guardian was needed, Sean would have to plunge his sword into the heart of either his father or his close friend.

Deni caught his sorrow—Sean had had to send one of his brothers to dust a dozen years ago—which laced through the sorrow in her own heart. Deni wished her cubs were here, her boys, but they were working at their jobs in the city, earning what little money Shifters were allowed to earn.

Dylan backed away from Ronan's onslaught, ears flat on his head. He didn't roar—Dylan's roar could shake apart the town—but his growls filled the space.

The sound caught in Deni's nerves, calling to the feral inside her. All Shifters had the instinct to throw off any polish of civilization, to revert to their wild forms, to return to the time when they'd been bred to fight and hunt. Even after a thousand and more years, Shifters retained the same basic instincts—fight or be killed, hunt or be hunted.

Shifters had come up with strict rules made to tame their inner beasts. To keep themselves from tearing each other apart after they'd fought free of their Fae masters, Shifters had agreed to certain rituals that must be performed in regard to mating, fighting, and even death. Take those away, and they were simply animals who could make themselves look human.

Deni's motorcycle accident last year had robbed her of the veneer of calm Shifters strived to learn. The wreck must have jarred something loose in Deni's brain, because she'd been fighting her instincts ever since, often losing. Knowing the bastard who'd run her down was dead had helped her begin to heal, but she wasn't there yet.

In the midst of the growls, snarls, roars, and cheers, with the scent of blood and sweat pouring from the ring,

Deni's thoughts began to tangle. Her scent sense heightened, bringing in the excitement of the Shifters, the bloodlust in Dylan, the singed-fur smell from the sparking Collars, the strong male scent of Jace Warden next to her.

She probably would have been all right with Jace's calming hand in hers, if the fighting Shifters had been anyone else, but Dylan had a powerful Shifter presence. Being alpha didn't simply mean winning fights and scaring Shifters into submission. It was an indefinable something about the Shifter—scent, timbre of voice, subtle compulsion to follow this male. In animal form, it was more apparent, and Dylan was broadcasting his force loud and clear.

Since the accident, Deni had been able to use her animal senses fully in her human form. All Shifters retained some of their superior senses of hearing, scenting, and tracking ability when human, but they were muted, distant, able to be pushed aside so the Shifter could live as human without going crazy.

Not so for Deni. She had to constantly fight herself not to shift, attack, or even kill when she was confused, afraid, or angry. Going feral was the term. Her Collar tried to shock sense into her, but that only resulted in more pain, more confusion, more anger.

Deni smelled Dylan's fighting blood, which announced to everyone there he was far stronger and meaner than the giant bear he battled. Ronan continued swinging his enormous paws, landing blows on the smaller lion. Dylan's lithe body moved and flowed with the hits that would have crushed any Shifter who'd stood still and taken them. Dylan's lion's paws moved in a flurry, batting back the bear with the swift, manic strength of a cat.

Deni's wolf howled to life. She wanted to leap into the ring, rush to Dylan's side, and help him fight. He was her alpha—he'd been leader of all Shifters for a long time before conceding his position to his son. Ronan was lesser than Deni, and he dared to confront Dylan. Now Ronan must pay.

Deni clenched her free hand into a fist, jaw so tight it

ached. She shouldn't be here—she should have gone home
and not let the compelling Jace talk her into watching the
battle. She now wanted more than anything to break all the
rules of the fight club and run into the ring. Ronan would
knock her senseless before he could stop himself, but her
wolf didn't care. The bear needed to go down.

Deni started to growl, the sound rising in her throat. Her
Collar snapped a spark into her, but she didn't stop. She
couldn't stop. And that terrified her most of all.

"Hey," a deep voice in her ear rumbled. "Hold it together."

Jace. His warmth covered her side, his stern command
reaching her inner beast and stilling the need to shift. Deni
realized her fingers had already changed to wolf claws, and
fur ran from her head down her back, which was bared by
the sarong.

Jace didn't let go of her hand, though she felt her claws
pierce his skin. He ran his other hand, warm and broad-
palmed, up and down her back, which returned to human
smoothness.

"Want to go?" he asked her.

Deni nodded. She couldn't see much anymore—the
fires and lanterns blurred into one whirling light, the shouts
and growls blending into a mass of animal sound.

Jace tugged her away, again becoming the lifeline that
drew her through the crowd. In the howling, swirling madness, Jace was a constant, his warmth pulling her onward.

He took her into the parking lot, turning her away from
the lights. Once the cool night air touched her, darkness
erasing the maddening lights, Deni drew a long breath. Her
fur and claws receded, leaving her on her human feet,
shaking.

"I shouldn't have done that," Jace was saying as they
threaded their way through parked vehicles. She heard his
voice but didn't pay much attention to the words. "I
shouldn't have taken you in there. I didn't realize it was
that bad."

"It's bad," Deni said, nodding. She wasn't concentrating

on her words either. "I should have stayed home tonight, but I needed . . ." She shivered. "I don't know what I needed."

Not true. Deni had needed escape, life, not hiding in the dark. Her sons had gone to work, Ellison had taken his mate, Maria, out for dinner and probably sex, and the rest of Shiftertown had emptied to attend the fight club. Sit at home and mope or go out and be with her friends and neighbors? She'd been tired of moping, so here she was.

Deni's uncontrolled instincts were punishing her now. Jace had known to take her out of there before she did something stupid, but the wildness in her didn't calm. It needed release.

Deni's wolf needed to fight, to hunt, to kill. Robbed of that, the she-wolf in her wanted the nearest thing to it.

She swung to Jace, his scent filling her, his strength calling to her. He was solid, strong, alpha, male, and he was here with her in the dark. She couldn't have stopped herself even if she'd wanted to.

Deni slammed both hands to Jace's chest. He caught her with a strong grip but fell against the side of a pickup, carrying her back with him. He had a musky male scent, a little wild, like the woods on a moonlit night. The moon was high and full tonight, always irresistible to a wolf.

Jace's eyes were unusual, jade green, the color heightened by his tanned face and brown black hair he'd buzzed short. He was large too, but agile and athletic.

He watched her, not shoving her away, not angry. Just watching.

Another surge of sound came from the arena, human and animal crying out for blood. Deni snarled, pinned Jace against the truck, and kissed him hard on the mouth.

FROM *NEW YORK TIMES* BESTSELLING AUTHOR

JENNIFER ASHLEY

FERAL HEAT

SHIFTERS UNBOUND

Jace Warden is sent to the Shiftertown in Austin to find a way to free all Shifters from their Collars. But pulling off the Collars can drive Shifters mad or kill them outright.

In Austin, Jace meets Deni Rowe, a wolf Shifter who was deliberately run down. And while her body has healed, she still has episodes of total memory loss during which she retreats into her pure animal self.

Jace has never met anyone like Deni. Courageous and beautiful, she volunteers to help him test the Collar removal. And as Deni and Jace work together, they feel the mate bond begin. But can Jace help Deni believe she will ever heal enough to be anyone's true mate?

AVAILABLE EVERYWHERE E-BOOKS ARE SOLD!

jennifersromances.com
facebook.com/ProjectParanormalBooks
penguin.com

M1394T1013